MW01131111

PRAISE FOR
BREACH

"Kelly Sokol delivers harrowing emotional intensity with writing that is fierce, compassionate and insightful. *Breach* is the stuff of book club legend."

—Jayne Ann Krentz, *New York Times* Bestselling Author

"*Breach* tears at your heart [and] embodies grief and fear, sexual tension and maternal love, poverty and hope, and the shrapnel that destroys when men go to war. It's impossible not to pull for Marleigh in this story of scrappy survival in a world that keeps throwing punches."

—Janine Latus, Author of the International Best Seller
If I Am Missing or Dead: A Sister's Story of Love, Murder and Liberation

"*Breach* breaks your heart. It also fills you with courage and gratitude and the will to fight to the bloody end."

—Ellen Bryson, Author of *The Transformation of Bartholemew Fortuno*

"This virtuoso story draws the reader into the character's hearts and souls, to feel what they feel, love whom they love, grieve when they grieve, exult when they overcome."

—Mike Krentz, Retired Navy Fleet Surgeon and Author of *Dead Already*

"The characters all feel like people I have known and cared for . . . At its core, *Breach* is a narrative about hope and the heartbreaking sacrifices a person sometimes must make just to keep living."

—Chera Hammons, PEN Award-Winning Author of *Monarchs of the Northeast Kingdom*

"*Breach* is a heart-pounder. Kelly Sokol has gifted us a passionate story with language inked like a raw, vibrant tattoo on the heart."

—Diane Zinna, Author of *All-Night Sun*

Breach

by Kelly Sokol

© Copyright 2022 Kelly Sokol

ISBN 978-1-64663-649-5

This is a work of fiction. The characters are both actual and fictitious. With the exception of verified historical events and persons, all incidents, descriptions, dialogue and opinions expressed are the products of the author's imagination and are not to be construed as real.

Published by

◤köehlerbooks™

3705 Shore Drive
Virginia Beach, VA 23455
800-435-4811
www.koehlerbooks.com

BREACH

A NOVEL

VIRGINIA BEACH
CAPE CHARLES

To all of the men and women in the fight at home and abroad.
Keep battling hard and loving harder. You're worth the fight.

• • •

For D. J.

CHAPTER ONE

Marleigh looped the tail of the letter *y* on her note card to complete the word *autophagy*, transforming the letter into a pointed trident. Multitasking was a survival skill; still on the clock at the gym, she learned her biology terms while practicing her art. Outlining and shading. She should have forked the tail, instead, into a mouth that turned on the open arms of the letter. She liked when form and meaning matched. Couldn't a letter self-devour as much as a cell? She slid the card to the bottom of the stack. She only had a few more minutes to review the terms before she had to close Box-n-Go and leave for class.

The fake prizefighters bell dinged as the gym door opened. Marleigh looked up as two new guys entered. The first one, bigger and better looking than his friend, flinched at the smell and the heat. Box-n-Go regulars stopped noticing the stink—sweat and blood and yeast and leather all wiped down with Clorox.

Hot new guy spoke first. "We want to box." He had no accent. His hair was buzzed. He had a lopsided dimple bigger than Marleigh's pencil eraser on one side of his smile. Managing her grandfather's gym had few perks, but a view like this was one of them.

"That's what we do here. Drop ins are twelve dollars, or you can prepay three sessions for twenty."

Often, wannabes were caught cold by sore muscles after their first workouts and never returned. *Projection bias,* a term she'd learned at night school at ECPI. People told themselves that paying guaranteed that they would show up. School cost her a lot, too, and she never missed a class. She'd need all the tricks she knew and plenty she didn't to keep Box-n-Go's doors open and her plans on track.

New guy dug into the pockets of his mesh shorts, muscular forearms tightening, opened his wallet and slid out a credit card. Marleigh tapped the laminated wall sign: *Cash Only.* He scratched at his freshly buzzed scalp, the skin still bright white above his ears and at the base of his neck.

His buddy thumped him on the shoulder. "I've got cash," he mumbled. On the other side of the thin wall, the real round bell sounded. The speed bag started, the clang of the chain as it was struck. The treadmills revved.

New guy took his friend's money and handed it to Marleigh. He yelled over the din. "Two three-packs."

Marleigh nodded. She pointed to the spiral notebook open in front of her, facing the men. Each line had hand-drawn sections for *Name* (your REAL name), *Date* and *Paid Y/N,* and *Manager's signature.* The new guy signed Jace Holt. Then he thrust his hand out between her nose and the notebook, forcing her to shake.

"Pleasure to meet you!"

His eyebrows were thick and light brown above big, dark-brown eyes. Marleigh twitched him a half smile and nodded at the book to get his friend to sign in. The round ended with a ding and the treadmills and speed bag slowed. She set two release waivers in front of the new boxers. Both signed without reading the language she'd cut and pasted from a Wiki how-to. No one ever read it. No one wanted to think that far ahead. Basically, the paragraphs said that if you got fucked up in here, you knew what you were getting into. Box at your own risk.

"Do you have your own gloves?" Marleigh asked. The friend held up his pair. Jace shrugged and shook his head. She plucked a pair from the metal rack behind her and sprayed them liberally with Lysol, holding them out to him with her fingertips. "Wrap is right there. You can use ours tonight, but bring your own or we'll start charging you next time. This isn't your mama's house."

Jace held up his hands as if to guard his face. "These are deadly weapons," he said. "The wrap just protects the other guy." He smiled wide at her, and it connected, sending a dangerous twinge deep in Marleigh's gut, somewhere he wasn't supposed to be. His triceps strained, a curve of navy ink showed at the edge of his shirtsleeve, almost certainly an anchor. Of course. Working in a gym only a couple miles from Norfolk Naval Base, the largest base in the world, Marleigh could spot a sailor.

"Good luck." Marleigh crossed her arms and leaned back in her chair. "Go on and wrap up and find Terry." Marleigh was trying to save the gym financially until her grandfather found someone he trusted to run it permanently. She was the only business head left. Terry made boxers and boxing trainers. He could identify anyone's strengths and weaknesses in minutes. If Marleigh could find a way for the gym to make money, Terry would be the perfect person to take it over for Pops.

After checking the clock, she tilted her head down to her notebook and found the paragraph she'd been annotating in her textbook. She forced herself back into the biology notes she was taking and reeled her mind back in when she was tempted to peek around the doorway to see what Terry had Jace doing first. The classes at ECPI, a school billing itself as a college, cost way more than Tidewater Community College, but they offered a fast track to hygienist school. Marleigh had a plan and a schedule—bust ass short-term for that long-term life of her dreams. She loved how dental offices all coordinated—décor, dress code. Front desk staff clad in blue shirts and black bottoms on Wednesday, orange and black the whole month of October. The hum of air-conditioning and swish of wealthy patients with time and money to spend on their teeth. The cool, neutral scent of fluoride, X-ray equipment, and air-conditioning.

She had to be out of there in ten minutes. Six months into courses at ECPI, Marleigh would begin her hygienist apprenticeship in less than a year. Clean, minty fluoridated teeth replacing rot and disuse with orderly, uniform beauty. The first step in her real life. No time for distractions.

Biology she could learn from a textbook, but Ocean View's Box-n-Go was an anatomy lesson. None of the guys ever had their shirts on after round one. She was going to ignore Jace. She resisted sneaking a glance into the gym.

The gym never really washed out. The odor was yeasty, a musk with a sharp edge, sweat in leather, used wraps, shared helmets and groin protectors, the plastic gloves the trainers wore when the boys sparred, rusty blood when a lip or eyebrow popped open, a bright straight line, thick and resinous, Lysol sprayed into gloves after every match, the bucket of bleach used to wash everything down. It all coalesced, somehow.

The strongest smell, the one that made her try to hide the rise and fall of her chest, came from the men's bodies. Almost like in high school when she left her shin guards in her bag after a game, forgetting to air them, to wash the socks. No ventilation. Rich people didn't reek like that. But there was something more. The perfect stink that originated in all the *V*s of men—their armpits and where their thighs met. The deep cuts that started above their shorts, at the hips, and finished under. As they sweated off pounds during a bout and their shorts slipped down and their bellies tensed and twisted. That's the smell that lingered. Sweat and hair and crotch and pheromone. Man stink, animal and visceral. She went to sleep with it in the curls of her hair. She imagined running her fingernails up the back of the new guy's freshly shorn neck.

Focus. He didn't have twenty bucks on him. He had to be low-level enlisted, even if he looked a little older. She reviewed the material for tonight's quiz one more time, mumbling the vocab aloud, confident that between the music, the grunting, and the misery in the other room no one would hear her, though the "wall" forming the reception-slash-office didn't go all the way to the ceiling.

She double-checked the cash in the box with the sign-in sheet for the day. It was short by fifty-two dollars. She added and re-added the columns but couldn't rectify the difference. Shit. She didn't need this tonight. The gym was dangerously in the red. Her grandfather had been far too lenient on people making their payments over the years, always prioritizing training over profitability. Her efforts were probably too late, but Marleigh couldn't let Pops lose his gym.

Marleigh turned over the page and there was a sticky note from Serpent (not his real name, his ring name). *I O U.* He was late on his payment plan and should have paid eighteen dollars the last two visits. He was, of course, long gone, and now she was running behind. And Serpent's missed payments only accounted for thirty-six dollars. What about the additional sixteen dollars? The gym had Q-tip-thin margins in its best years, but no one besides Marleigh and Terry, and Pops, when he could remember, had any clue how desperate the gym's financial situation had become. If the fighters kept acting like this, there would be no gym for them to stiff. Where was the remaining cash?

She clicked the exterior light from open to closed. The trainers, fighters, and the two new wannabes could stay past ten, but on Marleigh's school nights, no new boxers could sign in past seven, unless her parents showed up to take over. But that happened never. Her father, Parrish, had been a hot-shit boxer. He'd quit before she was born. Her mom, Jackie, ran the gym's front office until Marleigh was in high school. Jackie hadn't kept many records; Marleigh was certain Box-n-Go fell off the financial cliff under her watch. Jackie no longer had a key to the cash box.

The clock read 6:53. Marleigh had to be in her car by seven so she could slip on a change of clothes and stuff her gym clothes in a plastic bag. She scanned the list of boxers still in the gym. A few of them had problem friends or girlfriends that she had to remind the trainers not to let in. She saved that for last. She locked the cash box in the gun safe against the wall and ran a copy of the week's receipts so she could bring it to her grandad's tomorrow. Marleigh stacked her books and notebooks on the edge of the desk—she left her bag in the car, too. She repeated the vocab for the quiz. She turned out all but one light in the front room and made her way into the gym—a fancy name for three cinder-block walls with a cement floor. The boxing ring took up half the room, a speedbag hung in one corner and two treadmills squeezed in next to the bathroom door. Two weight racks and benches took up the other wall. Jump ropes hung over every door frame, and large white buckets were strategically placed around the room for snot and spit and puke and blood. It was small and old school. But three trainers had up to twelve guys sweating their dicks off at any one time. Even women sometimes, usually scary Marines with something to prove. Marleigh only trained when the gym was empty.

The room fell quiet when she entered, just as it always had for her grandad. The new guy, Jace, was shirtless on the weight bench. She knew she'd be able to sense him somehow, even if she couldn't see him. She kept her back to him. "I'm shutting it down out front. Y'all know the rules, nobody else comes in. Marco and D'Ash, I'm looking at you."

The fighters in the ring held out their knuckles for a bump, signaling agreement.

"We won't cause any trouble, Marleigh," D'Ashandre told her.

She fist-bumped the guys in the ring over the ropes. "Good. Terry can let y'all out and close up." She'd known Terry since she was a kid. He showed up in OV Box one day after months in a group home for adolescents somewhere across the long Hampton Roads Bridge-Tunnel Marleigh could see from the beach. "My mom gets another shot at me," he'd said, his voice and mouth tight. "Least I'm out of that dump."

"Marleigh, huh?" Jace said from behind her. He stood up and re-racked his weights. "Like Bob?" He mimicked smoking a joint and stepped closer to her.

She rolled her eyes and ignored him. "I've gotta go," she said to the room. "And remember, he's watching." She pointed to an old glossy photograph on the wall—her grandfather before he was a father himself. The colors were faded, but his eyes were clear and bright and present. His body hard as cement. She turned to walk out.

Jace took a big step closer, his body intimidating but his expression goofy and boyish. He had a dimple even without smiling. "Marleigh, don't we get fist bumps too?"

"I'm leaving. And those are for the guys who stick around."

He jumped between her and the door. "I'll stick around."

"Get out of my way. I'm already late."

"Not without a fist bump." He held out his fist. "We'll be back tomorrow." She'd be down the street bartending, but Jace didn't need to know that. Marleigh shoved her body around him. He leaned to the side and pinned her to the doorframe. "We bought three packs, remember?"

"Fine." She bumped him with her left hand and pushed him out of the way with her right shoulder. He let her move him and exaggerated his reaction to the shove.

"I'm going to walk you out. This is a shitty neighborhood."

"No kidding. I grew up here." *Stop talking*, she reminded herself. *Go!* Another bell sounded. Jace stood in the doorway as she turned the exterior lock to the building and got into her car. The dash lit up. "Shit!" *7:08.* Checking that he'd gone back inside, Marleigh pulled the smelly T-shirt over her head and replaced it with a button-down—no time for a bra change—and shimmied into jeans. She tore out of the parking lot.

• • •

If not for the lane closures at Military Highway, Marleigh would have only been ten minutes late to class. The parking lot was full, and there were no stragglers into the school that looked more like a business. She ran from the car to the lecture hall. She'd watched students come in late for months. The door to the room was closed, though, and a neon flyer posted: *Quiz being administered. No admission until completion of the examination.*

No, no, no, no. She'd never once been late for class, let alone missed a quiz. And finally, she was taking classes that had something to do with what she actually wanted to study. Quizzes accounted for a quarter of her grade in this class, and she needed to maintain a 3.0 to make it into the hygienist track. Her neck burned. She could smell the gym.

She swallowed hard and prepared to plead her case. Marleigh walked down the hallway to the teachers' shared office. She knocked on the open door. Her teacher sat with his large back to her. "Mr. Shunk?"

He twisted around in his chair. "Yes? Ms—?"

"Mulcahy," she said. "Marleigh Mulcahy."

"You're very late."

"I know. I got stuck at work and then this construction. Please, I've—"

"Class starts at the same time every night."

"I've never missed a class. I've never been late before tonight. Can I please take the quiz?"

"No. Everyone always has an excuse. If you don't make these classes a priority, you'll never finish."

"But—"

He had no idea who she was. She wasn't like the rest of them. She was bettering her life.

"You get a zero on the quiz, Ms. Mulcahy. You know the policy. You can rejoin the class after the quiz, though, so you won't be marked absent, and you won't miss out on the material."

A zero.

She sat in the hallway beside the classroom door and drew. She had designs that she wanted to add to her tattooing portfolio, and they had to be perfect so she could keep advancing beyond her scripts and fonts and characters. She'd blown it on the quiz, at least she could accomplish something.

CHAPTER TWO

Marleigh followed her usual Thursday-morning routine: gym, cash, deposit, Pops, double at the Thirsty Camel. Mornings were the only time she had a good chance of finding her grandfather lucid. Her parents were becoming similar—the bad hours outnumbered the good ones anymore. Despite a lucrative and fun shift at Azpiration Ink Tattoo Parlor the night before, Marleigh's favorite of her three jobs, the zero she received on the quiz on Tuesday rankled. She couldn't quite shake her foul mood, and having to stop back through the gym didn't make her any happier. She told herself to perk up: on Wednesday and Thursday nights, the gym was someone else's problem.

Until the night six months ago that she was robbed, Marleigh saved the extra trip and brought the night's cash home with her ahead of the morning deposit. Now she picked it up in the morning and went straight to the bank. It hadn't taken a genius to figure out that the thief had to have been a *client* of OV Box who knew Marleigh's schedule.

Her attacker wore sweatpants, a hoodie, and ski mask. Minus the ski mask, it was a boxer's uniform, so initially being approached by a big guy dressed like that didn't seem so threatening. Being thrown against the hood of her own car, chin then forehead cracking into the windshield, had been terrifying. The clang of the lockbox hitting asphalt, blood spurting from a split lip. She wasn't about to let it happen again. Definitely a shit neighborhood.

All she saw was pale forehead against dark fabric. The gym had its own kind of justice. Self-named Mickey Two Fists never bothered Marleigh or showed up around the gym again. Last she heard, he looked like Sloth from the Goonies after the other fighters were done with him.

Pops had started to decline, so she didn't have to explain the money situation to him. He wouldn't go looking for the five hundred in cash, though he and the gym needed it, bad. And bruises were easy to explain away if you worked in boxing, whether or not you stepped in the ring. She didn't have to admit her stupidity, the sloppy laziness that made her an easy target. Marleigh was supposed to be the one protecting the gym. Unlike her parents, Marleigh never asked Pops for handouts, or, worse, grabbed what cash was visible. She wasn't loyal to her parents, or necessarily to the gym. People mistook the gym for a family, but Marleigh knew better. She was deeply loyal to Pops, though, and nothing mattered more to Pops than Marleigh or his gym. He had always taken care of her. He would have killed Mickey Two Fists, or whoever, for putting his hands on her. Thank God she didn't have to explain. She would not let him down again.

At the gym, she propped open the front door to let some fresh air in. She shouldn't be inside so long that the smell would stick, but if it did, it would get her grandad talking. He loved that smell. In the morning, the gym was silent. No *snick snick snick* of the jump rope against concrete or *bappita bappita bappita* of the speed bag. Thin soles skritching on canvas, propelled by muscular calves. Spit hitting a plastic bucket. Barbells clanging back into racks. The heavy exhale that the boxers knew would keep them from holding their breath and passing out. Cotton cloth drying sweaty skin. Lockers opening, banging shut, re-opening to retrieve a forgotten mouth guard. *Clang.* That was the soundtrack to her homework hours every afternoon, and the background to Saturday morning cartoons for as long as she could remember. Today there were no men's voices. No "fuck you, move your feet, faster, protect your fucking face" she had to tune out. No gymnasium symphony.

She bumped into the desk as she transferred the cash from the lockbox into a deposit envelope. A piece of carbon paper fluttered to the floor. She bent to pick it up. A man's attempt at handwriting. *Why do you have a credit card swiper but don't take credit? Your books looked heavy. Did I make you late? Call me. 757-655-5500—Jace.* She laughed and thought about throwing it in the trash. There were several other pieces of carbon crumpled up in there already, first and second drafts of the same message. She tucked the note under the paperweight on the desk. She never understood why they kept the clunky machine either. Her grandad said it made them look more professional when he picked it up, but that was twenty years ago when Marleigh was a baby. Now it just looked silly.

As a child, she'd used the carbon-copied receipts to practice her letters as she signed in fighters. Jackie taught her how to sign the guys in, back when Marleigh was too young to be home at night alone. The pink copy she tucked in the metal drawer with the cash, the gray one she handed to the customer. Every name that came, she scribbled and then scrawled then looped in cursive into the ledger had music. Sometimes the mouthful of four consonants without a softening, slowing vowel. Others had apostrophes or were old words spelled backwards to make new words. On notebook paper, Marleigh tried to draw a fighter's tattoos, recreating the lettering and the shading. She sketched everything and everyone. She dragged her thumb across Jace's note.

Marleigh reminded herself that she was pissed that he had made her late. Still, she made the drive from the gym to the bank, and then to her grandfather's in a much better mood than she'd left her apartment that morning. She rode the elevator up to his room. Pops was on the fifth floor of a run-down old-folks home. The better-off residents had scant bay views through a row of big beach houses. He had a view of Ocean View Avenue, a bus stop, and Burger King. He didn't go outside much, so the view didn't really matter. And this wasn't a facility for people with Alzheimer's or dementia, so she had to help him seem much more self-sufficient than he was. He'd be out on his ass if anyone knew he could forget to turn off the oven, let it burn for a day or more. Anyway, Pops never wanted a diagnosis. "Boxer Brain," he called it. "What a lifetime of gettin' roughed up'll get ya." He'd lived longer that he had any right to, he would say. "Boxing gave me everything I got."

She had no idea if her grandmother was alive and, if so, where. She had left when Marleigh's dad was three, during Pops's brief prison stint for bookmaking. Marleigh rang the doorbell and counted slowly to fifteen before putting her key in the lock and opening the door.

"Hi, Pops," she called into the unit. After closing the door, she smoothed over the construction paper taped to the inside of the door—*NOT BY YOURSELF!*—and hoped he heeded it. "It's Marleigh. Hi, Pops!" The TV was on, but she was pretty sure he left it on all the time.

"Marleigh girl?" It was a good morning, then. On her last visit, Pops had confused her with the wife who had been gone twenty years. "Where the feck ye been?" he'd asked then and tried to reach up her skirt. Marleigh hated the bad days.

Her grandfather shuffled into the den from his bedroom. He wore his shearling slippers year-round now, and his favorite threadbare pajama pants and a T-shirt from the Ocean View St. Patty's Day parade in 1991. "Hi, Marleigh girl," he reached a trembling hand to pat her shoulder. "Good week at the gym?"

"Yes. How about you sit and I'll make us some tea?"

He sat on the small couch and Marleigh handed him the ledger copies and sign-in sheets. He fumbled around his lap for his reading glasses. She pointed to the top of her own head.

"Right," he said, placing them down on his nose. "Sneaky bastards."

"We still have only forty-three fighters who have an annual membership, Pops."

She put the tea kettle on the stove and fished out tea bags; Assam was his favorite, hers, mint. She hid his tea-making equipment so that he didn't try to make it himself and burn the place down. He liked his tea a little milky and sweet, "the Irish way," he'd say, and Marleigh thought it was disgusting. She opened the refrigerator and found four open quarts of milk on the door shelf. It had only been a week since she visited last and there had only been one quart then—the one she'd brought. Today was a good day, but he'd had a long week. She sniffed the cartons to find the freshest milk and poured it into a teacup for him.

"Forty-three?" he asked.

"Yup," she said. "We signed up five people this month. They have to pay three times a year instead of whenever they feel like it. Remember?" The kettle whistled and she poured the water over the tea bags.

His hand shuddered a bit as he blew at the steam. Her parents added vodka to their tea—"just a splash"—to take the morning's edges off. Their fingers would stop shaking. "Making the gym a business," he mused, smiling.

"It's not enough, Pops. We need at least fifteen more. Or we need to raise the prices."

"I'm proud of you, Marleigh girl. You're a chip off the old block. You and your dad make a good team." Did he really think Parrish was still helping at the gym? "I know you'll figure something out."

Marleigh tried to turn a wince into a smile. Her parents hadn't been to the gym in at least a month, and it was better without them. If Pops didn't own the small old garage bay that housed the gym, they wouldn't be able to make rent. The trainers routinely bitched about how little they made, how well the guys at the big gyms were paid. "Get in at one of them, then," Marleigh always countered without animosity. But they came back. Everyone had a day job or worked other shifts elsewhere. Boxers and their trainers were dreamers. Dreamers were always broke.

She sipped her tea. "You taught us well, Pops," she answered. He had taught them well, wanted to teach them everything he knew. Her parents just weren't interested. Happy hours had always been more their thing. Parrish hated his father. He swore Pops made him this way. Fought him too hard as a kid, used him like a bait dog. Marleigh's father had an excuse for everything, speedy on his toes with blame.

Pops could have sold the whole enterprise when Marleigh was in middle school. One of the franchise gyms wanted the space. He wanted a legacy for his family, though, and a place for local kids to turn their lives around like he did, so he kept it. Pops was crazy then and demented now, but Marleigh didn't want to see the gym flounder either. And until she finished school and found a full-time job, she needed extra income. They needed more fighters, and they needed the fighters they had to pay in full.

"Do any of the boys have fights coming up?"

She pointed at the spreadsheet in his lap. "This guy, Stinger Santana. He's fighting next week in Hampton. He's gonna get whipped. Everybody knows it but him. The gym will get some good exposure, though. And D'Ash is prepping for a fight up in DC."

"Pretty good purses in those regional fights," Pops said. The boxers had to pay their own entry fees, but the gym took a percentage of the winnings and momentum for the gym. Everyone wanted to train where winners sparred. "How's he goin' do?"

"He's a brawler from the get-go, you know that. He's got a chance if he can land some early and keep from fading."

"Terry got him running sprints?" Pops had always loved Terry, from the day he arrived at the gym offering to trade hard work for a chance to learn and the promise of a fight. He'd been the lead trainer for as long as Marleigh could remember.

"Uphill and wearing the weight vest."

"Good, good." Pops was always convinced everything worked itself out in the end.

Before she left, Marleigh wrote down all the upcoming fights and where her grandfather could go to see them, or if he had to get his buddies to chip in for a pay-per-view at the gym. She put asterisks around a fight or two that was on when she wasn't working, so if they had to go to a bar showing the bout, she could take him. He never seemed more himself to her than when he watched a fight.

She rinsed and put away their teacups. Before heading to work, Marleigh opened the breaker box and switched the oven to off, just to be safe. Was there anything worse than being old and poor and alone?

CHAPTER THREE

Marleigh finished her opening shift behind the bar at the Thirsty Camel, and it was time for getting out onto the floor for dinner and turning the bar over to Lynetha. The Camel, windowless and dark, teetered on pilings above the Chesapeake Bay. A cement camel welcomed visitors to the parking lot, draped in a plastic sheet proclaiming the night's specials. The bar was always the steadiest business, but Marleigh had agreed to take one of the girls' dinner service shifts.

Saturday night was the Camel's version of surf 'n' turf—greasy prime rib served with a pound of peel-and-eat shrimp. The air was thick with gristle and Old Bay seasoning, but it was the one night a week when the tables and booths were packed, and dinner service ended at nine, so Marleigh could go drop in on the gym and lock up for the weekend.

No boxing hours on Sunday—her grandfather's old Roman Catholic tradition. The staff observed it, whether they went to church. She'd make some money, close shop at OV Box and shoo everyone out of the parking lot and go home. She only worked the Bloody Mary shift Sunday mornings and spent the afternoon studying. After the zero quiz grade earlier in the week, she had to step up her school game.

Work and school would buy her stability. Stability, self-sufficiency would mask the desperation that had shrouded her since birth. The indelible mark of poverty, of a banged-up home. Desperation attracted the desperate. Marleigh wanted more.

"Someone came round asking about you yesterday," Lynetha told Marleigh as she clocked in. "Real cutie."

Marleigh restocked the cherries and olives and sliced lemons and limes. It had to be Jace. She was secretly pleased. He was resourceful, persistent, if a little stalkery.

"Huh," she said, scanning the people sitting down for dinner. The guys all had sunglass tans—stripes from their eyes to their ears. A few took off the faded ball caps and ruffled their hat hair. She knew several of the couples from her old neighborhood. Many of them looked like her parents—lined gray faces with a permanent sunburnt red swath across their cheeks and noses, pouched under eyes. This was a big night out for them and look how they're dressed—tight coverups over bathing suits that never touched water for the ladies. Stretched-out T-shirts with holes in the neck over baggy cargo shorts for the men. Flip-flops and yellow toenails. They were her future if she didn't get out of Ocean View for good. She took her order pad from her smock and tucked a pen behind her ear.

"Are you going to tell me about him?" Lynetha pressed, drying the rim of a pint glass with the bar towel. "Jace Holt. Sounds like Top Gun or some shit."

Marleigh turned back to Lynetha and shoved the pad back into its pocket. "He's just a new guy at the gym. He was here?"

"Cute for a white guy. Midwestern cowboy type."

His name gave her a tingle. Lynetha thought he was cute, too. Marleigh knew that cute didn't mean faithful. Her last boyfriend had been cute. He knew how to fill his time when Marleigh was in class or working. Cute didn't mean shit.

"You know more about him than I do. Just a squid like all the rest." A younger couple walked in. The woman wore a short floral shift, the man a sport coat and khakis with crisp pleats. They must be lost. He held out his date's chair and draped his sport coat over his own before sitting. Eventually, these would be the people she'd surround herself with every day, not some weird anomaly. They would be her clients, her friends.

"Bomb tech. EOD. Not your basic seaman," Lynetha said with a throaty chuckle. "He ordered a beer and asked about you. He's so disappointed you weren't here that he had another. I was only supposed to tell you about the first, though."

Normally, enlisted men held no interest for Marleigh, well, except maybe for Navy chiefs. Officers usually arrived with wives and children in tow. Young enlisted were—as the saying went—young, dumb, and full of . . . but EOD.

"Damn Terry."

"You know that's who sent him." Lynetha and Terry had history.

Marleigh shook her head. "I'm hitting the floor, girl, bye."

Marleigh greeted her first table. Two dinner specials and happy-hour Buds. She could do this in her sleep. She went to the well-dressed table next, ready to impress. These were her people, even if they didn't know it yet.

She greeted them with a smile. "Hi, I'm Marleigh. I'll be taking care of you tonight."

The man pressed a thick finger to his lips, shushing her. His date looked down at the table. The part in her very blonde hair flushed pink. The man slid a tall stack of dollar bills to the corner of the table and smacked it with his palm. "That's a lot of money, right?" he asked Marleigh.

"Graham, stop," the woman across the table pled. Marleigh would take five times that to the bank on Monday, though she'd spend the rest of the week writing checks to bleed it out.

"Whoa," Marleigh intoned, trying to play along.

"That's your tip, honey," he said, patting the stack again. "Any time you screw up, I take some back." He lifted the top bill from the pile and put it in his pocket.

"I understand how it works," she said, trying not to roll her eyes.

"I don't like her tone," he said. "Do you?"

"Graham," his date whispered.

"Two dinner specials. A Maker's for me. Do you have Maker's Mark? I want it neat. And a pinot grigio for the lady." He gestured, again, to the dwindling stack. She glanced around at the six other tables.

"Sure thing. I'll be back with your drinks."

Graham grabbed her elbow as she turned to leave. "Aren't you going to ask how we want our steaks prepared?" The woman silently mouthed *"sorry"* across the table.

"Right, of course. Sorry, I figured you were thirsty."

"The lady would like hers medium well," he said, shaking his head like he was embarrassed by the order.

"Absolutely," Marleigh answered, pretending to write it down.

"I want mine Pittsburgh rare."

Did the guy realize he was ordering fifteen-dollar steaks? And what did that even mean?

"It means charred on the outside and rare on the inside. Got it? Charred on the outside, rare on the inside."

Marleigh wrote A-S-S-H-O-L-E on her notepad. "Got it," she said, knowing that all the prime rib came out looking and tasting exactly the same. She ground her jaw as she approached the computer at the bar to punch in the order for her first two tables. On specials nights, everyone arrived at the same time and the bar and kitchen were flooded with orders.

When she dropped the drinks off, the woman thanked her as she placed the glass in front of her, but Graham slid another bill off the shrinking pile. "Took a while," he said.

"Your food will be out shortly," Marleigh said, then greeted her other tables. Two groups came in with gift certificates. *Shit!* Gift card users never tipped. She found herself looking forward to getting to the gym, reminding herself never to take another shift on this side of the bar.

Despite the cook's bitching, he'd made a valiant effort to fulfill the order. Graham's steak wasn't a muddy brown, but had dark striations from the grill across the top. In response to Marleigh's, "How is everything? Can I get you anything else?" Graham dabbed the grease slick off his lips and said, "So, you couldn't be bothered to bring us our food?" His date eviscerated her steak, cutting it into smaller and smaller bites without eating any of it. No matter what Marleigh said, the outcome would be the same.

"Fresh is the name of the game around here. Wanted you to get it hot. Can I get you another drink?" Brown liquor rarely made any man less a jerk, but it would at least up his tab.

He swung his index finger in a circle. "Yes, another round." There was less than fifteen dollars left in the pile on the table, though they'd both consumed double that amount in booze alone. "Make sure *you* bring them." As if there were anyone else. Lynetha would never leave the packed bar. Marleigh brought the drinks and closed out the remaining customer's tab.

When Fancy Graham finally left there was four dollars remaining on the tip pile for a fifty-two-dollar tab. Marleigh made less than eighty dollars for the night. She would have easily cleared more than that behind the bar, and without breaking a sweat. She waved at Lynetha on her way out. "Go have some fun," her friend called after her.

CHAPTER FOUR

As Marleigh pulled into the parking lot, she saw two cars and a crotch rocket parked outside the gym, but no stragglers. Plenty of the guys walked or ran over from the neighborhood, so she never knew how many people were there until she got inside. It was already ten o'clock, so she would only have to wait a half an hour before turning off the lights and locking up.

The gym's heady, humid smell had been almost welcomed when she entered. She always knew where she stood here. It was a small cement box, but she garnered something like respect when she walked in. It hadn't been earned; she knew that. Her grandfather's creation and dedication was a shadow she stepped into and tried to lengthen. But plenty of people enjoyed a security in the world that they did nothing to create. Fancy Graham, for example. Marleigh had to put up with his bullshit—he was a customer for a couple of hours. That girlfriend let him treat her like that, like they both deserved it. And for what?

The only people inside were Terry and the new guy, Jace. Back again. She tried not to stare. He was shirtless and had his shorts gathered high on his muscular thighs, crouched in fighting stance.

His gloves were up, protecting his face. They were in the ring sparring. Terry had him moving through a complicated routine and seemed to make the guy drop lower each time to avoid being clocked in the side of the face with the sparring pad. Terry saw Marleigh first and gave her a quick nod, then got back to business. As Jace stepped, jabbed, crossed, and ducked to make contact with and then avoid Terry's swing, he saw her. He stood, losing his boxer's stance—the crouched ready position, weight on the toes, knees bent.

"Marleigh!" he said, his voice deep and masculine, but with a child's excitement. Terry's mitt whacked him across the side of his face and split the corner of his lip. She winced. Jace grinned at her like she was a marvel, not some tired waitress covered in shrimp peels. She studied him, too, she couldn't help herself. His compact muscle on such a tall body, those perfect Chiclet teeth. The curve and bounce of his hamstring, undoubtedly her favorite part of the male body. Remembering that Lynetha told her Jace was EOD, Marleigh wondered what would happen if he hurt his fingers boxing. It was a rookie mistake to clench your fists inside your gloves. *Can you disarm bombs with broken fingers?* A bomb tech. That meant there was a brain inside that stupidly perfect body. She didn't really care. She was just happy for any distraction from the shitty night, and how she'd been treated. No one respected waitresses or bartenders, one reason she wouldn't be one for much longer. It felt good to have someone so happy to see her.

"One more go, Terry. I've got this." They moved through the maneuvers again. Jace was focused and quick. He landed a punch over one of Terry's mitts.

Marleigh tilted her nose down and sniffed herself, suddenly self-conscious of her dirty T-shirt and shorts, knowing she carried a greasy, shellfish stink, wondering if Jace could smell it. Marleigh picked up one of the cleaning caddies and headed to the bathroom like she was going to restock the toilet paper and clean up for the night. She planned on doing that, of course, but she also wanted to see the damage the night had inflicted upon her. The bathroom wasn't so bad. No one made it that far to puke, so she almost never had to clean that up. The trainers had to dump and spray the buckets.

She looked in the mirror and dabbed beneath her eyes to clean up the smudge of mascara, holding a wet paper towel to her cheeks to pull the flush from her skin. She clucked at herself. If anyone but Jace was out there, she wouldn't have given herself a second look before heading home and washing off the day in the shower. Her white T-shirt was short and tight, the Thirsty Camel logo stretched across her left breast, and the hem grazed her belly button. Her black shorts were high-waisted with a minimal inseam, highlighting her tiny waist and perky ass. The uniform didn't leave much to the imagination.

The round bell sounded, muffled through the bathroom wall. Terry didn't dawdle at the end of the night. "You gotta work on your foot speed and keeping tight. You're too tall and goofy to be a boxer." Terry was just like her grandfather. No bullshit. No puffing up a boxer so that he'd keep showing up and paying and training just to keep getting his ass kicked in the ring. That was for the big money gyms. Marleigh could hear in his voice that he liked Jace and could see something in him. She didn't want to hear that.

She could get this bathroom clean and just wait him out. They'd be leaving soon, and then she could vent the night's bullshit on the heavy bag. Nothing could squash her libido quite like cleaning the can. He'd realize he wasn't really that interested and leave her alone. She gave the bathroom the most thorough cleaning ever, but as she slipped the plastic gloves off and threw them in the trash outside the bathroom door, Terry and Jace were still there, bent over a table. Both turned to look at her. Jace smiled that smile again.

"Don't tell the other guys," Terry said, before tearing off a piece of paper and handing it to Jace. He nodded at Marleigh, "And don't tell boss lady I'm giving you workouts outside the gym, neither." Marleigh cocked an eyebrow at them. Terry rarely did that.

"Just make sure you're paid up, new guy." She wiped down the ropes on the far side of the gym from them. Then she moved to the first heavy bag.

"Don't stand around staring," she said, keeping her back to Jace as she cleaned. "We're closed. Y'all get out of here."

"Don't have to tell me twice," Terry said. "See ya Monday."

Jace walked to the ring and pulled wipes out of the plastic canister. "I made this mess. Can I help you clean it?" She should tell him no. Terry would walk out and they would be alone. She wasn't afraid of the new guy. He stood there, shirtless and still breathy and sweaty, two Clorox wipes dangling from his hands.

"Sure. Wipe down the weight benches and racks and I'll finish over here. And how 'bout putting on a shirt first? You keep sweating on everything and I have to keep wiping it down." Clothed and across the room. Yes, that was definitely best.

"Yes, ma'am," he said with a mock salute. "I brought a friend with me, a different guy. He didn't make it all the way through the workout, but he'll be back."

"Do you want an award? And what's with the note you left?"

"Nah." He wiped the benches as well as the sweat puddles on the floor around them. "Where have you been? What've you been up to?"

She remembered when her grandfather lived with her, how he'd come home from the gym all keyed up, how he wanted to hear about her day, and how she would stay up too late to tell him because no other adult had asked. Pops stayed with Marleigh each of the three times her parents tried to quit drinking. They weren't interested in sitting in meetings surrounded by a bunch of drunks. "What good will that do?" they asked. Each time, they took off for a cabin in the woods, away from Ocean View, the beach, and all its temptations. Each time, Marleigh hoped her biggest hope, it swelled inside her so big it hurt, that they would really do it and come back to her sober and reliable and normal. That they would come home and at least like her again. After the third time, Marleigh realized hope was just a tease. It only let her down and made her feel worse. But she always had Pops.

Jace moved quickly, from station to station, flinging used Clorox wipes like basketballs into the trashcans.

She recognized that same Pops energy in Jace. "I'm like that after working late," she said. "Tired but wired."

"That's it," he said.

"What does EOD really mean?"

"It means Ever On Duty or long-ass time in the Navy."

Most squids she knew planned on four years and out, found the simplest duty they could.

"I'm like a really expensive one-man roadside cleanup crew. Except instead of cigarette butts and beer cans, I get rid of bombs. Explosive ordnance disposal."

"No wonder you're good at this." She shrugged at the mop and bucket. "And instead of highways, you clean up—"

"Desert markets, Humvee corridors, jungle shit. You name it."

He wasn't what Marleigh had expected. "Don't you need all of your fingers for that? What if you break one boxing?"

"So long as I can control my robot, I'll be fine. Anyway, it's a miracle I still have ten."

She mopped the last corner of the floor, letting that thought sink in.

"You're not going to worry about me now, are you?"

"Hardly."

Gym clean up took less than fifteen minutes with the two of them. She clicked the sign to closed and put the *CLOSED SUNDAY* placard in the window. "We're closed tomorrow, so don't try and show up."

He stepped closer. She could feel the heat coming through his T-shirt. He reached out as if to sweep a sweaty curl across her forehead. "I like it best when the gym's closed."

She bobbed just out of his reach. He wasn't allowed to touch her. Not yet.

"Ah, are you training with Terry, too?"

"Wouldn't you like to know."

That little pinch, down low, when Jace got too close. She hadn't had a boyfriend in a while. The guys she knew were all lazily okay with falling in step with the same life as their parents, living in the same neighborhood. Same shit, different day. Her responsibilities in the gym most of them could tolerate, if not respect, as it was a family business and all that. But school and her other jobs were like luxuries and annoyances to them. They distracted her from them. Her family someday would be a real family. A mom and a dad, a checking account with a balance at the end of the month, and kids they loved.

Marleigh *never* dated boxers. She saw how the boxers treated their girlfriends when they showed up at the gym. Sometimes, in high school, those girls would corner Marleigh to find out who else their boyfriends were seeing. Marleigh never told, so the guys looked out for her. More than a couple of the girls accused her of sleeping with their guys. Marleigh just wanted out, as none of these boys or girls was going anywhere.

"Since we're both wide awake, go out with me. Let's do something."

Marleigh ducked out from underneath his arm. "We're both disgusting. And no way in hell I'm going back to the Camel." She straightened up the front desk. Jace cleaned up the rolls of pre-wrap, and sprayed Lysol into used gloves.

Her mother often taunted her for not having a boyfriend. Jackie would think Marleigh wasn't good enough for Jace. "I was winning contests when I was your age," she'd say. "You shouldn't waste your youth."

Wet T-shirt contests. "Nice, Mom," Marleigh'd say. Her mother wore her hair way too long, down past mid-back. And Jackie cut her own bangs. From far away, she looked almost pretty and almost young. But her face up close was wrinkles and broken capillaries, like she was constantly blushing. She was a walking scam.

"You're nothing special," she'd told Marleigh over and over. "If someone asks, you'd better say *yes*."

At first, the girls in high school called her a slut for hanging out with the boxers. Then a dyke when she got serious about sports. The hours of jumping rope and heavy bag work built her endurance. She was a strong soccer midfielder. She wasn't sure it would take her anywhere past high school, but it got her out of the house and the gym.

Instead of sleeping around, Marleigh figured out how to make herself feel all tingly and hot. Some of the girls did it on long bus rides in the dark. She made the few guys she slept with come on her belly, though she'd never be able to get pregnant anyway, according to her mother. "Trash in, trash out," her mother said. "Simple as that."

Enough with Jackie's crazy; maybe Marleigh just needed to scratch an itch. Maybe Jace was leaving town soon and that would take care of that.

"Ya ain't gotta go home, but get up out of here," Marleigh said. Jace had sprayed and resprayed the gloves. "I need to lock up."

"Sorry, yeah. I'll get my stuff. But once you lock up, walk with me?"

"What?"

"I haven't been on the beach at night yet. Show me?" He held up two fingers. "Scouts honor, I won't pull any shit."

She shook her head.

"You're right, I was never a Scout. But you don't have to worry about me."

Maybe she could go and forget about the night.

CHAPTER FIVE

He sighed. "You're tired. I should let you get home," he said, an opening for Marleigh to back out. His eyes were intent on hers. He seemed hopeful. His fingers thrummed against his thighs.

"You don't get to let me do anything," she said, rattling the gym keys in his face. "I do what I want."

He reached for them, but she snatched them back against her chest.

"I'm counting on it."

"And anyway, it's nice outside."

She locked the exterior door and pulled hard against it, just to be certain it had closed.

"Do you know you have a handprint on your ass?"

She laughed. "I have a bad habit of wiping my hands off on my pants. Why didn't you tell me when we were inside? I could do something about it."

"I didn't want you to know I'd been looking."

"I thought you said you wouldn't be trouble."

"If you're in the room, I'm always looking."

So, it wasn't just her body that sought his out.

It was dark on the beach, no city lights, just a dim moon. They couldn't really see one another, but their arms bumped together as they walked. The sand was cool around her feet. It was just Jace, Marleigh and the waves. She couldn't remember the last time she had walked on the beach with nowhere specific to go.

"I can't ever see enough water in this lifetime," he said. "I'll never be stuck on land in the middle of nowhere again."

It was easy to talk in the dark, almost like talking to herself. Speaking just to each other's profiles. "I've never given that any thought. The water's always just been here, or maybe it's me who's always here. Nothing special."

"I think you should go out with me," he said.

"I'm out with you right now."

"God you've got a smart mouth. I want to taste it."

"Don't push it." She shoved him with her shoulder. Their bodies settled even closer to one another.

He moved so that their thighs touched. Fine hairs tickled her skin. His calves were hard and muscular. They felt good moving in step beside her.

"I'm not asking for some big deal. Maybe dinner or a beer. Something where neither of us is smelly."

She snorted before answering. "I don't date guys from the gym." She paused. "Or Navy guys." She tipped her face up to the moon.

"You sure have a lot of don'ts, Marleigh. And I'm not just some guy from the gym or some Navy dude."

"Plenty of squids have come and gone through this gym, Jace."

"I'm a special operator, not just some squid."

She'd injured him. She could hear it in his voice and feel it as he picked up his walking pace. "I know. I'm sorry. Why did you join?"

"I wanted out of nowhere Nebraska, as far as I could go. I'm good with electronics, circuits, and wires. I worked all year fixing farm equipment but knew there had to be more out there. I liked the thought of deep dark water, and turns out I'm a solid diver, too. So it worked out. My dad was a Marine, and no way in hell I was going that route. And they're pretty choosy about who gets to go to dive school and then EOD training. And even then plenty of dudes wash out."

"But you didn't."

"No, I didn't. Now, I shouldn't overdo it. We're mostly asshats," he said, scoring another laugh from Marleigh. "But I'm not that bad."

She sighed. "Never said you were."

"And that's a pretty strict policy. Rules out a lot of guys. Who do you date?"

"I don't. I mean, I'm in school and working. I plan to get out of this shitty neighborhood and stay out."

"I didn't mean anything by that," he said. He stopped and looked at her.

Marleigh felt herself waver. If she just stopped. If she leaned into him. No. "It's not like you were wrong. I'm just too busy. It's late. I need to get back to my car. I'm working in the morning."

"What about after work?"

"I need to study."

"You're going to study all night?"

"Yup."

"I'll walk you back. Don't you need to eat when you study?"

"I eat while I study."

Back at her car, he watched her jiggle the handle as she unlocked the door. Her car still had a key that needed to turn in the lock, but the lock was jammed. "Don't laugh at my car," she said.

"I wouldn't dare. Can I help?" He walked over to her and pressed the handle in smooth and steady and turned the key all in a fluid motion. She looked at him, a mix of annoyance and relief washing through her. He held the door open for her. She paused, for just a second, as she got in the car.

"I don't have time," she said. She spoke her internal admonishment aloud.

"For food?"

"For you, for anyone. Thanks for the walk, but I'm not interested," she said as she turned the key in the ignition.

"Whatever you say, princess." He shut her door and walked to his crotch rocket. Clearly, he wasn't going to beg.

CHAPTER SIX

Three days later, Marleigh swigged her Diet Coke as she walked into Azpiration Ink. "Mornin', Crest," Jameson said, like he did every day they worked together. The shop was a block and a half from Pops's gym. She'd started apprenticing there in high school, honing her craft for free and cleaning for cash. Now she was the junior tattoo artist on staff. Jameson was only a few years older. They'd shared the same bus stop when they were kids. He was nearly covered in tattoos now, arms, legs and neck sleeved.

"Hey there," she responded, knowing she should have never admitted her dental aspirations. Someone had immediately called her Crest and it stuck. "Your teeth really are very white. Shiny." He was right. Her mother hadn't been very handy with advice except to say, "The difference between rich white people and poor white people is their teeth. You can cover up poor, but bad teeth always give you away." Marleigh had taken very good care of her teeth.

"You're up for our first walk-in." Jameson nodded to the man sitting in a chair just beyond the front door. "Dave over there is paid up and ready to go."

"Perfect. Come on over. We can talk while I set up," she said. Marleigh liked the daytime shifts just fine. Unlike the rest of the staff, she didn't groan about walk-ins. She had no problem accepting $200 from someone who simply had to have a peace sign or a Chinese character that they couldn't pronounce. When couples walked in hand-in-hand and wanted each other's names tattooed, she'd nod their gaze to the *Bad Tattoo Ideas* sign but wouldn't try and talk them out of it. Maybe the couple would make it. And there was no such thing as a curse. A tattoo didn't doom a relationship. She did give the couple odds, though, in her head. She knew someone had been caught cheating when he put his wife's name somewhere prominent and showy. As if, like a wedding ring, that would stop him. She rationalized that if the couple was determined to get matching tattoos, they'd get it done somewhere. Might as well make some money on their bad decision.

She motioned for the man to take a seat in her chair. "Do you have an idea of what you're looking for?" Marleigh laid out a clean set of tools on the tray beside her chair, inventoried the pigments.

Three days a week her shift started at eleven o'clock, when the tattoo parlor's doors opened. The day hours were almost always filled with appointments—the long-planned tattoos, the kind that the customers came in for a consultation and discussed concept and Marleigh would sketch out her interpretation and take their non-refundable deposits.

The man pointed to his chest. "Yeah. My wife just had a baby. Her name's Robin and the baby is Birdy."

"How cute," Marleigh said, a design crystalized in her imagination. "You want it over your heart, right?" Often, she read the customer well and he'd love the design. Rarely did anyone need anything but a minor alteration from her design. Women usually sought out the male artists. She couldn't see any tattoos on him. He wore a button-up shirt, the sleeves rolled up to his elbows, and jeans. Plenty of her customers didn't have visible tats.

"Yeah, exactly." He looked a little pale.

"Is this your first time?"

He nodded. "I mean I always wanted one, I just didn't know what. And this seemed like the perfect idea."

"It'll be great. Your wife will love it." She bent over her sketch pad and outlined a simple robin landing on a twig, wings extended, all in black and white, except for a gentle wash of orange on the breast, and a smaller bird just beside. "Like this?" She held up the pad.

"Wow. That's beautiful." What she did felt a lot like art sometimes.

"I like to start clean and simple. You can always add to it over time, or if you guys have another baby. Do you need time to think about it?"

"No. No, let's do it." His voice was little squeaky and unsure.

"Hit the bathroom over there. And I promise it's not nearly as bad as you're thinking it'll be."

When Dave returned, she shaved his chest and wiped him down with antiseptic. She gave him a candy to suck on. "Breathe," she instructed. She began.

"Oh," he exhaled. "That's not so bad." His chest relaxed under her palm.

The design was simple, and the client didn't need any breaks, so Marleigh finished in just over an hour, just as her first consultation appointment arrived. Dave couldn't stop looking at the finished product in her mirror, despite his aggravated, pink skin and the salve she smoothed over her work. He left her a thirty-dollar tip. It was going to be a good day. The customer had to pay seventy-five cash just to reserve her time. For a no-show she got fifty and the shop took twenty-five. When a customer did show, and they almost always did, she made 75 percent of the cash payment for the piece.

On bad days, Marleigh felt like those artists whose patron wanted portraits of a homely daughter or beloved hunting dog. Those days, at their worst, were fine. On a slow day, she made way more than she did waitressing and the flexibility was fantastic, but the lack of benefits sucked. Cash every day was great, but it went fast. Slow days gave her hours in her station drawing for herself.

Other than the zero benefits, Azpiration Ink could almost be mistaken for a dentist's office. Each artist had a station. Autoclaves glowed; magnifying mirrors were wiped to a squeaky shine. All the reclining chairs matched. The artists decorated their spaces with tchotchkes of their own. More had Little League or kiddie soccer photos taped up than their clients expected. They often said so. And everyone wore mostly all black every day, so they matched. It was an unspoken thing. Perhaps because of the staining dye, or maybe it made the artwork look more vibrant. They joked that it matched the color of their souls. They all decorated for holidays, especially Halloween. They had a kickball team. Add floss, some gargling and rinsing fountains, and they'd be there. Oh, some health insurance, too.

. . .

Marleigh left the tattoo parlor with a few hundred dollars in cash, changed her clothes, and headed to school. She managed to finish her homework in the study corrals before the evening's class started. Her day would end just in time to catch the fight airing at the gym. Tonight's ECPI offerings were biology and composition. Her class was dismissed at nine, and she drove back across town to Ocean View.

She came straight from class and was wearing a pair of gray shorts and a blue-and-white striped scoop neck T-shirt. She had straightened her hair that morning and worn it down all day, winged out her eyeliner and slicked gloss on her lips. Her hair was much longer straight than when she let it air dry; the ends dusted the tops of her shoulders. The trainers would pretend they didn't recognize her or act like they had forgotten she was female.

The guys started arriving fifteen minutes before the fight. She had wolfed down a sandwich in the car and sat sipping a sweaty iced tea. Terry and Pops were the second to arrive. Pops was always offered one of the office chairs, but he usually spent the fight pacing in the ring below the television, his neck craned up. Only the most serious boxers came to the gym for the televised fights, though she posted every fight they were hosting on the whiteboard in the office along with the three-dollar walk-in charge. Most guys preferred to go somewhere loud and that had more than one or two women present, places that smelled like beer and buffalo wings, not pre-wrap and antiseptic.

"Hey, Marleigh," Terry called as they walked in. She and Terry had taken to trying to use everyone's name as frequently as possible to minimize Pops's frustration. He hated to ask. Knowing he'd forgotten someone he knew made him collapse into himself.

"Hi, Terry! Hi, Pops!" She walked over to hug her grandfather. "Nice jersey." She winked at Terry, who must have helped him out. Pops wore a Mexican soccer jersey and sweatpants in honor of the fight.

"It's going to be a good one," Pops said, as he always did. Marco Antonio Barrera versus Eric Morales. Pops opened a can of grape soda, his favorite. Terry nursed a red Solo cup as usual. Fights were bring-your-own everything.

Everyone called Marleigh's grandad *Pops*, regardless of whether they were freckled white or dark brown. Pops called each of the guys *son*. No one knew for sure if it was out of confusion or ease. He'd done it forever and no one seemed to care. His affection was a warm place to be. Marleigh wheeled the two chairs from the office into the gym. She assembled the box jumps and weight benches in a semi-circle along with the trainers' folding metal chairs around the flatscreen in the corner. She fired up the two a/c window units. Fight nights were the only nights OV Box was climate controlled. On these nights, for however long the fight lasted, Pops was himself again. All the prep and logistics were worth it. Tonight, Terry had offered to pick him up, so all Marleigh had to do was get the gym ready. No one outside of the gym understood why she would want to watch the fights. She had talked Lynetha into coming once. Terry had been between women, and Marleigh thought they might hit it off. Lynetha made the mistake of talking while the fight was on and expecting answers to her questions. There was plenty of yelling at the screen, sure, but no one actually conversed.

"Half the time they not hitting nobody, but y'all just watch and watch two dudes bounce around a ring," Lynetha said. And the gym stunk, even when no one was training. Marleigh always forgot that. So, she went solo. If it was her one night off for the week . . . oh well. And she never knew if the fight would last five minutes or all twelve rounds, but that was boxing.

The door dinged and everyone turned to see who had arrived. It was Jace, and three guys with the same haircuts. She recognized Matty from their first night at the gym. His hand was bandaged. "Squids in the house," he said. They all dropped twenties in the pot to pay for the fight. There was way more than the PPV amount in the pot. Possibly enough to make up for how short the gym was that week.

"You made it. Nice, bro," Terry said.

Jace wore a slim gray T-shirt, dark jeans, and boots. Marleigh didn't know what to do with herself. Her face burned. Heat spread across her clavicle. She felt like a jerk for how she had treated Jace the other night, but at least he'd left her alone for a few days. She kept expecting to see him walk into the gym or the Thirsty Camel, but he didn't. She wanted to be angry at him for showing up again, for being around so much, but she wanted to apologize more. He had a motorcycle helmet tucked under one arm and a six-pack of Coors dangling from the other hand.

She started to stand from the weight bench where she'd been sitting to go say something to him, anything, when Pops climbed out through the ropes of the ring, yelling, "Parry! Get your arse up here." Jace looked around and behind him. "Finally, ye made it." Oh no. Pops's accent always thickened to a parody of itself when he got lost in his memories. Parry? Christ. Parrish. He thought Jace was Marleigh's father, Parrish Mulcahy, and that it was twenty-five years ago. Pops rattled the office chair beside his. "C'mon. Saved you a seat up front. This'll help you prepare."

Marleigh stood abruptly and touched Jace's arm. He flinched, then looked at her. "You don't have to," she mumbled. She felt panicky. If she corrected her grandfather, he would get angry, then embarrassed. And then he'd get scary angry.

Jace leaned into her. "Who's Parry?"

She shook her head. "My dad," she said, pointing to a poster of her father wearing the one and only belt he'd ever won, a picture taken five years before Marleigh was born. He'd been a promising fighter, but he was lazy and disinterested. That's what everyone but her father said, anyway.

"It's no big deal," Jace said, his voice warm on her neck. "Hey! Your hair is different." Jace didn't have a face that made her ask what he was thinking. Plenty of the time he probably wasn't thinking anything at all. But in his still, slothy moments, he never missed a detail. He noticed everything about Marleigh. She had to tune out plenty; taking everything in made her jumpy.

"C'mon, Parry! S'is about the start." Pops's eyes shimmered, bright with excitement.

"I'm sorry," Marleigh said, their faces too close together. She meant sorry for all of it. Fights had been the protected time. Until tonight, they kept Pops present. Hopefully, it was just a bad week. Maybe he needed more rest.

"It's okay," Jace answered, pushing a lock of hair behind her ear. She wasn't sure if he meant her grandad or the other night.

She gave him a look. "I was an asshole," she said.

"You were," he said and tugged on that lock of hair until she shrugged away. "Fight time, sweetheart." He turned to walk up to where Pops stood expectantly.

Her grandad didn't snap out of it. Not for twelve full rounds and a majority decision. "Shoulda been a draw," Pops shouted at the screen. "Toe to toe, punch for punch, the whole way." She'd barely seen any of it. She watched Jace listen patiently to whatever pointers Pops thought he was instilling and nod solemnly.

Twice he turned around and caught her looking. She mouthed *"thank you"* and meant it. As the gym emptied, Pops remained agitated. Marleigh couldn't tell if he was mad at the judges, his memories, or what. He didn't seem to know, either.

"I'll get him home, Terry," Marleigh said. "It's on my way." Pops wasn't Terry's responsibility.

"You sure?" They all watched Pops pace around the gym.

"Let's go to the Knights of Columbus," Pops yelled. "S'too early for bed."

"C'mon, wild man," Marleigh said. "The Knights is closed. And I'll clean up here tomorrow."

Pops tugged his jersey out from the elastic waist of his sweatpants. He rolled the shirt up over his small paunchy belly and began scratching the skin red. Marleigh hated when her grandfather embarrassed himself. She didn't want anyone to think this was actually him. She gave Terry a look and he herded the stragglers out of the gym. Pops had done so much for her and everyone in that room. He deserved better.

Marleigh reached for Pops. "Stop it, ye little bitch." He flung her hand away. "I'm not ready to leave. This is my place." He started scratching his balls.

"I'll come along," Jace said, steering Pops by the shoulder out of the gym. "Let's go have some fun." He directed Pops toward Marleigh's car.

"Yes, m'boy. But I don't want that little cunt to come. She'll ruin everything." Marleigh winced. She knew Pops had no idea who she was in that moment or what he was saying. Still, his words hurt. She could tell by Jace's expression that he didn't like hearing them, either.

Marleigh wasn't sure what to do. She didn't want to take Jace's help and allow him to expect anything, but her grandfather seemed calmer with him nearby. Pops was still strong and quick enough to do some damage. He'd put his fist through the new dry wall separating the office from the gym. They decided to leave the hole, and Terry had written *your face* beside it. Pops had taken a swing at Terry once, confused. He had not gotten violent with Marleigh, not with anything other than his words, anyway.

"How about that fight?" Jace opened the car door for Pops, and climbed into the passenger seat. "When Barrera caught Morales on the jaw. His arm was a blur."

"S'right, Parrish."

"Pops, this is—" Marleigh began. Jace shook his head to quiet her. He didn't mind that Pops's head was all over the place.

"And he kept his feet moving the whole time, shifting his weight. Morales couldn't tell where the punch was coming from. Keep working on your speed, you could be great like that, too, Parry."

"I will." Jace caught Marleigh's eyes in the rearview mirror.

"It's late, Marleigh," Pops yelled from the backseat. "Let's go home."

Marleigh sighed. "Yessir."

Back at his apartment, Marleigh and Jace sat with him until he fell asleep on the chair in front of the television. The couch was barely big enough for two people and their thighs touched.

"Thank you," Marleigh said. She wasn't sure what would have happened if Jace hadn't helped her. And more than that. He was so kind and patient with Pops, and he knew Pops wouldn't remember any of it. He was being kind just to be kind, not to get any special favors at the gym.

"I hate this. He made me promise not to dump him in a home. He wants to live alone."

"I got more time with you," Jace said, bumping her knee with his. "And you were actually almost nice."

She wanted to explain how she had too much going on, how this would never work, but she was too tired, and his body felt good. He kissed her, and she let him. He lifted her over, onto his lap, and it felt good to lean into him. His hands in her hair. His body hard beneath her hands.

Pops snored and caught his breath. Marleigh pulled away. "I need to go home. I'll drop you back at your bike." She expected him to argue, wanted him to argue, press to go home with her. He didn't. He stayed quiet for the quick car ride. It was a comfortable quiet.

"I'm worth the risk," he said as he stepped out of her car.

She let herself wonder.

CHAPTER SEVEN

Marleigh slept in the next morning. She'd had such a hard time falling asleep. Whenever Pops had one of his episodes, she wondered what it meant. Was he getting worse? Would a day come when he had no memory of her, when he'd run away forever to the years before his own son broke his heart? She needed to alert her parents, though she doubted it would do much good. How had she ended up his caretaker? What had he done to end up alone? Would he be okay this morning on his own?

She slept in and barely had time to grab a cup of coffee at 7-Eleven. She hated coffee and pumped it full of Coffeemate, but it woke her up and was way cheaper than any of the energy drinks. She would check on Pops after the lunchtime bar rush. There was always a mid-afternoon lull, and all the waitresses owed her one. She called her parents' house and got the machine, hoping the ringing woke them up and initiated pulsing morning-after headaches.

"Pops had a bad night yesterday. You should check on him. I'm worried." Damn it, her voice caught on that last part. She needed to be all business with her parents.

She wiped the last bite of chicken tender off her face, thankful for the owner's allowance of one free kid's meal per shift. The midday was steady business and pleasant, but Marleigh was distracted. She'd been so exhausted that making out with Jace seemed like a dream. If that was real, all the bad stuff that happened was real, too. Just thinking about his body against provoked her. She needed to get laid. Maybe they could just do it and get it over with and that would be that. It probably wouldn't be that good anyway. He'd fumble around and get off, leaving her to finish for herself. Still, her mind was happy to explore. He probably wouldn't be in Norfolk that long, anyway.

As the crowd thinned, Marleigh pulled one of the floor waitresses behind the bar with promises that she could keep the tips she earned and that Marleigh would be back in an hour. She meant to clock out before she left. She punched in an order for a grilled cheese and the waffle fries Pops liked, instead. Sometimes he forgot to eat. Other times he would eat three boxes of Ritz crackers in a day, never remembering the last handful. She'd find the brown sleeves all over the kitchen. She'd put up a dry-erase board for him, a smaller version than the one at the gym, and made a section for him to jot down what he was eating and when, but the system had proven unreliable.

Pops's apartment was five long blocks from the bar. When she reached it, she hoped he had slept in, too. Maybe the fights were on too late. Certainly, she could get one of the guys to help her figure out how to record them for him. He wouldn't know the difference between that and a live broadcast. He would just be happy to watch it. Wasn't that all that mattered? She was eager to see daytime Pops, the good guy who would never confuse Jace with her father.

She knocked hard on the door before reaching for her key. "Pops, it's me, Marleigh," she called through the open doorway. It wasn't unusual for him not to answer right away. Maybe he was napping. She stepped inside.

The kitchen faucet ran hard and fast, spray spitting up onto the countertop. She glanced at the stove to make sure everything was off, turned off the water, plunked the takeout onto the counter. The TV was dark. The remote was on the floor next to his recliner. Maybe he went out for a walk. He loved the sunshine on the beach and petting the dogs out for walks.

"Pops," she called again, waiting a few seconds before she walked into his bedroom. No answer. She stooped over to replace the remote back on the arm of his chair. Crouching to get the remote, she saw movement through the doorway, on the floor, a twitch. Fingers. Her grandfather's body, shirtless, crumpled was on the ground in the small walkway between his bedroom and bathroom. He lay on his bare stomach, still wearing his sweatpants.

"Pops!" she screamed. The only part of him moving was his fingers. She tried to roll him over, afraid he would suffocate against the carpet. It was like dragging the heavy bag. She checked his neck for a pulse. His skin was clammy, the base of his neck, damp. She pressed so hard, up and down his neck. A thump. That had to be a pulse. "Pops, I'm going to get help. Everything will be okay." She ran to the kitchen and pulled the phone from the wall and dialed 911.

She sat on the floor and held his twitching fingers in her hand. He must have known she was there. He relaxed. The paramedics arrived ten minutes later. When the two men lifted her grandad up onto a gurney, she saw a bruise that ran down the entire left side of his face. Marleigh gasped. Dark purple pooled beneath his skin. She must have made a horrified look. The paramedic spoke. "Ma'am, he was probably dead before he hit the ground."

Any second, he would open his eyes and tell the men to get their hands off him. He would move between Marleigh, and any threat, just like he always had. "Wait. What?" Marleigh asked. "I felt his pulse." That guy had to be wrong. Pops could still jump rope. He could walk and walk and walk. He couldn't be dead. He just forgot himself sometimes.

"Aren't you going to try?"

"I'm sorry, ma'am, but any chest compressions would simply be abusive to the body."

He's a man, not just a body. This was Pops.

"Strap him up and take him to the hospital. What are you waiting for? He needs a doctor!" She tried to lift him. He was stiff, heavy. Cold.

"We don't take dead people to the hospital, ma'am."

The paramedics radioed in, referring to Pops as DOA. "Elderly man, died at home."

"The sheriff's deputy will be here soon. Do you know what funeral home you're going to use? It's time to arrange for them to pick him up. Or his body will go to the morgue first."

Marleigh's head spun. Pops had died alone on his floor in this piece-of-shit apartment. Marleigh let this happen, after everything he had done for her. She nodded at the men.

Pops said he wanted to be buried with his buddies in the big cemetery on Granby Street. But she had no idea how to connect the dots between here and there. First, she called Lynetha. She started sobbing at her friend's voice asking her to leave a message at the tone. Next, she tried Terry. Where was everyone? She riffled through her purse, the pink carbon paper crinkling in her shaking fingers. She dialed Jace's number and got his voicemail. Before she could think and stop herself, she unloaded in a rush. "I'm at Pops'. He's dead. I don't know what to do next." She hung up, wishing she could delete the message. Her stomach flipped. She had to call her parents. The only safe person, her safe place, was dead. She hadn't been able to tell him goodbye. Or thank you. Nothing.

CHAPTER EIGHT

An hour later, once she'd forgotten her voicemail, Jace texted. *On my way.* In the time she spent alone with Pops, with what was left of him anyway, Marleigh talked. "Thank you for raising me. Thank you for teaching me how to fight." She sat on the floor with her back against the couch. It was easier if she didn't have to see him. "I'm so sorry I was late today and that I wasn't here. I'm going to miss you so much." She already did.

Jace barreled through the open front door, cheeks flushed and out of breath. It was nice to have another living person in the apartment. "Hey, Marleigh," he said quietly as he kneeled beside her, his breath cold mint on her face. "I should have been here sooner."

"I—I'm sorry I called you. I didn't know what to do," she said. "The EMTS laid him out on his bed."

"I'm not sorry you called." He put one arm, hesitant, around her. She rested her head on his shoulder. With his free hand he plucked the loose threads of her jeans that pulled across her knees like guitar strings and wrapped them around his fingers until the tips turned red.

"I finally got a hold of my parents," she said. "They gave me the number for the funeral home. My dad has to sign some papers before the people from the home can come pick up Pops, his body." She was trying not to cry.

"You've done good, Marleigh. Ya handled a whole lot today."

She held onto his sleeve. "You should probably go. The shit show could roll in any minute."

"You talk like a sailor." He smiled. "I'm not going anywhere."

"You don't want anything to do with them, Jace. I'm sticking around to make sure my dad signs off on all the funeral stuff, to make sure they actually show up. I just can't leave Pops alone again." She turned into him, her mouth so close to his neck.

"You took good care of him. And you let him live like a man, not a child. You know that's how he wanted it."

She was quiet, then, and leaned against him for what felt like a long time. He kept his arms around her, and she settled into him.

There was a commotion in the hallway, and two middle-aged people clambered into Pops's apartment. She should have smelled her parents coming down the hallway—way too much mouthwash. "And here they are," she mumbled and pushed away from Jace so that she could stand.

Marleigh's mother, Jackie, spoke first. "So, this is what you were doing when your grandfather was dying, playing grab ass?"

Her father said nothing. He walked heavy to the bedroom.

"The funeral home people will be here any minute," Marleigh said. "You both need to stay here until they get here." Her voice was icy and flat. She kept her expression hard.

Sounds like coughing or choking came from the bedroom. "Jackie, are you going to check on Dad?"

Jackie didn't move. "I'm your mother. Speak to me like it."

"Taking that as a no." Marleigh squeezed between her mother and the bedroom door. She put her arm across her father's heaving back. She couldn't help herself, even though her dad deserved to feel like garbage, knowing how he'd let everyone down, how he blamed Pops for caring about every street kid more than his own son.

Marleigh walked out the bedroom door to where Jace and her mother stood. "We're going to leave now," she said.

"Of course you are," her mother said. "You can't get anything from the old man now that he's dead." Jace was getting pissed.

"At least Dad's sad that Pops is gone," Marleigh mumbled. She looked once back to the bedroom, pausing for a minute to decide if she should go back in there. She shook her head and walked to the door.

Once outside Jace asked, "Where can I take you? Home? I can pick up my bike later, no problem."

She shook her head and walked into the parking lot. Home, alone, was the last place she wanted to be. She walked straight past her car to his motorcycle. "Take me for a ride?"

"Very good idea," he said. "Speed and forget, this I can do for you." He handed Marleigh his helmet.

They rode down to the end of Willoughby Spit and back again, her arms tight around his waist, the helmet bobbing gently against the back of his neck. She could feel each exhalation, his heart clamoring against his ribs.

They stopped at a seafood dive near the Hampton Roads Bridge-Tunnel. "Hey, Jace, who's your friend?" the hostess asked when they walked in.

Marleigh squinted at him. "I thought you weren't trouble," she said.

"Not the bad kind," he said. "You hungry? I haven't eaten all day."

"Starving." She finished a monster cheeseburger topped with a crab cake and a side of fries.

"Not sure where you put all that, but I'm impressed." He gulped his ice water and picked through his fried seafood basket.

When the waitress asked if they needed anything else, Marleigh shocked him by saying, "Tequila. Ice cold." She smiled at his surprise. "You want one?" she asked.

"Uh, sure. Just one, though. I'm driving." The waitress winked at him. "I didn't think you drank," Jace said.

Marleigh shrugged. "I don't really. But I don't want to feel all this right now."

"That I understand."

When the waitress brought the shot glasses, Marleigh raised hers and said, "To Pops and skipping class." Her eyes filled and she swallowed the tequila, jamming a slice of lime into her mouth.

She started feeling a little loose after her second shot. Jace waved off a second shot, paid the tab, and ignored the waitress's, "Look who's on his best behavior tonight."

"Oooooo," Marleigh teased. "I don't wanna go home," she said, a tipsy pout forming.

"Okay," he said. "You gotta hold on, though. Tight."

She slid the helmet on and tilted her chin up for him to fasten the chin strap. He grazed her lips with his.

• • •

By the time they got to his place, Marleigh was sleepy. His apartment was clean, but he looked a little embarrassed when Marleigh said, "Nice poster," pointing up at the St. Pauli girl above his bed. "Shquid," she slurred.

"C'mon, wise guy. Let's get you to bed." She lay down in all of her clothes. He lay beside her. She fell deeply asleep.

The room was still dark when she wriggled against him, her body a tight C-shape beside his. He didn't react at first. She tried again, stretching against him. His dick stiffened against the curve of her ass.

Marleigh pressed harder, tilted her head back. His mouth was full of her hair, lips grazing her neck. He slid his hands the length of her body from shoulders to the points of her hips. He held on and tugged harder still. His body asked hers for permission. She took one of his hands off her hip bone and wrapped his arm farther around her, pressing his fingertips inside her waistband. Soft belly, the edge of panties, a soft thatch of hair and down, grinding against her as his fingers worked into her wet folds. Slick. His dick pulsed against her.

He turned her onto her back. "Is this what you want? I can stop, but it'll be fucking brutal." Jace sat up and back from her.

She pulled her shirt over her head, and grazed her breasts against his mouth. She groaned as he clucked her nipple, tongue and teeth and her hips mashing against his. Their kiss tasted of tequila, lips and chin, salty. An indelicate yank and he had her panties off and his mouth in the wet spot his fingers had found. She wasn't hard or quiet or restrained. She fed herself to him. Nails on his neck and down his back.

He wiped his mouth and positioned himself over her, moving slowly. Just as he started to enter her, she whispered, "Wait." He gritted his teeth and stopped moving. "We need a condom," she said.

Jace groaned and opened the bedside table drawer, rummaging. "It's okay," he said, one hand plumbing the drawer as his dick ground against her thighs. "I'm clean." She shook her head. He found the square packet and tore it open. He slid it on and was inside her, finally.

CHAPTER NINE

Marleigh took her birth control pill and three ibuprofen as soon as she got home. Her head hurt and her heart too, but her body hummed. Jace's effect on her couldn't be reasoned with. Pops was dead and she'd slept with Jace, and she had a shit-ton of homework. She wished Jace was there.

She had four missed calls from the Thirsty Camel from the prior day. Not only had she forgotten to clock out when she left for Pop's, but she'd clearly never returned for her night shift or let anyone know where she'd gone. She had no idea when her next tattoo appointment was. It didn't make sense that all of that happened in one day— yesterday. Pops had been around for all her twenty-two years, and in one day he went away from her forever. There was no referee to call an eight count. No one was there to help, including Marleigh. Her body wanted to cry, wanted another release, but her eyes stayed dry. They had always counted on each other, she and Pops. He had loved her well, always showing up the minute her home life became unbearable. He taught her that love and loyalty were one thing— the inhale and the exhalation, one can't exist without the other. She would never see him again. Something inside her dimmed.

She should call work. They would understand, but she couldn't bring herself to do that, either. She needed to call Terry and the other trainers, let them hear it from her. She just couldn't make her mouth move right. Jace had wanted to take her to breakfast, but she had no appetite.

He'd driven her, instead, back to her car. Hugged her tight and said, "I'm really sorry about Pops." If she were going to cry, it would have been then. "Please, if I can do anything to help, I really want to." She laughed when he said that. He was so nice and earnest and honest. She had no idea how to take it. Then she just felt like a jackass. He'd taken care of her, and this morning felt so good, the way their bodies simply fit.

"Jace, I didn't mean to laugh." He gave her an *"it's okay"* look. "I have late class tonight. Won't be home until ten, and I plan to crash, and crash hard."

She couldn't solve any of it. She might as well just study. She was behind enough as it was.

He kissed her forehead. She rested her head in his palms.

• • •

Her ears rang the entire drive back from class that night. She could barely recall anything from the lecture. Her eyes were heavy, but her brain rolled like the tub in the laundromat. Over and over, she spun. Marleigh got home from class at ten thirty and knew she wasn't going to fall asleep. She had started to work on the paper due for next week when the doorbell rang. It was a Dominos delivery driver. "I didn't order pizza," she said, wishing she hadn't been so honest. Her stomach twisted. She hadn't eaten since the night before.

"You're 404 F?"

"Yeah," she said.

"Sign here." He handed her a credit card receipt. She signed on the line for Jace Holt. She ate three pieces and found the energy to cry. Afterwards, she texted Jace. *Thx for the pizza. Sry abt this morning.*

I'm not, he responded. *Get some sleep.*

Marleigh slept late and ignored the gym for another day. She let the angry voicemails from the Thirsty Camel linger. The last one said, "I'm sorry to hear about Pops. Call if you want to get back on the schedule." They already took her off the schedule? She needed to make that call. And Jameson from the tattoo parlor. "We're covering for you, but I'm worried. Call me." She couldn't talk about Pops. That would make it all real.

· · ·

After class the following night she drove to the gym instead of going straight home. Sleep at night was hard enough; waking up early seemed impossible. She wasn't sure what she'd find. Had Terry opened the place without her? Had it just sat inexplicably locked and dark? If word about Pops had made it to the Camel already, certainly the fighters heard. She smiled at the lights and open sign as she arrived at OV Box. Terry's car and Jace's bike were parked there, along with a couple of vehicles she didn't recognize.

The desk was a mess, but Pops would have been happy that guys were still training. She waved into the gym before digging into the books and tallying cash, reminding herself to lock the front door and to remind Terry to do the same when there was no one at the front desk. Someone had affixed *RIP Pops 1938–2013* above his picture, *A feckin' legend,* below.

"He'd love that," Marleigh said, imagining Pop's laugh.

"I know," Terry said. "We've got new T-shirts coming."

She shook her head. "Can you come see me when you're done? Sorry I've been MIA." She was sure there'd be some gaps in the sign-in and payment records without anyone manning the desk. Hopefully, Terry could fill them in.

"Yes, ma'am," he said.

"Even though you didn't ask, I'm going to come see you, too," Jace said with a sweet, dopey grin.

"Okay, okay! Finish your rounds first. I have work to do."

Marleigh sat behind the desk and began organizing the bills that had been shoved into the desk drawer, comparing them to the sign-in roster and trainer time cards. The front door flew open, slamming into the wall. Her parents stormed in, a vapor of smoke and alcohol and ruin. Marleigh went cold. Had she forgotten to lock the door? They hadn't had a key for over a year when they tried to sell the place out from underneath Pops.

"Hey, baby girl," her mother said. Jackie hadn't called Marleigh that in years. "I'm sorry about the other day. It was such a shock." Her mother sounded sincere. "Why do you look so scared?"

Because fear was the healthiest reaction to her parents' presence. "We . . . we don't normally get walk-ins this late. I was just surprised." Their eyes were red as their cheeks, and every bit of them looked rumpled.

Marleigh winced at her mother's hand, reaching out for her, stroking her hair. "It's me, Marleigh." She shoved the bills and cash beneath the desk. Her mother's eyes filled with tears. "What are you hiding? Why are you treating us like this?"

What the hell was going on? What kind of response was she expecting? Marleigh couldn't remember the last time her mother touched her kindly, tenderly. A hug could so easily turn into a slap. Kindness couldn't be trusted. She shrugged her mother's hand off her.

"What are you doing here?"

"We want to help."

"Since when?"

"Marleigh, girl," her father reached around the desk. No. It was too much like Pops. He wasn't allowed to talk to her like Pops. That wasn't fair.

"Stay away from me."

Her father's wince was exaggerated, cartoonish. Had he really thought she'd let him touch her? "I see." Normally Parrish scrupulously avoided s words when he was drunk so he wouldn't get caught slurring.

Tonight, he didn't care. "She's already got her hands in the cookie jar."

Her mother pointed. "Pops isn't cold and you're in here ripping us off."

Her father pushed her mother out of the way. "We'll take care of that," he told Marleigh, motioning for her to hand him the cash. "Probate, the estate. We need to get it settled."

She shoved the cash in the safe and locked it. "Not without a lawyer or someone."

"Give me the key, Marleigh. I'll take care of everything." Her dad took big, slow steps toward her. She shrunk into the wall. He kept his voice low.

"You're not the boss, you little slut!" her mother needled.

"You okay out there, Mar?" Terry called from the gym. After the mugging they had developed a code word for trouble. She couldn't remember it.

"Everything's fine, Terry," her father said, trying and failing to get a hold of his slur. Terry wouldn't need a code word.

Terry and Jace were through the doorway from the gym in an instant.

"We'll do this in the morning. Mom and Dad," the words rusty in her mouth, "meet me here. We'll get the lawyer and sort it all out." *Deescalate, Marleigh, deescalate.* The energy in the room was terrifying. Jace was tight as a held breath, his eyes locked on her father.

"Just give me the key," her mother said. "None of this belongs to you."

"I can't. We'll do it tomorrow." Always tomorrow. She was always waiting for the pass out and the storm to blow through. "I'll make an appointment with the probate lawyer tomorrow."

"Let's do like Marleigh said," Terry interrupted. "We'll handle this in the morning. We was just closing and settling out the day. It's been a bad week for everyone." Terry could always keep it cool, but she didn't trust the look of either parent.

"Which one of these guys is your favorite?" her mother asked.

Her father lunged at Marleigh, reaching for the money. Normally they saved their crazy for when no one was around.

"Don't touch her," Jace yelled.

Her father ignored him. Like that, Jace had him on the ground, a knee at his neck.

"Stop it," Jackie screamed.

Terry knelt beside Jace and put his hands on Jace's shoulders. "He's down, man. Let's go back into the gym."

Jace waited a moment, one fist still raised, Marleigh's father pinned beneath him. He stood silently and walked through the door.

"You animal," Marleigh's mother yelled.

"S'enuff, Jackie," Parrish said, rising to his feet.

Marleigh was shivering. She could hear the beating Jace gave the heavy bag in the other room. The skin on canvas, a louder slap than when struck with a glove. He hadn't gloved up, he was so angry. What would have happened if he'd hit Parrish? What made him stop?

"We should call the cops," Jackie wailed.

Marleigh's knuckles were white around the cash and receipts she clutched.

Terry stood in the doorway. Marleigh wasn't sure whether he was keeping her parents in or Jace out. "Mrs. Mulcahy, ain't no one pressing charges tonight. No one's doing nothing. Just get on home."

Terry locked the door behind them. "They gone," he called in to Jace.

Marleigh locked everything away.

Jace's hands were raw and bloody, cracked across the knuckles. Terry fetched him antiseptic and gauze. "Not worth you tearing up your hands, man," he told Jace.

Marleigh didn't recognize the look in Jace's eyes, but she could see him trying to master it. "That was a green-ass move, Jace. Not putting on gloves."

"Better than it could have been," Jace mumbled. "Nobody has the right to touch you like that, put hands on you."

"Damn straight," Terry said.

Marleigh imagined the way her old man's face would have crumbled beneath Jace's fists. The way Jace had attacked the heavy bag and destroyed his hands was personal. There would have been the crack of cheekbone and crunch of septum. Sticky blood and snot and spit. Begging him to stop. Parrish would have bled, fast and alcohol thin. A bloody pulp.

"Do you want me to stay, Marleigh?" Terry watched Jace tape up his raw knuckles.

"No. It's late and I'm okay."

"I'll be here in the morning. We'll get the lawyer scheduled, and the Mulcahys an' I'll handle it." Marleigh hated being lumped in with her parents, but she understood what Terry was doing. Seeing Jace would just set her parents off again. What would happen with the gym in the morning? What did she want to happen? She'd had no idea the end could be so close.

"Do you want me to leave, Marleigh?"

"No." She put her head down on the desk. "I don't know." Why did she try so hard? No matter what she did with the place, the furniture was so cheap any of the boxers could fold the desktop in two. The dented filing cabinets didn't match. The walls were cracked, but Marleigh worked hard to make it look professional. All for what, when her parents could simply knock files around, treat the gym like trash. She kept the desk organized, the shelves of used gloves and supplies, too.

"You're whipped. Can I get you home? Sounds like you have a big day tomorrow. What day isn't busy for you?" His breathing had slowed. The anger receded at least below the surface, and he gave her that damn smile again.

"Thank you for being here. For standing up for me. I'm sorry you saw all that."

"Don't worry about it. Let's get you home. We'll take your car. I'll come back and get my bike."

Feeling the weight of responsibility slip from her and into Jace's jacked-up hands brought immediate relief. She nearly fell asleep on the short ride back to her apartment. He walked her to the front door and kissed her, first on the forehead and then on the lips. "I want you to come in," she started. And did she ever. But she was so exhausted she was swoony on her feet. He brushed the sweaty hair off of her face. "But—"

"You're so tired. I'm not going anywhere. We have plenty of time for that."

CHAPTER TEN

Marleigh and Terry were the only two who arrived for the appointment with the lawyer the following week. Marleigh was relieved, and not surprised. Her parents weren't exactly morning people. Pops had left no will, but he'd left OV Box to Marleigh in a letter. He'd always told Marleigh he'd never expected to amount to anything, and that owning his own gym was outside of his wildest dreams. The probate attorney said there really wasn't much left of the gym, anyway. She told Marleigh what an admirable job she had done keeping the place afloat and the trainers paid and the boxers fighting. In total, Pops owed creditors nearly $70,000. The sale of the property seemed to be the only way to pay them.

"The other night with your parents wasn't a coincidence, then," Terry said to Marleigh outside in the sunshine, the awareness that their jobs were gone soon, too, dawning on them hot and fresh, along with the gym. He gently placed a thick hand on Marleigh's shoulder.

"Nope. They knew there was nothing left and came to grab whatever cash they could," Marleigh said. "I shoulda let Jace keep wailing on him."

"Maybe," Terry said.

Like Pops, they decided if they were going down, they'd go down swinging, not dancing. Terry, Marleigh, and the boxers staged two fights as fundraisers over Memorial Day weekend to try and raise enough money to pay off the creditors. No one wanted to see the gym close. The entire neighborhood came to work out or donate a few dollars. The top boxers and their amateur promoters hyped the fight.

Jace signed up twenty-three of his Navy buddies and their friends to sell tickets, volunteer, and cheer on the fighters. The week of the fight, Jace arrived before anyone else to help set up, and he stayed until Marleigh locked up the gym each night. He was tireless. No one had ever shown up for her like that. Jace'd only known Pops a few months, but there he was day after day, trying to save the small gym. No errand she asked of him was too big or too small. He assigned Gurley and Matty Harbich to Marleigh. "Anything she needs, boys. Don't even make her ask."

Marleigh's parents kept their shit together long enough to put on the shirts Terry had made with an image of young Pops in his shiny trunks, two hefty belts slung over his shoulders, and cheer on the fights. Marleigh kept her distance and a sharp eye on the proceeds, but she was happy they'd made it. In between bouts, Jace worked with the other trainers and regulars to teach the gawkers how to skip rope, what a combination looked like, how to stay light and coiled up, ready to strike, at the same time. He'd been paying attention all spring, by the looks of it. Where had the four and a half months since Jace walked into the gym gone?

This was Pops's goodbye. Marleigh was so pissed he didn't get to see it, all of these people who cared about him. And her. It was much more real and far more painful than the brief service beside his burial plot, another bill he'd left unpaid. Pops had built a legacy. He'd mattered. Marleigh knew she'd miss him the most.

Terry held court and ran the event like the gym owner he should have been. Pops would have been proud of him. They sat alone and counted the weekend's take of almost twenty-five grand. They'd worked their butts off but hadn't come close to the seventy thousand needed.

The valuable part of the gym was the tiny real estate it occupied. It didn't matter how many lives had changed inside the walls, the difference Pops had made. Marleigh's whole childhood. Like Pops, it was gone, suddenly and completely, and Marleigh's life was left riddled with holes. After June 1, OV Box N Go would disappear, and some shiny Planet Fitness or Mattress Plus would take its place.

"I need eight grand for the funeral and expenses," Marleigh told Terry. He passed the pile of bills to her.

"It's yours. There's three times that. You can get him a baller headstone. Go all out!"

She counted out $10,600. She packed the rest of the money into the pouch and handed it to Terry. She knew he wanted to get up to New Jersey where his sisters and their families had ended up. Terry deserved a fresh start. He studied her.

"Take it," she said. "We probably owe you way more."

"I can't take that," he said. "Pops would want you to have it."

"I'm too tired to argue, Terry."

"I can't believe this," Terry said. "Any of this shit." He shook his head but smiled. He gave her a quick, tight hug. "You take care of yourself."

"See you 'round," Marleigh said. She was sick and tired of taking care of herself.

CHAPTER ELEVEN

After the gym was sold and Pops's headstone had been carved and placed, Jace received his orders. Her time with Jace was running on empty. Jace made cheering Marleigh up his fulltime preoccupation. She'd been desperate to be free of her responsibilities at the gym hadn't she? She would take every one of them back on if Pops could come back, too. As Pops's small estate was gradually settled, Marleigh never had to see her parents again. But rather than free, she felt freshly abandoned, orphaned. Jace was convinced that an escape would shake her out of it. His golden retriever style persistence and loyalty were catchy, irresistible.

Marleigh told Jace no the first three times he asked her. "No, I'm not going to Nebraska." She had only been on an airplane once, for an invitational soccer tournament her freshman year. Pops had paid for the ticket and signed her school note.

"You deserve a vacation," Jace said.

"Who goes to Nebraska on vacation?" she said, though she'd never had a vacation, and nothing in the world sounded better than uninterrupted time with Jace. She had nothing left in Virginia—no Pops, no gym, and no job. She hadn't worked or studied since Pops died. Planning for the fundraising fight had taken all her time. She could beg her way back to the Thirsty Camel; same with the tattoo shop. School she had to wait to pick back up at the next session. She had already lost a month and a half. Jace had been there for all of it. He'd helped her box up personal items at the gym. Held her hand as she turned in the keys to the bank holding the mortgage. Told her what a killer (and crazy) chick she was for giving Terry nearly all the money raised. She hadn't needed to ask; he was just there and happy to give. Never had anyone done that for her. Jace earned more points in her book for not asking anything in return or rubbing his efforts in her face. And at least he had a family who wanted to see him, though he'd rarely talked about his parents. A change of scenery could be a good thing, right? And it was only a question of when, rather than if, her parents would come sniffing around for the fight proceeds.

"I can't argue with that, but I'm not leaving you here for the few weeks I have left before my orders."

She didn't want Jace to leave, either. With the insanity of the preceding weeks, she'd almost forgotten he was going, too. But she wasn't going to ask him to stay. His dress uniform hung in crisp lines in her closet. She had yet to see him wear it. His clothes took up so little space.

"It's a big decision," she said. She also couldn't afford a ticket; certainly he knew that.

"It's not like I'm asking you to marry me." She rolled her eyes. "Not yet anyway."

Heat crept up her neck. Marleigh didn't know how to be around siblings and aunts and uncles. "Can we talk later? I need to go."

• • •

Marleigh knew she should stay home and take summer classes and find another job, string together another hundred days identical to the ones before. She could up her course load since the gym no longer gobbled up her time. She could nearly get back on schedule.

Jace would leave, first for Nebraska and then for Afghanistan or a ship somewhere, and forget about her, and she could put her head down and make forward progress into the real life awaiting her. She'd tell Jace she wasn't going to Nebraska, she'd decided. Forget his goofy smile. Forget how damn good it felt, the way he looked at her. How much he made her laugh. The way their bodies searched each other out in sleep. It was just a passing thing, her and Jace. It could never be anything else. She needed a real way out of her life, out of the life her parents had lived. And that wasn't Jace. It didn't matter how she felt about him. She'd figure out her life without Pops and without Jace. She had little left to lose.

As soon as she got home, she'd call Jace and let him know. That would be easier than saying it to that hopeful face.

An envelope corner stuck out from beneath her apartment door. It wasn't a bill for rent or utilities; those were paid for another month. She tried pulling the edge to her, but it stuck. Once inside, with the light on, she recognized Jace's handwriting on the envelope. *Mar-open me!!* Inside was a plane ticket with her name on it, Norfolk, VA, to Omaha, NE, connecting through Chicago, June 9, and a neon green sticky note, *Get packed.*

She didn't own a suitcase. And they would be gone nearly a month.

· · ·

On the night before they left, Jace unzipped the duffel bag, pulled it open like a wound on his bed. "I can't believe you haven't started packing," she said. Although, really, she could believe it. Jace never seemed to worry about anything ahead of time, not until the moment was in his face. It was charming and boyish most of the time, but less so when she was getting ready to leave for one last night at the Thirsty Camel. Lynetha was sick and asked her to cover, and he needed help.

"There are rules, right?" he asked, digging his forearm into his bag. "Rules about what you can and can't bring? I've only flown military."

She'd only flown once and looked up how to pack. Her clothes were folded in neat piles. Jace had brought her a large backpack. She'd never been west of the Mississippi and didn't know what she needed, but she wanted to be prepared.

"Yeah. No pocketknives. No guns, obviously."

"No pocketknives?" Jace asked, what the hell just hanging in the air unspoken.

"Terrorists used box cutters. So, nothing with sharp edges."

"Box cutters should have been suspicious. Who brings box cutters on an airplane? But what kid doesn't get a pocketknife?" He turned the bag over and dumped out the contents. Six knives lay on the bed. One looked like a fishing knife, the kind men used on the pier to crack open oyster toads or fillet a striper. Three of the knives were small; two had foldable blades. One had a clip attached to the sheath, like for a pocket or a belt loop. They reminded her of the ones the goth kids in high school pretended to carry, attached to a long chain. Except that the chains attached to a wallet or something. Not an actual blade, or they would've gotten suspended. The last knife was almost as long as the duffel. The blade was notched, straight, and uncovered. She couldn't stop staring at it. Jace picked it up and twisted the hilt in his palm. "Scary, right?" Jace said, both of their eyes on the knife.

"Sure is," Marleigh said, wondering where all of these had been. Didn't it seem like a stupid number of knives?

"It was my dad's. From Panama."

Had it killed someone? Several people? Jace rarely mentioned his father. She knew now that she would have a curve of a bloody steel in her mind's eye where a face should be whenever she thought about Jace's dad. How would that go as they were traveling to his hometown for three weeks? A kid in her class had been knifed once. But by the time he was back in school and showing off his wound, the skin was growing back together, a dark pucker. Most of the blood—all of the blood except period blood—that she had seen was at the boxing gym. The pink to scarlet spit into the bucket after a fighter rinsed his mouth. Red trails from the nostrils if he didn't protect his face. A split lip or a busted eye or cheek. That blood came from skin rupturing at the surface. The cut-man swabbed epinephrine solution to make it coagulate quickly, then coated the fighter's face in Vaseline so his face didn't look so bad for scoring. Those cuts were minor, sloppy baby knicks. But Jace's knife would bleed you from the inside. She thought of the old slasher horror movies, the *"reet-reet"* sound of background music. But you couldn't cut deep from afar. You'd have to get as close as boxers to do that. Stabbing or slitting a throat was intimate and up close. A thrust and a pull. Violence had never bothered her. But these knives made her feel a little sick.

"Is that where he was killed?"

"No. I wasn't even born then."

Marleigh blushed. "Oh, right. Oops. I'm not great with dates."

Jace kept messing with the knife like a boy with a toy. "He made it out of that jungle just to die in a desert ten years later."

"Oh," was all Marleigh could conjure.

At the restaurant, prep cooks and line cooks were always nipping off pieces of their fingertips or grating their knuckles on mandolins in the kitchen. "Be careful," she said. "Don't cut yourself."

Jace smiled and put the knife back on the bed. "Doesn't your shift start soon?"

She checked the clock and nodded. "Make sure there aren't any more in there. No way they'd let you on a plane." Had they been in the closet in the bag the whole time she'd known Jace? Where would he put them while she was at work?

He picked up one of the folded knives. "Here," he said and tossed it to her. She didn't want to catch it, but instinct took over. "I'd feel more comfortable if you had it with you, walking around out there."

She dropped it into her purse. "It won't do you any good if you can't find it when you need it." He fished the knife from her purse and slipped into the tight front pocket of her black jeans. She felt dangerous and unsettled as she left the apartment. All those knives would be there when she got back from work around midnight, but where?

• • •

Their flight into Omaha was late, but Marleigh had no one to call. No one was worried about her safe travel. In a way, Pops's death had freed her, but it was a mooring she hadn't wanted cut. It would have made more sense to fly into Denver or Rapid City and drive to Scottsbluff, the actual city closest to where Jace grew up. Both were much closer than Omaha. But Jace had left his truck with a buddy in Omaha before he'd gone to Norfolk so he and Marleigh could drive it back home and sell it before he moved to the East Coast for good.

Before they left Omaha, he was going to take her to the zoo. It was the biggest he had ever seen, he'd told her, with a miniature rainforest indoors. He had a key to his buddy's house. They'd stay the night there, then see the zoo and catch a few innings of the AAA Royals game, and then tackle the nine-hour drive to Mitchell and Scottsbluff. Two days in the city before they crossed the state and met Jace's family. As they drove west, they stopped to pee and gas up in Norfolk, NE, and laughed over the different pronunciations. In Nebraska, it's *Nor-fork*. In Virginia, *Naw-fuk*. They climbed into the cab of Jace's truck, silly and handsy.

"How 'bout we naw-fuk?" Jace asked, and they did it in Jace's truck, in view of the giant *Home of Johnny Carson* billboard. "Heeeere's Johnny," he said in her ear as she tensed around him.

Marleigh had never seen so much open space. On the interstate they covered miles without passing another car or truck. Exits had signs on them reading, *Last service station for 30 miles. Check gas.* She could believe it as they careened through the great, dusty flat with only fence posts and windmills to mark distance. She leaned back against the seat, lolled her knee out the window, her feet on Jace's dashboard.

"Whole lotta nothing, right?" Jace asked her.

"This is the biggest place I have ever been. I didn't know space like this existed." She knew she sounded like a kid, but she didn't care. She felt like a kid for the first time in a long time. Wind whipping through the cab of the truck, Jace's hand on her thigh. Her head tipped back. Eyes closed. She'd be perfectly happy riding this way forever. Maybe they could just keep going.

"Why would you leave all of this for the Navy?" Marleigh asked.

"Home always feels like a trap," he said, eyes straight ahead on the ribbon of highway unspooling ahead of them. "Doesn't matter where it is."

"Why are we going there, then? Why were you so happy to bring me here?"

"I wanted to show you this. And this part I love. Home, our house, that's a different story. Kind of like yours." She understood that. Tourists were always going on and on about how great it must be to live by the water. Real life was always real life, even if you lived where people go vacation.

"The Navy has been really good for me. I mean it. The military helped me unfuck myself."

She shrugged and nodded. She didn't need more explanation.

"Not as good for me as you are, though," he said, tracing her chin with his free hand.

They pulled into town after midnight. They would be staying with Jace's aunt and uncle, Ed and Donna Holt. Jace said they had been asleep for hours. "Early to rise, early to bed," they've always said. Marleigh knew Jace had spent much of his childhood in their home, miles from his mother and sister, although she didn't know why. She knew plenty about complicated living arrangements. The night was absolute dark. Thick clouds cut off the moonlight. She could feel the strain in her pupils when Jace turned off the truck and its headlights. Marleigh stood still for a moment, sifting through darkness.

She wasn't sure where Jace was. He moved in total silence. He tapped her shoulder. She gasped. He kissed her neck. "Sorry, baby. Didn't mean to scare you." He had their bags looped over his shoulders and he pulled her to the front door, a small, illuminated rectangle. Bugs circled the front porch light, a frantic halo.

"Do you have a key?"

"No. But it's never locked."

Marleigh imagined her response to hearing someone open her door in the middle of the night. She would grab her pepper spray—not welcome the intruder into her home. He tugged her hand. "Don't worry. I used to sneak in here late at night all the time. Anyways, they know we're coming."

They walked quietly in the front door and Jace set their bags down beside a small table in the kitchen. Ed and Donna had left the kitchen light on for them. They had also set out a pitcher of ice water that had begun to sweat, two glasses made from mason jars, a loaf of what smelled like banana bread, and a note.

Jace and Marley,

We're so glad you're home. Sorry we couldn't stay up to greet you. Have a nibble and a good rest and we'll see you in the a.m. Your old room is all ready.

Love, E & D

. . .

Marleigh heard footsteps and whispers, the sounds of people telling one another to be quiet. She opened her eyes, blinking to remember where she was. Must be Donna and Ed. Jace snored lightly against her, their legs entwined in the small bed. She was groggy and tired from the drive and hadn't seen much of the room before they had collapsed into sleep the night before. Her bladder was full, but she wasn't ready to leave Jace's warm body and the bed to venture out into the hallway. The room was paneled in wood, bleached in places from the sunlight already glowing through the window shades, and the ceiling was popcorned and off-white. A wooden ceiling fan wobbled above them, the chain dancing. She was snug and happy.

Jace's muscular back twitched in sleep. He was too big for this bed. The two of them were preposterous. It was perfect. And it really was Jace's room, like the note said. He was everywhere in this space.

She had to pee. There was no fighting it. Marleigh gently removed herself from Jace's limbs and off the bed. He flopped over, still asleep, until he was face up and both arms hung from the sides. She picked up her backpack and skittered to the bathroom down the short hallway. The toilet lid was covered in the same fabric as the bathmat on the floor, a faded granite color. An embroidered quotation framed and hanging on the wall read, *Give thanks* above two hands in prayer.

Marleigh washed her hands and brushed her teeth. She couldn't wait for a shower; the long trip showed on her. But she was feeling sleepy again and decided to put it off. She finger-combed through her curls, certain she would not make it back to Jace's room without seeing either Ed or Donna. Her face was heart-shaped as ever in the mirror, but she'd looked worse. Her breath was fresh now, and her green eyes looked more rested than she felt. She had slept in one of Jace's Navy T-shirts and gym shorts, and hadn't taken her bra off, she was so tired.

As she walked out of the bathroom, Marleigh heard, "Someone is awake!" A woman's voice. She smelled bacon. Normally she loved the smell of bacon, the smoke and sizzle. This morning, though, it made her throat feel thick. All she could picture was the jiggly white fat the hot grease became.

"Leave 'em be," a man said. Ed, certainly.

The door to Jace's room remained closed. Marleigh took a deep breath and walked into the kitchen. "Good morning," she said. A man and a woman sat at a natural wood table, the table where she and Jace found the note and water last night. Steam wafted from ceramic mugs. Four plates sat empty, forks and knives beside them. Bacon popped on the stove. A carton of eggs was open on the counter. The woman, Donna, was up and out of her chair as soon as she saw Marleigh, dimpled arms extended.

"Oh! You must be Marleigh!" The woman said and wrapped her arms around Marleigh.

"Don't suffocate the poor girl," Ed said from the table. Marleigh was released from the woman's hefty bosom.

"We're just so glad you're here. And you brought Jace home!"

Ed stood from the table. "Welcome, Marleigh. We've been so excited to meet you. Can I get you some coffee?"

Marleigh was about to comply when Donna said, "Nope. Ed, remember. She likes Diet Coke in the morning. Jace told us."

"That's right. Silly me. It's in the ice chest in the garage. I'll go get it." Marleigh was overwhelmed by the simple, thoughtful gesture, the fact that Jace had thought ahead to tell them her preferences.

"Thank you," she said. And she was grateful.

Ed opened the can and handed it to her. "Offer her a glass, Ed!" Marleigh shook her head and took a big drink.

"You're up early," Ed said. "At least compared to Jace, anyway." Both smiled.

"Must be the time change," Donna said. "Just enough to mess with your clock."

Marleigh nodded. "Thank you for having me." They had included her in the place settings, their grocery purchases, everything. No wonder Jace was happy in this house.

"I've heard so much about you."

Ed walked to the stove to flip the bacon. "Just making some breakfast. Can I fix you a plate?"

Donna cracked eggs into a bowl, shook heavy handfuls of salt and pepper and whisked furiously.

"Is it okay if I wait for Jace to eat?" Despite the Diet Coke, Marleigh was feeling sleepy again.

"Of course, honey. Whatever you like. Ed and I have to watch our blood sugar, but there will be plenty when he wakes up. You're such a tiny thing. We need to put some meat on those bones while you're here!" Donna lightly squeezed Marleigh's underarm.

Marleigh wrapped her Diet Coke in a paper napkin and walked back to Jace's room. She curled up beside him and fell back to sleep.

CHAPTER TWELVE

Their first full day in Mitchell would be a picnic at the park, Jace said, her big introduction to his whole extended family. "Everyone can't wait to meet you."

Marleigh was tempted to ask how many *everyone* was, but she didn't. Jace's excitement about showing her his world—and showing her off—was catchy, though she didn't entirely understand why he considered her such a catch.

She asked him if he was going to introduce her to his mother, Guylene. "Yes," he said. "Once. If Guylene behaves herself, fine. If not, screw it." He refused to make Marleigh meet her at the house, and Guylene refused to go to Uncle Ed and Aunt Donna's. Marleigh was relieved to know it wasn't just her family that was a mess. So, it would be at Agate Fossil Beds National Monument, a family picnic. Marleigh could get to know everyone at once. "Hopefully all of the good will at least water down my mother's bad," he told her. "They've all done it for me most of my life. Why wouldn't they now?"

"If they're like you and like Donna and Ed, what's not to like?"

"Agate Fossil Beds is pretty cool, believe it or not. Donna and Ed take such pride in the park, always have." They were both park rangers, he explained. "This way we can avoid some long deal at Guylene's." She'd never heard him call his mother anything but her first name. Just as she never called Jackie "Mom."

"You don't have to sell me on it," she said, rolling over towards him, laying her head on his chest, groggy from so much travel. "Of course we'll go. I'll look for work Monday. Restaurants are too busy Saturdays for interviewing anyway." The bedsprings creaked under their shared weight. Jace's bed and room still looked like it housed an adolescent boy. Not that either of them was that far from their teens.

"They haven't changed it much," Jace said. "Not since the first day I moved in." She rubbed the dark blue comforter with the rip in the top right corner. The stitches had been pulled apart. "I was so dumb. I thought I could make a big hole and hide in there, make myself look just like stuffing."

"You were a little kid." She didn't know why he lived with his aunt and uncle. She hoped she would find out soon. "Baseball was your thing, huh?" Donna had dusted his many little league trophies and medals.

"Yeah. I was okay. I don't know where Donna found those. I thought Guylene chucked them." His Cornhusker doll and teddy bear were on the bed when they arrived, too. "Donna was obsessed with making me feel comfortable here. And I was comfortable here. It was safe." Ed and Donna were Jace's Pops. She understood.

She squeezed his hand.

"I lived in this room until I left for boot camp." He shook his head. "That's funny."

"That would be quite a change! Is boot camp as bad as they say?"

"No. All that bitching's just part of the big-dick display. I didn't mind it that much. I'm coachable—remember even Terry at the gym said that. Every coach I've ever had said that was my ability. Not speed or strength."

She curled against him, drawing his arms around her. "From where I'm lying, you feel strong."

He kissed the top of her head. "And dudes get close quick. I've been around long enough to see that's what happens when people are separated from their daily lives and turned into a team. Guys come from all over—every color and build and background, same uniform."

"I spent a week at YMCA camp once," Marleigh said. "Sounds a lot like that." She turned to face him.

"Pretty much the same damn thing," he said. "No one ever has to be alone in the Navy." He positioned himself over her, holding his weight just inches over hers.

She groaned and reached to pull him down. She arched her back, craned her neck to reach his mouth.

• • •

Later that morning, they climbed into Jace's truck. It was high and grumbled and shook. The leather seat had his butt imprint. There were two other houses visible from Ed and Donna's windows. One was within shouting distance. The other was at least three soccer fields away. There were few trees, but so much space. Green grass and an endless horizon of hills and plateaus. Marleigh had never been so far from water. Much of the land was sectioned off by split-rail fences. Cows munched lazily by the side of the road, yellow rectangular tags flapping on their ears. She slid closer to Jace on the bench seat. They turned onto the highway.

"I told Ed we'd bring some beer," he said, pulling into a gas station advertising, *Cheaper liquor prices than Wal-Mart!* "Do you need a bathroom?" When she started to ask why, he said, "The park is forty miles away."

A forty-mile drive for a picnic. At home, if she got in her car and drove forty miles, she'd be almost to North Carolina's Outer Banks. She shook her head. There was so much space between everything and everyone out here. He left the car running, the air-conditioning blowing. She heard him slide the cases of beer into the truck bed and slam the tailgate shut. Felt his weight shift the balance of the seat when he climbed into the cab. He placed a six pack of Budweiser at her feet.

He drove with one hand on the steering wheel and the other on her thigh. "Best way to get somebody lost in Mitchell is to tell them to turn at the light with the church on the corner." She scooched closer to him, blood running hot to the center of her as it always did when they touched. He signaled a right turn at the second stoplight.

"That's funny," she said. "There's a church on every corner."

Jace squeezed her knee. They drove past the high school's four short rows of parking spaces, more than half of them filled with big pickups like Jace's. On the rare occasion when a car passed heading the other way, he'd raised four fingers to wave, keeping his thumb on the wheel, and the passing driver inevitably did the same.

"At home we just raise one finger," she said with a laugh, her hand on top of his.

"Everybody's pretty pissed off all the time in Norfolk. The traffic does suck, though." He nodded toward her side of the car. "Wanna open one of those for me?" She looked down at the beers at her feet.

"Sure." She hesitated before pulling a can free from the plastic ring.

"I haven't been home in a while," he said. She popped it open and handed him the can. He took a long pull and tucked the can between his legs, then ruffled Marleigh's hair. "That's better," he said. "You want one?"

She hadn't eaten much that morning. The time change, long drive, and sleepiness had sagged her appetite. But it was revving back up. "It's just a beer, Marl. I've got some mouthwash in here somewhere. It's just a picnic."

"What the hell," she said and opened a beer for herself. It was almost noon, right?

The forty miles of rolling hills and ranch land passed so quickly, a blur of gold and dots of black cattle on the hillsides. She couldn't stop gawking at how pretty it all was.

"Oh my god," she said, pointing out the window. "Is that an actual tumbleweed?" A large ball of tangled golden grasses bounced across the highway.

"Sure is, little lady," Jace said, straightening in his seat and smiling, laying the Midwestern cowboy talk on thick. They crossed a river and turned. "Only three more miles to the visitor's center and we're there."

She could ride in this truck with him and never stop, just the two of them in his cab pointed at the horizon. She slid both of their hands up her thigh, just a little, instead of talking.

"Yes. More of that," he said. "I have a plan."

They passed a Smoky Bear sign and a low brown sign: *Agate Fossil Beds National Monument.* He turned again into a small parking lot. She counted eight cars and two white park ranger vehicles.

"Park, ha!" she said, shaking her head. "I pictured swings, maybe a slide." Graffiti, kids ganging up on each other. But no. Golden sandstone hills rose in the distance. Hawks swooped low over a marsh of purple-brown cattails. Prairie grasses danced in the wind, winking sunlight. To think, she almost missed all of this.

"I'm sorry there's no one sleeping on the benches to make you feel at home," Jace said before hopping down out of the truck and wheeling around to her side to let her out. "Guylene isn't here yet," he said. "Good. You can meet the nice ones first."

The sky was blue-streaked white and endless. "It's unreal," she said. He squeezed her hand. "Where are all of the trees?" she asked. Miles of river and grass undulated out from where they stood.

"It's all this damn wind. Enough to make you crazy after a while," Jace said.

She could see it now; she understood. The wind sheared and rounded everything in its path. Rolling mounds of hills, some of the oldest were wind-blown straight-edge-razor flat.

"I picture shapes and cutouts like these in the Grand Canyon, not Nebraska," Marleigh said. "But I've never really been anywhere until now."

"This place isn't anywhere," he said. "But it feels fucking perfect with you here." She thought Jace had the same effect on just about any place.

Marleigh pointed to a diamond-shaped sign, brown and white, with a snake in the middle, a rattle curved all the way up to the forked tongue. "What's that about?"

"Rattlesnakes," Jace said. "We have them here. No place is perfect, right?" He laughed as Marleigh lifted her feet high, looking down at the path. "People make a bigger deal about it than they need to. Rattlesnakes warn you before they strike. Polite that way."

"What?" Marleigh asked.

. . .

Before they reached the tailgate of the truck, Ed and Donna were on them. They were dressed almost identically in long khaki shorts and pine-colored polo shirts, tucked in over soft bellies. Sneakers and white socks. Donna had pulled back her graying hair and secured it into dark clips on either side of her head. Her face was peachy, made up since they'd met in the kitchen in the early morning. Ed kept smoothing thin, errant strands of hair down onto his head as he walked toward them. He and Jace shook hands, clapped one another on the shoulder before pulling into a hug. Jace dwarfed Ed.

Donna reached a plump hand to the back of Jace's neck, patting the tightly buzzed hair. Hugs smelled of Avon Skin So Soft. "Best bug repellant and not full of stuff that'll give you cancer," Donna said with a look to a man smoking while leaning against a *Danger, Fire Threat Level 2* sign. Donna trundled off to the picnic tables to help fasten clips onto the table to hold the tablecloth down before they brought the food out of the car trunks.

"Come get some lunch and a beer," Ed said. "I'll let Jace give you the grand tour himself. But you've got to be hungry, and I'd like to let you in on some of the history of this place." Ed was bigger here, at the park, crackling with excitement and pride.

Donna called over to Ed. "We're off today, honey." She smiled and gestured to the T-shirt and shorts she was wearing. "No uniforms. No name tags."

Marleigh loved their easy way and the playful banter, their loving teasing. She filled her plate with corn, grilled in its husk, baked beans thick with bacon, salad full of peanuts and shredded cheddar, and a hot dog. There was a line of more condiments than could ever fit on one bun. The thick paper plate sagged in the middle. Jace offered her another beer. Her head was still fizzy from her first. Jace had finished two on the drive and was well into another.

As she ate, Ed told her about John Cook and how this park had been his ranch. The way the rancher had befriended Red Cloud and how the Cook family maintained a close friendship with Red Cloud and the Ogallala Sioux tribe. Was this why the overwhelming space felt like too much to her? Because this open wild space felt like Jace's home, yes, and she wanted to walk and walk it, trail the grasses in her fingers, but it felt a little haunted, too, so vast and powerful. Too big and open to be any one man's land. What had that friendship earned the Sioux? Marleigh wasn't a good student, but everyone knew how that story ended.

Even so, Marleigh was fascinated with all the old Indian stories. She was far more into those tales than the fossils that earned the park its name. Ed was a natural storyteller. His love for this place accented every word.

"If the fossils hadn't been found," Ed said, "this'd just be another spread, just part of someone's spread."

"Or, maybe, the Sioux would have regained this land," Marleigh said quietly.

Ed shrugged and nodded. "Maybe, Marleigh."

Marleigh couldn't believe she was still hungry. She added another scoop of potato salad and a second ear of corn to her plate.

Donna beamed in response. "Glad to see you eating. You're a tiny little thing."

Marleigh blushed. Everyone at the park was tall and strong; even most of the children's legs and arms were thicker than hers.

Jace ruffled Marleigh's hair. "My little waif," he said with a laugh. "Now you know what the expression *corn fed* looks like."

Marleigh spoke through her last bite of potato salad. "I'll eat anything you cook. Ever."

It was Donna's turn to blush.

CHAPTER THIRTEEN

A car turned onto the gravel road. Jace tensed at the sound, alert. "Shit," Jace said. "I hoped Guylene changed her mind and decided not to come."

"It'll be okay, Jace," Marleigh said.

"No it won't. She'll ruin this picnic faster than an overturned hornets' nest. If she's here, you really shouldn't worry about snakes. She's way more dangerous. And crazy."

Marleigh had never seen the look in Jace's eyes. He looked a million miles away. He stood so still Marleigh could barely tell he was breathing. When she put her hand in his, he gripped it hard.

"She can act normal for a while, but that crazy always leaks out," he said. He seemed to be talking more to himself than to her.

"I mean we'll be okay, Jace."

"Of course we will. Damn it, Ed, don't we have anything stronger than beer?"

Ed looked down and shook his head.

"Give me your empty plate," Jace said. "I need to go get something from the car and I'll throw it away. I'll be right back."

A car door slammed, and a tall woman climbed out of the dusty vehicle. Marleigh had lost sight of Jace and was mad that he'd left her alone. But before she realized it, Trish and Donna each stood on one side of her.

Guylene loomed over all the women. She wore her long hair in one long, scraggily ponytail looped over her shoulder. It looked more horse than human, the hair coarse and ragged.

"I hope we're not too much for you," Donna said, a light touch to Marleigh's elbow. "We're so excited to get to know this girl our Jace can't stop talking about." Marleigh smiled as she saw him approaching. She gave him a quizzical look. He ignored it but wedged himself in between her and Trish.

"Our Jace," Guylene muttered, shaking her head. "*Our* Jace who couldn't be bothered to tell his mother anything about some girl before announcing he was coming back."

"How about you get some lunch, Guylene?" Donna suggested.

"Don't try to manage me." Guylene sucked her teeth as she looked Marleigh up and down. "As if she's anything special."

Marleigh looked from Guylene's face to Jace's, back and forth. The resemblance shocked her. They had the same dark eyes, same shape, same lashes. Looking at his mother's face was like staring into some skewed crystal ball. She was Jace's past. Nothing anyone could do about that. For damn sure, she wouldn't be his future. Marleigh felt an overwhelming need to protect Jace. She could sense this woman's danger.

"Are you kidding?" Marleigh asked, ignoring Guylene's comments, and sidled closer to Donna. "This has been wonderful. You've been so welcoming."

"Must be different," his mother said. Jace stared at his mother, his expression hard. A silent *"watch it."* "Seeing as you come from nothing."

Marleigh squeezed Jace's hand. He fumbled for something to say, to interrupt. Instead, Marleigh spoke. "Big families are new to me. It's nice to meet you, Guylene." Marleigh extended her hand.

Guylene just stared at her. Marleigh went into waitress mode. Kill 'em with kindness.

"I'm surprised he brought you," Guylene said. "Let's put it this way: I'm not half so bad as he says, and you're not half so good."

Marleigh stood taller and took a step toward Guylene. "He hasn't said a thing about you." His mother's jaw tightened. Jace extended a protective arm across Marleigh's waist.

"I've heard all about you. Father went to prison. Grew up in a boxing gym. Parents who want nothing to do with you."

Marleigh scowled and looked at him, confused and angry that Guylene had this ammunition. Had Jace told her all of this?

"What the hell, Trish?" Jace kept the anger at his sister stoppered.

Trish formed prayer hands and mouthed, *"I'm sorry."*

"At least my mother raised me," Marleigh said, always the scrappy fighter from Ocean View. Guylene had misjudged her, underestimated her.

Donna and Trish shared a tense look.

Guylene's nostrils flared. "Who do you think you are, coming here and talking to me like that?"

"I should ask you the same thing." Marleigh had some idea now of how Jace felt when he wanted to beat her father that night at the gym. She would love to land a sharp uppercut on Guylene's masculine jaw. Pull a fistful of that ruined hair.

Jace stepped to Marleigh's side. "I'm taking this young lady on a walk, whether you're done interrogating her or not."

His mother sputtered. "We certainly weren't—"

"Try to be nice, just for a minute, Guylene," Donna said, her voice unusually stern.

Jace's mother stepped around Donna, closer to Marleigh. "She's city trash. I want to know what designs she has on Jace."

Marleigh took a step back. She wasn't the only one with horrible parents.

"My boy's going places," Guylene continued. "He doesn't need to mess around with a port townie. He's never stayed with just one girl for very long. You're not going to change that."

"Shut up, Guylene," Jace said, his voice low. "Marleigh came all this way to meet you and everyone else. I'm not going to let you ruin it."

"I'm just tryin' to talk to her," Guylene said, moving in closer to Marleigh.

"Jace, it's fine," Marleigh said, her voice low and calm. "Say whatever you need to say, Guylene." But they both knew Guylene was anything but fine.

"He better not be acting like some hero, just because he joined the Navy. The war's in the desert."

"Do you have any idea what he actually does?" Marleigh asked.

"Don't you tell me about my son. You don't know anything. But you'll see."

Donna stepped between Guylene and Marleigh. Jace put his arm around her waist and steered her away from the women. Marleigh's eyes widened, and Jace wrapped his hand around hers. "I'm sorry about her," he said, loud enough for everyone to hear, as he led her to the path to a bridge over the marshy, slow-moving Niobrara. "Let me show you around. Walk sound good?"

"God, yes." She laced her finger through his. Tall grasses swished by her calves. "She didn't say anything about me that wasn't true. I don't come from war heroes or school principals or park rangers. I come from assholes."

"Uh, you met my mother," he said. Marleigh paused when they reached the bridge. "I'm sorry. I don't know who gave her your life story. Maybe Trish. Her intentions are good, her communication skills, not so much. That's not how I told it."

"I forgive you." She reached over the railing and rubbed a thick cat tail between her fingers. He moved to stand behind her, holding her, pressing himself against her. "Oh," she said. It was a long *oh*, not surprised but happy sounding. She wiggled her butt just a little, the same way she did in bed when they spooned and he got hard. She knew it was impossible for him to sleep that way, and she wanted to let him know she was game. Then she slipped out from under him and walked off the bridge onto the trail that led up the hill. She turned to look over her shoulder at him, wagged her eyebrows. "You coming?"

"You're such a tease, Mar. A perfect, infuriating tease. And you bet I'm coming. Not yet. But soon, very soon," he said, jogging to catch up with her. They came to a sign. One pointing left and up said, *Fossil beds.* The sign in the other direction read, *Bone House.*

"Y'all just love some skeletons around here, huh?" She looked down the path; they had to have walked almost a mile. "You can see everything so clearly and so far here."

"Keep walking up to the fossil beds. We'll take the long way. Once we get behind the hills, we won't be able to see them. Out of sight, out of mind, ya know? Then we can cut across to the bone house."

"I'll go anywhere with you." There, she said it out loud.

CHAPTER FOURTEEN

C ould they really have all this space to themselves, this open sky, the bending grasses and dry warmth of the sun? His hand holding hers, and every inch of her that brushed against him, aware. Everything was brighter, louder—the meadow larks singing their long call and response, their footprints on the dry grass of the path. Crunch. And the wind. Always the wind. It could eat words and sounds, swirl them away in a loose fist.

She had enjoyed the picnic. Jace made even more sense after meeting the people who formed him, including his piece-of-work mother. She looked forward to getting to know his sister, Trish, better. Dressed head to toe in black—T-shirt, yoga pants, and clogs—she swam upstream in this family, it appeared. But it felt so good to have him to herself again. There would be plenty of time to get to know everyone. She realized that the crowd assembled today was at least in part to buffer Guylene. Marleigh wouldn't be greedy with him while they were here. Ed and Donna didn't get to see him often, and Norfolk would become his home base after all.

"Are there usually other people on this path?"

"Not really. Mostly people stick to the paved ones and the fossil sites. Just us and the rattlesnakes out here."

"The what? They're out here, too?" She had a healthy city girl fear of snakes. She leaned into him before she realized it.

"That's right, hold me close. I'll protect you," he said and copped a feel.

She swatted his shoulder and looked around her. A sound at her foot like an expertly shuffled deck of cards. She gasped as a huge bug launched itself at her out of the tall grasses.

"Grasshopper, Mar, not a rattlesnake. You won't mix up the sound of a rattlesnake with anything else."

"Good to know," she said.

"We're making enough noise that we won't see one. They want nothing to do with us. And if we got bit, they'd only use a little venom."

"How do you know?"

"It's a fact. They only have so much, and they want to use it on what they can kill and eat. Not on what they want to scare off."

"That's comforting, thanks."

"The babies are more dangerous than adult rattlesnakes."

"I kind of love that."

They reached a small building in the shadow of a still windmill. It was painted bright red. It was old, clearly, but meticulously maintained. "This was where the archaeologists and Indians stayed when they visited the ranch."

Marleigh stepped up to the door, partially screened and wood framed, painted white. There would be room for a bed, a neat painted table, and a small kitchen. She needed to see inside. This place was so powerful. She wondered if the power would be more concentrated inside. Something about this land and all the lives that had inhabited it called to her. The door felt permanently sealed. She stepped back.

"I can see why they'd all want to be here," she said. This little, perfect place. Self-sufficient and surrounded by all this beauty and guarded by rattlesnakes. Like a cottage in a fairy tale. If Marleigh ever sought to picture heaven, this was it. She felt the pencil in her hand, whiskering in the grass on paper, just the way she'd sketch it.

"Ed and I camped out here all the time when I was a kid." He smiled at the memory. Jace reached down to a small space below the concrete step up to the house and lifted a flat-head screw driver. It glinted in the sun. He slipped it between the door and jamb and the door opened. They stepped inside. No table, no bed, just the original wood, aging raw timbers, and Jace. He took up most of the room. Perfectly too much.

He stepped back from her and raised his forehead in his cartoony attempt at wagging his eyebrows. "It's called the bone house for a reason, baby." She laughed and then covered his open mouth with her own.

He released her and tugged his shirt off of his shoulders and spread it on the floor. Faint, sweet smell of rotting wood and their pheromones. The windows had been covered long ago.

"I've wanted to get you naked all day." He bit lightly around her throat. She tilted back for him.

"They won't start banging on the door, right? Or come looking for us?"

His belt buckle clinked as it released, and he dropped his shorts and boxers to the floor. He returned his attention to her mouth while his hands yanked at the waist of her skirt. She stepped out of it. He sat on the outspread shirt, ready, always ready for her and he gently pulled on her hands.

"Sit down with me. No splinters." She straddled his Indian-style bent legs and took him inside her. She wrapped her arms and legs around him and rocked. She moved slow. They were both on an edge, and otherwise it would be over too soon. His hand found the back of her neck, her shoulders, then slid down to her waist. He lifted her up, just a little, and she came down, hard, a yowl neither of them had ever heard before coming from below her throat. She shuddered, almost dizzy with pleasure. His breath hitched, his hands tightened around her waist. They held each other, panting on the floor of the bone house. She didn't move off him until her hips started to ache.

After their slow walk back down to the picnic area and visitors center, the picnic had dispersed. Guylene could scatter people as well as Marleigh's own parents. The day had been so perfect, though, except for her, that Marleigh wasn't going to let her dampen it. As soon as they returned to cell service, their voicemails flooded with messages from Ed and Donna and Trish about how wonderful it was to meet Marleigh, how happy they were to see Jace so happy, and how excited they were to get to know Marleigh better. The voicemails made her feel warm and included, almost like part of the family.

• • •

The following Sunday, after a mountain of scrambled eggs and bacon, Ed and Donna left for church, and Jace and Marleigh lazed around in their pajamas. Ed and Donna's three-bedroom house had carpet in the den so thick that it buried Marleigh's feet. Like Jace's room, the walls were paneled wood. The hallway between the two downstairs bedrooms and the kitchen and den were lined with pictures of Jace and Trish. One frame was shaped like an old-timey schoolhouse. It contained thirteen small portraits of Jace, each labeled for a school year—kindergarten through twelfth grade. Some of the years, Jace had rewarded the photographer with that smile of his, the one that formed one perfect dimple, deep, just to the left of his mouth. Many, though, captured a wary boy and a tough-guy teenager. She could picture Donna sitting at the kitchen table, trimming the edges of the photographs to fit perfectly inside the small borders of each opening, sticking tiny pieces of tape to hold them in place. She had no idea where her school pictures ended up. Jace had been truly loved by these people. He was lucky and he knew it. She was so happy he'd had them. Marleigh wouldn't have minded an Ed and Donna for herself, but she'd had Pops. God, she missed him. He would have loved it out here.

Above the upholstered couch, where they sat tangled in one another, hung Donna and Ed's wedding photos. They were both young and lean and smiling. The couch sagged perfectly into the middle beneath her and Jace, and in places the upholstery was so worn that it shone.

Jace suggested they camp out for the night. He wanted to show her the stars, he said. She'd been too tired and tipsy to appreciate anything but her head hitting the pillow the night before. First, they would have to run by Guylene's to get his camping gear out of the shed. Marleigh was hesitant. Why would they chase after trouble? She could happily spend the day with him on this couch.

"We could wait a few more days," she said.

"She makes a big show of Sundays, always tearing off into town, for church, brunch, the whole shebang. It's the opposite direction from her place," Jace reassured her. "We won't run into her."

Once they were dressed and in Jace's truck, they took a right out of Ed and Donna's onto a ribbon of gray asphalt that spooled out ahead of them forever. She thought the plains would be flat like a piece of paper. She had been wrong. They passed one farmhouse in half an hour. A white-capped mountain stood blurry in the distance.

"Wow," Marleigh said, looking over Jace's shoulder out the window.

"That's Laramie Peak, near Cheyenne. It's about ninety miles west."

"There's still snow. It's June!"

"It never melts all the way."

She'd never seen snow—not more than flurries that turned immediately to gray slush, anyway.

"We can drive there while we're here."

She smiled. "You're crazy for trading this place for the Navy, you know. But I wouldn't have met you otherwise, so I'm glad you did." They both came from towns people were always saying they were desperate to leave but never did. He'd told her that he thought Virginia was exciting—the beach, the long summer, all the sand and bars and girls, and thank you for your service. But as soon as he'd shown Marleigh his Nebraska, she'd fallen in love.

· · ·

Jace turned the truck onto a dirt road. About a mile up, he stopped and opened a rusting white mailbox, *Holt* in shiny letters on the side, scanned the contents, and flipped it shut. "We won't be here long," Jace said.

He parked closer to the shed than the house. It looked like every other farmhouse they passed, weathered and tall. But unlike Ed and Donna's home, or the Bone House at Agate Fossil Beds Park, Marleigh did not want to go inside. She could sense that it would be one of those places that left her panting for air. Nowhere had ever felt less welcoming, not even her parents' house where she never knew if she'd be coming home to a party or a battle, or which one of her father's friends she would find passed out in her bed. Hopefully everything they needed was inside the shed, and they wouldn't need to cross the threshold. The wooden farmhouse had one large rectangular window under the narrow gable, but no shutters. It reminded Marleigh of an eye without brows or lashes, unblinking and dark. The front of the house was two stories. A longer, single-story section jutted to the left. She wouldn't dare stop there to ask for help if her car broke down on the county road out front.

Jace rummaged in the shed and handed her tight nylon pouches, folded-up chairs, rolled Styrofoam pads. "Lay these out, will you?" She put them on the grass in the sunshine, preparing them for Jace's inventory. His arms full, he dumped a pile of equipment at her feet. "We'll do your first wilderness experience right," he said.

He shook out a blanket onto the grass. He sat and motioned for her to lie down beside him. "Don't worry, she won't be home for hours," he said. "Check it out." He pointed to the sky. She shimmied beside him so their shoulders touched and watched the clouds blow across the endless sky. She hadn't done this since she was a kid on the beach. Now she had someone to speak shapes to.

"There's an elephant," she said.

"Where?"

She pointed.

"I got it. And there's monster truck at fourteen hundred."

She found the cloud truck where the clock face would read two o'clock.

A siren wailed. "Shit," Jace mumbled.

They were so far from any big town. It wasn't a police siren, at least not one that she'd heard before. And she'd heard plenty. Jace looked up to the bright sky, squinting. He looked just as he had when they were playfully identifying cloud shapes. She looked away from his profile, the short hairs glinting. There were no threatening clouds above them, first sun and a sky so bright the blue turned white. He looked left and right, though since they got to Nebraska he'd begun saying east and west, north and south. He stood and began quickly picking up their camping items. "We need to get inside."

"What is it?" she asked.

"Tornado siren."

He offered her his hand to get up. He was always doing things like that. She playfully tugged him back down to her. There was no one in the house behind them, his mother's house, no neighbors for acres and acres. "Come on. We need to get inside." She pulled against his arm and stood, unfamiliar with this serious determination. She didn't understand the worry; the weather was beautiful. Hot and clear. Only a shelf of clouds off in the distance to her left, west.

"Do you have a key?"

Jace shook his head. "She never locks it, like she's daring someone to break in. She'd just love that." He spoke with something like awe.

By the time they stepped inside the heavy front door, she heard rocks pelting off the roof and windows. "Hail," he said. The house smelled musty, as though it hadn't been opened in weeks. The front door opened into a small sitting room with a fireplace. She could see the corner of a kitchen table, shiny linoleum through the doorway.

If it weren't so clean, Marleigh would think the house was vacant. There wasn't a spider web or dust bunny in sight. No clutter of any kind. Sparse and spare.

"Come on," Jace said. He seemed angry. He tugged her down a small hallway. There was a door with a padlock on the outside, the key in the lock. He unlocked the door and pulled it open. Jace tugged the chain on a light above his head, a bare bulb at a slant above steep, narrow stairs. It stunk, this basement, but not like the too-wet-too-long Norfolk fug long after sump pumps have stopped working. It stung her nose, made her gag.

"Jace," she stopped on the third stair down.

"I know. I fucking hate this fucking basement, but we have to get underground. The siren means a tornado is down and close. It shouldn't last long. I'm really sorry, Mar." His voice started to crack, and his hand was sweaty on hers.

"They happen all the time, right? You just go in the basement and wait it out." That's what he'd told her about tornadoes.

When he pulled the chain on the bulb at the bottom of the stairs, she wished he hadn't. The basement was partially finished. The walls were painted. Half of the room had carpet. He clicked on a small radio at the foot of the stairs.

"Sometimes, when the storms were real bad and the power'd go out, I thought we'd get trapped down here and never get out."

In one corner were boots, fatigues, dog tags. A shadow box with a folded American flag hung above them. Jace saw her stare. "It's what came in the box that's assembled and sent home for a KIA." On the walls were seven guns ranging from the size of her fist to longer than half of her leg. She started to sweat. "They're not loaded," he said. "Look," he said and pulled one off the wall.

At home only drug dealers and pieces of shit had guns. "I—I believe you."

His father was from way out in the middle of nowhere Wyoming, said they had a lot of wildlife and better to be safe than sorry. Jace held one of the guns out to her. She shook her head. "An unloaded gun can't hurt anyone, nothing to be afraid of." She could hear he'd been admonished with just those words. "I guess unless you hit me with it." He smiled at her. She turned her back to the guns. Across the basement was, she presumed, the source of the stench. A few dead animals, what looked like deer, and a few birds on stands, parts of their bodies covered in fur or feathers, others not.

Jace pointed. "Those were the old trophies made before modern taxidermy. Creepy, right? She swore she was going to fix them up. They're just down here rotting."

Marleigh walked over to an overfull magazine rack, bursting with old, yellowed magazines—*Soldier of Fortune, Good Housekeeping, Highlights*. Fun for the whole family.

"You need something to do down here," he said, like he was attempting a joke. "Just like your average waiting room, right?"

Marleigh had loved everything she had seen in Nebraska until this. Now she understood why Jace was so happy to leave. "Why is there a lock on that door upstairs?"

"So I couldn't get myself into any more trouble."

"She locked you down here? Jesus fuck," Marleigh said.

"Ed and Donna's was so much better."

The radio crackled an all clear. They both ran out into the daylight.

CHAPTER FIFTEEN

S he tried to hide it, but Marleigh could tell she wasn't fooling Jace.
That place made her sick. She didn't trust herself to talk about
Guylene's house-of-horrors basement because she knew tears and a
flood of questions would follow.

"I'm so sorry we had to go in there," he said.

"It's not your fault, Jace," Marleigh said after they emerged from
the basement.

"You sound like my sister. And anyway, I spent way more than
enough time down there as a kid. Let's leave it behind us."

Outside, the air was cool and still. Wet piles of grass scattered
across the driveway, and something bright red dangled from the
fence—the bag with the tent. Otherwise, it was hard to tell a storm
had blown through. The little pebbles of hail that collected on Jace's
windshield wipers were melting.

"Whoa," she said. "In one direction it looks like nothing happened."

"That's how tornadoes work, Mar. Fast and specific and deceptive
destruction. They can drop down anywhere and flatten a school or
cut through the center of a single room, leaving one side destroyed
and the other perfectly intact, teacups full."

They walked to recover the tent. It had been dragged at least a hundred yards and appeared pretty beat up. Marleigh kept looking up and around at the sky, twirling slowly, keeping watch. How could something so big and violent be so suddenly gone?

"Will it come back?" In her experience, storms tended to dissipate, then regroup.

"It's all gone," he told her. They were sudden and violent, but over so quickly. "They disappear as quick as they drop in. The weather should be nice the rest of the day." He lifted the torn tent and shook it for emphasis. "Tent's fucked, but we don't need it. We'll car camp."

"I've never slept outside before," she said.

He stacked firewood in the truck bed. "Glad I can be your first," he said. "Get ready for a sky like you've never seen. Why don't we go find a spot now?"

"I don't have any of my stuff with me," Marleigh said. "I left everything at Ed and Donna's."

"You don't need anything. We'll go back tomorrow." They drove across the state line into Wyoming and stopped at the first gas station they found. Jace bought two bottles of cheap wine, hot dogs, buns and Jiffy Pop. "We'll do this high school style." She plunked a small toothbrush and tube of toothpaste on the pile at the register.

"Don't laugh," she said.

"I can't wait to taste that minty mouth."

. . .

He parked them near a river, the truck cab under a tall tree, the bed extended out into the open. "Out here, a copse of trees means water."

"A cop . . . what?"

"A *copse,* a thicket of small trees."

So often, Marleigh forgot what Jace was trained to do, how he could read threats in terrain as well as hideaways that provided advantages. Special Forces Jace and silly, flirty, lovable Jace were one and the same.

He was right. The ground was softer there, and the trees provided a little break from the incessant wind. It was making him edgy. She wrapped her arms around him and reassured him just as he'd taken care of her earlier.

"Thanks, Mar. Fucking Guylene and her house. She's worse than the tornado."

He was right about that, too. "It's over now. And this place is so beautiful," Marleigh murmured as she inspected their home for the night.

"Your body and maybe a little of that wine are all I need to wash off the day, baby." He stretched out foam roll pads over the bed liner and unzipped both sleeping bags, shaking them out flat like blankets. "I want to feel you beside me, not sleep all cocooned and separate."

"Sounds perfect to me." She opened one of the wine bottles and took a big pull, wiping her mouth with the back of her hand.

"Goddamn, you're perfect," Jace said. "Donna and Ed love you, and so does Trish."

She handed the bottle up to him and he took a long swig. He hacked two branches off a tree and pared them down to kindling. He steepled the wood for a fire, rammed two hotdogs onto sticks for each of them to roast. The foil belly of the Jiffy Pop swelled and then burst just before dark. They finished the second bottle sitting in each other's arms by the fire.

"We should have bought a third."

Coyotes yipped in the dark. Marleigh's back stiffened, and she looked around for the source of the sound.

"Nothing to worry about," he told her.

"Are you *ssshure*?" she asked, feeling even tipsier when she moved.

"I promise," he said and she relaxed against him again.

"Do you ever get scared out here? It's so dark and we're so far away from anywhere."

"No."

"What about the animals? What about the cold?"

"The first cupla times," he said, shrugging.

"What happened?" she asked. "I know you weren't a Boy Scout."

The speed of his breathing increased. She could feel his body inhaling sharply and the effort it took him to draw out his exhales, get it back under control.

"I feel so comfortable with you, Marleigh. It'd be so easy to spill my guts and tell you everything."

"So do it."

He shifted away from her, just a little. "I don't want to scare you away. Every special operator makes that mistake once, tells his girl more than she can handle and ruins everything."

"I'm not asking for war stories," she said. But as soon as the words slipped through her lips, she paused and wondered. Maybe in a way, she was. Maybe his childhood was even worse than she imagined.

He shrugged. She wiggled her fingers under one of the palms he pressed into his knee, and he let her hold his hand.

"I was five or six the first time they locked me out."

Marleigh realized she was holding her breath.

"It was the middle of the night."

"Jesus Christ. You were so young. What did you do?"

"I don't know." He paused. "Probably being a pain in the ass and waking them up."

"You don't have to tell me anything you don't want to. But if you're going to talk, don't lie to me, Jace."

He sighed. "I'd pissed the bed." He told her that he remembered walking to his mother's side of the bed. He'd already changed out of his wet, stinking pajamas and stripped the soaked sheets from his bed. He tried to sleep on just the mattress, but it was wet, too.

"You were just a little boy," Marleigh said.

"The way her face scrunched up when she smelled the pee. I was trying to stay quiet and keep her quiet so we didn't wake my dad. She told me I needed to learn my lesson." Jace cleared his throat.

Marleigh tightened her grip around him. "They could have just locked their bedroom door. Fuck." That's what normal parents would do.

"Yeah, they could've. Guylene shook my father by the shoulder." Marleigh felt sick.

"I was such a pussy. Sorry, a baby. I begged her not to wake him up. I told them that I'd cleaned everything up. I just needed a blanket. So weak."

Marleigh leaned her full weight against Jace. She wanted him to feel her growing closer, not farther away.

"My father, he was a huge dude, he got out of bed and led me out of their bedroom. He said, 'You wanna piss your bed like an animal, go be an animal.' I was so stupid I didn't realize what he meant until we got down to the front door."

"Not stupid, Jace. You were a little kid."

"He turned the deadbolt and opened the door, but stopped halfway and stared at my bare feet. He asked me where my goddamn socks were. He already knew the answer. I'd put them in the sink with the other wet things. So stupid. I thought because I hadn't left anything wet or dirty on the floor that I'd done better this time. He pushed me out the door as he reminded me, 'Never piss your socks, son.'"

"I was stupid," Jace said with a shrug. "I was sure he'd let me back in. He was just trying to teach me a lesson, right? I counted to one hundred, certain that by the time I got there he would open the door and let me into the warm house. I was wrong. He didn't let me back in, and he turned off the front light. It was so dark I couldn't see to the end of the driveway."

"Oh my god. That's just cruel."

"It taught me how to take care of myself. Survival skills have come in pretty handy the last few years. It's weird. The land here, the topography, the wind. It's not so different from Afghanistan. I hadn't realized since I haven't come back in so long."

"A survival gift," she said, shaking her head. "No one is trying to kill you here." Thank God for black humor.

"Definitely the biggest difference."

"Is that why you went EOD? You get to stop the wreckage before it happens?"

"I never thought about it that way. Maybe, I guess. I have so much control on a bomb call. It's silly, but I can, like, slow down time or slow myself down inside of it."

"There's no way I could do what you do."

"The call, the Humvee, the long walk—that's what we call it, the walk in the suit to whatever's ready to blow—it calms me. How fucked is that?" He nudged her with his thigh.

"I would freak out, no question."

"At EOD school you learn to find a phrase, something you can repeat to quiet the chatter around you and in your own head. Yogi Trish calls it a *mantra*, but whatever. It just needs to get me outside of my head. Everyone has his own."

"What's yours?"

"This is nothing. You are nothing. You have nothing to lose." His voice was blank and monotone, probably just like the voice in his head when he repeated it to himself. But the sadness behind those thoughts was sharp and sliced quickly.

"You're not nothing, Jace."

"It doesn't have to mean anything. I don't even think about it. I just repeat it."

"You have me now." So much for resisting. So much for her plans.

"Do I?"

Marleigh pressed her face into his chest. "We'll take care of each other," she said. He was worth it. They could be equals, taking care of one another.

"I love you, Marleigh," he said. "I fucking do, you know. Might as well get all of this scary shit out of the way."

She moved in closer. She could see the scared little boy inside this hard, self-sufficient man. She wanted to protect them both. Her mouth tickled his throat when she spoke. "Really?"

"You're so good for me," Jace told her. "You make me want to be a better man."

CHAPTER SIXTEEN

At first these sounded like compliments, but Marleigh realized he wasn't saying nice things about her so much as how he felt around her. Men often confused that and tried to fool her with movie quotes and song lyrics. But it felt good, making Jace feel good.

"How much better do you have to get?" Marleigh asked. "Have you been arrested or something?" Not that it would necessarily disqualify him for her. Maybe Nebraska cops had as much of a hard-on for poor kids as Virginia cops. But Marleigh could never picture Jace looking like anything but a mini soldier. He'd probably gotten into a fight or something, and who hadn't?

His sister and aunt kept saying, "Thank God he found someone like you." They said that a lot. She was lucky to find him, too. Couldn't they see that?

He answered her by standing up and holding his hand out to her. She stood and he kissed her, hands in her hair, her body wanting to erase the space between them. He lifted her up onto the truck bed, unbuttoning her pants before she tumbled onto the sleeping bag.

They made love, and as she lay in the perfect crux of shoulder and chest, sparse hairs tickling her cheek with each inhale and deepening exhale, he fell hard into slumber. Her mind took longer to unwind. He slept like she imagined a child would, dreamless, eyelids still, his breath just a woosh, not a snore unless he'd had a few beers. Unguarded and vulnerable. Open, all his soft spots unprotected. She didn't imagine she could ever sleep with someone's eyes, a focused gaze on her. He didn't seem to notice when she rolled off him, their bodies too hot for her to sleep.

Marleigh envied Jace's sleep, much as she wanted to wake him and share the starry night sky he'd given her. She had never seen anything like it and wished she'd paid attention to the constellations to learn them. There were so many stars competing for her attention, a rivery swath of them curlicuing across the sky, she could never make out just one shape.

They had piece-of-crap fathers in common, what a bond to share. His had been almost entirely absent. She envied him that, too. Her father's incarcerations felt more like reprieves for her. It always took her a few weeks to walk into the house without holding her breath. It was embarrassing the first time he went away, sure. But he'd been a bigger, more immediate, and present embarrassment plenty of times. And at the gym where she'd largely grown up, jail was more of an inevitability for most of the patrons than an anomaly. It was funny, in a pathetic way, that her grandfather had opened the gym to keep the neighborhood kids out of trouble, and his own son was the biggest screw-up of all. Marleigh boxed there far more often during her life than her father had. She watched her mother handle those boys, most bigger than she, and handled it all, for so many years. But it made her weary. She faded out too, and left Marleigh in charge.

Her mother expected Marleigh to be hard, like the boys, and most of the time she was. Marleigh knew that it was different for mothers and sons. The way the dads or coaches would yell and push and berate. Do better, get leaner, faster. The moms would celebrate and coddle and swoon over their sons. Jace's mom liked to play both parts. The boxers' moms would side-eye the girlfriends when they showed up at the gym too, the ones that snuck past her own mother at the front desk.

"I love you, too." In Jace's arms, she could be soft.

. . .

Marleigh spent less than a week at Ed and Donna's home before she found two jobs. Mitchell was a town with two stoplights, so she had to venture to Scottsbluff, the only town of size for a hundred miles. She was added to the shifts at the Log Cabin Diner, which only served breakfast and lunch. At nights, she worked the bar at the Silver Saddle, which had an acre of motorcycle parking and a sand volleyball pit. Everything was less expensive in Nebraska than in Virginia, so she wouldn't make as much, but, hell, she was finally back to work, and she wouldn't be spending much anyway. Rent, car payments, student loans, and cell phone bills never went on vacation. She'd work four of every seven days for the three weeks they'd stay in Mitchell—that was the deal she made with Jace, who wanted to spend as much time with her as possible. Norfolk seemed so remote, maybe, she thought, it could stay that way.

After her first shift at the diner, Marleigh agreed to meet Trish at her new holistic wellness studio, the first professional space of her own—a massage table in the center of one room and two overstuffed chairs and a small desk shoved in around it. There were little sayings painted on old barn wood hanging on the walls. One said, *Happiness is your birth right.* The other, *The light in me thinks the light in you is freaking awesome.* Marleigh brought her a coconut cream pie from the rotating dessert stand to celebrate. They ate at Trish's small desk.

"He has the biggest heart, you know, Jace does," Trish said. "Even now that he looks like a tough guy." Jace's older sister couldn't get over his buzz cut, though he had been in the Navy for years. She kept running her palm over his scalp at the park that first day. Jace told her he hadn't been home much. Marleigh realized he meant he hadn't been home at all since boot camp. He'd been gone for four years, but to his family, Jace had never left.

"I've never known him to look any different," Marleigh said. "High and tight is pretty common at home. That or surfer hair." She smiled at Trish. "I love how you talk about him. He told me how close you were." Marleigh loved that Trish was happy to talk and not pry. She never asked Marleigh uncomfortable questions. She seemed so open and kind, so unlike Guylene, whose conversations felt like snares ready to spring.

"He told you about how much time he spent at Donna and Ed's, right?" Trish asked. Marleigh nodded, inhaling the candle scenting the room, sandalwood, and cedar.

"It was because of me he had to move there. I want you to know that." Trish closed her eyes. "Yoga breath," she said in a whisper, a reminder. She took a long inhale. She exhaled in a slow hiss, her eyelids fluttering. Marleigh could see the muscles, tense, the length of Trish's neck.

"I thought it was because he and your mom—"

"Mom's impossible to live with, alright. I was twelve, so Jace was nine, and I was really into making up plays back then and casting them and making everyone act them out. For one play I needed a soldier, so I made Jace go get Dad's uniform."

"Oh, down in that room." It slipped out before Marleigh could catch it. She pressed two fingers to her lips.

"It gets worse," Trish said. "I made him get it and put it on."

Marleigh's stomach flipped.

"He was never allowed to touch it or smell it or anything after Dad died. She didn't display the flag or his shadowbox, back then. So Jace has his uniform on and he's mixing up the lines with things Dad would say, 'semper fi and hoo-rah and shoulder down,' and then mom walked in. At first, she froze and got this dreamy smile. Then she snapped out of it." Trish was talking faster and faster. She kneaded the toes of her left foot with her right.

"You don't have to tell me," Marleigh said. She wanted Trish to stop.

"She picked him up and threw him on the bed, hard. She was yanking at the buttons and the collar, trying to get everything off Jace. I tried to get in between them. She shoved me against the wall and I hit my head hard. 'Do you think this is funny?' she screamed, and 'Don't you ever touch his things. You're not like him. You can't touch his things.' But she was scratching Jace, had him pinned down with her knees. He couldn't breathe."

The thought of this happening to Jace turned a key in Marleigh's insides. How could his mother be so cruel and him turn out so good? She wished she were back at the diner. Trish's voice was high and pitchy. Her nose was running.

"Jace tried to get up, and she smacked him so hard his nose bled. Bad. I told her to stop, that it was my fault. My idea. She said something about being a man and pushed him off the bed onto the floor. Always gets nosebleeds, she said. I don't remember him having one before that."

Marleigh didn't know what to say. She hoped Trish was finished. She felt sick to her stomach, feverish. Before this trip, all Jace had said was that his mother was pretty torn up by his father's death and that he'd been closer with his aunt and uncle. Marleigh wouldn't have wanted to relive it, either. Maybe that's why he never told her. He was very good at acting like none of this had ever happened. It felt like a betrayal, hearing this story from Trish.

"Nothing I ever did set her off like the sight of Jace. I called Donna the next day after school and asked her if he could come over and play. He never really came home. I packed his stuff for Donna, but he never told anyone that it was my fault or why she had beaten him up. I don't think Donna or Ed know all the details to this day. He always wants to protect everyone."

Marleigh nodded, at a loss for words. Jace's backstory was worse than hers. What a competition to win. The sweet, happy Jace she knew didn't fit with the horrible stories of his childhood, but this description certainly did. *Thank God he escaped,* she thought. *Thank God he got away.* Maybe those women were reliving it all because they were stuck out here in a small town and they couldn't avoid constant reminders of the past. Look at what Jace had already accomplished. A tour in Afghanistan. Jump school. EOD school. He was already so far ahead of his parents. The bullshit in both their pasts didn't have a chance at catching them cold.

· · ·

Jace came into the bar half an hour before she was scheduled to punch out. She had already begun slicing lemons and limes for tomorrow as the bar had started to empty. Unusually worn out, Marleigh felt off and unsteady on her feet and was ready to clock out. She told him that she saw Trish earlier in the day. He asked for a Bud and shook his head. "She called me. Trish is a little too into her emotions sometimes, a little dramatic." His face closed off when he talked about his childhood, his features smoothed and hardened to stone, even the dimple faded into his skin. Is this how he'd looked in the dark, telling that awful story?

"Okay," Marleigh said, popping the cap off his beer and throwing it away. "Still, I wish you'd told me." As she slid the bottle across the bar, she kept her hand around the belly of the beer until he met her eyes.

"I'm sorry, Mar. I've worked hard to forget that shit, leave it behind me. I barely think about it anymore."

"I get it." No one should be forced to relive abuse like that, but she was confused, a little dizzy. One moment she felt as thought she'd known Jace her entire life, but there was so much she didn't know.

"I trust you, baby. Trish can get things a little twisted, though. And she's always more worried about other people than keeping her own life together." He took a long drink. "Damn that's good. Before my sister settled down here, she used to teach on the reservation. Used to drive Mom crazy," he said.

"An Indian reservation?"

"Yeah. Pine Ridge, the Sioux reservation. She's always been obsessed with other peoples' problems."

"That sounds like Trish," Marleigh said. Were Jace and Trish and Ed and Donna really as kind and as good as they seemed? She was starting to believe so, however impossible.

The last time Marleigh had really thought about Native Americans was in social studies as a child. She remembered her thick textbook, the heading "A Trail of Tears," and an inset painting and two paragraphs. Other than that, it was all Powhatan, Pocahontas, Jamestown. She was close to a reservation, a place where the people who'd first walked this wild, huge place had been parceled and bundled together. Her belly hurt, just like it did in social studies in elementary school. That's why she'd stopped thinking about it.

"Why'd it bother your mom?"

"Because she was sure Trish would get taken by some Indians." He rolled his eyes. "She swore they were after white girls."

Marleigh nodded. Sounded awfully similar to her own parents and their condescending, racist attitudes toward the Black and Brown kids who once kept the gym afloat.

"The rez isn't the safest place for women after dark," he said.

"What place is?" Marleigh asked, wondering about the women who lived there day and night.

He leaned across the bar and pulled her close. "Anywhere you're with me." She stood on tiptoe to kiss his neck. She believed him.

CHAPTER SEVENTEEN

On Marleigh's first day off, Jace woke her in the dark by kissing her bare shoulder. It tickled. "Good morning. Today I'll show you the bluff that put the *bluff* in Scotts*bluff*." He was so damn chipper in the morning. "We need to get there for sunrise."

She hadn't shaken the queasiness, going on a week now, and would have liked to spend the morning in bed. But Jace's energy was contagious, and he insisted they get outside before the mid-June heat warmed the day. Marleigh threw on shorts and a T-shirt and pulled her hair back with an elastic. She munched on Saltines from Donna's pantry to settle her stomach. The bumpy county road ride to the highway didn't help.

Jace twiddled his fingers on the steering wheel and shifted in his seat. Marleigh had seen the sandstone bluff almost every day she had spent in the area. The natural formation was visible from every part of Scottsbluff as well as most of Mitchell, which was twenty-five miles away. It was startling in so much flat land. It looked like an ancient serpent winding its way through the plains. When they parked, Jace took a golf club out of his truck bed. She gave him a look.

"In case we see a snake. I can shoo it off the trail." Marleigh tensed.

"It's still pretty cool out this morning, so we shouldn't see any."

He handed her a flashlight and walked a step in front of her, golf club extended. The path was longer than Marleigh expected—and steeper. Jace had no problem finding it in the dark. The trail cut through the rock in places to form tunnels. They entered each one, proceeding through pitch black and emerging to warming sky.

As the sky glowed and the sun prepared to break the horizon, they reached the top. Scottsbluff looked like an actual city from this height, and she could see for tens of miles. Since they were on a plateau and the highest point around, Marleigh had a 360-degree view. She didn't know where to look first. Green irrigated squares, bisecting roads, fences, livestock, streams, the whole world was below her feet. The sky was afire—burgundy and orange and pink and purple. She thought only sunset on water could be so beautiful. She was wrong.

Jace coughed. She turned and found him on one knee, a small box in his hand. He had that big dopey grin. His hand holding the box shook.

"Will you marry me?"

"Are you crazy?"

"Maybe. Marry me, Marleigh. Like you said, we'll take care of each other."

She looked down at the simple gold band glinting in the sunlight. "That's just for now," Jace said. "I want you to pick out the diamond you want when we go back."

Back, right. Norfolk and them meeting felt like a decade ago, a lifetime and half of a continent away. She'd not planned on being married at twenty-three, but she hadn't planned on Jace, either. They were more than hot for each other. Since Pops died, they hadn't spent a full day apart. Marleigh had never had a best friend. She'd never trusted anyone enough to let them know her or burrow into her heart. She'd never wanted to risk herself for anyone. Until Jace. The fact that merely a look from him lit her up like neon was just a Megaball bonus. Jace felt more like her home than any place she had ever lived.

"Yes."

He stood and picked her up and swung her around.

"Just you wait and see!"

They sat together, feet dangling off the cliff as the sun edged up into the sky, warming the rock and sand beneath them. She couldn't stop smiling. Jace held her hand. He ran his thumb over and over the band he'd just put on her finger. She rested her head on his shoulder and looked at the world below them. They could build a good life together. They had already started. She had been too busy enjoying it to notice. She felt limitless with Jace by her side.

"Goddamn I love you, Marleigh!"

• • •

When they walked down, Jace's golf club swung lazily at his side. Marleigh held Jace's hand with the one that wore his ring, and the held the flashlight in the other. Every third or fourth step one of them stopped to nuzzle or embrace the other one. She had awoken to her most perfect day.

They didn't hear the warning rattle as they entered the tunnel cut through the stone. A rattlesnake coiled tight at the other end, a car length from them. Jace threw the golf club at it. The snake spooked and slithered away. Marleigh's heart throbbed in her throat.

"Where is it?"

"We won't see it again, just a lazy rattler. Hardly *Unhcegila*."

She gagged, spit and bile on the dusty ground. "*Un*-what?"

"Never mind. A Lakota Sioux myth." Jace collected his club and waved her on. "He's long gone," he said. "How's that for an exciting story?"

Marleigh smiled, but black dots bloomed across her vision. Her knees felt noodley. "I love you, Jace. I'm sorry. I think I have the flu."

"And a stop at doc-in-a-box. What a day!" His smile was unbreakable.

CHAPTER EIGHTEEN

Jace pulled his truck into a small strip mall in Scottsbluff. Marleigh saw the red cross painted on the white wall of the urgent care office. "In the Navy, we call this place the 'I and O.'"

Marleigh looked at her reflection in the rearview mirror. Definitely pale, maybe even a little yellow. "What does that even mean?"

"Itch and odor clinic."

"That's disgusting," she said. Her mouth felt overstuffed with her tongue and too wet.

"Sorry, poorly timed raunchy squid humor. I just want you to feel better, baby."

"Me too. Later, I want you to tell me about that myth. The snake one."

Marleigh signed herself into the clinic and they took their seats in the nearly empty waiting room. An elderly woman with a walker and oxygen tank, and a white-haired man, his shoulders permanently slouched, sat in the chairs directly in front of the check-in area. The couple held hands. Their skin was spotted and thick with dark veins.

Jace placed his palm across her forehead. "A little clammy," he said, "but I don't think you're feverish."

His concern was so sweet. She could tell it made him physically uncomfortable to not make her feel better. "I'm sure it's nothing." She spun the gold band around her finger. "I'm so sorry to ruin such a great day."

He squeezed her hand in his. "Nope. That's impossible. You make every day better. And no day could be better than today. You said *'yes.'*" His voice rose, directed to the old couple at the front of the room and the women at the check-in desks. "Holy shit, she said yes! Can you believe it?"

Marleigh felt the color rise in her face. "*Shh*, Jace." But she couldn't help but smile. She rested her head on his shoulder, and he sidled his body even closer to her.

"I hoped you would. I thought just maybe you would say yes. But part of me wondered if you'd just laugh in my face. Especially after Guylene and all of that."

"Of course not, Jace. And look, it's like a little preview of in sickness and in health."

"This shoulder, my body. You can use it up. Lean on it, lay on me. Anywhere and always."

A door swung open and a nurse stepped through. "Marleigh Mulcahy?"

Jace stood with her and held onto her fingertips as she stood releasing them only when she walked through the doorway. She could picture him out there, pacing, flipping through old *PEOPLE* magazines, restless until he knew she was okay. No one had ever loved her like that.

In a small, windowless room, Marleigh wore an examination robe that was a hundred sizes too big for her and a pair of socks with rubber on the bottom. A towel made of nubby paper draped across her legs. She needed Jace. Why was the nurse taking so long to bring him back? She needed the solid heft of him next to her to remind her that she was real, that they were real, that this was really happening.

"Where is she?" Jace's voice, nervous and strained, but close by. She smeared her hands across her wet eyelashes and got herself together.

"Mr. Holt, please come with me."

"Is she okay?"

"Yes, she's right back here. Just follow me."

His smile spread wide across his face when he saw her. He'd lost the nervous mask. Now it was Marleigh's time to panic. Maybe she had ruined the day.

"Hi, Mar. Your color looks a little better, pink almost. Have you been crying?"

She couldn't fool him. Her chin quivered and she nodded.

"Marleigh, girl. What's going on?"

"Not the flu after all," Marleigh said with an unsure smile. How he reacted to this news would change everything.

Jace looked from Marleigh to the nurse. The nurse looked at a technician seated in the corner of the room on top of a whirly chair. Then they all turned to Marleigh.

"It looks like we're pregnant?" Her voice got all high on the last word.

"Pregnant! A kid! *Our* kid? Oh my God! Are you serious? Is she serious? You guys wouldn't shit me about this, right?" He buried his nose in Marleigh's hair.

"The pregnancy test came back positive. It's a standard procedure," the tech in the corner said.

"It might be too early, but they said we could try and listen for a heartbeat."

Marleigh gripped his hand with hers. "I didn't want to listen without you. Is this okay? Are you good with this?"

"Of course, let's try. Oh my God. Marleigh!"

She inched the gown up and looked down at her stomach. She certainly didn't look pregnant. The nurse squeezed a tube of jelly all over Marleigh's stomach. Marleigh found Jace's fingertips with her own. The tech slipped on plastic gloves and touched a microphone-looking thing to her skin.

"Breathe," Marleigh whispered. Jace hadn't taken a breath beside her, he was so still.

At first, all they could hear was sloshing and gurgling. And then *whump whump whump*. Jace pressed two finger to Marleigh's neck to get a pulse.

"That's so much faster than yours," he said.

"Is that . . . ?" Marleigh looked up at him. His mouth hung open, just a bit, in wonder. His eyes shone and his hand clutched her tight.

"That's your baby," the tech said.

"There's another heartbeat in you, Mar."

"Holy shit, Jace." She smiled and fat tears squeezed out the corners of her eyes. As she wiped them away, the ring he gave her that day glinted in the fluorescent light. The happiness was so profound it was painful.

"Holy shit is right. I can't decide if I should cry or smile. I want to shout and dance and put my fist through a wall and stomp and shoot off fireworks and turn a goddamn cartwheel."

The nurse smiled. "That sounds about right. Congratulations, you two."

After Marleigh dressed, the nurse pressed a thick jar of prenatal vitamins into her hands. "It's still early. Maybe six weeks, so anything can still happen. But make sure you take these every day."

"I'll make sure," Jace told them both. "I'm going to take care of you, Mar. No harm is ever going to come to you or our kid."

· · ·

All the way back to Ed and Donna's, Jace drummed his fingers on the truck's steering wheel and sang along with the country songs, howling "Carrying Your Love With Me." At the end of the chorus, he squeezed Marleigh's knee.

"I bet George Strait can hear you wailing your heart out, wherever he is," Marleigh said. He lost his volume button when he was worked up.

"You're incredible, Mar, you know that? You've changed my life in one day. My whole life!"

"I think this," she said, pointing to her abdomen, "was a joint effort. And we've changed all of our lives." Three lives changed in one day. Jace's, her own, and that miraculous *whump whump whumping* life growing inside of her.

"What a day! How are you feeling? What do you need?"

"I'm just trying to get a hold on all of this. Today can't be real."

"Just you wait, Mar, what an adventure!"

"Are we ready for all of this?" Marleigh asked, rubbing his ring on her finger. Excitement still pulsed inside of her, but reality had nosed its way in, too, like a stray dog. She looked out the window as she spoke. "A child. That will be so much more. And think about what our parents did, what messes they made."

"Look at you! Look at us, Mar. We're going to do it right." She'd turned her face to him and looked at him straight on. "I choose not to let that shit ruin my life." He smiled his perfect, dimpled, Jace smile.

They both believed him.

CHAPTER NINETEEN

Donna and Ed were seated at their kitchen table, hands clasped and heads bowed, when Marleigh and Jace arrived. After a whispered, "Amen," Donna looked up at Marleigh. "I didn't know if you were joining us for dinner tonight. I've made plenty if you want to fix a plate." Donna was a great cook. Marleigh remembered stuffing herself at the picnic and nearly every meal that followed. Tonight, the smell of the fried chicken, baked beans thick with bacon, and yeast rolls slick with butter turned her stomach.

Marleigh still wanted to cry and smile. She needed to throw up, first. Just that morning, saying yes to Jace had been the biggest commitment she'd ever made, thought she'd ever make. She'd never admitted to anyone her dreams of motherhood, of the type of mother she was going to be. Not everyone should be allowed to have children. Marleigh knew what mothering looked like in TV and movies, but she endured a real, flesh-and-blood mother. No way, though, that her parents had ever loved each other like she and Jace did. They were different. They had to be. Jace was certain that their threesome—daddy, mommy, and baby—would make the best family the world had ever seen. His excitement was contagious. She wanted to believe him—and did. They were going to do so much better than their parents. There was no alternative. Except she had barely kept herself going before she met Jace. Clothed, employed, working on a degree. She already had more responsibility than she could handle. And now motherhood. Could dreams come true too fast?

Jace piled food on his plate and ate it nearly as quickly. "You're not late for a ship," Marleigh said. "You have time to chew." She couldn't watch him swallow. Her tongue was high in the back of her throat, her mouth sticky. She didn't want Donna to think it was anything she had prepared, but Marleigh couldn't pick up a plate. She wanted to escape the smells.

Jace exploded like a child who had been holding a secret all day. "She said yes! We're going to get married!"

Donna stood and extended her arms to Marleigh for a hug. Ed scooped up a big bite of potatoes from his plate. Just as Donna and Marleigh embraced, Jace said, "And it gets better!" Marleigh shook her head. They hadn't talked about who they would tell and when. She was barely pregnant. Hadn't the nurse said it was too early, that anything could happen? Her mother had so many miscarriages. Surely their engagement was surprise enough.

"Mar's pregnant and we're going to be a family."

Ed coughed on his bite of food.

Donna's arms drooped at her side. Her face betrayed something before she mimicked Jace's smile. "Wow. What a day you've had." She motioned Marleigh out of the kitchen to the couch, leaving her nearly full dinner plate in the kitchen. Marleigh was happy to melt right into the soft, old cushions. She could be perfectly happy in this room, in this house for the rest of her life, with Donna and Ed looking after them. Jace bounced around the room, finally bounding over to the kitchen table where Ed remained seated. Ed shook his hand and pushed his glasses up his nose. Donna pressed on the old armrest to ease herself onto the couch beside Marleigh.

"What are your plans?" Donna's voice was gentle, as though she expected the answer.

"We haven't had time to make any," Marleigh said.

"It's perfect," Jace continued as though she hadn't spoken. "Marleigh's always worried about money. But now we don't have to be. Married guys get better housing and they make more."

The Navy did seem to want its sailors married. She saw lots of women her age and younger married and kidded. They were loud and confident, and they'd lived in Germany and California and Spain. He flopped down on the couch on the other side of Marleigh.

"Once the kid's older, Marleigh can go back to school if she wants. Or she can draw and paint all day. That's really what she loves to do."

Once the baby is older? School? She could stop worrying about living hand-to-mouth. Someone else could take care of her for a while. She leaned into Jace. His lips were warm on her neck, his arms strong and steady around her.

"Money is a big consideration," Donna said. "And there are plenty of others."

Just as quickly as he'd sat, Jace was up on his feet again.

"Do you want something to eat, Mar?" Jace asked. "I'll make you a plate." She shook her head. He ducked into the kitchen and emerged with the box of Saltines that Marleigh had nibbled part way through. "Don't pregnant women always want ice cream or pickles?"

"I'm—" He thrust the box at her. "Fine." She smiled up at him. She wanted to catch his energy, but she was worn out. From the hike, the proposal, and news of her pregnancy. It was starting to make sense, how she had been feeling. Seasick on dry land. Achy and tired. She twisted the ring on her left finger.

"Congratulations," Donna said, tipping her head to Marleigh's.

"Yes, congrats!" Ed mumbled over another bite of food.

"Thank you both so much," Marleigh said. She was happy, too, so happy. She knew that with a good night's sleep she would wake up as thrilled and excited as Jace. Donna put her arm around Marleigh. The warm heft of her plump shoulder and thigh felt so good. She felt drowsy.

"Got any cigars?" Jace asked Ed, who responded by scratching his head. He'd turned back down to his dinner. "We need to celebrate!"

"Jace," Donna said, "your bride-to-be is exhausted. Maybe hold off on celebrating until tomorrow."

"I'm too excited to sleep! Baby, I'll tuck you in tight. Then I'll go meet some of the boys down at the lodge." Ed and Donna shared a look. "Ed, you can come, too. I'll be back so quick you won't know I was gone. We're getting married!"

"Your life is about to change, Jace," Donna said.

"I know!"

"You've been doing so well. This visit has been wonderful."

"And it keeps getting better, Donna! Aren't you excited for us?"

Marleigh studied their back-and-forth, confused.

"Of course I am. Just suggesting you get started off on the right foot is all."

"Ed's coming too. And I won't be gone long," Jace said. "Marleigh doesn't care. You don't care if I go out and celebrate, right?"

Donna sighed.

"You don't mind if I stay here and sleep?" As long as she was headed for bed, she really didn't care what anyone else did.

"Hell no! That's what you need to do."

Once she was settled in bed, he kissed her forehead and patted her stomach. "I love you, Marleigh."

Sleep dragged her. "Love you, too, Jace." He kissed her ring finger before tucking her hand back under the covers and walking out, easing the door closed quietly behind him.

. . .

Marleigh rolled over in the empty bed, her bladder too full to ignore. She heard the rumble of tires and wondered if she were still dreaming. Her dreams in Nebraska had been so vivid. She thought it was the place. Maybe it had been the baby. Her vision was blurry.

She couldn't make out the numbers on the alarm clock. She could hear voices outside the house, Ed and Jace.

"No way for a father to act," Ed said.

"You're no one's father," Jace said. "Get off my dick."

Sounded like the night had taken a turn. After Marleigh emptied her aching bladder, the front door banged open. The men shuffled loud and heavy into the house. The television clicked on, *America's Great Histories Revealed* blared through the wall.

"Sleep out here. You can't go in there like that," Ed said.

"Stop telling me what to do."

"I *juss don* want you to ruin the best thing's ever happened to you."

"Listen to yourself, old man. You're the one who can barely talk. Don't fucking worry about us. We'll leave tomorrow," Jace said. Marleigh hoped maybe she was dreaming. She loved this little house.

She woke to morning sunshine and the sounds of Jace muttering as he packed their suitcases.

CHAPTER TWENTY

Marleigh hadn't been dreaming, and Jace was adamant that it was time to leave the following day.

"What happened at the lodge?" Marleigh asked. "Ed always seems so mellow."

Jace handed her a pair of underwear, her bra, a T-shirt, and her jeans. Everything else they had brought to Nebraska was zipped up tight. "The old prick can't control himself and had too much to drink and somehow that's my fault." He made the bed, corners tight, lines straight. "Nope. I don't need to stick around for more of that."

Marleigh looped her arms around his waist. "It's so obvious they love you, Jace. Is one bad night a good reason to leave ten days early?"

"Baby, don't you get on me, too," Jace said, tightening his arms around her. "I thought you needed to get back to school. And remember that apartment you have to pay for even if you're not there." They both knew that the fall session of classes didn't start until August. And when she had used her bills as an excuse not to leave Norfolk after Pops's funeral, he had said he had it covered. No big deal. "It'll be cool. We'll drive to Denver this time and spend the night then fly home. I want you all to myself, on a bed bigger than this one."

Marleigh had loved their time in Nebraska, but they did have to return to Norfolk sooner or later. It didn't seem worth the fight. They had probably overstayed their welcome with Ed and Donna anyway. "I've never been to Colorado," she said.

"That's my girl, my fiancé," Jace said with a smile. "Damn right! We're starting our own family."

. . .

Ed was gone before they left. Donna watched Jace load the bags in his truck.

"I hope you'll come visit us next time," Marleigh said. Donna hugged Marleigh so tight she could barely breathe.

"Ha! Ed won't make that trip," Jace said. He stood with his arm on the open truck door.

"He isn't much of a traveler," Donna said, her eyes on Jace. "That's true. But I hope we do get out to see you, Marleigh."

"Real nice of him to see us off," Jace said. He gave Donna a stiff hug and climbed into the truck.

"He loves you, honey," Donna said.

"He needs to get himself squared away before he tells me how to live my life."

Marleigh rolled her eyes and swatted her hand. "Please tell Ed goodbye for us. And thank you both so much." The corners of Marleigh's eyes pinched. Pregnancy hormones already? She just wanted to stay.

Donna took Marleigh's hands into hers. "You take good care, you hear? You two be careful." Marleigh wasn't sure which two Donna meant. She squeezed the woman's hands goodbye and walked around to the passenger side of the truck.

Marleigh slept nearly the entire way from Denver back to Norfolk. She felt rested and more in control of her nausea by the time they landed. She was eager to get back to work and prepare for a new school session. She wasn't as fond of the midsummer heat. It was only the beginning of July; the days were only going to get hotter and steamier for another two months.

"There are plenty of bars and restaurants," she said. "I called Bella Italia, and I'm on their schedule this week. No more Thirsty Camel. I'm sure Jameson would give me a good recommendation at a tattoo shop with openings."

"Two jobs and school," Jace said. "That's a lot for someone who isn't pregnant."

Of course it was. "School is so I can end up with one real job. A job without shifts and tips. A job with a salary and health insurance. But I need to make money while I'm in school, now especially." She rolled her eyes at her stomach, still flat, hiding what was growing inside.

"You won't have to. That's another reason we should get married right away. You won't have to carry heavy plates or stick needles in people." Marleigh loved tattooing. She would have loved to open her own shop one day, but that wouldn't happen.

Guylene was convinced Marleigh had gotten pregnant to trap Jace. She'd made that clear. Yet, he was the one trying to convince Marleigh to rely on him and let him provide for her.

It would be nice. So much better than nice. Fantastic to just be able to go to school. She could finish in less than two years, even with a baby. To not have to take deep breaths when her credit card bills arrived or try to figure out if she should pay cash for groceries or put them on a card in case she didn't book enough tattoos or earn enough in tips to make it through the month. To see if she could make more than the minimum payment, open a bubble of room. Move ahead in life instead of falling back. "And I fucking love you, Marleigh. You love me, too. We should just do it. ASAP."

She knew he was right. Why was she trying to talk him out of her? When he said nice things and goofy things, told her how pretty she was and how they'd be a family and love each other like their own parents never knew how, she could hear her mother's voice. *Just wait. He'll figure you out. Think you're better than everybody? You're not.*

The offer he was making was real. She'd already talked to plenty of Navy wives and girlfriends, several of whom had "forgotten" to take a pill—always said in air quotes—because of the healthcare the Navy offered, and for the housing stipends for married sailors. None of those women worked. None of them had to. She would still be working on her degree and finding a place on a dental staff; she wouldn't be giving up her independence, her equal footing as a breadwinner. It was the perfect job for a Navy wife because she could find work anywhere Jace was stationed—in the US at least. She would always earn her own money. And surely, she could hold onto a shift or two a week tattooing until her belly got in the way, bringing in some cash and keep her skills sharp.

"Okay," she said, smiling.

"Okay, you'll marry me? Okay? How about today?" He tried to sound gruff, his grin wide and eyes bright.

"I'm pretty sure we need a license or something."

"This week then!" She swatted his shoulder. He picked her up and swung her around. "I'll always take care of you, Mar. All of this Navy stuff will be worth it. I promise." She relaxed her weight into his frame, the strong arms around her.

Jace only had three boxes of things to move into her apartment. She hadn't realized how little he had and how almost all of it already resided with her. Stepping up on the sidewalk, Jace asked, "Why do you live here?" He gestured to the old, funky Victorian-lined neighborhood street in Norfolk's historic and trendy Ghent district.

"Because Ocean View is a dump, like you said. Well, not all of it. But the restaurants and bars are nicer here and the tips are bigger." Big brick homes with columns. Art galleries. People with enough money to dream. No public housing in sight, at least not on the main streets.

"I could see the ocean from that bar. Looked pretty nice to me."

"It's called Ocean View, but you can't see the ocean. That's the Chesapeake Bay. OV is the poor man's oceanfront." The poor man's everything. She hated OV for the same reason she hated her parents—she was born of it. Ghent wasn't rich like Virginia Beach, not by a long shot, but it was a big step in the right direction; so what if her apartment was smaller and hotter in the summer in Ghent. She wasn't looking back, and she definitely wasn't going back. What was so great about sand, anyway? It just made your sheets gritty. There wasn't real salt water, just a mix of salt and freshwater. Brackish. Even the word sounded dirty.

"How's it living on base?" she asked.

"You've been there, right?"

"A few times. I haven't known all that many people in the Navy. Navy kids came and went so much in school we didn't make good friends with them."

"I went to school for twelve years with the same dumbasses. It never changed. The first airplane I ever rode took me to boot camp."

"If I got on a plane out of here again, I don't know if I'd ever come back. You barely got me out of Nebraska."

"I understand. Join the Navy and see the world!"

He didn't have a lot, but his slacks hung in her closet, ironed into tight lines. They barely took up any space. Her clothes were soft and loose, his starched and crisp. The old beer poster didn't reappear, and for that she was thankful. After Jace was unpacked, he said there was someplace he had to take her. "We can walk. And, no, it can't wait." He tugged on her hand, and she followed.

. . .

"Oh, this is pure romance," Marleigh said as Jace pulled open the door to Bress Pawn Shop and held it for her. But she said it with a smile. Neither of them was used to firsthand anything. Jace made them both shine like new pennies. In a way, their love was kind of secondhand, but it was still the real thing.

"I know, baby," Jace said. "Who knows what we'll find. And this is just till I get back." She wiggled her fingers in between his. He looked from her fingernails up the length of her arm to her face. "Goddamn, you're so pretty. Why are you with me again?"

"The baby," she teased.

"Sure," he said. "Sure. We both know it's more than that."

"Of course it is."

He tugged her past the hocked musical instruments and radio equipment to the jewelry cases. The eyes of the guy behind the case went straight to Marleigh's belly. There was nothing to see, and Marleigh knew Jace had proposed before they knew about the baby. That's all that mattered. Jace tightened his grip on her hand.

"This dick better not ruin this," he muttered. "You know this is only for now. I'm going to give you the world."

"How can I help you two?"

Marleigh didn't say anything. She just looked at Jace.

"We're shopping for an engagement ring and wedding bands." Jace lifted their interlocked hands.

Marleigh wiggled her fingers for emphasis and smiled.

"Congratulations are in order, then!" the man behind the counter said. "And doing it all at once," he said. "I can make you a good deal that way. When are you getting married?"

"Next week," Jace said. "I ship out a couple weeks after." Marleigh touched her belly then dropped her free hand.

"A Navy man, eh? Thanks for your service." He turned to Marleigh. "What's your ring size, sweetheart?"

"I have no idea," she said.

"Let's start there," the man said. "He's the sailor, but you're the important one." He winked at her. "This is just to get an idea. We can resize almost anything."

He reached below the counter and held out a loop of brass circles. "My name's Al," he said, gesturing to Marleigh to hold out her ring finger. He slid a ring on. Too big. Her hand trembled.

"I'm Marleigh." He went smaller with the rings. Still too big.

"Marleigh, you're a delicate size five," Al said.

"Size five," Jace repeated "I'll remember that for when I can afford a real ring."

"What kind of engagement ring have you been dreaming of since you were a little girl?"

Marleigh laughed. "My childhood was more taped up wrists and bloody knuckles than Disney movies."

"Something else I love about her," Jace said.

"I don't think I ever really thought about it," she said. "Just something simple."

"Come over here and browse. Let me know what sparkler catches your eye. And, big guy—"

"Jace."

"Jace, come over and look, too. If you were gonna surprise her and it had to be perfect, which one would you choose?"

"Mar, turn around," Jace said, and with his hands on her shoulders, he gently turned her away from the jewelry case.

"Don't pick anything crazy," she said. She blushed. He kissed the line of heat creeping from her neck to her jaw. He saw a brilliant round diamond in a gold setting and pointed to it.

"Can I see that one?" he said to the store clerk.

"Princess cut, very nice," the man said. "I have all the appraisal documents on this."

Marleigh stood still, her eyes closed. The tinkle of keys, and the slide of a plexiglass drawer. She pressed her thumb against the band that Jace had used to propose.

"That's the one," Jace said.

Something tickled the back of her knee. Marleigh opened her eyes and found Jace kneeling before her. She opened her eyes and gawked at the ring in his hand.

"Take off that trashy piece of tin," he said. "This is the ring that belongs on your finger."

The diamond looked bigger on her small finger. She kept opening her mouth, trying to find something to say, but closed it each time.

She'd never imagined a diamond like that on her hand. It was so brilliant, so bright.

"You already said yes to that little piece of crap," Jace said, showing the clerk for emphasis.

"I don't need—" Marleigh began. She fanned her fingers out and turned her hand side to side, mesmerized by the sparkle. "Jace. This is the most beautiful thing I've ever seen."

"You're the most beautiful thing I've ever seen."

CHAPTER TWENTY-ONE

Marleigh splurged on a short, white dress to show off her legs and flat-ironed her hair for their July 21 courthouse wedding. Jace took her breath away in his dress whites. The Norfolk City courthouse provided a witness. She wished the baby counted. They didn't need anyone else in the world. A stranger who was walking by offered to take their picture on the courthouse steps, Marleigh still holding her bright bouquet. Jace scooped her up into his arms. Flags whipped in the wind. She was blissfully dizzy from it all.

The first wedding gift Jace bought her was a pack of five pads of good drawing paper and two sets of pencils. "I like watching you sketch. You always curl your knees up and get all scrunched." He tried as hard as he could not to talk to her while she was drawing, but couldn't help himself. Most days she used the bright primary color spiral notebooks you could find anywhere. "You deserve better." She practiced her new name, *Marleigh Holt*, in cursive, print, calligraphy, the *H* shaped like an embrace.

Every couple of years she had splurged on those items for herself, she'd told him once when he caught her doodling in the gym. The thick paper beneath her fingers, the pencil that would erase without smearing or leave unwanted shadows behind.

"I don't know shit about art," he said. "But you're good."

She'd felt the urge to draw always, but recently she'd been almost compelled to draw every day, like the baby inside of her fed her creativity as it fed off her. "Thank you. These are so expensive. You didn't have to." But as she said it, she held them close. They felt too good to give up.

"Think of them as coming from our rich uncle," he said and winked at her.

"Wouldn't that be nice? A rich uncle!"

"We've got one," he said. "Rich Uncle Sam. He's going to take good care of us, and I'm going to take good care of you and this little guy." He pressed his hand against her stomach that gave no indication of the baby growing inside. "Seriously, you can relax."

Could she, finally?

With Jace back on base each day, prepping for his upcoming deployment, Marleigh told the restaurant she was giving up her shifts so she could focus on school. "You're always welcome here," the manager told her. She was never going back. Her days of having to kiss ass in the hopes of the smallest tip were over. Having to laugh at stupid jokes and pretending to ignore a hairy hand on her ass. Folding pizza boxes until her knuckles ached. No more restaurant work for her.

"Thanks so much," she said. "Call me if you're ever short staffed." That happened always, but she'd never answer that call. A husband, a baby, school. The route to an actual career. It was everything Marleigh had ever wanted all at once.

She called her mother and left a message. "You're wrong about me. I'm married and we're starting a family. You're not part of it." As she spoke, she had the sense of her mother sitting there, a cigarette between her fingers, listening without picking up. Laughing.

• • •

It was less than a month after they returned from Nebraska and six days before he deployed when Jace came with her to Portsmouth

Naval Hospital to hear the baby's heartbeat again. When Marleigh'd called the OB-GYN covered by Jace's insurance, she was told, "If you peed on a stick and it says you're pregnant, congratulations! We don't need to see you until at least nine or ten weeks." She knew that most miscarriages happened early, so that must have been why.

To her core, Marleigh knew she was pregnant. Her body told her, and yet it still seemed impossible. For her entire life, Jackie warned Marleigh that she'd probably never get pregnant. Her mother had gone all the way cold after an emergency hysterectomy when Marleigh was eight. "Thought I'd started the change," Jackie said, when Marleigh asked how she didn't realize she was pregnant when she was missing periods. "Not like it happens all that often," her mother said, Marleigh fake retching at the thought of her parents having sex. "He still slumps down heavy on me sometimes," she'd said before Marleigh left the room. Maybe it was better that she always heard fighting instead.

Marleigh almost had a sibling, but you were supposed to stop drinking when you got pregnant. Her mother cut back. "You coulda helped take care of it, too," her mother said. She had a feeling that much of the caretaking would have fallen to her for whatever was refusing to grow and refusing to bleed away. It began rotting inside of Jackie, giving her an infection that made her sweat and seize, eyeballs rolling blankly in their sockets, foamy spittle gurgling from her throat and out her mouth. From the ambulance to the ER and then to the OR, all her mother's reproductive organs were found strangled by this wouldn't-be life.

Some days Marleigh thought the dead baby had it easier. All her mother said she remembered was feeling a tremor and then falling to the kitchen floor. Next, she awoke in a gray room feeling hollow as a jack-o'-lantern and so, so cold. Likely a reaction to anesthesia and antibiotics, the doctors said, her body trying to play catchup with the rapid decrease in febrile temperature to normal body temperature. They also said the word "withdrawal." Her mother couldn't stop shivering. But that didn't change when she left the hospital and could drive herself to the liquor store. She wore sweatshirts inside the fetid heat of the boxing gym, wool socks in Virginia August.

Jackie cooled every other way, too, hardening like wax. She had never been cheery Holly Homemaker, but she'd at least had fire and wit. Jackie'd always cried when medal winners at the Olympics became teary atop podiums, thanking their mothers, certain, Marleigh thought, that one of her "adopted sons" from the gym would be up there, one eye distended, lip bloody, but still victorious. When he thanked Mama, he'd be thanking her. After the surgery, it was all gone. Jackie was brittle calm at best. She could sit so still at the check-in desk that she could be asleep. Marleigh wondered what else they had scooped out along with dead alien baby and her uterus and ovaries. Or maybe they'd put something in her IV. When she'd come to, her mother was muttering something about not being a woman anymore.

But in that dark room at the obstetrician's office, nothing mattered but Jace, Marleigh and the life they'd created. The swooshing sound of their baby's heart echoed around them, Jace looking at Marleigh like she was a miracle. "That's a strong, healthy heartbeat right there," the doctor said.

Jace wiped the goo from Marleigh's belly. He had a six-month deployment coming up, so he would miss the ultrasound and seeing her get big, but he would be back to meet his child. "We'll see you in a few weeks for your ultrasound, Marleigh. She can send you pictures, Dad." Marleigh could feel how badly he wanted to stay right where he was.

· · ·

Marleigh upped her course load, bought some new clothes, and started picking out items for the baby's nursery. One of her regular customers asked for her at the tattoo shop. She went in and gave the guy his piece. He only wanted some Roman numerals and shading to add to her previous work on his shoulder. The work only took her an hour and a half and she left with two hundred in cash.

She wanted to surprise Jace with something. He'd been spoiling her since Nebraska. She wanted to send him off to the desert with a hot reminder of her. A photographer had tried to rope her into posing for a pinup for charity once; plenty of the girls she worked with participated, and he was known for his boudoir photo shoots. She wanted Jace to remember this body, the one he fell in love with. Marleigh had planned to use the money for books, but another custom tattoo would more than cover those. And wasn't Jace always telling her to relax about money? He'd flip looking at the pics. She had enough to book the session. She needed some sexy lingerie, and let Jameson know that she had some open time the next few days if the shop could use her.

Jace was getting edgy. He had ten days left until his deployment. He was packed, restless and ready. Anticipating the desert was worse than the desert itself, he'd told her. "You're magical. I forgot all about war and duty and everything but you this summer, Mar."

She went straight from her sexy photo shoot to the tattoo parlor. The photos and prints were already paid for, and now her books would be, too. A little something for both Jace and her. She was washing some splotches of iodine off her forearms when Jace walked in. The alcohol-soaked cotton balls were cold and left her skin pink, but they got the job done.

"Hi, baby," she said, wondering why he'd come looking for her here. Jace leaned in to kiss her but stopped and looked down at her hand holding the cotton swab.

"What the fuck?" He grabbed her hands and turned the palm-side up.

"I'm scrubbing off iodine. No big deal." Marleigh pulled away.

"I thought you were done with that shit. What about the baby?"

"I wasn't giving myself a tattoo. And everything is clean and sterile. You know that."

"Why are you sneaking around? You said you were done with that. All the jobs, hiding cash."

"*You* said I was done with that. *I* like tattooing. Art, drawing— you know that. It's perfectly safe."

"Is that how it's going to be when I'm gone? You being all sneaky." He squeezed the container of rubbing alcohol. Any tighter he would smash it.

"What are you talking about? I haven't been sneaking around."

He poured the rubbing alcohol down the drain.

"What the fuck? Does that make you feel better?" She cupped his face in her hands. He looked more scared than anything. "What's wrong?"

He pushed her hands from his face. "My wife telling me the truth. That's what makes me feel better." Each day had wound him tighter. He wanted to know where she was all day, how was she feeling, had she felt the baby yet? She'd heard pre-deployment paranoia was common, but this was ridiculous.

She stomped away from him and refused his ride home. When Marleigh walked back into their apartment, she yelled, "You know what? I have been sneaking around." She slapped the folder with the photos on the counter and walked back to the bedroom. The top pictures were the surprise lingerie photo shoot Marleigh took for him. Her face was tilted sideways, but her stare was dead-on straight. Her eyes were lined thick, lashes dark and heavy. Her legs looked a mile long in stilettos and fishnets. "I wanted to surprise you, you ass."

"Baby," Jace called from the kitchen. "I'm so sorry."

"You'd better be," she said from the doorway.

It only took him three large strides to reach her from the kitchen. "Oh my God, baby, you're so beautiful. And you did this for me. In this one, somehow you're staring right into me." He picked her up and set her gently on the bed. "And this one, all you need is a lasso. You're my sexy superhero. I'll look at them every goddamn day I'm gone." She leaned back against a pillow and he rested his shoulder on her thigh. "I know you wouldn't sneak around."

"Of course not."

"I've never had anyone to leave behind before. I've always been so ready to go." She dusted her fingers across his scalp, buzzed again just this week.

"And after you come home, there will be two of us to love on you."

Jace held the bottom photo, the smallest, gently between his thumb and index finger. The image was black and white and blurry, the oval inside of Marleigh that was becoming their baby.

After putting the photo back into the folder with the rest, Jace pressed against Marleigh from behind and wrapped his arms around her. His hands were warm against the firm mound of her belly. "Godfuckingdamn, I hate leaving you!"

She tipped her head back and rested it against his clavicle. She knew he was telling the truth; she also knew he was restless and ready to get back to work.

"I'm going to miss you so much, but it's okay that you feel ready to go. This is what you've trained for."

"It feels like what I was built for and I've never been home so long before. But that was before you, Mar, and this little guy."

"We'll do our things, and you'll do yours. And we'll all make it through."

"Roger that, Mar."

• • •

Jace watched her that night as she dressed. Marleigh had no idea what to wear to meet the wife of Jace's CO and the other wives and girlfriends of the unit, or what to expect. Only wives were invited, none of the men.

The house was beautiful and in an old and tony off-base neighborhood. It sat on perfectly mowed grass that reminded Marleigh of Jace's buzz cut. She knew the couple had children, but there were no plastic toys, no bikes, just a small basketball hoop above the garage.

Join me for sunset on the creek, the invitation said, a subtle announcement that they lived on the water. In Norfolk, property was worth a mint if it had water access, even if that property were right across the street from public housing projects. Growing up, her mother went on and on about how they had water access. At the end of the street and through two families' yards there was a marsh. She certainly wasn't hosting sunset cocktail parties there. Actually, maybe her mother did. But just her regular cocktails for one in a plastic bottle of Burnett's vodka. Start time, as early as you want. End time, never. She cringed, imagining her mother in this home, smelling of smoke and sizing up one valuable object to another. She saw her mother's hunger, that same awe, in the eyes of the other young wives and girlfriends. Except for the CO's wife, who probably wasn't forty, all the women were exceptionally young. "Oh, your house is soooo beautiful," they all said.

"Thank you for having us in your beautiful home." The young women lined up to greet her. Marleigh had learned to act like she'd been here before, like wealth and power didn't impress her, even if she planned to study the woman and figure out how she had built this life. Jace would likely never be an officer, but he could still do very well, especially with the right kind of support at home.

"It is scary when we first think of our men preparing to leave us," the CO's wife said.

A young woman beside Marleigh, her voice trembly whispering, said, "I mean, isn't it? I don't know anyone here and I'm about to be all alone." Marleigh patted her hand.

"It'll be all right," Marleigh said. She nodded toward the woman speaking. How nice it must have been for this girl to have had parents that babied her, and then she moved from their house into married life with a sailor. Marleigh had been alone since she was born, and was certainly safer away from her parents. Alone she could handle. She would have a leg up on these women. She had the baby; she would never have to be alone again.

. . .

The morning before he deployed, Jace woke Marleigh up and said they had an appointment. He tugged her hand like an eager child four blocks up the sidewalk from her apartment into the nicer section of Ghent, to one of the renovated old buildings.

"It's not the first floor," he said. "But wait till you see it." He led her up two short flights of stairs.

A young woman in a pants suit stood beside a door marked 303. She handed him a key and said, "Welcome home!"

Marleigh looked from her to Jace and back again. The woman smiled and walked down the hallway. Jace opened the door into the most beautiful apartment she'd ever seen. "I wanna build you a desk over there so you can draw. And look at how big the bathrooms are."

The realtor chimed in. "Two bedrooms, two bathrooms." Marleigh couldn't speak.

"See, my family man allowance from our rich uncle! Do you like it?"

"Oh, Jace," Marleigh said. She knew she'd never want to leave it. But she had no idea how they could afford it.

"I know you'll have it feeling like home before I get back!"

CHAPTER TWENTY-TWO

Marleigh received her first letter just three weeks after Jace left. That was sooner than the CO's wife told her to expect anything to reach her. The envelope was heavy and battered, covered in stamps and post markings. She could feel the distance it had traveled. She slit it open. Inside were several pages written in Jace's small, slanted man-scrawl. Words were crossed out if he caught the misspelling. Two pages had no paragraphs, just long blocks of sentences. Just like Jace. When he was quiet, it was as though he barely breathed. But when he got to talking, watch out. She held the papers to her nose, hoping to smell him. She shook her head. *Dumbass, it's been way too long for that.*

Dear Marleigh,

I MISS YOU BABE. I missed you the second I left and that hasn't stopped. I know it won't. How are you? How are you feeling? How's little one doing? Tell me about Norfolk and about you. Tell me everything.

I've been back inside the wire a week and my teeth and the inside of my ears are gritty with sand. It makes me think of how you refuse to go into the house with sandy feet. The shit really does get everywhere. We stopped in Germany first and then on to Kabul. All a blur.

So far there's only one other SO in my tent and a Snake Eater who was on my chopper into base. There's an empty cot, so maybe someone else is on the way. They're both ok. They call me Smoky. No one else in this tent wears a crab badge, and can't anyone else cleanup the shit like I can, so they're smart enough to stay out of my way. The tent smells like hot dip spit. Nothing like sleeping with you. I really can't wait to do that. Your pictures are getting a workout wink wink. I try not to make the guys jealous telling them about my super hot wife. You don't even have to try, Mar. That's the best kind of hot. I LOVE YOU. It took me a few days to get my head on straight here. You changed my whole life. You are my life. You and little man inside of you. My life used to be over here— disarming IEDs and clearing routes. That used to be what made my dick hard, sharpened my mind into a trench knife. Now that's work. My life is in Norfolk. And I fucking love it. I hope you're not worried about me. Worrying isn't good for you or the baby, right? It's the same old shit, different day. Clearing routes and taking the bomb calls as they come— usually right when I've fallen asleep. Ha. Fuckers. We have quite the collection of jury-rigged devices. Some are hi-tech— the rich terrorists have gotten fancy. Labels and internet-based designs. Most are trash. Those are the most dangerous. I know all about being trash. Trash gets underestimated. Techs can be tempted to cowboy that shit. You know what I told you. There are bold EODs and there are old EODs. There are no old, bold EODs. I'm going to get old with you. I've got Fang—my bomb robot. We'll get our jobs done and I'll get the hell home to you. Promise.

I can't believe I'm going to be a dad, Mar. What a fucking club, fatherhood. I'm going to make you proud.

I got the first drop your cocks/grab your socks call three days in. The rear tire of a Humvee sat on an IED. They missed the first muffled whumph under one tire, then stopped. Honestly, you gotta listen. There were five people inside like always. Fang and I got to work balancing the trigger mechanisms under the Humvee tires. I wish Fang was the one who had to wear sixty pounds of Kevlar and foam and plastic in the damn desert. Fucking hot in there. The Humvee was stopped in a bowl of sand, desert plateaus on either side. It did look like Nebraska. Remember how you can see far? I couldn't see an enemy. But that's the shit. Just because I can't see them, doesn't mean their not there. Somebody's always watching. We got one guy out—and a chick, the super butch type, always busting balls—and Fang and I finished stabilizing the IED but then some towel head started shooting at the Humvee to blow all of the IEDS. The driver is always last. That job has to be the fucking worst, sitting duck. All he wants to do is gun it and get the hell away from the bomb. I held his life in the remote control I use to work Fang. If Fang applied too much or too little pressure, it'd be over for him. He had nothing to worry about. Not with me there. We got them all out and the Humvee rolled on. My fingertips get so cold doing that. It's like a thousand degrees out. Makes no sense. So that's what I do here. When I'm not on a call, all I think about is you baby.

Write soon. And send some more hot photos.

Love,
Your Husband Jace

She remembered the nicknames Jace had told her. Snake Eater meant Green Beret. SO was a SEAL. All she could think about, though, was that during the entire time Jace was saving the Humvee and its crew he'd kept telling himself, *This is nothing. You're nothing. You have nothing to lose.* Both had everything to lose now.

Marleigh wrote him every other day, keeping in mind the advice from the CO's wife: *keep it light, the boys need always know we're behind them; they shouldn't have to worry about the home front.* She told him about her growing belly, the shapes the limbs of their baby boy made across her skin. He'd guessed right. She picked the clearest ultrasound photos to send to him, drawing a little Sharpie arrow to his penis. "We're having a boy!" was her opening line. He told her he saved every letter, printed each email. She used email for her quick, regular check-ins. Snail mail was thoughtful time spent on Jace, their baby. She sent him sketches.

Marleigh wrote about the apartment, how she was opening boxes and placing items on shelves she'd assembled herself. How the smell of chicken—any poultry—cooking made her throat gummy and tight. She wrote of her checkups, the extra supplements the doctor recommended and how he wanted her to fatten up a little.

She didn't tell him about how she couldn't take a shit, that she popped a blood vessel in her eye straining so hard. She didn't tell him that she'd grown scared of walking up their street after dark, the way the homeless man from the park on the corner moved closer and closer to their front steps every time she worked nights, husband gone and baby on the way. She didn't tell him about the man, it was always the same man, who sniffed loud at her approach down the street to her apartment. He said he could smell her. "Fuck off," she told him the first time.

"I can smell that baby inside you. You smell sweeter than ever. That smell calls to me." He lunged at her. Marleigh didn't want the man to see her hurried steps, to smell her fear as well as her crotch. She started carrying Mace and flashed it at the man.

She also left out that she had been working, just a few shifts at a new tattoo parlor and Bella Italia, to pad their income and give her mind something to do besides worry about Jace and count down to the birth of their son. She tried to imagine Afghanistan, desert and sand, but instead saw golden grasses rippling across rolling hills. She started her letters on her breaks and finished them at home, often after awaking in the dark hours of morning, her bladder cracking, her cheeks slobber-glued to the pages. She'd wake up again, face bruised with ink. *I love you. The baby and I can't wait to have you home.*

CHAPTER TWENTY-THREE

Jace made it home on leave two days before Marleigh was due. He strode through the airport terminal and scooped her up in his arms.

She wasn't certain what to expect during childbirth—the library copies of *What to Expect When You're Expecting* were worn and pages were missing—but she anticipated pain, everyone talked about the pain. Jace flipped through the pages, too excited to follow the paragraphs through. "You're going to be amazing, baby."

There was something so hot about Jace assembling baby furniture, so reliable and sturdy. He would never let them down. He surprised her with a mobile he made. Elephant gray, it looked like propellors or a rotor twirling over the crib. They had fumbling but pleasurable third-trimester sex on the floor of the second bedroom, their son's crib half-built against the wall.

Neither of them had any doubt when she went into labor, four days after her due date. She'd been adamant that her son not beat his father home. A warm wet rush down her legs. The experience put her inside her body in a way she'd never known. From her toenails to the follicles of her scalp, her body felt of one single piece working with the new body inside of her to move it out of her. There was pain, yes, before the epidural, which she'd first declined knowing the bill for it months down the road would enrage her. "Get it," Jace urged. "You don't have to suffer, baby!" He was calm and watchful throughout her labor, brought her ice chips and gently wiped the sticky curls from her face.

She could feel the wave of tension building, her muscles tightening and then releasing, the baby moving down through her. She knew—a moment before the doctor directed—that it was time to push. She could tell the baby was ready, too. Beside the necessity of open, ready arms to catch the baby, she wished she and Jace could have labored alone, in the dark somewhere, without the scratchy gown and bright lights, the blood-pressure, pulse-monitoring clamp on her finger. Throughout labor she closed her eyes, imagined herself on that grassy plain, windblown, near the fossil beds where Jace grew up. Jace's abs were hard beneath her foot. He cupped her bent knee. Told her, "Give it all you've got."

Her body didn't need help. She'd scoffed at the hippie waitress she worked with, always smelling like patchouli and BO—those crystals don't work—when she told Marleigh what a mystical experience childbirth was. As soon as she told Marleigh that she'd given birth in a baby pool, Marleigh'd written her off. Turns out she was right, only *mystical* wasn't the right word. It was a profound change. Everything in her shifted and realigned to create the space and power to move this baby into the world. Her vertebrae restacked themselves; her jaw relaxed. Her pupils dilated along with her cervix, despite the lights. So much opened. Her mind shifted, too, expanded as colostrum leaked from her nipples, cooled and stuck to the gown in folds around her.

She hadn't known until this moment that gaping, stretched, painful moment how she would really feel about this baby. Yes, she was still an idiot in love with Jace, but this baby, the unexpected family, had come so quickly. Work and exhaustion and worry and constipation dominated her pregnancy. She never worried about her unborn baby's health in the womb. She had an unspoken certainty of his vitality. His near-constant kicking and hiccupping reminded her that he was there, he was real. That wasn't it. She'd worried about everything after. Would she know how to take care of him? Would she want to? There weren't a lot of pointers to be picked up from her mother, except what not to do. What if she couldn't breastfeed? Formula was so expensive. Would she ever finish school? When would she be able to go back? In that moment as he crowned, though, Marleigh understood that she had all of it within her—love, the ability to nurture, food to sustain him—all there waiting for her and for him. She just needed him to be real first, not an idea, something growing inside her. She hadn't been indifferent while pregnant. She was crying and smiling and eager to feel his warm messy body against her own.

This hot, wrinkled thing, was cone-headed and bruised and swollen. Jace cut the knot between them; severed, it still pulsed. The charge of this baby in her arms, on her skin, the way their bodies anticipated each other was a base, fundamental pleasure, a need she never knew she had. She and Jace had made this. Jace barely spoke that first day of their son's life. He just kept looking back and forth between mother and baby, saying thank you.

They both signed the birth certificate, and small inky footprints pressed onto paper. Jason Matthew Holt.

• • •

They spent less than two days in the hospital before being discharged. "Get some rest, baby," Jace said and kissed her forehead. "Little man's konked out, and you did all the hard work." He tucked her into their bed. The room was warm and clean and home.

She had her own family already, and they were a good family, a happy family. She had no idea people could love each other so much. Maybe it was the hormones, but her throat was thick with happiness. Her body was so full of gratitude. She would show these men what love was, but first she had to sleep. Jace was right. He'd barely left her at the hospital, and yet there it was, the little portable crib and a stocked diaper-changing station that her coworkers surprised her with when they heard she'd gone into labor. Assembled and ready. She would love these two like no one had ever been loved before.

Their bed felt like heaven, especially after the pneumatic hospital bed and the around-the-clock nurse checks. She could sleep knowing that Jace had the baby. It always made her a little jumpy when one of the nurses took him out of the room, even if it was just for a bath or to the nursery. It felt too good to have both her boys with her. Jace's hands were steadier, smoother and surer than her own. When Jason cried, Jace kept his molasses pace and it soothed the baby, soothed Marleigh. Nothing to it. Nothing to worry about. She slept. Jace only disappeared on his motorcycle when both Marleigh and Jason slept. She could smell the exhaust on him, feel the cool of high speed on his wind-whipped cheeks.

The morning of Jason's first well-baby check, Jace helped Marleigh down the stairs from their apartment, cushioning each ginger step. She stepped outside the building and looked for her car. She always parked in the same spot, but the beater was gone. In its place, a shiny new Subaru. On the back windshield were two stickers—I love my sailor, and baby on board. She was too tired to panic, so she looked at Jace confused.

"Do you like it?"

"Like what?"

"The car."

"Where's my car?"

"The Ford POS has been retired, Mar. You can't be driving my son around in that thing." Marleigh looked closer. Jason's infant car seat was buckled inside, behind the driver's seat.

"Oh my god," Marleigh said.

"Baby, I can't ever thank you enough for him and for us," Jace said. "Let's see how she drives." Marleigh was a wife, a mom, and she had her first new car.

Marleigh eased herself into the driver's seat. The only new car smell she'd ever known came from an air freshener. This was different, real. No warning lights illuminated when she turned the key in the ignition. Her seat adjusted with a touch. When she shifted the car into reverse and checked her rearview mirror, she realized how close the bright motorcycle, chrome pipes shiny, was to her bumper. It looked like the bike Jace drove when they met, but much nicer.

"Easy does it," he said.

"Oh, I see. Don't want me to accidentally tap it?"

"Just a little upgrade, baby. We have one perfect family car and one ride built for fun."

CHAPTER TWENTY-FOUR

Lynetha came by to see Marleigh when Jason was a week old. She carried a three-tiered cake made of newborn diapers and decorated with bottles of diaper rash cream and baby soap and wash cloths into their apartment. "Wow," she said. "This place is gorgeous."

Marleigh blushed. She still couldn't believe that she lived in this light-filled space. "Thank you. I'm so glad to see you. And the diaper cake. That's so great. This kid goes through more diapers in a day. I had no idea." She patted the couch beside her. "Take a seat."

"I couldn't picture you sitting here, nursing a baby," Lynetha said. "But now I see it, you're such a natural." Marleigh could barely keep her eyes open. The letdown of her milk was so powerful. She felt dreamy and sleepy when Jason nursed.

"Is there anything she can't do?" Jace asked, bounding into the room. "And come on, isn't he perfect? Look at my dark-eyed boy."

"He's the perfect mix of both of you." Lynetha smiled and allowed Jason's fingers to curl around her pinky. "I see the honeymoon period is still a thing for y'all. It's impossible not to feel like a third wheel with you fools, but I'm happy for you, Marleigh. You deserve it. I hope we never see you back at the Thirsty Camel."

Marleigh gently swooped her index finger through Jason's mouth to break his grip on her nipple so that she could switch him to the other breast.

"Damn right," Jace answered from the kitchen.

"I miss you, Lyn."

"No you don't. When everything slows down and you're sleeping again," she dropped her voice to a whisper, "when he's deployed, call me." She picked up her keys and walked to the door. "Bye, Jace. Bye, Sis."

"Bye, Lyn," Marleigh called softly behind her as she walked through the door.

Their world shrunk to a perfect triangle. They didn't need distractions from each other, or other couples to hang out with.

"Lynetha's great, but I'm glad people feel like third wheels," Jace said. "I have no interest in sharing you. Everything I need in the world is between these apartment walls."

• • •

Their routine was simple those first few months. Marleigh was surprised and thankful at how quickly she mastered breastfeeding—certainly Jason deserved some credit, too. That boy was born ready to eat. She could feed Jason sitting, laying on her side and standing up.

"I'm kinda jealous of that little fucker," Jace said with a smile as wide as the horizon. "He's got round-the-clock access to my wife's tits."

Marleigh sighed. "And they're still so big and heavy."

"Yeah, I hadn't noticed."

Jason's hair grew in curly like Marleigh's. "He'll have to be a special operator with a mop like that," Jace said with a smile. Military special forces were granted greater leeway when it came to regulation grooming appearance. Marleigh had learned a few things in her crash course in becoming a Navy wife.

Marleigh dozed when she could, and for the first time in her life she felt no guilt about resting.

"I want you to do nothing while I'm home, babe," Jace told her. "This is my time to help on the home front. I've always got you covered."

Marleigh was only a few weeks healed when she reached for Jace the first time after giving birth. She'd put Jason to bed and walked out to the couch where Jace sat watching television. She slid his hand up the oversized T-shirt she was wearing. His fingers moved slowly up her thigh, his touch intensifying.

"Are you sure? I don't want to force you—hurt you."

She turned quickly for the bedroom. His fingers caught the edge of her shirt and he followed. "I'm sure."

She yelped when he cupped her breast too hard. He had his mouth on her nipple and his hand on the other one, her normally tiny breasts were heavy and thick. Oh no. Her breasts were trained to let down.

"Jace," she said, trying to warn him. She was too late. She expected him to sputter and turn away the second his mouth filled with milk.

Instead, he swallowed. Once, twice. She moaned, a low, guttural sound she'd never made before. The intensity of pleasure coursing from her breasts through her blood, across her skin, down to the aching space Jace filled between her thighs shattered her body. She bucked hard against him and pressed him in deeper. He swallowed another mouthful, the other breast weeping warm against his hand and down between their bellies, cooling and sticky.

He came hard and fast, juddering into her, against her. They sat, wrapped around each other, her cheek resting against his new traps, where the dip down to his shoulders used to be. She felt the slowing of his breath as he softened inside of her, every subtle movement he made sent pulses through her.

"Can we stay like this all night?" His fingers traced her soft belly, the extra soft skin that had grown their kid pressed against his abs. This, right here, made sense. Like they were back in Nebraska and combat was so far away, theoretical.

She told him six weeks later that she was pregnant again. She hadn't taken a test; she just knew.

"That's how we do it, baby," Jace said. "Life's just getting better and better."

She had no nerves about this pregnancy, she was so confident in their happiness. And Jason would barely remember life without this new sibling. He'd never have to be alone.

They took walks each day, Jason bundled against the spring chill in the crocheted hats and sweaters Donna sent.

"Hey! Look at this," Jace said, his face bright and pink. He pointed both hands at his chest. He learned how to slide his wiggly kid into a pouch he could wear on his chest, the same one Marleigh wore around the house if Jason got fussy. "Now I just need to master that cool hip wiggle you do that puts him right out." She knew that both of their fathers would mock a dad like Jace. She'd married the right kind of man.

Jace ignored the cards that came with the handmade clothes—*Ed isn't well. He needed two stents. Please call.* Ed and Donna ate too much and moved too little, he said. It was a simple, losing equation, and there wasn't anything he could do about that. That last night in Nebraska was distant to Marleigh, but Jace hadn't softened to Ed after their fight. "My focus is the here and now, my wife and kid," Jace said.

"Please make up with him. Before it's too late."

"I'm sure it's not nearly as bad as she says." Jace danced Jason's bootied feet. "They just want me to apologize."

"Is that so horrible?"

Marleigh wrote them letters and sent pictures of Jason, of their family. She snuck in a phone call or two when Jace took the baby out for a walk by himself.

"Stubborn as mules, those two," Donna said.

"That's the truth. Thanks for keeping us posted, Donna. We love you both, so much." Marleigh surprised herself with the articulated burst of emotion. Becoming Jace's wife and Jason's mother had fundamentally changed her. She did love Donna and Ed. And she was brave enough to say it.

Marleigh made Jace dinner every night. Healthy stuff, heavy on the vegetables.

"Oh, good. Roughage," Jace grumbled in jest. "The weight has fallen off you. You can eat whatever you want, Marleigh."

"He's eating what I'm eating, right?" she asked.

"Well, damn. I hadn't thought about it that way."

"And he's growing so well, if it's working, I don't want to screw it up." Jason had started grabbing, reaching out his starfish hands. His head filled in with soft dark curls. He rolled from one side to the other and straightened his dimply arms, raising his tiny chest to the sky.

"No shit. This kid can press them out like no other baby. Pushups in a diaper. What a trip."

It took more than six months for Jace's patience to wear like the carpeting that Marleigh walked so many hours to ease Jason into sleep. His movements were crisper, sharper. His eyes regained the furrowed intensity she remembered from the weeks before he deployed when she was pregnant the first time.

On their way to the park, Jace walked so fast she could barely keep up with him. Jason cooed and giggled, loving the breeze on his face and the sturdy safety of his father's chest beneath him.

Marleigh put a hand on Jace's shoulder. "Slow down and look at me."

He slowed, but avoided her eyes.

"Jace, spit it out."

"I have to leave again."

"How long have you known?"

"Two weeks."

"When did you plan to tell me?"

"I didn't know how. I'm sorry. Everything is so perfect. I knew this would ruin it. I didn't realize it would be this hard."

"So soon?" Marleigh asked.

"Yeah. There's some extra pay in it, too."

They had started a savings account right after Jason was born with the money he brought home, the first Marleigh ever had.

"I told them I really shouldn't leave, with Jason not even a year yet, and you pregnant." He knew she would appreciate the extra money. She was always so stressed about money.

"Combat-zone pay isn't taxed by the feds."

"It's gone so fast! I thought we'd have more time." She could see the disappointment roiling off of her made him antsy. Her eyes flooded, and he grimaced and looked away.

"Don't, please. I should've waited longer to tell you and just gone. Stop with the weepy eyes."

"As if I had any control of that," she gestured from her eyes down to her breasts and back to Jace, "or any of this."

"I could hardly turn down the money," he said. That part was true. "And it's just how it goes. We don't deploy like ships, for some predetermined amount of time. We just get called up when we're needed."

Marleigh was no dummy. She knew how it was. She'd given his new motorcycle a look and shook her head. She also knew that some guys volunteered for duty. Most of the wives knew it, too, but it was easier to hate the Navy than their husbands, or at least more convenient. She didn't choose the Navy; she'd chosen Jace.

"I love you, baby," she told Jace when he prepared to leave at zero-dark-thirty that summer morning. "We all do. We'll be right here waiting for you."

He kissed her, hard, his hand in the curls at the back of her neck. "I miss you already."

She pictured him on a plane high above a dark ocean when she sent her first email to him. *We miss you already, baby. We can't wait to have you home. Be safe, SO! All our love—Marleigh and Jason*

CHAPTER TWENTY-FIVE

Dear Marleigh,

You know what I dream about out here? Normal everyday life. Our life is so good, Mar. You, of course I'm always dreaming about you. That hasn't changed, and it won't change. How are you feeling? I get hard thinking about you. I can't help it. You've made me a teenager. How do you do that, woman? I love you. I don't tell you that enough.

    How's little man? Has he changed so much? I keep picturing his little hairless chest, and his soft belly. I think it's because everything here is gritty and rough. Dry mouth and sweat inside this heavy ass suit, helicopters. Unending noise. If I never hear another tarp or sheet of canvas flapping in the wind, I'll be just fine. Coming in country has always been cut and dry for me. Making the world a safer place. Taking the fight to them, so these bastards don't bring their shit back to the US again. I'm doing my job and my job protects people— kids, especially, now my kid, but all the kids, American, Iraqi and Afghani, the kids who deserve to grow up without their way of life being shit on. I know that. But goddamn it gets confusing sometimes. Hits you in the balls how much they need protecting. I look for you and Jason everywhere. His perfect face. Those curls. But I know better. Women here walk like they're carrying bundled babies against their burkas. Those aren't babies. They could be carrying something dangerous or acting as a distraction, decoys to draw the soldiers' attention away from their surroundings, off their patrol routes. Still, I paused. A few days ago I was out, we saw a group of kids who looked at us like we're God. They touched my fatigues, kicked my steel-toed boots, asked for candy. Someday Jason will be that age. They were cute. But at first my back stiffened when they approached us. I watched them to make sure they really moved like kids. That shit happens you know, people turning their kids into weapons. My guard dropped the second they got close. They all reminded me of Jason. What happens when we fuck kids up? I guess look at you and me. No one broke us.

I'm sorry it's taken me a while to write. I haven't been on base a whole lot. The calls have been a lot of the same hurry up and wait. Irregular becomes regular. Roadside IED, wired package. Inside, outside. Day and night. The most recent was inside a marketplace. Would've killed kids, women, grandpas. Who the fuck does that to their own people?

Good news is, looks like I'm coming home early. I'm tired and I need you and my son and I can't fucking wait.

I love you, baby!

Jace

The letter looked to Marleigh like it was written in installments rather than in one feverish sitting. But it was hard to tell. The way Jace gripped a pen, he often smeared letters with the heel of his hand. She realized, after she finished reading, that she had been a little jealous of the pull war and the Navy and EOD had on Jace. A fear that she couldn't compete. But she was happy he wanted to come home, and hopeful that he wouldn't have to leave again so soon. And she'd get to see Jason's face light up like the morning horizon at seeing his daddy again.

CHAPTER TWENTY-SIX

Even in the sea of men—same uniforms, same haircuts, same purposeful, angular strides—streaming across the pier at Naval Station Norfolk, Marleigh found him. Her Jace. He looked bigger as he walked to them. His chest was wider, and his arms hung out, away from his body. His waist was a narrow *V* cinched in the thin belt of his uniform. Marleigh's heart fidgeted as he moved closer. He walked different, too. Long legs bending and extending, mechanical and crisp.

Jace had been home, just a couple miles away, on base. Marleigh was allowed to know he was home and safe, but he had to stay on base for fourteen days. She'd heard this was commonplace for special operators, so she tried not to worry. It was easier, though, when he was thousands of miles away and she couldn't see him than knowing he was just across town and still completely out of reach. Now he gave her his Jace smile and closed the gap between them. Nothing else mattered.

Still standing on the pier, Jace kissed her neck. "You look so sexy," he said. She hoped her breasts, already tight against the seams, held up the top and drew the eyes away from her giant middle. She'd matched her lipstick to her bright-red dress. "Sexier today than those old photos you gave me. You're so real."

Marleigh couldn't stop smiling. Jace was home for a couple of months. He was back and safe. She was so thankful. So relieved to have him back. She sucked in her stomach. She scratched the back of his neck with her fingernails and spoke into his neck. "I love you, Jace Holt. I'm so happy you're home."

He ran his hand down her spine, grazing the curve of her butt. He hadn't written her in three weeks, except for the email telling her he was in the States again. "Where's little man?"

"Oh, right, he's not so into being held anymore." Marleigh pulled back, tottered on her heels.

Jace dropped down to a squat to greet Jason. "Hi, big boy," he said.

Jason ducked his head behind Marleigh's leg.

"Say hi to your daddy, Jason," Marleigh instructed. Jason peeked out warily and hid back behind her leg. Jace looked hurt. He had to realize Jason was only fourteen months old and he'd been gone for a third of those months. "Jace, he's so little."

Jace reached down and scooped Jason up onto his shoulders, ignoring the arms that reached for Marleigh, steadying him with his hands. "Peekabo, little man! You might not remember me, but I sure missed you."

"Eeee!" Jason squealed, clapping his hands.

Good boy.

A man with a large camera tapped her on the shoulder. "I'm a photographer with the *Pilot*. I just got a great shot of your reunion. Can I get your names for the caption?"

Just like old times, neither Jace nor Marleigh had any idea they were being photographed. They were their own perfect island.

The next day, Marleigh cut out and framed the front-page of the *Virginian-Pilot* that ran two weeks and a day after Jace landed at Naval Station Norfolk. In her imagination, Jace's first steps on American soil were those moving him back into her arms, one day ago. In the newspaper photo, Jace's hand, hairless and unlined, framed by the sharp cuff of camouflaged sleeve, cupped the curve of Marleigh's stomach, which stretched the rouching of her bright-red dress. His other arm encircled her shoulders. A scarlet lip print on Jace's cheek. Marleigh's hair blew behind her. Jason, dressed in a white sweater with a Navy anchor on the front, miniature khakis, and shiny faux-leather shoes, clutched at her knee. The caption read, *Next generation U.S. Navy. Explosive Ordnance Disposal Technician 3rd Class Jace Holt, his wife, Marleigh, and their son, Jason, reunite after four months.* Marleigh placed the framed photograph on the kitchen counter. She knew it would take some time for everyone to settle in to being a family again. She just had to be patient.

"I'm going to owe every guy in my unit who sees that a six-pack."

Turning around, Marleigh saw Jace reach up to the *Welcome Home!* banner that hung over the cut between the kitchen and family room. "We worked hard on those decorations, buddy," she said.

His arm froze. "Right, sorry. Not sure what I was thinking. Let's leave it a couple of days." A frown she didn't recognize reshaped his face.

"We've only just gotten you back," she said. "Barely twenty-four hours."

"Is that all? Crazy." Jace rubbed the top of his head and smiled down at her. "I knew he wouldn't be the baby I left behind. And even with all of the pictures you sent and the updates. . . I wasn't prepared."

She wrapped her arms around him, angling her stomach to his side. "Don't be hard on yourself. Or him. It'll just take a minute."

"How about you, Marleigh girl. You're still you, but damn look at this missile." He placed a protective hand on her belly. "Where'd that little pooch go? And your arms. Those are fighter arms. Lean."

Jason babbled to himself on the floor, and they sat on the couch, touching with all four limbs, Marleigh's belly, and never losing contact. "We've kept it together while you were gone, but it's been busy," she said. "At first I didn't know days from nights. I was so tired," she gestured to her stomach, "you know, pregnant again and all of that. And Jason has the energy and will of a bigger kid now, but he's still not beyond having an explosive diaper, and his blast radius has only grown as he's gotten bigger."

Jace winced. "Seriously, explosive."

"Shit, Jace. I didn't think."

He brushed her legs off his and stood. "Don't worry about it." He paced around the room like he was inspecting.

"Are we shipshape?"

He laughed and Marleigh relaxed.

"Way better than that. You'd pass the most anal chief's inspection. Where's all the shi—stuff? Where are his toys and those plastic teething things?"

"This apartment is too beautiful to mess up. I really wanted it to feel special, homey to you this time."

He walked back to where Marleigh sat and gently rested his hand on her head. She turned up to his palm. "It's incredible. Like you guys don't even need me!"

"Jace—don't be silly." He sounded like he might be joking. Maybe. "You better believe we do. Check out that wall." She pointed to the framed and hung photographs. One of Marleigh and Jace when they got married. Photos of Jace as a child.

"I don't even remember those. Where'd you get them?"

Donna and Ed, of course. "Who do you think?" she asked. "You know, they'd love to hear from you now that you're home."

He stared at the photos, one after another. He stopped in front of a picture of Jace holding Jason on his chest, skin-to-skin, one she'd taken in the hospital right after Jason was born.

"That's my favorite," Marleigh said. "You were both asleep when I took it. You and Jason will be thick as thieves in no time. And I'll get you all caught up on this newest crew member," she said.

Jace knelt and kissed her belly. "Do I smell lasagna?" Jace asked, standing. "It smells so damn good. Though I bet it won't taste as good as you. That bed in there," he nodded to their bedroom door, "looks pretty inviting. I can't wait to see you naked in it."

That's my guy. Marleigh bit her lip and smiled at him suggestively. "Glad that your appetite hasn't left us. Take a load off, sailor. How about you grab a beer while I put the big boy to bed?"

• • •

The next morning while Marleigh double-checked her grocery list, Jace swooped in behind her and slid the list out from under her hand. "Whole milk, can do. What else do we need?" He squinted at the list. "Cheerios, bananas, bread, blueberries, almonds."

"Just a few things, but milk's definitely key. Jason goes through it so fast." She smiled. "Breastfeeding was almost easier. Almost." She gestured to her breasts. "That milk I could make on premises."

"About those beautiful breasts—I have plans for them. And all of you, later."

Marleigh blushed. They had fumbled and kissed last night, once they'd finally gotten an overexcited Jason to sleep. But that was all. They were tentative in the dark. His body felt new and strange beneath her fingertips. Marleigh knew how pregnant she looked, much more so than at this point with Jason. And they were both so tired.

She kissed his cheek. "Yes, please," she whispered into his ear, leaning back with a soft tug on his earlobe.

Jason toddled into the kitchen. *"Mmm-mmm-aaaa,"* he said. *"Mmm-mmm-aaa!"* His version of Mama.

"You sound like an engine revving, son," Jason said with a chuckle.

Jason stopped at Jace's feet and looked up at him and extended one chubby finger. "Dada?"

Jace swooped him up over his head and caught him. "Damn right." Jason giggled and squirmed to be put down. "Mar, how about I take Jason with me and we pick up everything. We'll hit the *p-a-r-k* on our way to the grocery store."

Jason seemed intent on figuring out the word Jace had spelled. Marleigh was so thankful. She could sit, put her feet up, actually rest a minute. Use the bathroom by herself. She flopped down onto the couch. "Really, oh yes. That would be great! You don't mind?"

"Little man and I've got it' don't we, Jason?"

"Go Dada! Go Dada!" His chubby thighs bounded across the apartment to the storage closet by the front door that held his stroller.

Jace looked from Marleigh to Jason and back, puzzled. Then walked to the closet door and opened it. He saw the stroller. "Damn this kid is smart!"

"He doesn't miss a thing, Jason. And he's going to pick up that word if you're not careful."

Jace covered his mouth in mock horror. "Ma'am yes ma'am!" He saluted her.

"Babe, you can teach him every word in the book if it means I get an hour off of my feet."

"At least that long. Are there extra diapers in here?" He patted the pockets of the stroller.

"Dada! Here!" Jason pointed to a mesh section containing diapers and a packet of wipes.

"Be good for Dada, Jason," Marleigh said, her eyes already drooping closed.

"We've got this, Mar. See you later."

CHAPTER TWENTY-SEVEN

When they returned two hours later, Jason's face was puffy and red, his dark eyes wary, lips twisted into a pout. *Uh-oh.* As soon as Jace unclipped him from the stroller, Jason ran to Marleigh's legs and thrust his arms up at her. When she picked him up, he twisted his legs around her hips, trying for a tight hold. Her belly thwarted him, but he wrapped his arms tight around her neck and buried his face in her neck.

"Right back to mom. Just like I thought," Jace said. Marleigh couldn't read his face, but the tendons in his neck were tight, fighting for control, just like his voice.

Jace pulled six Harris Teeter bags from beneath Jason's seat in the stroller, before he folded the stroller up with a clatter and shoved it back in the closet.

"Should I ask how it went?"

Jace looped plastic bags around his wrist and carried them to the kitchen counter. "Fine. He's going to have to man up, though."

Marleigh smiled. "You bet. By two he should be ready for boot camp." She aimed for light.

"Dada scream," Jason said, looping her hair around her fingers.

"*Shhh*," Marleigh said. "It's okay. Did you try to grab fruit again? Get out of your stroller?" His hot forehead shook hard, side to side, against her neck.

"Damn right he did. What's with that, the reaching out and grabbing from the shelves?"

Marleigh knew that in another mood, Jace would be praising his son's reflexes and reach. She also felt this wasn't the time to remind him. "Shopping with a toddler is the worst," she said. "You saw how happily I let you take him with you."

"But I didn't yell at you, Jason. Not one time."

Marleigh watched him try to empty the bags, searching for the place for each item. It looked like he bought so much. "I'll put everything away, Jace. Thanks for taking him."

"I didn't yell at him, Marleigh!"

"Of course you didn't." She put a steady hand on his elbow. "I'll get all of this."

"There was this chick on our way home. She was running and not paying attention to anything." He pointed to his ears. "Wearing headphones. She almost crashed into Jason's stroller and then crossed in the middle of traffic. Two cars honked at her, and she didn't even look up."

His temples pulsed. He straightened and then balled up the hands at his sides, over and over. "We caught up with her—"

"You what?"

He continued as though she hadn't spoken. "She finally turned around, and when I told her it wasn't safe what she was doing, that she should take out those fucking air pods and pay attention to the world around her, she told me to back up and give her some space. Like I was dangerous. I was just trying to help.

"This is why I risk my dick in the desert? So some dumb bitch can get in everybody's way, then get herself killed because she's listening to Britney fucking Spears and then she can go into a goddam Starbucks and order some foamy ass coffee, pick from twelve ready-made sandwiches, buy a hard-boiled egg already peeled the fuck for you. Then she complains about me? Even in a military town everyone's soft." Mouth and eyes closed, he exhaled in a huff through flared nostrils, reminding her of an angry stallion.

Jason still wrapped around her waist, Marleigh filled a glass with icy tap water. She handed it to Jace. "I'm sorry that happened," she said.

He gulped the water and then leaned against the sink, his arms straight and braced. "I get it. I overreacted. I . . . I forgot how chaotic it is, being back. Chaos in-country . . ."

"Is deadly. I know." She leaned gently against his back. Jason's body relaxed between theirs.

"You'll put this stuff away?" His voice was quiet and unsure.

"Absolutely. Go relax. I'll get Jason his lunch and we'll come see you after that."

He turned to face Marleigh and Jason. He kissed Jason's sweaty curls and drew them both gently against him. "I'll figure my shit out. It won't take long."

"We know you will."

Jason reached a palm up for Jace's cheek and rested it there. After a moment, he walked into their bedroom. The door closed, but she could hear the muffled sounds of the TV.

Jason wriggled down to the floor and Marleigh emptied the grocery bags onto the counter. There were four different boxes of cereal—Apple Jacks, Life, granola, and Chex—bread, bagels, Pop Tarts, two six packs of Coors and Coors Light, a half-gallon of apple juice, blueberries, raspberries, grapes. But no milk. She'd find a minute to sneak off to the store for milk later. Jace had wanted to help, and tried. She'd never hidden anything from him, but this errand she would. She could tell he wouldn't take it well.

· · ·

Marleigh clawed for air. Jace lay on top of her, yelling. It sounded like "*Abno! Abno!*"

She was pinned beneath him and could barely breathe. He had one finger pressed against her lips.

"Jace! Wake up!"

He didn't respond. She dug her fingernails into his biceps. He didn't release his grip. His muscled thighs wrapped around and under her. He was rock hard against her.

"*Alab!*" he cried. "*Alab!*"

She shoved at him, but he held her so tightly she could barely move. She bit the finger he'd pressed over her lips and his eyes flew open. His sweaty chest pulsed and then relaxed.

"The fuck?" He went rigid and flung himself off her. "Oh my God, baby. I'm so sorry."

She took deep gulps of air. She couldn't keep herself from shaking. Tears leaked out as she realized that the crisis was behind her. She was a tangled snarl of sadness for Jace, and anger. Fear.

He wiped the tears from beneath her eyes, and the roots of her hair where they fell, heavy. "I—I'm okay," she said, trying to remember a time where she was less okay. "It's okay." It was too dark to see his face.

"Did I hurt you?" His touch was feather light, now. His voice trembled.

"No. You didn't hurt me." That was the truth. He had not physically injured her. Still, she found it hard to swallow. "I think it was a bad dream. You're awake now, right?"

"Yeah, Mar. I'm awake. Jesus! I'm so sorry."

She ran her fingers through the hair at the back of his neck. It was growing in again.

He stiffened and pushed away. "Don't. I'm so sorry. It's not your job to make this right. Are you sure you're okay?"

She put her hand in his. "Yes. I'm fine. Can you tell me about it?" They weren't under the Nebraska sky, but the room was full dark. Maybe he could open up to her here. And she wouldn't have to work so hard to hide her expressions if he did.

"About what? The dream or war?"

"Both. Either."

"I don't remember it, baby. You know how dreams are." He leaned toward her and traced her face with his fingers. "Do you want me to sleep on the couch? I understand."

"No way I'm letting you out of this bed," she said. If only she could keep him here, safe, always. "What does *abno* mean?"

"Is that what I said?"

"Yes. And *alab*."

"That's weird. That's Arabic."

"What do they mean, Jace?"

He leaned in to kiss her. She gently pushed his face away. "Tell me what the words mean."

"Son, my son." He cleared his throat. "And father."

Oh. When he pressed his mouth to hers again, she let him. He'd told her enough for tonight, certainly more than he'd ever planned. She didn't know what it meant, and she wondered if the dream was tied to the reason he came back a few weeks early. He kissed her throat, down and up her neck, and found her mouth again. This would make them both feel better, for a little while, anyway. She'd save more questions for later.

. . .

A few mornings later, Marleigh tried again. Jason babbled happily in his crib, his laughter and play carried into their room by his baby monitor. Her head rested on Jace's bicep. They'd made love in the morning sunlight and were still drowsy and smelled of one another.

"What happened over there?"

Jace spoke without opening his eyes all the way. "Everybody's girl asks that question, Mar. Every guy on the teams talks about it."

"What do they tell their girls?"

"When they tell them what they think they want to know, what you think you're ready to hear, their girls never look the same way at them again. I don't want that."

"I'll never look at you different, Jace."

"They all say that, too, before. You're the best thing that ever happened to me. You and Jason, and this kid." He grazed his palm over her naval, and down.

She slid his hand back up.

"I don't want that. I want to tell you everything. But so much of it makes no sense here. But it does there."

"You say I'm different from the other girls. Give me a chance to understand."

He sat all of the way up, leaning against the headboard. She sat up beside him.

"I fucked up, Mar."

She licked her lips and willed her features to stay relaxed. "What do you mean?"

He'd stopped looking at the ceiling and studied her face as he spoke. She was being tested. "It was the day after the market bomb, the one from the letter. A span bridge. Simple, really. I've done this thirty fucking times."

She silently counted through her inhales and exhales, sipping air slowly, to try and keep her pulse from rising, keep blood from coloring her cheeks. "What was it like?"

"Like every other goddamn call. Burqas fluttering, people wailing, hands grasping for nothing. I can always silence it, so the people are like a reel streaming by. I was so close to my position, almost ready. But this old fucker started yelling at me. '*Ab-no! Ab-no!*' Sounded like something from when we played cowboys and Indians as kids."

The baby, something pressed so hard against her sternum that she had to open her mouth to breathe. Jace's nightmare fresh in her mind. Son, he'd told her. *Abno* meant son.

"I told the man to shut the fuck up. In my head I took a minute to shut it all out again. I wondered if he was the same age my father would be if he lived."

"But that's good, right? You shut it out."

"It was too late. You don't have that minute out there. I knew better."

His hand went clammy in hers. She squeezed a little harder.

"I started moving Fang to the spot, but the fucking thing blew. It was half-buried in the hillside under the bridge. I wasn't even as close as I should be, but that shit shook so hard, it shuffled me like a deck of cards."

"What if you had been any closer?" Marleigh knew what Jace did for a living. She understood, rationally, that he willingly put himself in danger for other people. Those were facts. But she managed not to think of that each day while he was gone, otherwise she would have gone crazy with worry. "Thank God you weren't closer."

He shrugged.

She forgot her false composure. She straddled him and covered his face with kisses. Just like that, she could have lost him.

He cupped her face in his hands. "No one died that day, but the bridge was FUBAR. Because of my fuckup, my brothers had to take longer, more circuitous routes deep into Taliban country. So my mistake will cost someone."

The old man distracted Jace, which may have saved his life. But Jace's delay got the bridge blown up. All Marleigh could think of was how happy she was that he'd returned. His story hadn't ended in bloodshed or death. But Jace's face showed no relief. It was a mask.

"That old fucker hung around. He smiled at me."

"Thank you for telling me," she said. "Jason and I are so happy you're home safe and in one piece." She had a sense she failed Jace's test. She didn't know this unreadable face.

"Back inside the wire, team leader took me off rotation. 'Every soldier has a day when he has to reconsider his life in the military,' that arrogant bastard said. 'Today is your day.'"

CHAPTER TWENTY-EIGHT

Jace was home for ten days before he returned to the base for what he and Marleigh joked were banker's hours—0830 to 1700. Jason watched out the window for his father's motorcycle. Even if she couldn't hear his tailpipe, Marleigh knew Jace was close by how feverishly Jason jumped up and down on the couch.

"The days on base are so effing boring," Jace said, trying to keep his language PG. "But it's great to know I get to see you two at the end of each day."

Marleigh made dinner for the three of them every night, and for an hour after dinner Jace took Jason for a walk or to the park. Both routine and fatherhood suited Jace. At first, Marleigh accompanied them. There was nothing like the sight of her son and his father, the way Jace hunched his powerful shoulders over so he and Jason could walk half of the block hand-in-hand. Slowly, though, she realized that this time was theirs alone. She put her feet up and enjoyed this new life thumping around inside of her. The astonishment of the sole of a foot pressing out against her, a tiny elbow. Her big and little boys returned smiling and pink-cheeked, Jason's curls sweaty against his forehead.

All three of them went to Marleigh's seven-month prenatal appointment. Jace insisted on bringing Jason to see his little brother's ultrasound. As the technician pointed out images on the screen, Jason's head swiveled to her belly to the screen and back. "Brudder's on the TV?"

"Your brother's in your mom's belly. But we get to see him on the TV."

No matter how many times she experienced it, Marleigh couldn't believe it when the sensations she felt inside of her showed up on screen. Even though she hadn't met this little one yet, Marleigh couldn't imagine her life without these three men.

Afterwards, Jace said they needed to decide on a name. He winked at her. "Not such a no-brainer as last time."

"How about Edward," she said. Of course, she'd already been thinking about names. They couldn't prevent Ed's death—and Marleigh regretted not going to his funeral—but what a beautiful gift having a namesake could be.

"I don't know what I think about naming the kid after my uncle. How about Nicholas. We can call him Nick."

"Or Nicky." Marleigh liked that. "Where's that from?""

"My dad was Nicholas."

Oh. "Nicolas Edward Holt sounds pretty darn good."

"Damn straight it does. You're going to have a little brother named Nick, Jason."

"Nick! Nicky!" Jason said, clapping. "Brudder Nicky!"

. . .

Marleigh knew she'd gotten too comfortable in their perfect routine, even if her body was stretched and hot and swollen. Each day she waited for it.

"It's time for me to start working up again," Jace said Monday morning.

"So, you've reconsidered your life in the military," she said. "And this is your decision?"

"Screw that guy," Jace said. "I'm good. It was a horrible fuckup, that bridge. But this is what I was made for, Marleigh."

She could hardly argue that point. "And you've done it. Over and over again. What about orders here? On base or another base."

"I know it's hard to understand. But I do better when I have time over there. It's like a puzzle. No one else, not even someone cross-trained, can fill that space. Who knows what the kids coming out of EOD are like?"

"This is part of it, our life. I just want you here and with us."

"I know you do, baby. And that's what I want too. Look at how much time we've had together. And we'll have so much more, I promise. I'll do what I'm trained to do and get back to you and the boys. This last time, it was the fuckup with the old man. I was too close to the blast. I'll make sure that never happens again."

It seemed to Marleigh that all he wanted when he was away was home—and all he wanted when he was home—was to feel the rush, the stress, the peril. This was the bargain she'd made, the only sacrifice Jace asked of her after giving Marleigh her dream family.

CHAPTER TWENTY-NINE

Only a month of workups and a ninety-day mission and Jace was back home. Their family had grown by one very small human in his absence, Nicky. Marleigh was dead tired. If one boy wasn't waking up in the middle of the night, the other was. Jason was so excited to be near his little brother, and also antsy for Marleigh's attention.

This time she brought both boys to meet Jace at the pier, but there was no red dress and stilettos. She wore a dowdy A-line shirt and leggings to pick him up at the pier. Her hair was unwashed, and she hadn't worn makeup in weeks. She felt guilty that she couldn't do more for her husband, the guy who had started all of this, but, God, was she worn out.

Jason dropped her hand at his first sight of Jace. "Dada! Can I go?"

Marleigh nodded, and Jason ran full speed toward his dad. Jace's face glowed with the smile he saved for his son. He picked Jason up and swung him high in the air before catching him. He reveled in Nicky's still-scrunched-up newborn face. "He looks like you, Mar." Marleigh loved Jace exponentially more seeing him through Jason's eyes.

She loved him for the children he'd given her. The family they'd built. The way he had helped her break free from a sad life and replaced it with this one. She loved him for how hard he worked to befriend his older son, how he gave and gave and gave of his energy to entertain and teach Jason. She could tell the transition was difficult, being home, and she knew better than to take it personally. She told herself to enjoy seeing Jason so happy and entertained all the time, to relish the quiet time she had with Nicky, for the first time since he was born. Marleigh'd had almost a year and a half to moon over Jason, and she barely ever had to share him. And she knew Jace would only be home for a few months, just long enough to settle back in. Their timing had never been good, but sometimes a ticking clock ramped up the excitement.

When he was awake, Nicky's second favorite place to Marleigh's breasts was a quilted mat with the half circles hooped over it. He'd grab at one of the dangling animals—the zebra that squeaked when squeezed, the snake that rattled when shaken, and the giraffe that sounded like paper being crunched in a fist. From the floor, the baby's viewpoint, it made sense. Marleigh had stopped noticing the sounds.

"I hate this thing," Jace said when he walked by it the first time. Nicky was swaddled and asleep in Marleigh's lap. The snake rattled and Jace shivered.

"Little more cluttered than when we had only one," Marleigh joked. "Kind of like walking a minefield in here."

"Funny," Jace said. His voice said it wasn't.

"Not a real minefield . . . I mean. The other moms say wait until they're big enough to leave Legos out. Those really hurt."

Jace bent over to pick the playmat off the floor. He unsnapped one of the curved arms from the quilt. She watched him. "We don't need stuff all over the floor."

"I put him down there like ten times a day," she said. "He's supposed to have time on his belly and on his back."

"It takes five seconds to put away. Not a big deal."

"He likes it."

"What if one of us is carrying him and it's dark and he needs a bottle or something. We could trip over this and fall on him and crush him."

She turned her palms skyward. "That's dark." That goddamn thing had been on the floor for weeks.

"Apparently I'm the only one who worries about the kid's safety around here."

"We're not on a ship, Jace."

"No shit," he said. He unsnapped the last arch and folded the mat in half under his arm.

When he returned, empty-handed, from the nursery, Jace appeared calmer. Yes, he was ridiculous about the mat, but she reminded herself that he deserved a say in how the household was run when he was there. And the early weeks were always hard. She was too tired to worry.

Nicky scrunched his face up and wriggled. His fingers found their way out of the swaddle and flexed open. He grunted. "So much for that nap and for a clean baby," Marleigh said. She stood to get the diaper-changing basket.

"I'm sorry, Mar. I'll change his diaper."

Marleigh handed Nicky to Jace. He unswaddled the baby and placed him in the middle of the changing pad. He set up a diaper, the pack of wipes and tube of diaper rash cream immediately beside him. So orderly and precise.

With Jason, Jace laughed about how fast he could change a diaper. How he could basically do it one-handed. He got the messy diaper off Nicky and wadded it up, trying to contain the stench. He ripped the adhesive tabs off the first diaper. Then stuck the two together on the second. His forearms were tense. Finally, he opened a clean diaper and slid it beneath his son.

"Why does he look like that?"

"Like what?"

"Why are his balls so big? They're purple. Way bigger than his tiny pink dick."

"Jason looked exactly the same way. He's just new, babe."

"If everything is fine, why are you watching me all of the time? I was just changing a damn diaper. Remember, I showed you how to do this last time. You were the clumsy one."

"Yeah, and you were nice back then." She walked into the bedroom and closed the door. It would get better. It always did. She'd give him time, but she wasn't going to be a weak doormat either. She wanted to ask the other wives if their husbands were acting this way. She tried a couple of times when attending the deployment support group. Their reactions indicated that either it was disloyal to ask, or she was being overly sensitive. Of course, there were adjustments to be expected, or no, there weren't. She realized she didn't want to know if she was the only one struggling. That seemed worse somehow.

Two gentle knocks, then Jace opened the door. He'd reswaddled Nicky and held him against his shoulder. "Can we come in?"

"Of course you can."

"I'm sorry, Marleigh. I'm so proud of you and how you handle yourself. You run a tight-ass ship."

. . .

Jason began preschool just after Jace's return. Jace pushed Nicky in a stroller and the four of them walked to the Presbyterian church a few blocks away. Marleigh could hardly believe she was able to bring her son to this place. Most of the military spouses who had children at United Presbyterian Preschool were officers' wives. It was Jace's CO's wife who had offered to write a letter of recommendation, would speak to the director if Marleigh heard that the baby's age group was full. Jace and his job made this possible.

Marleigh knew the school existed; she'd seen the women with expensive strollers on the blocks around her apartment, the long line of shiny cars that sat puttering in the pickup line. But those impressions were made before she'd ever met Jace, before she'd ever given any real thought to becoming a mother. Had she ever given motherhood deep thought until she became one? Before motherhood she had known, deep down, that this kind of private, part-time education would never be accessible to her or any future kids. But here she was, walking her boy in Mondays, Wednesdays, and Fridays at nine and picking him up at noon, two if she needed aftercare. The Mothers Morning Out lasted only until noon. She laughed when she first puzzled out those words. *Out* meant out of the house. This was a preschool built for mothers who didn't have to work; they would pay extra for three hours away from their homes a couple of mornings a week. Maybe that was when their maids came. There was a whole world of these women, she realized, and a whole world who catered to them. She wanted to be one of them. She'd done plenty of catering.

The hallways of the preschool were loud as the children clutched their mothers' thumbs and led them to their classrooms. Yarn hair dangled from paper-plate faces. Acrostic poems spelled out *friendship* and *fall* and *fun*. Each classroom door was decorated with the teacher's name, the age group (ones, twos, threes, pre-K and K) and generally a seasonal theme. The insides of the classrooms were orderly, a big round woven carpet in the middle of the floor for circle time, open plastic bins spilling with toys and dress up costumes. A changing table against the wall, a few beanbag chairs, a couple of prayers on the walls. They looked like just about the nicest classrooms she had ever seen. There were no Head Start breakfasts being served. But the teachers. They wore the most expensive jeans she had ever seen, some over pointy-toed heels, and with jewelry, into a room for children eighteen months to two years. Their faces were expertly made up, and she couldn't spot a split end on any of them. It was because of Jace and his service that her sons would have this education. She felt so grateful.

CHAPTER THIRTY

Marleigh should have noticed how his sleep changed, sooner, anyway, after he came home. The muttering. The knees up. The way his hands grasped and groped the air. For her? It wasn't a loving touch. It had been hard to notice anything, what with Jason, baby Nicky, her excitement to have Jace home. *I can't wait to jump back into life, get back to normal*, he'd emailed her. She wondered if perhaps they were better liars long distance.

Neither of them was getting sleep. Jace usually spent the requisite hours in bed each night, usually eleven at night until six in the morning, far more time than she did with toddlers and a newborn. But when she came to bed after a feeding or snuck under the covers for some unpredictable length of time between the inevitable wakeups, the pillows were strewn, some punched flat, others squeezed from the sides, blankets twisted. The top layer was tossed off Jace, a sheet wound like a vine between his legs. She promised herself she would worry about it in the morning, after she'd gotten some sleep. She started leaving a thin, fleecy throw on the barely used rocking chair in their bedroom so she could curl up beneath it rather than wake Jace. She fell, exhausted, into deep and dreamless dark, often jolted awake by the baby or Jace's elbow errantly sliding her way.

"Marleigh!" Jace awoke one night. He put his hand over her mouth. "*Shhhhh!* There's someone in here," he whispered. He turned on every light, searching room by room. Ripped the shower curtain aside. Yanked open drawers. He woke everyone.

The next night, she unplugged the baby monitor. The apartment was small enough that she knew she'd hear the baby scream if it howled. But Nicky wasn't a screamer, whether wet or dirty or hungry. He knew his father needed quiet. Marleigh's breasts filled hard and tight and she'd wake before the baby most nights anyway, her own alarm clock.

Jace moved more actively in his sleep than when he was awake, his hands opening and closing into fists—not unlike her babies—but these were real fists he made. Knuckles hard, not the soft curving of his fingers. A different reflex. Some nights he fell asleep on his back with his knees drawn up. Those nights he muttered. She could rarely make out what he was saying. Words like "grinder." Or, "just a fucking hole. Gone." Sometimes he chuckled a low, deep laugh that she hadn't heard from him before. She told herself, each night, that she would talk to him about it in the morning. But the early dark morning hours were when the children both would sleep, and Jace was up and out of the house, his crotch rocket rumbling between his legs. He left earlier and earlier for work. She couldn't watch the way he wove around parked SUVs and moving delivery trucks, horns honking.

She knew her normal had certainly changed while he was gone. And try as she might, she couldn't picture what his life must be like in the desert. He had muscles in his jaw, his neck, when he came home. All of him was bigger, harder, than when he left. His embrace was different. Surely her body was different, too. They would have to figure out how to fit together again. Both of their bodies were eager.

• • •

One Saturday, Nicky napped and Jace had Jason for the morning. Marleigh needed to pick up the apartment and run some laundry. Jace had started and stopped countless projects while he was back home, always moving onto another one without completing any. The apartment had boxes of dangerous solvents and nails and hammers. "You can't wrap them in bubble wrap," Jace had said when Marleigh pointed out that they were hazards to the kids. "The world's a fucked-up place. Better they learn that now."

She knew he needed structure and a schedule, not the chaos that comes with two children under two. And she knew each mission left a serious mark on Jace. She wished she knew how to help. She wished she had the energy to dig into what he had going on. She was running on empty, even with an extra set of hands at home. She was in get-through-it mode. Get through deployments, get through babies in diapers, get through Jace's downtime.

Marleigh dumped the full laundry basket by the door to the stacked washer and dryer. The previous load was still spinning out, so she had a few minutes to declutter before switching over the loads. She'd spent her pre-Jace life walking laundry to a laundromat, watching her machines, and then folding clothes in public only to walk the clean load back home. Now she only had to carry the clothes a few feet. And thank God. These men, big and little, made a mess.

She went into her bedroom to check for any discarded socks, fallen breast pads, or tissues under the bed on Jace's side. Her first find, a pacifier. That would go to the kitchen to get steamed clean. She swept her hand beneath the bed and bumped something hard. She slid it out. A half-consumed baby bottle. Jace had fed Nicky the night before while she pumped. She touched something else, moved it into the light. It was the knife. All black. Long. The shaft pocked plastic, the blade curved at the tip. She'd had no idea it was there, or for how long. If it hadn't been sheathed, she would have cut herself reaching for Nicky's pacifier. Worse, Jason could have easily found it. He was into everything these days. The carelessness made her furious. She couldn't leave it there, could she? What would Jace do if she moved it? How many nights had she slept with it beneath her, in Jace's reach? Jace dumped that bag of knives out in her old apartment. The one he'd given her, she'd left at the restaurant almost two years ago. She hadn't thought about all those blades since then. She should have.

The following night, Marleigh tiptoed out of their bedroom. The floor creaked under her weight. She saw Jace twitch on the couch, and shove a glass out of sight with his foot. He didn't look away from the screen. His fingers toggled the controller.

"What now, Mar? Haven't I done everything you asked today? I'm not wearing the stupid headphones."

When he wore the gaming headphones, he lost control of his volume. She didn't mind the video games, but she definitely didn't want wide a wide-awake toddler and newborn in the middle of the night. The first-person shooting games couldn't be helping Jace get used to life at home, either.

"I know," she said.

"So go back to bed. I'll be in soon."

He'd never come to bed the night before. "I want you to be there with me," she said.

"I was gone for almost a year, and you slept without me. Or was there someone else here. Is that it? Is that why you're so needy? Why are you spying on me? I'm not one of the kids."

"That's not going to work tonight, you being an asshole. I'll sit right here until you're ready to come to bed."

"All you want is sleep. So take it. I can't sleep, and I don't want to wake you up, so I'm staying out here."

"I hear you snoring," she said. "You do sleep. You're not always awake." Perhaps his dreams were that bad.

"Then enjoy the break from the noise."

"Baby," she said, tracing a fingernail up his neck. He softened under her touch; they both knew she didn't deserve this shit.

"You must support your sailor, no matter what." How many times had she heard that? What's happening over there is harder than anything we can imagine, and they can confront reality once they get home. Timmy is flunking fifth grade? Get him a tutor, but all your sailor needs to know is you've got it covered. It's being handled. Everything is under control. Nothing to worry about.

What if she wished he were gone more? They all seemed happier, seemed to do better when he was away. Jace, too, seemed more content. Or maybe that was as much a lie as telling him everything was perfect here, just his way of telling her not to worry about him.

She knew, deep down, that it was Jace who was struggling. And bad. What if he got in trouble with the Navy? Could he get help? If he could, would he? No one in the Navy wanted anything questionable to end up in his personnel folder. Maybe he needed to get out. Maybe it was too much for him. What would they do? Would she end up a bitter, resentful, poor piece of shit like her mom? No fucking way. Marleigh, who had so many dreams, and plans, who thought she was so great. How had she gotten here? How had things gone wrong so quickly? She was trapped, and so were the kids. So was Jace. Where was the old Jace? He had to be in there somewhere. If she couldn't unearth him, no one could.

Marleigh promised herself she wouldn't screw him over and that they would take care of each other. Look at everything he had done for her, had given her. Those promises mattered. Jace was worth the fight.

· · ·

One night, Jace went to bed before her. Marleigh made herself feather-lite as she got into bed. Jace reached for her, his hands tracing her hip bones. Though tired in a way she didn't know was possible, Marleigh didn't shoo him away. He kept exploring with his fingers, down into her panties and up her belly, slim again, but skin still slack. Under and around her breasts. Her body was sore—from delivery, from nursing, from not sleeping more than a few hours at a time for several years. His dick hard against her ass. His touch was plaintive and pleading. He didn't need to whisper please. She wouldn't make him apologize or ask.

He needed her; she needed him.

"I don't want to hurt you," he said. He lifted her on top of him, harder than any of their wildest early nights together. His groan sounded like agony, but every muscle, save the one deep inside of her, relaxed. Hands on her ass or hips he lifted her up, down, up, down.

It burned at first, but her body drooled for him as it always had. First it was gentle. Then it wasn't. They were fucking for love and something more desperate. She found him again, deep in her center. He slowed down just before he came and sat up. He put his mouth over her nipple and thrusted slow, deep. Milk dripped from the free breast. "Jace," she said, backing away from his mouth. He sucked harder. She came like a grenade around him, her milk letting down into his mouth. Jace tried to stifle a sob. She held him with interlaced fingers, her hips aching with the force of her grip around him. His body shook in her embrace. She felt him relax, muscle by muscle. It was the most intimate moment she had ever shared. When they slowly inched apart, Jace's eyes shined wet, but he quickly wiped them dry with the palm of his hand.

"God, I love you, baby," he said into her neck as they sat entwined, him soft inside of her.

"I love you, too," she said.

She lay against his chest, lulled by his beating heart. They both slept less troubled.

CHAPTER THIRTY-ONE

"You're the big man around here while I'm gone," he told Jason. The little boy studied Jace, his eyebrows tight together and serious. "Take care of your mommy and little brother. You listen to her. She's the admiral around here." The boy bobble head nodded, and when Jace squatted, he wrapped his plump arms around his neck so tight he could hardly breathe.

He gave Marleigh a look she could read from a mile away. For the first time since he'd been home, her husband didn't want to leave. Maybe that was the best anyone could hope for.

"I love you, Daddy. I miss you."

"I haven't left yet, kid. I love you, too."

"You know what he meant," Marleigh said as she unwound their son from him. "We'll be fine," she said, rubbing her child-free hip against him. "Be safe. We'll be here waiting for you."

Jace pulled her tighter. "Careful," he whispered. "You still get me hard. Just a little move like that. I can't wait to put another baby in you. A girl this time."

She kissed him, hard. "Keep your end of the bargain, and we'll get to trying." She wondered if he hadn't already gotten her pregnant again. No matter what, their bodies couldn't refuse one another. But she didn't say a word. She'd agreed to the possibility of a third child only after Jace agreed to refuse the re-enlistment offer and the retention bonuses and promise of hazardous duty pay at the end of this year, his eighth of Navy service.

"I'd rather the third kid and staying in, but there are plenty of civilian jobs for a guy with my circuitry skills," he said. She'd dared to hope. They could leave this all behind. Head west and away. She had only to get through. Get through one last deployment. Get through a few more months of Jace's domestic Navy duty after that. Then she'd be able to suggest Nebraska and the idea of an extended family.

. . .

This time Jace was gone more than six months. He was hard to keep up with. He seemed to be moving from desert to European base and back again, but all the identifying information in his letters had been inked out by redactors. She wondered what the readers had thought of the almost naked photos from Jace's first deployment, more than two kids ago. They'd seen them, right? Didn't they see all the mail?

Marleigh sent pictures like last time. She grew her hair longer again, just how he liked it. Jason wasn't so chubby, and Nicky had three teeth when he smiled. Jason's head was closer to Marleigh's belly button in pictures. When Jace left, Jason barely reached her hip. And he could say so many more words now. Marleigh had been working with him while Jace was gone.

For the first month Jace was gone, she wrote that Jason had been largely inconsolable, tantrums and crying and saying he wouldn't eat until Daddy came home. Marleigh won the battles, but admitted, "This one isn't a mama's boy. We'll all be so happy to have you home." Jason was almost entirely out of diapers during the day, Marleigh wrote. "He only wants to pee standing up like Daddy." He had taken his little man role very seriously. In the envelopes, Marleigh included drawing after drawing Jason made for him. He said he was imagining the desert. But Marleigh said he and sometimes confused it with the old fossil beds Jace and Marleigh told him about from back home.

Baby,

I can't wait to be home! Not sure what amps me up more—your tight body in my bed, or the big eyes of my boy staring up at me. How did our parents think we were such disappointments? All Jason has to do is shit in the can and we're like oh my god start a parade. I never knew it was so easy to love your kid.

Tell Jason I'm proud of him and to keep up the good work. And give Nicky a squeeze for me. I've learned from last time, baby. And it will be different. Jason isn't a baby anymore. I know he hasn't forgotten me. That kid and I are like puzzle pieces.

Love,
Jace

Marleigh, Jason, and Nicky met Jace inside the Naval Station Norfolk. She managed hair and makeup this time, and arrived complete with the baby in a backpack on her shoulders. Makeup and a come-lay-me dress and heels, his favorite. And a belly, a tiny pregnant belly.

"Hot damn," Jace said on his way to them. "I had to stop myself from running."

As Jace got closer, though, Jason hid behind Marleigh's legs. "Get over here, sailor," Marleigh said, holding her arms wide for him. She kissed him, her breasts tight and full against his chest, her belly barely rounding and hard. Jace's tongue in Marleigh's mouth, he reached around to ruffle his firstborn son's hair. The boy jerked his head away. Jace pulled back.

Marleigh put her hand on his chest and smiled up at him. "We're so glad you're home, Jace," she said, lipstick smudged.

Jace reached with his other hand, but again the boy dodged. He pushed her away, gently. He bent down and tried to play peekaboo with Jason between Marleigh's legs, like they always did, but Jason buried his face in his mother's dress.

"Stop acting like a little baby, Jason."

"It's been a long time, Jace," she said. "You can't take it personally." Of course, he did.

Marleigh cleared her throat. "*Ahem.*" She nodded down to her belly. Jace gave Nicky a quick kiss on the pudgy cheek before kneeling beside Marleigh. He cupped his hands around her stomach and kissed the growing bump.

"I knew it! I'm not missing a minute of this kid's life. Not a chance." He looked up at Marleigh.

"We have an ultrasound next week. I didn't want to find out until you got back."

"It's a girl, I can feel it," he said.

"Whatever the sex, it'll be our last," she said. "And you're keeping your end of the bargain. Third baby and O-U-T," she spelled.

"Let's make this one a surprise!"

. . .

It was almost a week before Jace told Marleigh that he needed to go meet the guys for a few beers. "I can't abandon the guys now that we're home. Most of them don't have any family here." He collected the dinner plates, rinsed and stacked them in the sink.

"But you do. You have a family here," Marleigh reminded him.

He grabbed a dish towel and wiped his hands before looping it over the handle of the dishwasher. "We're the only ones who can understand what went on over there. It helps us to be able to get together."

Marleigh loaded the rinsed plates into the dishwasher. "What did go on over there?" she asked, wishing he would tell her and close the gulf between them, just a little. No, she didn't know what had gone on *over there*. She asked him to share whatever he wanted to share, but that she was proud of him and loved him no matter what shape those months away took and that he didn't owe her any war stories.

He edged out of the kitchen. "That's what I mean; I don't have to explain it to them. They were there. I wouldn't know where to begin, and it's not like we have five minutes to ourselves."

She wiped Jason's face and then Nicky's. "These two will both be asleep by seven. Won't you, boys? Yes you will." She scrunched her face at Nicky and he opened his mouth wide. To Jace, "We'll have hours together, but only if you don't fly out the door."

"Jesus, Marleigh. I've been home with you guys 24/7." He lifted Nicky from the highchair and set him on the floor. Jason climbed down from his chair, and carefully pushed it back in.

"For five whole days, Jace. You talk about us like we're a sentence you're serving."

"It's all fucking naps and toys and Mommy this and that. You guys don't care if I come home." She couldn't really argue with any of the points he raised—except that they weren't consistent. He moved from one to another. "And any time I tell either of them what to do, they both look at you first."

"So, work on it," she said.

He slammed his keys down onto the counter. "Fine. Boys, what do you want to do?" Nicky ignored him. He was chewing on a giraffe and sliding on his butt on the floor.

Jason nodded solemnly. He fastidiously unfolded a large color-by-number on the coffee table in front of the television and opened a pack of crayons.

Jace rolled his eyes at Marleigh and sighed.

"Oh, c'mon. What's wrong with liking to color?" Marleigh asked. Jace had loved the cartoons she'd drawn for him when she was first pregnant.

"Nothing. I mean not for you. You're really good. You still have those markers?"

"Of course."

"I start here, Daddy," Jason said, one chubby fist clutching a crayon, his tongue sticking out in concentration. Without touching it to the paper, Jason returned the crayon to the box. He picked up another one, but gripped it too hard and it broke.

Marleigh watched as Jace tried hard—really hard—to remain patient.

"Don't cry. It's a crayon. It'll still work."

Jason tried again. She could tell how nervous he was, how badly he wanted to impress his father.

"It's just a *g-guuhh* color-by-number, kid, not hard."

This time, Jason plucked a red crayon from the box, and he reached for the high middle of the paper.

"It's four," Jace said, reaching for the crayon. Jason yanked his hand back, out of reach. A pile of snapped crayons lay at Jace's feet. "The sky is number four. Four is blue. Why do you have that color?"

"I wanna make the sky a sunset, like at the beach."

"It's not the beach. It's a city." He thumped the paper to distract Jason. Marleigh saw the quick flash of an airplane bottle move to his lips.

"You wanna color, go ahead and color," Jace said. "No sense in me sitting here while you do it. Not sure what I expected from a kid home so much with his mother."

"Easy, tough guy," Marleigh said. She came by to give him a playful swat on the butt, to defuse the tension, but instead her hand grazed his thigh, low on the cargo pocket of his pants. Her fingernails clinked against the airplane bottle in there.

"Don't give me that sad, disappointed look. I don't tell you what to do all day."

Before she realized what she was doing, Marleigh pulled her hand away, and took a swing at him. Her jab wasn't what it used to be. He caught her by the wrist. He held it tight, raised it up to her face, a slow, humiliating uppercut to her jaw. The children stared at him, but she looked away.

"Got something to say?" he asked.

"Stop it, Jace."

"We're not operating heavy machinery around here. Coloring and eating dinner."

"Let go," she said.

He dropped her hand. Jason chewed on the crayon he'd been holding. "I'm sorry, son. You didn't do anything wrong. We'll finish later. Your mom ruined it."

"Real brave to run away, Jace. So much easier than staying here and learning how to do all this shit I've been doing. On my own."

"Mom!" Jason said. "Bad word."

"You sound like a warden to me. You're so fucking soft, sitting around here all day. Fucking lazy. You wouldn't survive five minutes in the real world."

"Daddy!"

"Quiet down, Jason. You don't make the rules around here."

"We live in the real world, Jace," Marleigh yelled. "I have no idea where you are." She was so angry, so frustrated, so sad. What the hell was happening? She felt Jason cowering beside her.

"That's right, no idea. You little princess with your soft ass and tits out. Come out of there, Jason. Face me like a man."

Jace lunged at the couch. She threw the television remote. It struck him in the shoulder.

"Stop it. That's enough. That's why he doesn't want to come near you. He's scared. And me not working was your idea, and you know it."

"That's right. I support you. I pay for this nice apartment and your car and everything."

"How about we don't do this in front of the kids."

Nicky squawked for his bath.

Jace already had his keys in one hand. "Goddamn, they're going to be such mama's boys," Jace said. "You shouldn't baby them so much."

"They are babies, you asshole." She rolled her eyes, and scooped Nicky from the floor. Jason kept one arm wrapped around her thigh. "Let's at least make it an early night."

He slammed the door on his way out. Angry as she was, his absence was a relief.

The way he tensed up with what little he did tell her, she wasn't sure how much she really wanted to know. How much she could handle. He was being so critical and demanding and hard to deal with it was easier for him to be gone so she could meet the boys' needs. Once he was out of the Navy, it would be all over—the unpredictable schedule, fucked up sleep, the pressure of disarming bombs. They would make it. It was less than a year; that was nothing. She'd waited out much worse before, hadn't she?

CHAPTER THIRTY-TWO

He'd been gone too long this time.

Marleigh made sure the boys were asleep and locked the door behind her before she went looking for Jace. Hopefully, this would be one of the wide-eyed nights, when he would light up at her arrival like they'd planned to meet for drinks and she was just running late, caught behind a train.

It took her a minute to find him in the haze. The bar was built on a dock, decorated to look like a tiki bar. All the windows had been slid open, but the smoke was thick. Jace was angled over the musician's tip jar. He clumsily stuffed some bills into it and made his way back to his bar stool. To his left, a woman was seated, barefoot. She'd kicked off her shoes, and rested her bare feet on the footrest. Jace's calves were brown and hard. On his right side was a large man who banged on the bar top and yelled, "Amazing Grace! Amazing Grace!" The shoeless woman nodded deeply, a neck stumble, eyes low, like she was nodding off to sleep, an alcoholic. An addict who looked like Marleigh's mother, Jackie.

Marleigh knew better than to sneak up behind Jace and tap him on the shoulder. That terrified, angry whirl around. The fists in ready position. She approached at an angle and forced herself to smile. He saw her and grinned.

"Come here, baby." He patted his thigh, turning his chair to meet her.

"Hi, love," she said trying to stay calm, keep him calm.

With an awkward cant of his head to the musician, Jace said, "He's about to sing 'Amazing Grace.'" His *s* sounds were endless.

"It's really late, babe. Can we tab out and go home?"

The barefoot woman turned to them. "You gotta stay for 'Mazin' Grace," she said, well above the din in the bar. Marleigh made eye contact with the bartender and nodded when the woman mouthed, "Check?"

The musician strummed his guitar and sang. It wasn't long before the entire bar was singing along. Jace snaked his arm around her waist, his voice whiskey sharp, he sang wet and loud in her ear. "You saved a wretch like me." He tugged her chin to face him. "I was lost and you found me, baby. I's blind but now I see."

Marleigh wasn't so sure.

• • •

At least the boys were still asleep when she got Jace home.

In the middle of the night, he rolled over to her. His breath beer hot and smelly. "I see the smoking crater, Marleigh. It's coming but I don't know how. If it just happened already I wouldn't have to wait for it. I'm always fucking waiting for it. You're beautiful. The kids are open. Do you see how open? Anyone could hurt them."

His words drifted as he passed out. When he started to snore, she knew they'd never shared a more honest moment.

She didn't yell at him the next day or the rest of the week. She stopped asking, "Why are you doing this? What is so bad here?" Marleigh knew *here* wasn't the problem. Here was perfect. The house was perfect. The kids were perfect, as perfect as kids get anyway. And she understood that Jace knew it, too. No wonder the only place he could sit still was the bar.

"I'm sorry, baby."

She couldn't hear him apologize again.

"Then get out," she said. Her voice was quiet, unemotional. "You've got your years. Get out. You promised. The paperwork is sitting right there. All you have to do is sign."

"But the kids, their school," he said. "My guys."

"You promised, Jace. We can make a living another way. This is eating you up and taking us with you. It's time for our family to come first. We have the entire rest of our lives ahead of us."

"Do you know how much the second reenlistment bonus is? It's mind-blowing, Mar. College fund starter."

He knew Marleigh was always worried about their bank account. He thought this was his ace in the hole. She grabbed his arm, held it gently so he couldn't turn away. "It's not about the money, Jace. Baby, please."

He sighed. "Okay, okay. I'll get out. I'll turn the paperwork in this morning."

• • •

Marleigh held Jace's Navy-separation party at Shucker's. Actually, she only agreed when two of his Navy buddies and former shipmates Gurley and Harbich asked if she would attend a party in his honor. By now, Marleigh hated military bars. The way the drinks just appeared before the guys. The wet slide of glass across the bar. The quiet after the gulp and swallow of the shot.

It was strange, how easy the process of separating from the Navy was. He just refused the automatic reenlistment and awaited his updated DD 214, the form he would carry as proof of his eight years of service. He was almost twenty-seven, Marleigh twenty-four, and they were on the cusp of the second chapter of their lives, some time to finally exhale.

She wanted nowhere near any bar with Jace. But he deserved a goodbye. And she'd never been any good at telling Harbich and Gurley no after they'd worked so hard to help save Pops's gym.

Gurley raised his rocks glass and cleared his throat. "Jace, you sumbitch, leaving us high and dry for a life of leisure."

"Keep it moving, you pussy," Harbich yelled.

"Shut yer yap, Harbich. Well, it couldn't have happened to a better guy than you, Jace. Happy trails, motherfucker!"

Harbich stood. "Enough with Jace. No *boo-hoo-ing* over his sorry ass. A toast to our wives," Harbich motioned to Marleigh, who smiled," and our girlfriends," a nod to Gurley's fiancé, who none of them seemed to like. "May they never meet!" Navy toasts were never very inventive.

Jace raised a pint glass. "I'm getting out," he said. "You suckers stick around if you want to. Cheers to tasting the end." He pushed a full shot glass to Marleigh.

She shook her head no.

"Why aren't you fun anymore?" Jace asked. "You used to be so much fun."

She gulped down the shot, belly-button-popped-out pregnant and everything. "I want to go home." She wiped her mouth. "I want you to want to come home."

CHAPTER THIRTY-THREE

The last thing Marleigh worried about ahead of her third baby's birth was labor and delivery. Jason, her first, was one of those miracles who was born on his due date. Jace had been there for that one. He'd told her she seemed powerful. And even alone with Nicky, her second boy, born three days after his due date, everything proceeded so smoothly, so quickly that she was up and around walking an hour after delivery. Birth was just a day, day and a half. It could only last for so long.

What she worried about was Jace's discharge from the Navy. His paperwork read *general discharge.*

"What's that about?"

"Just some clerical screw up. Fucking civilian government service morons can't even get the paperwork right. I've appealed it."

"What aren't you telling me?" Had there been a reenlistment offer? Did that bonus he dangled so often exist?

"Nothing, babe. I'll get the paperwork. Everything's like you wanted it."

Marleigh shrugged. At least the military was behind them. Finally. Jace was looking for work. He was out of the house each day trying to find them a new source of income. For Marleigh, days were breakfast with one in a highchair, smacking his lips and opening his mouth into a big wide *O*, squealing as he picked up a fistful of Cheerios and jammed most of them into his mouth, along with his slobbery fist. One on a booster at the kitchen table, Marleigh on high alert to keep him from toppling over. Jason was already fastidious about food, just like his father. He sliced his hard-boiled egg with a butter knife before he ate it and nibbled his toast from the outside in so that his last bite was "the jelliest." She rescrewed the top onto the sippy cup for the baby who wouldn't be the baby of the family much longer. The cup leaked no matter how tight she put on the lid, so she had taken to bringing his clothes into the kitchen and dressing him after he'd had breakfast. One less pile of tiny laundry. One less step. This pregnancy wore her out.

After breakfast, preschool. She felt pressure to look at least a little put together when she brought the boys to preschool. She'd still be put to shame by some of the outfits the other children wore, let alone the teachers.

While the boys were in school, she tattooed again. Jace's job search and the hours both boys were in preschool gave her freedom she didn't know she needed. She hadn't hid her tattooing from Jace. But he couldn't fight her on tattooing a few days a week until he figured out his post-Navy move.

Today, she had an early appointment with a return customer, the start of a complicated, multi-stage piece. She loved back pieces best; calf pieces came in second. Large back tattoos took time; there were often layers. She cleansed the whole back, always waxed or shaved smooth, with the big alcohol wipes. The customer shivered beneath her gloved hand. Sometimes goosebumps formed. A man's back didn't always remind her of Jace and his skin on her skin. But this guy did. Miguel and Jace were built the same. Broad-shouldered but lean. That's why back pieces were best—no eye contact. The customer couldn't warily eyeball her every movement, swallowing thick and loud as she prepped the equipment and the dyes. She didn't have to watch the bouncing Adam's apple or calm the fearful eyes.

"You ready, Miguel?" She applied the ink outline transfer to his back. He had given her old family photos, and she had drawn each person's face, inlaid them in the bark of a tree that rose up and across his back.

"Let's do it," he said.

"Remember, don't hold your breath. And let me know if you feel faint or like you're going to puke."

"Got it," he answered, rolling a Jolly Rancher from her bowl around in his mouth.

"Don't try to be a hero."

Almost no one started with a significant back tattoo (shoulder or tramp stamp, sure), so she was way less likely to end up swabbing up vomit or having a customer pass out when she did one. Other pluses. Miguel's back and shoulder muscles tensed, then released under her hands as she worked.

Jace's back had changed while he was deployed the last time. His entire physique had, but especially his upper body. There were ridges and valleys to him that felt like an exotic foreign country, no soft places left. Jace was different in bed, too. He'd never been a sloppy lay, but he also never went out to get loaded and stayed out before. Before what exactly? Or at least he hadn't when they were together—at least, not at first. Maybe this was his normal behavior and the stolen perfect months they'd had were the aberration. His back was hard, but his dick wasn't. It was going to get better. Nowhere to go but up.

She touched the needle to Miguel's back. He barely flinched and then relaxed. "The outlining isn't so bad," he said, releasing a held breath.

She wiped away the excess ink that pooled at the skin's surface and the bright dots of blood. "The anticipation is worse. Keep breathing, slow and easy." The candy in Miguel's mouth clacked against his teeth as he moved it, calming himself down.

After stashing Miguel's cash in her purse and sanitizing, Marleigh opened a gallon Ziploc, and fished out her breakfast of toast with peanut butter and banana. She dropped her pen. As she hinged over to pick it up, she wet herself, soaking the chair, fluid splattering on the floor. She'd never done that before. She guessed there was a first time for everything. It wasn't just her belly that stretched each time. She was almost thirty-one weeks pregnant. Peeing your pants couldn't be that unusual. She stripped off her soaked panties from under the long skirt she wore and stuffed them into the empty Ziploc and sealed it, thankful for the long stretchy skirt that had stayed opaque through three pregnancies. Careful not to fall, she collected towels to clean up the mess around her chair. Her body felt tight, as though the entire bulk of her belly, placenta, fluid, baby all now rested on her bladder. It ached. But she'd just peed. She collected the wet towels. As she walked by the full-length mirror used to gauge the placement of tattoos, she saw that her belly had dropped. She had to get home and change her clothes. One of the artists walked in as she was walking out, keys out, ready to lock back up.

"Why the face, Marleigh?"

"Oh, I think this kid is running out of space and fast." She felt like she had to puke. "I need to go home for a minute. I'll be back."

"We can handle it, Mar. You're white. Like white, white." she said. "Go get some rest or something."

The three-block walk back to her apartment was excruciating. She tried holding her breath, but the sidewalk went wavy under her feet. Black spots sizzled across her vision. She sucked in her cheeks tight so that she wouldn't groan aloud. She felt clammy, cold and sweaty at once. She was supposed to be at work. The kids were at school. They were covered there until five. She walked past the church that housed the school. Her ears were like the inside of conch shells. Something warm and wet trickled down her ankle. She pushed open the door to the apartment lobby. She needed to sit on the stair for a moment. Ceiling tiles swelled and swam in Marleigh's vision, their borders expanding, shiny surfaces and scuffs until suddenly the floor smacked into her forehead.

. . .

Marleigh awoke in the hospital, an IV dripping into her hand, a stretchy belt around her waist, a hospital gown. She opened her eyes to a nurse standing over her. "Good, you're awake. You gave all of us a scare."

Marleigh didn't feel awake. She was so groggy, her eyelids heavy. Her hands immediately cupped her stomach. "Is the baby okay? I need to call my husband."

"We've called him," the nurse replied, turning her face down to the buttons and lights at the base of the IV. "And the doctor will be in to see you shortly." So, no, everything wasn't okay. "But—" Marleigh didn't have the energy to press the nurse, to demand to know what had gone wrong. She knew that if she did, the woman wouldn't tell her anything anyway.

"What's in the IV? How long have I been here?"

"An antibiotic. You spiked quite a fever and passed out. You've been here a little over two hours."

"Two hours? Where's Jace? What's happening?" Marleigh asked. "It's too early, right?" The nurse looked distraught, as though she didn't trust herself not to answer. Marleigh cut her eyes to the door. The unmistakable ripple of a contraction rolled over and through her body. She couldn't be in labor yet, but she was. "It was my water breaking, wasn't it?" she asked through gritted teeth as the contraction eased. The nurse nodded but kept her eyes down. Marleigh clutched the bedrail in anticipation of the next contraction. She had the hands of an old woman, so pale, veins so bright blue and round beneath the skin.

The doctor entered in a whoosh. "Mrs. Holt, good morning, well afternoon, I guess." She looked up at him as a contraction ripped through her. "This baby isn't adhering to anyone's plans, is he?"

"He?" she asked. "We thought—" Marleigh shook her head and stared at the door. "What's wrong?" she asked.

"What we know for certain is that your water ruptured fully, so we can't stop the progression of labor at this point. You've already developed a dangerously high fever, which is a signal of infection. We're prepping antibiotics for your baby for immediately after delivery, which has to happen inside twelve hours." He slid two gloved hands inside of her. "A good seven inches dilated already."

"Will it hurt the baby?" she asked. The darker question she wasn't ready to ask—had it already?

"We're not sure yet," he said. "Have you been sick at all lately? A flu or cold? Could you have picked something up from your older children?"

Of course she could have; but she'd felt fine. Just tired. Hadn't she? She couldn't fully recall how she'd been feeling, her well-being falling below the scope of her notice at this point. "I don't think so," she said. "I've been really worn out, but I thought it was just pregnancy and two little kids and . . ." her voice trailed off. Jace.

As if summoned, Jace stepped through the door, his visitor tag bobbing against his chest from a run down the hall. Maybe it was the lighting in the room, but he looked terrible. His worried eyes shone through dark pits, his thin, angular face was puffy. When had she last taken the time to look at him?

When he reached her, he grabbed her hand, roughly. She winced. Jace leaned over her. He smelled worse than he looked. How late had it been when he'd gotten home last night? She hadn't noticed. Hadn't noticed. Hadn't noticed. Jesus Christ, he was hungover.

"What's going on?" he asked. She had to cut him some slack; neither of them planned on having a baby today. But she had to keep a better eye on him. "Why is my wife so pale? If she doesn't come through this okay, you're not coming out of here either. Got it?"

She squeezed his hand. Shushed him like one of their children. *There there.*

"So far it's going okay, Jace," she said.

Marleigh's contractions slowed. At first she didn't say anything. Then there were three weak ones in a row. She wasn't sure what to do. Her body had always led her before. She had been feeling the pressure build and was certain it wouldn't be long before she'd begin pushing. She felt dizzy, but she had to keep Jace calm. The core of her was so warm, but her fingers and toes were icy. Her head felt loose on her neck.

"Baby, are you okay?" Jace gripped her chin in two fingers, his eyes pleading. She laughed. She couldn't help it.

"I've been better," she said. "How are *you* doing?"

The doctor and nurse chuckled. Jace tightened. She wasn't okay. She knew it and so did he. Nothing felt sure or certain or strong. She studied the nurse and doctor's faces for any sign that they understood this, too, but she saw nothing. They prepped her to push. Jace held her hand and her knee. "It's almost over now," she told him, hoping she was right. "We're going to meet this kiddo soon." She could tell her efforts to reassure Jace were working. He stood taller, his jaw stopped twitching, he eased his grip on her hand. She was still nervous and uncertain.

"On three, take your first big push." Marleigh breathed in deeply, held it and then pushed her breath out as she clenched and pushed down below.

"*Ahhhhhhhh.*" It hurt this time, a deep, wet hurt, a twisted hurt. She hadn't caught her breath by the time she was instructed to push again. She was thrown off. With each push she felt as if the baby were moving deeper back inside of her, not down or out.

"Give us all you have on this one," the nurse said, as though Marleigh had been holding back. She sucked in air through her teeth and closed her eyes as she pushed. Something broke loose from her. The smell. The nurse scraped the shit immediately into a plastic bag that hung from the bed. Another first.

"Jesus," Jace muttered. "Like a fucking corpse."

An alarm sounded. "The baby's heartbeat is dropping. Nurse, can you see the baby's head?" the doctor called.

"No, he hasn't crowned yet." Gloved fingers searched her vagina, stretching her already stretched edges. None of this felt right. "The head is close. Maybe two inches from crowning. Push again and I'll see if I can ease him out."

Again she pushed.

"Good! You made some progress there. He's retreating. Push again!" And so she did. The room twisted and swirled around her. "We're going to need the forceps, nurse," the doctor barked. "If we can't get this baby out on the next push we're headed to the OR. Prep the room."

A nurse to Jace, "Sir, you should stay out here."

"Like hell I will." He clumsily scrubbed up.

Marleigh's heart climbed up her throat. They didn't need the OR. Jace began swaying, and one of the nurses pushed a chair against the backs of his knees and he crumpled into it, cursing. "Fuckers. How about you take care of my wife and baby?" He was still pale. The chair was a good idea.

On the next contraction, Marleigh pushed with everything she had. The doctor slid the horrible forceps inside of her. She was tearing like a seam, and there was a wet tug inside of her, like her insides were coming out instead of the baby.

"Why is there so much blood?" Jace's unsteady voice beside her. She tried to calm him with her eyes, but this was nothing like either time before.

A nurse and orderly pushed Jace from the room.

Marleigh wasn't sure she would make it out of this room. Was there really a baby inside of her or some toothy, many-clawed monster intent on taking her out of the world he was entering?

CHAPTER THIRTY-FOUR

M arleigh stayed in the hospital for four days after the baby's birth until doctors could stabilize her temperature. She needed rest, needed to heal, but she spent her awake hours worrying about the three boys at home—Jace and the children. He swore to her that he had it covered.

They named the baby Max. And Marleigh only knew him as the little dreamy baby she barely got to see. Raisin-colored skin in a miniature diaper, so many monitors, tubes and cords. His spine curved like it always did in ultrasound photos. He looked unprepared for life outside of her womb.

She had held him in the Neonatal Intensive Care Unit for the first time the morning after he was born. The alarms that sounded in the NICU were similar to those that had gone off when she was in labor. She could feel the cold of her own blood as she stood there holding her tiny, newest baby, and started to hemorrhage. She looked down on the linoleum floor, still polished to a squeak, to make sure there wasn't a pile of entrails at her feet. Her arms had slackened, her grip on the baby loosening. A nurse's hand was on her shoulder, brought her back. The baby was in distress, still struggling to get enough oxygen.

She had been sewn up after the placenta fell from her.

She needed to get it together and be strong for this baby. She needed to get home.

She left the hospital without Max and without a set date for when he would be strong enough to leave. On her second day home she walked Jason and Nicky to preschool, so slowly. Jason matched her pace without question. He helped push his brother in the stroller. Both boys' touches were surprisingly gentle. Her little young men. They had grown while she was in the hospital.

The preschool office assistant bounded into the hallway and looked Marleigh up and down, clearly surprised.

"I hoped I'd get a glimpse of your little one," the woman said.

Marleigh tried to smile, but her eyes flooded as she tried to speak. "He needs some more time before he can come home. He came so early. And his heart isn't pumping blood the way it should."

The woman raised her hand to her mouth. "Oh, I can't imagine."

Marleigh asked Jace, again, please, not to leave her alone with their son in the NICU. "Just hold him for a minute or two. He needs to know you." She shouldn't have had to ask, but she knew that look on Jace's face, his eyes scanning for the halls, any possible escape. She didn't want to be left here again. No parent wanted to be here.

Marleigh sat with her shirt unbuttoned and open, her breasts nearly too big for tiny Max, who kept trying to eat. The lighting inside the NICU didn't help. Max's little diaper glowed bright white in the fluorescence. Electrode patches connected to wires all over the baby's back. Thin threads of tubes up his nostrils. The rise and fall of those pumps. *Snick snick snick.*

"I know it makes you twitchy. But I need you to hang in with me." Max wasn't just small, he was impossibly small. The crocheted newborn cap slid down over his wrinkly skin. Jace wouldn't hold him. He said he didn't know where to put his hands around the countless monitors and tubes. He feared he could hurt him by accident.

"Wires don't belong on babies."

"This little guy needs them." She wrapped Max up, gently, and held her son out to his father.

Jace took a step back.

"C'mon, Jace. I'd like to put these away for five minutes," Marleigh said, nodding down at her breasts. She had milk for days, too much for Max. She stood and tried to move towards him. She pulled too far and one of the baby's monitors started chirping.

Jace held his hand out. Stop. "Back up, alright? Don't hurt him."

"I'm not sure what you're so scared of," she said, lowering herself back into the chair. Her patience was thinner than Max's translucent fingernails. She was too exhausted to coddle Jace while also caring for Max and the older boys. "But, fine. Don't hold him. Just keep me company." She was pissed. She asked very little of Jace these days—pack the older boys' lunches for preschool, schedule job interviews, hold your newest son. How low could her bar go?

Jace paced, but his strides were slow and methodical as Marleigh rocked Max, her shirt buttoned most of the way back up. Between the sounds of Jace's rhythmic footfalls and the rocking chair, Marleigh dozed lightly.

"Baby, I'm going home," Jace said.

Marleigh jerked awake.

"That way I can put Jason and Nicky to bed and send the babysitter home."

She glanced from Jace to the clock. It was just past eight. He'd lasted forty minutes.

Marleigh studied him. She desperately wanted to believe that he would go straight home, that the harrowing motorcycle ride would be enough, could replace the burn of the Old Crow and the cold beer chaser. She knew he played his bike back and forth over the solid white line of the tunnel lanes before rising and fast onto the overpass and into the humid night air, how he leaned deep and low to split off of the highway. She was too tired to argue.

"Give the boys an extra-long hug for me," she said.

Jace surprised her by taking five quick strides across the room to Marleigh and the baby. He kissed her worry line and then gently kissed the baby's head, skull still pulsing, scalp still full of chicken fluff.

"I love you, baby." She could hear the relief of escape in his voice.

"I'll see you at home, Jace." She couldn't stay at the hospital past ten. How much trouble could he get into in less than two hours?

"I'm going straight home." He sounded so convincing that she wondered if he actually believed his own words. "Promise."

CHAPTER THIRTY-FIVE

After spending the morning hours at the tattoo shop, Marleigh was dressed in near-scrubs, the outfit she saved for her hours in the NICU. She'd put it on after she hugged little Jason goodbye and kissed a sleepy Nicky's forehead, his afternoon nap a hard-won routine so she'd bring fewer germs into the hospital, pressing two twenties into the neighbor girl's hand.

"Jace should be home any time. Thanks for staying extra!"

Marleigh hadn't planned stops or seeing anyone before the NICU. Jace promised to be home by two so she could be at the hospital before the baby's late-afternoon feeding. She'd pumped the morning and midday feedings, ready to go to work, when Jace announced, "I need to go run some errands." He brushed Jason off his lap, who kept his lip from wobbling until his father left the room. She toyed with her ziti-noodle necklace. Jason had strung them on a flat purple strand of yarn. She put them in her purse before going in to extract Jace.

She searched for Jace's bike first at Shucker's, then Cantina, and finally the Brass Buckle. She hated those places and the chokehold they had on Jace. Nearly out of ideas, she saw a flash of neon parked in front of Cheetahs. "How did I end up here?"

Marleigh wore her scrubs into the strip club. The place smelled like pussy and sweat. Everyone in there needed to shower, Marleigh now included. Marleigh had sworn she would never do this. She would not be the wife dragging her husband home from where he really wanted to be, wheedling, cajoling, pathetic. Her mother when she was over the party. But Jackie had played the if you can't beat 'em join, 'em game. Not Marleigh. Not ever. But she also never thought she'd have a brand-new baby who couldn't breathe on his own, who had holes in his heart. She never thought Jace would fall out of love with Jason and Nicky, with her, and in love with the bottle. What an idiot.

She didn't hate strippers. Marleigh almost ended up working in a strip club once. "Your ass is perfect. Goddam, I'd take a bite outta that crease. But your tits are small, real small," the manager had said. "Think about surgery or how much harder you have to work than the big-titted girls. Extra hours"—a sharp raise of his chin. "Extra effort." What a pig. Everyone had to figure out how to get by, and she knew it wasn't the tits or the ass that brought Jace back in here. Sure, he appreciated the jiggly scenery, but it was men's company he sought. The liquor they drank all day. It was a package deal.

Marleigh's tits weren't so small now. They ached, gorged and bigger than nearly any of the girls on stage, blue-veined with milk for the baby waiting for her at the hospital. If touched, she would explode. Marleigh hated approaching people, hated interrupting. How often had this scene played out when she was a child, sent in to fetch her own parents. Her breasts stung.

"Oh, shit." Jace slurred when he saw her. *Come on*, she said with her eyes, silently screaming. *Leave with me now so you can return to your sons, and I can feed our baby.* He slung his arm around the empty chair beside him. "Get her a beer. She likes beer. One of the things I love about her."

Marleigh shook her head and remained standing. "Sir, it looks like maybe she needs you," said the boy to his left. *Yes. I need you. Your sons need you. We can fix whatever needs fixing later; just come home.*

"I take my orders from her, not you," Jace said. He stood, wobbly, from the bar stool. At least he didn't make a scene.

The babysitter kept her eyes on the floor as she hugged Jason and Nicky goodbye and Jace staggered inside the apartment. Marleigh remembered her teenaged self fleeing drunk dads, except that those guys usually held her babysitting money. "Thanks, Mrs. Holt," the girl called behind her.

. . .

A weary-looking new mother admired Marleigh when she arrived at the hospital with several bottles of expressed milk. "Wow. What a supply!"

"Oh," was all Marleigh replied. She was so tired. She wasn't sure what the woman meant at first.

"Mine is lucky if he gets six ounces from me a week." The woman's eyes were shiny. Her cheeks wobbled. "I can't seem to make more. No matter what I do."

"It's good," a nurse interjected. "You're doing good, Mom. Any amount, big or small, really helps." A small smile twitched across the woman's face. But she still seemed hungry for validation. "It's almost impossible to force your milk to come in when they don't latch right."

"And the pumps really suck," Marleigh said, wry. Breastfeeding was a language, a process she understood. Feeding her boys was regular, happened on a schedule. Predictable in an unpredictable time. The nurse and the other mom laughed and nodded. As Marleigh sanitized her hands in preparation for nursing Max, she wondered how she would feel if she couldn't do that much.

Marleigh had taken her ability to feed Max with her body for granted. This other mother came just as often to the NICU as Marleigh did, just to hold a bottle of some other woman's milk to her child's lips. It was touching, that kind of selflessness. The nurses would have done it for her.

"Mom," the nurse said to Marleigh as Max snuffled and gurgled at her breast, the letdown release so intense.

Her eyes drooped. "Uh-huh," she said.

"You know about the milk bank, right?" the nurse asked. "Our hospital lets you donate your extra milk. You usually have quite a bit extra every week. Would you consider doing that?"

"Of course." It was the only extra, the only extravagance Marleigh had ever had, her overabundance of milk; of course she would share. Even with all of her milk, Max remained so small.

The nurses assured her he was growing. "You seeing him twice a day every day makes it hard to tell. Not like when your cousin goes away for the summer and comes back fat. Thank you for the extra milk. All these babies need all the help they can get."

Didn't they all.

Max's feeding relaxed her; thank God for those soothing chemicals breastfeeding released. She never knew what she would find at home. She turned the radio up loud to keep her awake on the drive home from the hospital. Jason met her at the apartment door. His hair was wet and neatly combed. "Hi, Mama! We made dinner!"

The apartment was spotless. Blankets were folded neatly on the couch, rather than haphazardly strewn. The boys' toys had been placed back in their wooden bins. The room smelled of garlic. Nicky, too, looked freshly bathed. He sat in his bouncy seat on the floor in front of the TV, burbling happily.

Jace approached her warily. His eyes were clearer than this afternoon. He smelled of soap and cologne, not the strip club. "I'm so sorry for earlier, Mar. I can't believe I acted like that. I know it's just a start, but yeah, little man and I made dinner. And everyone is bathed. Even me." He leaned in to kiss her on the cheek. Marleigh wrapped her arms around him, breathed Jace in. Her mouth against his neck. She squeezed so hard, hoping to solidify this moment.

"Thank you," she mumbled. Her voice wavered.

"It's just spaghetti, not filet mignon or anything."

She stepped back from him and wiped her eyes.

"And bread, Mama. We made bread." Jason's *r*s still sounded like *w*s.

"Salad, too. We're really trying hard," Jace said. He unclipped Nicky from his bouncy chair and lifted him to the highchair.

Marleigh sat. Jace and Jason heaped their plates full, and proudly set them on the table. She was so thankful.

"I can't wait until we're all under this roof and at this table," she said. "The NICU nurses said it won't be long until baby Max can come home."

"So close, Mar," Jace said with a smile. "And I'll never let you down again."

· · ·

After a shopping trip to Target the following week, Marleigh waved the boys inside the apartment building and up the stairs. "Come on, Bud, let's get you a rest," Marleigh said to Jason. He was cranky; lunch eaten in the car on the ride home from Max's feeding in the hospital, an hour past their usual nap time. Nicky'd babbled in his car seat. Marleigh forced them to sing songs on the car ride, squeezed the extra skin on their knees to keep them awake in the car. She needed them to nap when they got home. She needed the hour or two on Mondays to plan out the week ahead: work, Jason and Nicky's hours at preschool, which feedings she could make it to the hospital for, how much milk she could pump and how often. Just another NICU mom.

She had no idea where Jace was. He had a second interview with a logistics provider, and she knew there were several defense contractors anxious to meet him. He was home every night. The boys piled into his lap for story time before bed. He played a savage version of this little piggy, which involved growls and roars and left Nicky and Jason begging for more.

Sweet Nicky, her little big boy, almost made it home before falling asleep in the car. He didn't stir when she lifted him out. She lay Nicky in the bed beside Jason, whose palms were slack, already deeply asleep.

She needed an extra-long nap from both. She could use some extra tips, some extra hours in the day, some extra time with Jace, a little sleep. She was thankful the boys didn't fight their naps today. They were as worn out as she was. She kissed Jason's perfect forehead—Jesus, did he look like Jace, especially when he slept—and whispered *I love yous* over open-mouthed Nicky. She tiptoed out of their room and into the kitchen to survey what she could put together for dinner before she had to work.

She wanted to have a warm meal waiting for Jace when he got home. When he was in the military, Jace was told when to show up and where. And when he did, he received and followed his orders. Things were orderly, more routine. Life afterwards, not so much. Her seven-until-ten Monday-night tattoo shift was mostly walk-ins. No appointments booked. She took whatever she could get until Jace found something permanent.

She dumped the chicken thighs she'd bought Manager's Special into the crockpot along with carrots and onions and potatoes. Maybe she could sit and close her eyes. Exhaustion would eventually dry up her milk. And Nicky and Jason deserved better than zombie mom when they woke up. She plopped down onto the couch and tipped her head back. She didn't remember falling asleep.

• • •

The buzzer from the doorbell rang. And rang again.

"Shit," she whispered and sprang up, dizzy, to hit the intercom. "Stop ringing! I'll be right down."

Marleigh grabbed the baby monitor she only needed for going outside and her key and stepped outside into the hallway. She ruffled her hair on the three flights down and checked the corners of her mouth for drool. Clean; she probably hadn't slept long enough to drool. She opened the door to a big, overgrown kid in his daily work fatigues. He wrapped her in a tight hug that propelled them against the doorway.

"Get off me." She pushed against his chest.

Gurley was his name, the kid who organized Jace's farewell party. Jace and the rest of the guys had lots of fun with that one. Gurley had a prissy fiancée who prided herself on picking someone from officer candidate school. Marleigh pushed against him until he broke his grip. His eyes were red and puffy, his mouth dangling open, lips wet. He clenched and opened his fists.

"Jace isn't here, Gurley."

"I know, ma'am."

"What's wrong? Is it Angela?" The fiancée.

"No, ma'am." His breath was minty on her face. Mouthwash or harsh gum. That was always Jace's first giveaway these days, a super minty mouth.

"Jace isn't here," she repeated.

"Um, I know. That's why I'm here," he said. The big guy swerved in his boots. Marleigh had never seen any of them tipsy in uniform. They always changed into street clothes first.

"What happened?"

"We just saw his bike. On the highway."

She dropped to the concrete stoop, only realizing what she'd done when her butt hit concrete. "Ow!" The left side of her throat closed. "What do you mean? Where's Jace?"

"They took him. One of us needed to get here before the police. To tell you." The boy slumped over and started sobbing. His cries broke like waves across his wide back.

"What are you telling me, Gurley?"

"I'm sure it was over real quick. That's what the EMTs said."

Marleigh stood up. "No," she said, "You fucking liar." She kicked Gurley in the ribs. "Get away from my house."

A shiny, jacked-up Jeep swerved into the parking lot.

"Take me to him," she told Harbich. "Take me to the hospital."

"He's not in the hospital, Marleigh." She flashed back to what the EMT told her about Pops. *They don't bring dead people to the hospital.*

She battered his chest and the three of them cried together. Silence from the baby monitor she clutched so hard in her hands that the antenna had bent. "No. He was done. He was getting better. Everything was better."

Harbich wiped tears and snot off his face. "The police are on their way. They'll take you to identify his body."

"No."

A police cruiser parked beside Harbich's Jeep. "Mrs. Holt?"

When her older sons awoke from their naps, Marleigh had to explain that their father was dead. Max would only know her as a single mother.

CHAPTER THIRTY-SIX

Jace's death made the newspaper. *Motorcycle crash kills one, injures three and cripples I-264.* Twice, then, he'd been in the *Virginian-Pilot*. The photo beneath the bolded headline showed chunks of neon-green plastic, one rear tire, the bike's tailpipe. Wreckage from the cars that crashed when trying to swerve out of the way. The front of Jace's motorcycle smashed into the concrete median separating east and westbound traffic. There were no skid marks left on the highway. By the time the photo was taken, Jace's body had been removed from the opposite side of the highway. Flares ignited and the area blocked off. "Traffic was re-routed for a one-mile stretch between Tidewater Drive and Military Highway yesterday afternoon. Excessive speed and alcohol were factors in the crash." Marleigh wouldn't cut out that article. The photo of Jace, Jason, and her, happy and young, was still up on the counter. That was less than three years ago.

Marleigh called Donna first. They had only spoken a handful of times since she and Jace married. Ed and Jace refused to apologize to one another after the bar brawl in Scottsbluff, and both women were caught in the middle. Still, she had to know. She called three times before she left a message asking Donna to call her. Jace's DD

214 listed Trish as his next of kin. He'd never bothered to update it, just as he never sought the appeal to improve his general discharge to an honorable one. Trish and Guylene had to know by now, but she called Trish, anyway.

Trish's voice was thick with tears after Marleigh said hello. "Oh, Marleigh," she said. "It's so horrible. I'm so sorry."

It was horrible. Jace was so much more than his last year. She knew that, but would her boys? Or would they only ever know the scorched earth their father left behind.

"Yeah," was all Marleigh could say.

"How are the boys?" Trish had never met them. They had all talked of visits, but they never happened. No one booked the flights or made the drive. There was always next summer, next year.

"Max is coming home from the hospital soon. He won't—" He would never know his father. "He's doing better, getting stronger. Jason and Nicky." She stopped to breathe away the tears. "Nicky doesn't understand. He's waiting for his dad to come home again like he always does. Jason is so quiet, it's scary."

The night after she identified Jace's body, she told her boys that Daddy wasn't coming home. "Dada?" Nicky asked. "Dada! Dada! Dada! Work?" He only had a few words at his disposal: Dada, Mama, Brudder, baby. One he never needed again. It was so tempting to tell them he'd been deployed. She was a lot of things, but Marleigh wasn't cruel.

"Not at work, honey. He's gone." Jason set his soft little jaw, put one chubby arm around his mother, and one around his little brother. He became the man of the house, again.

Trish had no problem crying over the phone. "He seemed so much better with you. I hoped—" She gulped. "I hoped it would always be good for you."

"He didn't slow down," Marleigh said. "He sped right into that concrete wall."

"He's been chasing death a long time," Trish said.

"I don't know what to do," Marleigh said.

"We'll have a small service here," Trish said. "You do whatever feels right."

Marleigh meant she didn't know what to do about anything, about her life. None of this felt right. She needed to have him cremated; there was so little left to bury. Trish explained how sharply downhill Donna had gone when Ed died. Trish was caring now for both Donna and Guylene. Donna had been improving, Trish told her. But she didn't think Guylene had much time left, and now they'd all lost Jace, too. "I'm terrified. Jace was discharged. We're completely on our own. Once you're out, you're out."

"I wish I could be more help," Trish said.

Me, too, Marleigh thought. "I understand. Bye, Trish."

· · ·

Marleigh brought Jace's ashes to Ocean View beach, a handful of blocks from the old boxing gym where they had met. She wore Max across her chest. Jason held Nicky's hand as they walked down the beach to the foamy edge of the Chesapeake Bay. Gurley and Harbich were down at the water's edge, their fiancées, too, arms wrapped around one another against the mid-October wind. Jace had loved the water, the way the sun set over the Bay after rising above the Atlantic. This was the beach where they had decided to risk themselves on one another. A pod of dolphins swam back and forth, surfacing and submerging.

Marleigh waded in knee deep and took the lid off the box, unwrapping the twist tie from the plastic baggie inside, scattering Jace into the lap of the waves, knowing Jason and Nicky watched from the shore. Gurley's fiancée held on to Nicky's hand. Jason stood stalwart, unwittingly at attention. Marleigh was exhausted. And angry. And devastated. She felt a century old. She felt cheated. She felt so fucking sad.

Part of her wanted to walk all the way into the water, give into the grief that would pull her out and under. Max's little feet kicked gently at her ribs. If she kept walking, his tiny-socked feet would be underwater, too.

"Goodbye, asshole," she said through a mouth thick with tears. "We loved you so much."

Marleigh gave the box a final shake and turned back to the shore, with Max squirming against her chest. Jason and Nicky ran to her, tugging on her skirt, holding onto her sopping wet legs. They walked to the top of the beach access, heading to the car. Jason stopped suddenly and turned back to the beach. Jason waved to the water, to his father, and gave him the quick salute they'd practiced for all those times waiting on the pier for Jace to come home.

CHAPTER THIRTY-SEVEN

The baby was boogery and warm—too warm. Max tugged on his ears and drooled and drooled. *Let it be teething; let it be teething; let it be teething,* Marleigh wished over and over. In the six months since Jace died, both Jason and Nicky had occasionally spiked fevers, worrying her, and then the next tooth would inevitably erupt. Their mouths dried up and their skin cooled. They quieted, comfortable and back to themselves. She couldn't waste a sick visit to the pediatrician on teething, or a cold, something that wouldn't merit antibiotics, something the doctors would wave away saying "push rest and fluids" after taking her twenty-five-dollar copay. Max was the only one of them with insurance. It was shitty, but she knew if she let it lapse, she could never cover him again. She tattooed and bartended every shift she could get.

Max's unlicensed daycare turned him away or called her back to get him if he had a fever. Hopefully she could buy herself a whole shift worth of hours if she gave him both a little ibuprofen and Tylenol. If he was going to need antibiotics, she was going to need to find a way to pay for them.

Neither of the other two ever had trouble with their ears, but Max was always catching something. More than his heart and lungs were underdeveloped, no matter what the nurses said. "He'll overcome this. He won't believe it when you tell him stories later." She just wanted to rush him to health, see if he could catch up to his brothers, get him old enough to join them at the church school. She was adamant about keeping them in the church preschool with its small class sizes and growing endowment fund. When she looked at the early-start programs and free preschools, it looked like just where she'd come from; she wanted better for them than that. Otherwise, what had everything meant?

Marleigh was outnumbered by boys, three-to-one, and they were all hungry. Hunger she could understand; she could harness it. She was (again) a boxer cutting weight. Self-denial was control and power. It didn't work that way for little boys, boys who grew overnight as they slept, who outgrew shoes from one day to the next. Thank God her milk kept up and Max was such a good nurser.

"I don't wanna," Jason told her as she put on his too-tight Sketchers, showing with her fingers how to scrunch up his toes.

"You need them for school today," she said.

"They hurt, Mom."

"It's just for today."

"You said that yesterday." She cut into the front seam and dug out extra space for his toes.

She probably had said that. When Nicky or the baby outgrew something, they had their brothers' clothes and shoes and pajamas to move into. Jason's had to be purchased. And if she bought something new, it might last long enough for the other boys to use it. Thrift store clothes had already been passed down again and again, all the boys' pants thin and discolored at the knees. New was so expensive, even at Walmart and Target, where so many women shopped for recreation, eagerly awaiting the new seasonal colors and accessories. Marleigh didn't care about having new things for herself; she wore the same items over and over anyway. She always had.

But she knew how important it was to have the right characters on the boys' T-shirts and how many colors of Swoosh their friends had on their shorts and shirts. It was part of their *just like every other kid* camouflage. Just like newish backpacks filled with all of the requisite colored pencils and dry-erase markers were at the beginning of the new school year. The teachers said none of that was mandatory. Jason was only carrying papers and crafts and lunch back and forth to school. He only needed a lunchbox, but Marleigh remembered the exacting difference between the teachers' lists and the students'. She had drawn a navy rectangle on the heel of her white sneakers so they looked enough like Keds from a distance to fool her peers. And by high school she could mimic the Adidas stripes and logo. Her friends paid her to draw theirs.

Marleigh told the boys how stuff didn't matter, how none of it made you any better on the inside where it counted, but she would do everything she could to help them fit in just enough. Best to be invisible.

She gave Max a squirt of ibuprofen and dropped the older boys at school and him at daycare. She had to shop, and she had to work. Marleigh had a process for shopping. When she was alone, she picked strip malls with bargain grocery store chains and dollar stores. She started at Family Dollar for all the household goods—so much cheaper than grocery stores—and lunch box items and snacks. She always had plenty of shelf-stable foods for them to use at the end of the month when fresh was no longer an option. When she had the boys with her, she shopped at Harris Teeter. Their prices were higher, but almost every aisle held free samples. Ham and cheese on toothpicks, orange wedges. Jason liked the California rolls offered between the sushi shelf and the dairy. Each boy left the store with sugar crystals on his hand from the free cookies offered to every child. She saved her WIC money for Harris Teeter. It didn't go far on purchases, but a few handfuls of samples each could see them through most of the day.

And Marleigh taught her kids how to barter. The contents of Jason's lunch box were objects of interest at school, different from the carefully curated bento boxes many of the other parents packed, full of vegetables and hormone-free dairy products. "He's so generous with the other kids," a teacher remarked. "He's always willing to trade a pudding cup for a banana or an orange." Of course he was. You could store those puddings in the trunk on a summer day and they'd be just as you left them. A piece of fresh fruit was never guaranteed.

One day, Nicky came home, his face sticky and orange. He wouldn't let Marleigh wipe it off. "Emily had mango in her lunch today," he said. "Mango, Mom. She hates it, but it's her sister's favorite, so her mom packs it anyway."

Marleigh smiled at him. "Yum," she said.

"Can we buy some too?"

"Maybe next month," she said. They both knew what that meant.

Marleigh asked at the school office about scholarships or tuition discounts. She was desperate to keep the boys together at a school that would keep them safe and give them a life so much better than hers.

"Only the Catholics give big family discounts, and they are phasing that out," the office manager said. "The school is the one money-maker for the church."

"I understand," Marleigh said, turning to leave.

"Regularly attending members of the church do get fifteen percent off tuition," the woman said.

"Where do I sign up?" Marleigh asked.

"Church Sunday. Fill out the newcomer card and turn it in at the fellowship luncheon afterwards," she said. The woman gestured for Marleigh to lean in close. She whispered, "And, you know, with everything you've been through, I can knock off another ten percent. Just don't tell anyone." She winked at Marleigh like they were in this together.

School tuition was three grand per boy. Aftercare hours were extra. She and Jace had prepaid the year, but re-enrollment was right around the corner.

Marleigh had to hold her children back that first Sunday at the luncheon. They stuffed their faces with tuna sandwiches and Goldfish crackers and ran around with their friends from school. Marleigh watched husbands and wives roll their eyes at one another conspiratorially as their children misbehaved, and she wondered what that felt like. She was all tightly held secrets and worries. What would it feel like to share a word of that with someone else? To exhale and let her shoulders fall if just for a moment? A one-bedroom apartment had opened in their building, and Marleigh had downsized their rent. There were so many of them piled together in bed that she felt like the mother of puppies, but also profoundly alone in every adult way.

She grabbed Nicky's hand. "No more today," she said.

His eyes flooded and his chin wobbled. "But—" he began, quickly stopping.

She wouldn't be cruel enough to suggest a big meal later. They both knew it would be a lie. There was an art to staying invisible.

Marleigh liked church coffee hours the best because all the children and the adults ate like they hadn't seen food in days. Soup kitchens were dead ends. Church coffees were hopeful beginnings. Little girls wearing giant hair bows and intricately smocked dresses— some of the dresses were themed, fairy tales or seasons and holidays, occasionally alma maters—sloshed pink lemonade and licked orange cheez-ball residue off their fingers before plunging their hands into the bowl of pretzels. Sunday mornings were the one time each of them could eat until they were overfull. They could do more than just take the edge off their hunger, and Marleigh didn't have to ration food between the boys, determine whose needs were greatest. The adults socialized some, but it was disinterested, distracted chatter. Nearly all eyes scanned the hall, awaiting the minister's appearance so the attendees could shake his hand, make sure their presence was noted. The choristers came in just before the minister, looking only vaguely recognizable outside of their matching robes. Max stayed in the church nursery, gulped down a bottle and some Cheerios.

Marleigh's kids fit right in. All the boys in attendance wore pants just a little too short or two long. They all wiggled inside of their tucked in shirts and belts. The little boys' hair looked fresh from sleep with the wet-palmed attempt to flatten and smooth.

"Enjoy," she told them. "But chew slowly. And be sure to thank the host family." A white-haired woman at every church always announced that Sunday's host family. Beyond that, Marleigh only had one rule for the children—they each had to fill a plate with only fruits and vegetables, and they had to eat every bite. After that, they could have all the brownies and tortilla chips they wanted. One woman complimented Marleigh on what healthy eaters her sons were. "Mine just beelines to the sweets," the woman said. "How do you do it?"

"I starve them until we get here," Marleigh said. "They'll eat anything at that point."

The woman trilled a light "ha ha" and touched Marleigh on the inside of the elbow. Hunger was one of the most powerful tools of all.

When Marleigh picked Max up from the nursery, he was tugging on his ear again. Shit, off to the doctor with him tomorrow. Twenty-five to see the doctor, fifteen bucks for the amoxicillin, another day she couldn't work.

• • •

The ringing phone was insistent. Of all the things that had been cut off recently, Marleigh wondered why she hadn't neglected the home phone bill. It was a safety issue, she told herself, a reliable way to call 911 if someone broke in. If there were an emergency, and she'd had to leave the boys home for a few minutes by themselves. She couldn't afford a babysitter every time she left the house. It wasn't because that was the number Jace would call her on when he was deployed. Before he came home and wasn't so much Jace anymore. She ignored the shrill ring.

Jason was brushing his teeth and would be ready for breakfast. She had Nicky on lockdown in the highchair, limiting what he could get into so she could get them all fed and out the door. Max crawled along at their feet into his bouncy chair. Finally, whoever was calling gave up. She took a few gulps of the Diet Coke on the counter. She'd left it sitting there, cap off, to let it flatten out. Coffee was for people who had time. She just needed caffeine.

She dumped Dollar Tree–brand Cheerios on Nicky's highchair tray and spooned strawberry applesauce into a bowl for Jason while his bread toasted. White bread with peanut butter, sliced banana. Just like Elvis. Just like Jace. The baby slurped his bottle from a bouncy chair.

"Ooooh! Applesauce! Applesauce for me," Nicky squealed. Marleigh scooped some into a plastic bowl. She dipped the spoon in, but as she raised it to Nicky's mouth, he pushed it away. "No. Mama! Do it myself."

She shook her head. "Get some in your mouth." His burgeoning independence was an adorable time suck.

The toaster pinged, and Marleigh assembled Jason's plate and poured him a cup of water. Like clockwork, he bounded into the small kitchen in an outfit of his own choosing, a bright-purple polo-type short-sleeve shirt over a too-big, emerald-green, long-sleeve T-shirt, long, navy mesh shorts, and socks pulled up to his knees.

"Brudder!" Nicky exclaimed, clapping his applesaucy hands.

Jason smiled and started climbing into his chair. "Hi, Nicky. Oh, I forgot something," he said and slid off the chair and trundled back into the boys' room. He returned with a construction-paper chain he'd made the evening before. At sight of his brother, Nicky saluted him like he was a senior officer, a ridge of applesauce sticking to his forehead. When had that started?

With the kids eating, Marleigh could finish her Diet Coke and take a few bites of a granola bar she used for packing lunches.

"I eat like you, Jash-Jashun," Nicky said. Marleigh smiled. He seemed to blend Jason and Jace in his mind. His memories were probably happier than his older brother's.

The phone rang again. At least she had finally stopped expecting and then hoping that it would be Jace on the other end of the line.

"Mrs. Holt, good morning. This is Mary Johnson with Cavalier Management. I've been trying to reach you for some time."

Shit. The granola turned to rocks in her mouth. The Diet Coke burbled, cold, in her belly. "But I—" She paid at least some of the rent every month. They couldn't kick them out if she'd at least paid some, could they? She remembered the tricks of her childhood, how to put a landlord off if you had to. Why did she pick up the phone?

"You're nearly three thousand delinquent in rent, Mrs. Holt. We've mailed notices." And stuck one on the door, which she ripped off so that Jason didn't see it. He was starting to read.

"Mommy, what's wrong?" Jason asked. She faked a smile and held up a finger—one minute.

Marleigh lowered her voice. "I'm working to make that up, Mrs. Johnson. My husband died last year. I know you know that." She was babbling, stalling. "I can pay two-seventy-five right now. I have it. I just need to get my kids to school."

"I'm afraid the time for payment plans and negotiations is well past. I need you out of the unit by Monday."

"It's Wednesday."

"It is. I could evict you by Friday, but wanted to give you the weekend."

"What a kindness," she said.

"Goodbye, Mrs. Holt."

The kitchen warped and stretched. She slumped into the chair beside Jason.

"Are you okay, Mommy?" Jason asked through a mouthful of peanut butter toast. He was worried, but still eating. Good. She could manage this.

"Mama, you okay?" Nicky parroted. He had fake Cheerios stuck to the applesauce on his cheeks. She picked them off.

"Yes, baby."

"*Mamamamamamamama*," Nicky burbled.

"Who was that on the phone?" Jason asked, meticulously wiping any residual peanut butter from the corners of his mouth and fingers.

"No one."

"You can't give no one two hundred dollars. That's so much money!"

You have no idea, son. "I wanted to buy something, but I can't afford it. Yikes! Look at the time, we have to get you monkeys off to school."

She arranged her face in something she hoped didn't look like a twenty-seven-year-old single mother of three on the verge of homelessness as she walked the boys to school. Her mother's voice in her head: *"You run with losers, that's what you end up."* Marleigh was fifteen, and Jackie had found her making out with Anton from the gym. "You should know," Marleigh had said.

As they walked, she pressed her bottom teeth against the backs of the tops to keep from crying. Nicky's body was warm against hers. He hung on to her hip with his legs. She had one arm around him and the other guiding the stroller. The knuckles of the hand pushing the stroller were white. Jason held on to the other handle. Max's feet kicked the air.

As soon as they got to school, Jason saw his friends, gave Marleigh a quick squeeze around her thigh, and trotted off. Nicky wriggled down from her. Max squirmed to get out of the stroller and toddle into the ones' classroom. She smiled at the moms who said hello or waved, her mind awash in panic, glad to have at least the empty stroller beneath her to steady her, keep her upright. She fought to calm her breathing. She had to keep it cool. After she left the school, she stumbled off the curb, narrowly avoiding the ground and received a nasty honk from a speeding Suburban.

Once home, Marleigh jumped an invisible rope until she broke a sweat and her racing heart made sense. Then she shadowboxed. Finally, she assessed what she had left to pawn. Her ring had kept them in the apartment and the boys in school. Jace hadn't left her with nothing. She could sell her car to stay in the apartment, but how long would that buy her? And without a car, they were dependent on the bus, or on places that were walkable. She had to keep the car.

Her car wouldn't fit very much. She took out all the cash she had and took it to the apartment's rental office. She negotiated a final month in her apartment.

CHAPTER THIRTY-EIGHT

Marleigh had thirty days to figure out a next move. She'd been surprised and relieved by Cavalier Management's reprieve. They must not have had anyone to fill the tiny one-bedroom. After school, Marleigh took all three boys to the park, the one that was close enough to downtown that not all of the neighbors could recognize an outsider. Yes, all the Norfolk city parks were indeed public, but they didn't always feel that way. In certain neighborhoods she could see the women angling their children away from hers to the children of the older, non-tattooed moms who clearly shopped at the same stores. Those women shrank in horror when her son offered another boy a few of his Cheez-Its, held out in his orange-stained fingertips.

Nicky cried. He was always crying when his feelings were hurt. Jason swung from one high monkey bar to the next over on the big kid section of the playground and either couldn't hear his brother or ignored him for a change, not swooping in to fix everything as he usually would.

The world would consume Nicky. He was so delicate. Marleigh adored that about him, but it terrified her, too. She thought of the boxers in Pops's old gym, some of them only a few years older than her older boys. The trainer told them to suck in their stomach, keep it hard and tight so that it wouldn't hurt so bad in the ring when they got punched. You couldn't fear getting hit because you were going to get hit. That was inevitable. And fear wore you out. For practice, the boys took off their shirts, if they hadn't already, tensed their abdominals, and the men pelted them with basketballs. Any time a boy went just a little slack, they'd hit him harder, the air blowing out with a whoosh. That had seemed mean and unnecessary when she watched as a kid. Why practice getting hit? But she saw what a nervous kid was like in the ring. Too afraid to take any opening, holding his breath, turning into sea grass on his feet.

Boys got tough by taking a few hits and then learning to throw their own. And wasn't the same true for girls? You just couldn't see the blows coming; the fists weren't wrapped in thick, bright gloves. The borders of the ring were invisible.

Nicky walked toward her. Snot and tears tracked lines in the playground dust on his cheeks, his shoulders, and neck, curved in, down. He swung the open bag of Cheez-Its against his thigh, the bag crinkling against the edges of his fraying shorts.

"They didn't want any," he said.

"I saw. You were nice to offer." He was always offering.

"They said 'gross' and ran away."

"Who cares what they think?" Marleigh had watched as the women's eyes flicked down to her ring finger, bare, then to Max in the stroller. To the children running around the playground. "Go play," she told him.

"I want to sit with you."

"I'm not always going to be here. You need to stop letting them bother you."

His eyes went watery. His chin puckered. "But Mom."

"Go play," she said.

He looked at her, betrayed, for a moment. Then turned around to face the playground. She reached out and pinched the skin at the back of the knee, hard. He jumped away but silenced his "ow." She felt it more than heard it. If she let him be soft, he'd stay soft. She would miss his soft. She knew it.

A red-haired man holding the hand of a similarly red-haired little girl walked to their bench. Marleigh's neck burned. They must have seen her pinch Nicky.

"I haven't seen that move in a long time," the man said. "My mother did that to me whenever I reached out for something hot—the stove, fireplace, you name it. She'd say, 'Hot! Hot!' and pinch me. I never knew how painful it was to actually get burned. I thought fire pinched." His eyes were a shocking blue.

Marleigh laughed louder and harder than she had in longer than she could remember. "I'm Mark," he said. "And this is Ariel." The girl twisted her long, freckled arms around his legs.

"My two monkeys are Jason and Nicky, over there, under the pirate ship. This little guy here is Max." Mark's eyes never moved from her when she spoke. He looked at her like a man looks at a woman. It had been a long time. She felt self-conscious in her faded black shift.

"Don't be shy, Ari, go play." The girl took tentative steps toward Marleigh's boys. "Can I sit here and pretend to be a great dad?"

Marleigh laughed again. "You've already witnessed my *A* material."

• • •

The following day, Jason was silent and sullen on the walk home from school. His silence had a different flavor than his tired quiet or his thoughtful quiet. This silence held static electricity. He brooded. The whole dynamic was off, come to think of it. The only teacher who stopped Marleigh to speak was Nicky's rising threes teacher.

"I'm not sure how to say this," the older woman began, "but Nick bit a little girl today." Nicky's plump hand went limp in hers. She looked down at him.

"What?" Marleigh asked, understanding what the teacher had said but trying to make sense of it. The woman had to have it twisted. Nicky got bitten. He never bit. Nicky kept his head tilted down. She could feel him shaking.

"I'm trying to get to the bottom of what happened," the teacher said, crouching down slowly to Nicky's level. "This isn't like you, Nicholas," she said. Looking up at Marleigh, she continued. "I wouldn't have believed it if I hadn't seen it myself. He's never laid a finger, or anything else, on another child."

Nicky always gave way, whether it was because Jason demanded he do something—Nicky idolized his big brother—or because the baby needed something and Marleigh made him wait. Nicky never came first. She was glad she had come to Nicky's classroom first, rather than Max's room. She hinged over and tipped his tear-stained face to hers. "What happened, Bud?" she asked. He shook his head. "Nicky?"

"I bit her," he mumbled.

"Bit who?" She was already trying to control the damage. The school policy on biting was frequently communicated—two strikes and you're out. No questions asked. But she was also panicking. Why did he bite someone? What happened to cause it? Part of her was the tiniest bit proud of her son for not just taking it.

"Caroline," he said. The teacher nodded.

"Shit," Marleigh whispered before she could stop herself. The teacher suppressed a smile. *Shit. Triple shit.* Caroline Winston was one of a set of identical twins, the late-in-life daughters of Emily and Larry Winston. Biting Caroline Winston could be an expulsion-worthy first offense. Emily had quit her law practice after giving birth. You learned that as soon as you learned her name. He owned a car dealership; their perfect twins smiled out from every ad. Emily organized the preschool carnival and the teacher appreciation breakfast each year. And she had mistaken Marleigh for Jason and Nicky's nanny once. Emily was closer to Marleigh's mother's age than her own, though very significantly better preserved. Jackie had been pickled, not preserved.

The teacher attempted comfort. "He didn't break the skin," she said. "But, obviously, Caroline's parents are very upset. Neither child wants to tell me what happened. They were playing and talking. Then I heard Caroline cry and I looked up to see Nicky's face on her arm. He pulled away as soon as he saw me. She came over and told me he'd bitten her. He admitted it right away."

Marleigh ran her fingers through Nicky's curls. "What happened, sweetie? Mrs. Rogers and I want to help." He pressed his face against her chest and shook his head, trying to burrow inside of her.

"It's very out of character," Mrs. Rogers said. "I have to write it up, but I'll be sure to include that. I assured the Winstons that Nicky's immunization record was up to date."

Rage flashed through Marleigh. "They're not dogs." Nicky woofed, just audibly, breaking the tension and making both women laugh.

"Between you and me, the Winston girls can be pretty nasty. I'll make sure the director knows that, too."

"Thank you," Marleigh said, so grateful for this woman. "I'm so sorry this happened."

"Me too. I hope you can get to the bottom of it. I'll send the incident write-up to you, the director, and the Winstons. This is the first incident Nick's ever had. Hopefully that will be the end of it." The teacher looked like she was about to say more, but instead pursed her lips and frowned.

"But if the Winstons want to push this further . . ." Marleigh trailed off.

Mrs. Rogers gave her a sympathetic nod. "The director has a good head on her shoulders. Hopefully the Winstons can't turn it."

On the way home, Nicky started sobbing. "She pulled at my shirt and pulled and said I smell like poo, and I only have two shirts and I smell like poo. I told her to stop. She wouldn't stop, Mommy. Do I smell like poo?"

"Of course not, Nicky."

"Why are you so quiet?" Marleigh asked Jason. Jason flinched, but he didn't answer. The baby burbled in his stroller. Nicky had one arm looped through her arm pushing the stroller and the thumb of his other hand in his mouth. Normally, he wouldn't be caught dead outside of his covers sucking his thumb. He was still sniffling.

"Nothing," Jason said, his face still down at his sneakers. What a role reversal. Generally, Jason didn't experience an emotion or sensation without verbalizing it. "This tag is itchy. It's too tight. My hands are sticky. Brother took my toy." She'd never had to work something out of him before. He held the straps of his small school backpack tight in his hands. Normally, the pouch drooped at the base of his back. His knuckles were white. Why must both of them have a crisis on the same day?

"Jason, what's the matter?"

"Worry about Nicky, Mom."

Max began squirming and fussing half a block from their apartment, angrily gnawing his fists, bringing a pinch of milk to her nipples. That happened less and less lately. She had to take the opportunity to nurse him when she could, both for his health and for her below-the-minimum balance bank account.

"See, Mom, worry about him," Jason said, an unfamiliar edge to his voice. He stomped off, but she heard him puttering around in his room while she nursed Max. The baby was warm in her arms, eyes closed, kissing the sky in his sleep. Nicky breathed deep and easy, curled up beside her on the couch. His breathing hypnotized her. Her body was too heavy to raise and so were her eyelids. Two of three were right here and Jason was just in the bedroom.

She had a nightmare. Nicky was snuffling over something like she'd seen a rat terrier do to a squirrel once, shaking it back and forth until everything flopped still. Jason appeared, too, red smeared across his mouth and cheeks, something like a bandage dangling from his teeth, the kind from an old war movie. She couldn't get the boys to look up at her, to stop what they were doing. Nicky, face down and growling. Snarling. "Boys, stop! What are you doing? You're scaring Mommy."

"So hungry," both boys murmured in unison, like zombies. "So hungry. So yummy." Marleigh patted the Baby Bjorn on her chest, certain to feel the baby, but it was empty, except for a gauzy blanket. She'd seem that gauzy blanket before, dangling from a mouth. She could hear crying, but she couldn't tell where it was coming from. Suddenly, Nicky lifted his head. A baby-doll leg, shaking side to side in his teeth.

"No!"

More crying. Louder crying. "Mommy!"

It was Jason, holding a frantic Max. She was awake. It had all been a dream, thank God. Jason held the crying baby out at her. "He fell off your lap."

She waited to feel horror, but all she felt was tired. Jason handed Max to her, and he slowly quieted. *"Shh shh shh!"* What she wouldn't give to have someone give her a break, to take someone out of her hands, something off her plate. For a moment, anger flashed through her when Jason put the baby in her arms. Couldn't he just hold him for a minute? It was hardly rocket science.

None of this—her aloneness, their poverty, her exhaustion—was Jason's fault. Or Nicky's. Or the baby's. Not directly. But if she hadn't gotten pregnant with Jason, none of this would have happened. She lied to herself; Jace could have been a summer fling, a forgotten fuck. She would have finished school. She would be able to pay her rent. She would be able to sleep at night. She wouldn't be taunted by Jace's face on those little bodies. It was all his fault. She was old and done and over at twenty-eight because of him. And there was no one else to help. He'd left them. He thought they'd be better off without him. Damn it, Jace.

"Go to your room," she said, thinking, *I don't want to see your face. Get out of my sight.* Isn't that what her mother always told her? Maybe everything was Jason's fault, but he didn't have to know that yet. They were all paying for it. She didn't want to punish her boys for her life. They were already being punished.

She had to wake up, get off the couch, and move around. Her body was leaden, held in place to the cushion beneath her like there was a magnet connecting her to the sleeper sofa rings beneath her. She had sunk so deeply into the tired, squished cushion that she could feel the springs, coiled and ready. She wished she could sink through the surface and fall down into the dark. Just the loose change that she'd already searched for and used, the hollow top of a marker, a broken toy. If they couldn't find her, couldn't see her, they wouldn't need her. She wanted to hide from her children, from everyone, from that look on Jason's face.

"You dropped the baby." Had she dropped him? Was that part of the dream? Max was back in her arms now and her elbows were achy. He was right there. She needed some incentive, a motivator to move. She chewed the inside of her lip, gently at first, searing the inside of her mouth. She kept chewing until the skin was lumpy, making cankers. She stopped only when she broke through, a sharp twinge, a taste of metal and salt. She could still bleed. She had to get off the couch.

She tucked the baby between cushions in the corner of the sofa; Max was almost asleep again. Nicky hadn't woken. Max had survived a slide off her lap, hadn't he? Marleigh walked to the bedroom door quietly. Jason was hiding something from her and that wasn't like him. It felt like sneaking up on his father, but with Jace, over time it became predictable what she would find. He hadn't been particularly good at hiding anything.

Jason stood over a little trash can, his back to the door. He was tearing something up and dropping the little pieces of paper like snow. He took a piece of paper—a few strips lay on his bed—folded it several times then ripped it into strips, just like he'd seen her do with credit card and utility bills, back when she paid them in full. She stepped into his room. He sensed her, crumpling the remaining papers in his fists and holding them tight.

"What are you doing?" he asked her before she could ask him, already turning it onto her. He had been paying attention all those years. He furiously shredded the papers as she walked towards him and spit on top of the small pile of trash. "It's nothing, Mom. Just trash."

"Jason. What—"

She grabbed his arms just as Nicky exclaimed, "Oh, wow! Are these for me?" Marleigh, confused, looked to him. Three T-shirts were folded nicely beside new shorts, new to him, anyway. "Are these mine?" he asked again.

"Yeah," Jason answered. "They don't fit me anymore." New clothes for his little brother so he wouldn't get teased. Marleigh was emotionally punch drunk. She was touched and disoriented by what Jason had done for Nicky.

"I'm gonna try 'em on," Nicky said, shimmying out of his clothes. "But I'll keep 'em nice for tomorrow."

Nicky would be okay tomorrow, walking into school with gifts from his brother, the clothes off his back, better than armor. "Thank you, Jason," Marleigh said. "That was really kind."

"He needs new clothes," Jason mumbled, fists still tight. He was too wary of her right now. She needed to back off. She couldn't get him to confide in her this way.

"I know he does," she said. "So do you. We all do. You're such a good big brother."

"That girl's a brat, mom," Jason said. "I wanna punch her. It's good Nicky bit her."

"She seems like a nasty piece of business," Marleigh said, her mother's phrase tumbling out of her mouth before she could stop it. She knelt beside him, and he let her hug him. "I wish we could beat up everyone who was mean to any of you, too. But you boys need to stay in school, and you can't do that by beating everyone up, right?" She was going for a laugh but didn't get one.

"Dad would let me. Handle it like a man."

"He did say that. But handling it like a man sometimes means not using your fists when you want to."

He nodded, but pulled away. "I'm hungry," he said. Conversation over for the moment.

CHAPTER THIRTY-NINE

Marleigh didn't have to wait long to discover what was going on with Jason. Normally, she remained in the hallway as Jason walked into his classroom, gave a quick wave, and left. The kindergartners and first graders all felt too old to be walked in by their parents. But as soon as Jason opened the door and walked through, into his classroom, his teacher walked out and into the hallway.

"Mrs. Ummm. Marleigh? Jason's mom," she said, sounding breathless. Marleigh turned around. "I have been sending these with Jason, but I haven't heard from you." Chubby fingers extended a folded white piece of paper, just like the ones she'd seen Jason tearing. Marleigh took the paper from her. "Please," she said, "it's important that we meet." Marleigh opened the note. *Urgent parent-teacher conference. I'll send Jason to aftercare at dismissal—no charge—please meet me in the classroom. Sincerely, Mrs. Shields.*

"Yes, of course I'll be here." Something leaden dropped in Marleigh's belly. Jason had been lying to her, and for how long? She saw the panic in his eyes as the teacher had flown out the door past him. Had he bitten someone, too? Or punched someone as he'd threatened? Surely the penalty for an older child had to be far worse.

When had Jason become so angry and secretive?

Marleigh had to be back to school at dismissal, no later, and she knew she had reservations for tattoos that would take her at least five hours. Now she had less than three. She prayed she would get into the tattoo parlor before anyone else arrived so no one would hear her make the call. She got lucky; the key turned the deadbolt, and she opened the heavy doors into darkness. She went straight to the computer to find the schedule for the day. A good tattoo shop was a business like any other. She found the customer and his number. She liked him, had worked on him before. She hissed out relief when her call went straight to voicemail. "I need to reschedule our appointment. I have a family emergency. I am so sorry for the inconvenience." She left her cell phone number, hoping he'd call her back directly and not the shop. Before she met Jace, she'd hated when the mom waitresses had called in to bail on their shifts because their kids were sick, or the babysitter hadn't shown up. Now she was that girl. And this would cost her a hundred fifty in cash. *Please reschedule. Please reschedule.* She hit delete on the appointment on the computer calendar, though the office manager was the only person authorized to make changes. Immediate crisis averted.

Now she had to clear her mind and focus on her morning piece. She still did good work and enjoyed it and the confidence that she would end the day with money in her pocket calmed her. It was a relief. She cleaned her tools and prepped her sketch. It was to be a tribute. A memorial piece. A trident with a team number to stretch the length of a muscular calf. The Latin *mal ad osteo*, forever bad to the bone. The guy had been her customer's swim buddy through BUD/S, and they'd ended up in the same platoon in the teams. He'd gotten quiet after that explanation, and Marleigh had no desire to press him. She had done plenty of tribute tattoos, probably too many. But she respected the desire for an external mark to reflect the internal wound. What tattoo could she create to tell her own story? She worked, and the tattoo pen buzzed, wiped clean, buzzed again, creating lines on flesh. Only twice in two hours did Jason and his teacher intrude into her thoughts, but each time she felt her hands sweat inside her gloves, so she forced the worry away.

The work was beautiful, and she was proud of it. She smiled at the man's quiet "hooyah" as he looked at his calf in the mirror. "Thank you," he said, giving her a fifty-dollar bill as a tip before paying the rest of it.

Marleigh felt herself gape, even though she'd earned it—the work was detailed and beautiful, just as he wanted. She couldn't stay cool in the face of cash. "You're welcome. Come back and see me!" She tried not to look like she was rushing to finish cleaning up her space, but she only had a few minutes until she had to be back at school.

As she walked by the front desk, the shop owner popped out of the doorway into the back office. "You have an afternoon appointment," he said.

"But—" she sputtered.

"You only deleted it on that screen. The system has an archive."

Fuck. "I called and told him I needed to reschedule. It's my—"

"Your kid. I know. He called back and rebooked."

"Oh, good," she said, immediately relieved.

"With Gabbi."

"Oh." Marleigh nodded.

"I've worked with you, Mar. I know shit hasn't been easy since Jace died. But I need to be able to count on you. You're canceling on people right and left."

"I need this job, Jameson. This is temporary. I'm sorry." She looked desperate.

"Look, he's coming back here. We didn't lose the business. But if it happens again, I'm going to have to let you go."

She tried not to puke right there on the floor. "I'll make sure it doesn't," she said. Of course it would happen again. She wasn't sure how much more she could take, not that there was much choice.

She had a fleeting impulse to skip the meeting with Jason's teacher. What had he done to make the woman so frantic? Something she didn't understand until becoming a parent; when a child is in trouble, the mother is in trouble, too, and generally deeper. And she was a mess, wasn't she? Three kids with a man who couldn't handle it and who left them with nothing. She'd made it as far as high school and was about to get fired from a tattoo shop.

. . .

Mrs. Shields, the teacher, was seated when Marleigh arrived. She kept smoothing her skirt. At least she looked like a real teacher, not the size-two designer-jean-wearing part-timers. She had pulled another small chair close to hers and facing her for Marleigh.

"Thank you for coming, Ms—"

"Marleigh is fine," she said and sat. *Out with it, lady.* The teacher looked nervous and kept starting to speak and then stopping. "What's wrong?" she asked, breaking the tense silence. She waited for it. A tantrum, a broken toy, a fight, pulled pigtails. Jason was so responsible that none of this seemed plausible, but she had to prepare herself for the worst.

"There isn't an easy way to say this. Jason has been stealing." Not Jason, the boy who folded almost brand-new clothes to give to his brother. Her hands wrestled in her lap. The bright primary color space. Letters in cursive on the wall. Toys in bins.

"What are you talking about?" Marleigh finally found the words.

"It took me a few days to figure it out," the woman began. "I was missing a few dollars from my purse last Monday, and a couple more each day after that. Then I saw Jason in the second-grade room during recess. He had only taken a couple of ones and seventy-five cents in change, and he put it right back when I asked him to. I followed him in because I was worried. He'd had a stomachache on the playground several days in a row and needed to come in to use the bathroom. Silly me, I thought he was maybe having gluten problems."

The room around Marleigh was swaying. She had a biter and a thief. She knew what her mother would do in this situation—threaten and scream and cajole, blaming the teacher and the school, forever marking Marleigh as one to watch. She chose differently. Her eyes filled. She clenched her jaw to try and will them back in. "I'm so sorry," she said.

"When I confronted Jason, he said he needed the money so you could stay in your house and for diapers for the baby."

The exposure of their situation hit harder than the revelation of Jason's stealing. Marleigh prepared herself to deny it, but a flush heat crept up her neck.

"I had no idea things were that bad," the woman said. "That's why I haven't gone to the director."

Oh, thank God. Marleigh had to control this, but how? She was dizzy on her feet but still dancing. "I have tried to protect the boys from as much as possible since their father died," Marleigh said, the thought of the woman's pity curdling in her stomach. But she had to grab on to the lifeline Mrs. Shields was throwing. "But it's been very difficult. With the baby still in the hospital when Jace was discharged from the Navy, there wasn't anything left." Marleigh looked down at her lap, knowing it was crucial to hit the right target. Too much and the woman would be on the phone with child protective services. "The hospital bills." Too little and Jason could be expelled. "It's all very humiliating," Marleigh said, slowly looking up to meet the woman's gaze. "Jace was from Nebraska. We don't have family here." An out and out lie. "But we're okay, getting back on our feet. I think Jason is exaggerating his role of man of the house." She shook her head.

"Poor guy," his teacher said. "That is some heavy responsibility for someone so young."

"This school, this environment, it's so important to the boys. It's all they've ever known. I just want them to be able to stay." Marleigh knew she'd do anything if it meant the boys could stay.

"I'm definitely supposed to report this," she said. "But I thought there might be extenuating circumstances. And Jason is such a bright boy. Under different circumstances, I could see inviting him up into one of the advanced classes."

"I'll make sure he pays it back and that this will never happen again." Twice she told the same lie in one day. "How much did he take?"

"As far as I know, he took forty dollars. He pulled the bathroom trick several times before I realized what was happening. I asked him if he'd taken anything from anyone else. He said no. There's no reason for children to bring money, and I haven't heard from any parents about items missing from backpacks. If I do, I'll have no choice but to turn him in."

"Of course," Marleigh replied. Where in the hell was she going to get forty bucks? She put her hand in her pocket, the fifty was still warm. She slipped it out of her pocket and handed it to the teacher, her fingers trembling. "I can't thank you enough for looking out for him."

"You don't have to pay it back today. It's not really an emergency for me."

Of course it isn't. "Yes, I do," Marleigh said. Money would always be an emergency for Marleigh. Until she was dead. Maybe afterwards.

"Your rent, your apartment. Is it really in jeopardy?"

Marleigh shook her head. The lies came so readily. "You know how kids are. So much worry and imagination. This is my fault. I must have said too much in front of him this month about some bills that have come due. He's so serious and responsible."

"That he is," the teacher said with a small smile. "I'm glad we had this conversation. I would hate for United Pres to lose Jason. And, of course, vice versa."

"Oh my god," Marleigh said, "me too."

She wondered if the teacher would make change for the fifty. She said Jason had taken forty. She was going to use that tip to pay for utilities, at least part of them. Marleigh knew she had almost two weeks past the bill's due date before they'd shut off power. The stack of all she owed and would owe kept getting taller. She'd let the teacher keep the extra ten since she hadn't turned him in.

Mrs. Rogers reached for her purse and extracted a ten-dollar bill. Finally, the tiniest break.

She swallowed hard, determined not to cry. "Thank you. So much."

. . .

Marleigh had to straighten her hair with her fingertips and soften her jaw before picking up Jason and the other boys so none of the teachers would sense anything was off. All she wanted to do was punch to transfer the energy she carried through her fists to something or someone else. She wanted to sweat until her body had nothing left to weep. She wanted to sway and move and bob and hold her belly hard against the punches. But she had to be Mom right now. She picked up Nicky and then Jason and walked them outside.

"Where's Max?" Nicky asked.

"We'll get him in a minute. We need to talk, boys."

"Mommy. I'm sorry. I—"

"No, Jason. Listen to me." She wanted Jason to have to ask her what happened with his teacher, but she was running so hot with fear and panic and worry she could barely walk the boys across the parking lot and onto the sidewalk before she hissed, "You can't ever talk like that to your teachers, Jason. Not ever. They can never know that I was worried about losing our house or that I can't pay the bills."

He looked up at her, confused. "I—I still have most of the money," he said. "I wanted to get to a hundred so we can have a/c for the summer. It's hot."

The things he remembered, her complaining that a/c cost her an extra hundred over the summer. They wouldn't even be in the apartment for the summer. "That was stupid, Jason." His eyes filled with tears. She was being brutal, yes, but he had to hear her and understand. "All of that money comes to me. I already paid your teacher. What would you do if you got kicked out of school at the end of the year? Huh?"

"I dunno. I'm sorry. I wanted to help."

"You help by going to school and watching out for your brothers and keeping your mouth shut. All of you." She crouched down and took the chins of the two older boys in her hands. "We have each other. But if your teachers think I'm not taking care of you or we don't have enough money, they will take you away from me. And who knows where you'll end up." Her voice shook. The boys studied her. "How we live needs to be our secret for a while. It's gonna get better. I'm going to make it better. But you look out for each other, and I'll figure out the money, okay?"

The boys' mouths drooped open. They watched her. She had to make them understand. If she lost them after Jace, after all of this, what would be the point? They were all she had left of him, of the life they'd promised each other. She grabbed one of both boy's hands in hers and squeezed. "You can't trust your teachers with our secrets. We can't trust anybody but each other. I can't have you taken far away from me. You're my babies and I'm your mommy." They were a unit, and she would collapse without them, their need and their mess, their hunger and their future pushing her always onward. She trembled with the knowledge of it. She squeezed their hands.

Marleigh was only eight, not that much older than Jason, when she'd ruined her relationship with her parents for good. She knew better than to trust the guidance counselor and her soft hair and sweaters, the brightly colored tights she wore each day. The woman enticed her into the office with brownies and an excuse to miss history class. The padded chair was soft beneath her, the brownie warm and gooey in her mouth. The counselor confused her. She asked her silly, meaningless questions like what her favorite animal was (dog, of course) and did she have a favorite TV show. She said *Full House*, and thought maybe life went smoother without moms in the house.

Marleigh relaxed, so when the woman asked, "Do your parents hurt you?" she answered, "Not really. Mostly just each other," before she could stop herself. She didn't know about her father's priors. And she didn't tell the woman that it was just as likely to be her mom wailing on her dad as the other way around.

"Ow!" Nicky whined.

"Do you understand?" she scolded.

"Yes, Mom! Ow! You're hurting us."

"Let's go home." Yes, home. She could lock them inside and no one could reach them. She could feed the baby and read to Jason and Nicky.

"Max, Mom," Jason said hesitantly. "We have to get Max."

"Right, yes. Of course."

They would watch cartoons and they would be safe from the world. They didn't have to go back outside until they wanted to. In there, everything was okay. Out here was where the world could get to them. They would stay inside possibly through the entire weekend.

CHAPTER FORTY

Marleigh awoke in the dark, each night, a running tally of debt in her mind. Food, school for the boys, diapers for Max, gas for the car, car insurance. Did she have room on either of her credit cards? Health insurance cancellation notices. How much she could pay Lynetha for the few weeks she said Marleigh and the boys could stay at her place before her boyfriend and his kids moved in. Nicky in trouble for biting and now the scrutiny of Jason's teacher. In the end, her landlord gave her an additional, final, month. If she didn't leave before then, the police would be called. She couldn't put the boys through that.

Marleigh had been caught in a rip current once when she was twelve, on one of those Saturdays, rare and disorienting, when her parents decided to act like parents. They had taken her down to the oceanfront, the actual Atlantic Ocean. She was an okay swimmer after long days on the beaches along the Chesapeake Bay, but not much was required in that water. It was shallow, tidal and the currents were minimal, low like the salinity. The bracing blue of the ocean was different. The cold tightened her calves and prickled her skin. She looked back to her parents, already asleep in the sun, her father's belly rising and falling regularly. Smoke from her mother's cigarette waning.

"Don't go out too far," they cautioned. How far is too far on the horizon?

They'd placed their towels in the residential section of the beach where there were no lifeguards, just marine flags posted every so often. A big red square snapped in the wind. The surf wasn't too rough but still a nice change from the warm, lazy roll of the piss-warm Chesapeake. She dove into a breaker and was softly tumbled. When she stood up and wiped salt water from her eyes it took her a moment to find her parents. She had moved swiftly and unknowingly down the beach. They certainly weren't looking for her. Why would she bother looking for them? She went back into the water. There appeared to be a sand bar just out past the breaking waves. She could get beyond the surf and stand half in the sun and half in the briny Atlantic. She dove under and couldn't keep her eyes open long in the salty water. She gave it her best guess, her strong legs kicking, lungs tight in need of air.

When Marleigh burst through the surface she was facing the horizon, a glittering sun sparkle that splashed her face. She flailed around trying to find the shore. She finally saw the sand, so much farther away than it should be. So far away that she couldn't make out any of the people on the shore. Dots of color and flesh. She tried to swim to shore, but with each stroke she was pushed farther out to sea.

"Mom! Dad!" She yelled, knowing as she screamed that it was pointless. She couldn't get their attention in the small gym. Or at home. No way she could in so much loud water. She swallowed salt water and choked, her arms and legs tiring as she treaded water, trying to keep her head above the surface. She knew how to fight, but fighting was making her weak. And regardless, her body was being carried by a current she couldn't control. That was how her life felt now.

She was being towed along and slowly drowned by her life. She may pop her head up a few more times and lap up clear air, but just enough to fool herself that this time she would stay up, which made the inevitable plunge back beneath the surface that much worse.

That day at the beach, she could remember the moment she decided to stop fighting. She was going wherever the water took her whether she liked it or not. She loosened her body and made herself long, wondering what it was going to feel like to drown, and would she know it as it happened? She was angry that her parents didn't know what was happening to her. Maybe this would scare them enough to care.

She turned onto her back and floated, eyes closed to the bright sun. Salt spray on her face. She didn't sink as she expected to. Instead, she kept floating. She began hearing voices. Children squealing in the surf. Feet splashing. Sand grazed her butt. She lay in the surf a moment, exhausted and a little amazed. She'd been gently rolled back to shore, but once on her hands and knees and then wobbly on her feet she realized the hotels on the boardwalk were much closer, too close. They'd shimmered, hazy in the distance when she helped her parents lay out their blankets and position their cooler in the shade. She had gone such a long way. She had to get back. She would be in so much trouble for being gone so long, for making them worry. She was so thirsty. Her lips stuck together, crusty with salt. Her lips blistered from the sun. She tried to run on the sand, but her feet felt floppy and strange beneath her, so she walked as fast as she could, staring straight ahead, certain she'd encounter her parents headed right for her, angry, towels rolled under their arms, "We need to open the gym" on their tongues.

Marleigh saw many other families. Parents burying their children in the sand, dads teaching their sons how to surf cast, elaborate castles being shaped in the sand. Babies shielded by umbrellas, kids in floaties, hats with ties under their chubby chins. She started to panic that maybe she had gone too far, or in the wrong direction. How long had she been gone? And then she saw them. Her mother lay on her stomach now, her freckled back red. Her father hadn't moved, his belly pinking.

No one had come to rescue her then, and no one was coming to her rescue now. That drowning would have been simple, clean; she wouldn't have brought anyone down with her. But now the responsibility for her family's success or failure was hers alone. She had always been scrappy. She had always been a fighter. She would at very least keep the kids' heads above water even if she couldn't keep her own up.

• • •

Regardless of where Marleigh and the boys lived, she worked to foster friendships with the kids in the boys' classes by offering to the mothers, and occasional fathers who dropped them off, to pick their kids up when she picked hers up and take them to the park nearby. When it had been one of those rare, good weeks, she would treat for small cups of froyo or a bomb pop from the ice cream truck. Eventually, the parents felt compelled to reciprocate and invited her kids over.

Jason and Nicky came home stuffed with snacks and cool from an afternoon spent in wantonly cold air-conditioning, eyes glazed from playing video games. It was worth the inevitable complaining about their own lives and possessions by comparison. Each of them had packed every bag and suitcase they owned to bring to Lynetha's. They slept on mattresses on the floor in the house that waited for its new furniture, its new occupants. But they were safe and indoors. Marleigh was so thankful to her old friend, who kept refusing to take her money.

Through visits to their school friends' houses, Marleigh was giving them glimpses into another world, another life that was possible for some people. "Work hard and you can have all of that," she said, over and over.

"But you work hard, Mommy," Nicky said.

Her parents had told her a better life was impossible for her, that she didn't deserve any better. She wouldn't fill her sons' heads with that poison. "Stay in school and work hard," she said. "Don't get distracted." She'd gotten distracted.

Nearly every day after Vacation Bible School, blessedly free summer care, Marleigh took the boys to the park to play with Ariel while she talked with Mark. She swiped on mascara and lip gloss in the car on the way there. "Fancy Mommy, oooh!" Nicky said. Mark arrived each afternoon with a small cooler stocked full of Diet Coke for her and waters and fruit for the kids.

Mark wiped a sweaty can off on his pant leg before handing the Diet Coke to her. "Those seem to be your favorite."

Her fingertips brushed his. "Yes. It's the fuel that keeps me going."

After a week of sweltering park playdates, Mark suggested that next time they could meet at his house. "There's some outdoor play space and we wouldn't have to pack up provisions."

"Whoa! This is way better than the park," Jason announced when he saw the fenced-in yard, playset, and overflowing tub of soccer, basketball, and kickballs through Mark and Ariel's sliding glass kitchen door.

Ariel took his hand and waved for Nicky to follow. "C'mon, I'll show you." Max half-toddled, half-crawled behind them.

They stood for a moment and watched the children from the doorway. The ceiling vent blew cold, even though the door was open. Marleigh closed her eyes. "So much better than the park."

Mark brushed his hand against her hip, then rested it there, just for a moment. Testing.

"Mom! Come *ousside*," Nicky said. "You gotta see."

Mark moved his hand to the base of her back, and they walked into the backyard together.

Mark couldn't have been less like Jace if he tried; he always wore his short-sleeved shirt tucked in and appeared ready for an imminent round of golf, twill pants and no-show socks. That was a holdover from the pre-Ariel days, he said, when he had free time. Women must justify their leisure whether they were the breadwinner or not.

Men who worked and had children seemed free from that worry. Funny how that worked. And Mark had full-time diaper duty.

"I think it's really cool that you stay home with Ariel. Not many men would do that."

"It's a great way to meet women, though, don't you think?"

God, it felt so good to laugh.

"At the end of the day, economics won. Heather's job can pay the bills solo. It just made sense. And it cost a small fortune to get pregnant with Ariel, so if we ever decide to try for another one . . ." His words trailed off.

They were gentle and sparing with the names Heather and Jace.

Marleigh had never considered what it would be like not to be able to get pregnant. "We're on opposite ends of the spectrum that way." And so many others. Small fortune. She wanted to see one of those one day.

"Let's just say I dropped the ball." His pale face flushed, and he cleared his throat. "My boys aren't good swimmers. I'm the weak link. So, it's a miracle Ariel is here at all."

"I can't imagine what that's like."

"Luckily, she hasn't asked for a sister or brother, but she thinks Jason and Nicky are so great I'm sure she will soon. Not sure what I'll say. But you do it all on your own. I have nothing to complain about, zero."

"I don't have a choice, Mark."

He rested his palm on her shoulder.

Nicky bounded over to them, one sneaker nearly falling off. "Mr. Mark, can you tie my shoe?"

Mark kept his hand on Marleigh's shoulder, his eyes on her face, until Nicky landed a filthy, worn shoe on his knee. Mark tied it without breaking eye contact.

"There you go," Mark said. "Have fun, guys. Your mom and I are going to go inside to cool off."

CHAPTER FORTY-ONE

On the last Sunday in August, Marleigh was dizzy with hunger as she walked into a large Methodist church in a fancy neighborhood, a quick three-block walk from the bus stop. The hungry gurgles of her insides were audible over the chorus. Her mouth was dry, the corners of her lips stuck together. She gulped lemonade and tried to look casual. She must have drunk too much, too fast, because she knew she would vomit. She told the older boys to stick together and watch Max; she'd be right back. She ducked into the women's room and flushed the toilet to mask the sounds of her gagging. She cooled herself with a wet paper towel and went back into coffee hour to find her children happily stuffing their faces.

"My dear," an oldish woman said and put her hand on Marleigh's forearm. She wasn't old enough to have Kleenex stuffed in her cuff, but she was somewhere between Marleigh and that old. Marleigh looked up at her. She seemed familiar, but the well of church ladies tended to look alike. "Your children are growing so quickly."

How did she know which children were Marleigh's? Right, at this church, the children had to sit through the mass. They were together in the pews, and then they walked in to coffee hour together. Other denominations sent the children to nurseries or Bible studies during the church service. Each Sunday she told some curious older woman or another, "We're visiting the church. But I've already filled out the newcomer card"—she intercepted the follow-up question, smiling. Each church, regardless of denomination, wanted her name, phone number, and email address. The body and blood of Christ weren't spilled for free.

"I'm sure you have," the woman who touched her arm responded.

Marleigh was sure she recognized her. "Have we met?"

"Not officially," the woman answered. "I'm so glad your middle boy seems to be feeling much better."

"What?" Marleigh asked, feeling panicky and trapped. Nicky had heat rash for much of the summer. His neck had been red and angry for weeks. How did this woman know?

"No need to raise your voice, Marleigh. I'm Belinda."

Marleigh stared at her. Like the good witch from the *Wizard of Oz*? No, that's not right.

"I've seen you here, and at St. Paul the Apostle, Christ and St. Luke's, the Unitarian Church on Freemason and Sacred Heart, too."

Marleigh could feel the color draining from her face. She hoped it was empty stomach nausea, not the free-food-on-Sundays-jig-is-up nausea.

"Don't panic, young lady. I'm a choral floater." Belinda winked. "An impostor, too, but a paid one. I sing in choirs at churches all over the state."

Marleigh exhaled her held breath. "I, I see. The hymns were beautiful today."

"I love to sing, and I love to bring families together, so it's perfect."

Marleigh couldn't figure out if the woman was batty or serious. "That's nice. I should probably collect my children."

"One boy is right there filling up his lemonade again, and the other is over there at the dessert table with your youngest. They're just fine. But how are you? How are you feeling?"

Who was this Belinda, and why was she so damn nosy? "I'm fine, thank you. I, um, didn't get what the boys had."

"I meant, how are you feeling? How far along are you?"

She had gotten quite thin and no longer had regular periods. One less thing to worry about, the cost of tampons. "I don't know what you mean," Marleigh said, barely above a whisper. She wasn't pregnant. She couldn't be.

"I can understand your modesty. I've never seen the father with you."

Marleigh's jaw hinged open before she could catch it. No more at this church. She'd get her kids and leave, and they'd never come back here. "I need to leave," she said, trying to act insulted rather than scared. She nodded at Jason from across the room, their signal. *"Go get your brothers."*

The woman tightened her grip on Marleigh's arm. "I meant what I said. I love bringing families together. I know so many couples who would treasure that extra mouth to feed. I can get you the care you need, money for expenses, and you won't have another child you obviously can't afford."

Marleigh pulled her hand away.

"Think about it," Belinda said. "I'm sure I'll be seeing you around. The real money is in surrogacy, but we can talk about that next time."

What exactly did the woman mean? Marleigh chomped on a cracker as her boys came back to her, but it turned to sand in her mouth. That woman was crazy; she had no idea what she was talking about. *Shit. Maybe some idea.*

It had only happened a couple of times. The off-handed suggestion of moving the playdate from the humid park to Mark's house for a change. The comfort of a warm, full belly as all the kids napped on the floor of the playroom ("daycare has them well-trained") and the comfort of a man's heft, his skin against her skin, a reminder that she was real. She was so tired and stressed out and trying to save money and make money, but money was always going out faster than she could ever bring it in; her reality had become filmy and hard to count on.

• • •

Their time at Lynetha's was nearly up. Where would they go? Marleigh needed to ask her mother, she knew it. What woman would refuse her own grandchildren? Jackie, Marleigh knew. She could do it. Her mother was poisonous, her awfulness contagious to everyone around her, and Marleigh had spent the boys' lives protecting them from her. How would she explain to them their grandmother's sudden presence in their lives?

Jackie would laugh in Marleigh's face if she went to see her by herself. "Always a drama queen, thinking the world owes you. Blow that big government payout already?" Both of Marleigh's parents had been convinced that the government picked and chose individuals to prop up. Since the American dream hadn't come true for them, it shouldn't be real for anyone else. Nope. Her only hope was a surprise arrival and the boys' innate goodness and sweet faces to convince Jackie. Marleigh had always been disposable to her mother. Hopefully these boys wouldn't be.

Screw that! Staying with her parents would be her last option. She had to try something else first. Anything.

Marleigh had hoped never to return to OctoPharma. But Jace had been gone for a year and a half, and she was past selling-her-blood desperate. She'd found a hotel she could rent weekly, cash, and it seemed safe enough. It would keep her and the boys out of her mother's house for a while, anyway.

The plasma center wasn't anything like the blood drives Marleigh remembered at school, the shiny white Red Cross Bloodmobile that pulled up to Holy Trinity after three of the foot football players had been injured in a car accident. The line of students snaked down the sidewalk. She had gone with her soccer teammates. All the athletes were expected, if not explicitly required, to go. Only Marleigh and the goalie had enough iron to donate that day. Picky, picky, they decided. So much blood they could just keep turning people away.

The OctoPharma Plasma center was crowded. She didn't see anyone who resembled the healthy and vital girls who had gone together to donate to the Red Cross, herself included. Based on looks, she was one of the youngest people in the waiting area, but with the women it was difficult to tell. From one angle a face would appear soft and youthful, but at a second glance the face was harder and lined; maybe it was the tank top and short shorts that gave the illusion of youth. Ridden hard and put away wet, her father used to say.

There were only a few other white people in the chairs lined up in rows like at the DMV, but it was a more diverse room than any classroom or locker room or restaurant she'd ever been in. Poverty was a bitch.

"This your first time?" A man in a white coat, *OctoPharma* embroidered over the pocket, asked as he pulled on gloves, blowing in the fingers first to make room.

"Yes," she said. "No. I gave blood a few years ago."

"We'll count you as new. We'll both get a bonus," he said. "Hold out your hands," he instructed, "one at a time." She lifted her right arm and he pushed up her sleeve, his gloved fingers powdery against her skin. He turned her wrist side to side and then inspected her hands, the skin between her fingers and underneath her fingernails. "Remove your shoes."

Marleigh squinted at him. They hadn't begun the questionnaire on his desk. He nodded to the paper she had signed, her careless initials beside each bullet point, including "donor consents to unobtrusive physical examination to rule out intravenous drug use." Ah, junkies. This place probably did attract a lot of them. They advertised paying up to three hundred a month for plasma through a debit card, almost good as cash. And junkies probably weren't afraid of needles.

The only people being turned away were those smelling of alcohol, and the ones who had returned too soon to donate. "I know it been two weeks," the man standing at the next cubicle argued.

"It wasn't five days ago," the man on the other side of the cubicle countered. "None of us, no one at any of our facilities, can take your blood for another forty-eight hours."

"Two days? Shit. What's the difference? Two damn days." He left the big, cold room muttering.

Marleigh drank plenty of water and ate eggs and greens the night before. They were expensive meals, and she needed to make them count. When she arrived, a woman was arguing with the security guard. "They won't touch nothing," she said, motioning to the two children leaning into her. "They've been here before."

"The sign and the policy haven't changed. No one under eighteen allowed," the security guard said.

The neighborhood around the blood center was bad. There wasn't a 7-Eleven within two blocks, and the nearest grocery store was at least eight blocks away. Marleigh didn't feel safe alone in the parking lot, lacking a destination, vulnerable. The woman gave the older child her phone and pressed both against the building's exterior wall. "Don't talk to nobody. Don't go nowhere, you hear?" Both children nodded.

At least Marleigh's kids didn't know where she was or their mother's desperation. She wondered how long those kids would be stuck outside, waiting.

She was asked brief, vague questions about her medical history and confirmed her consent to being tested for HIV, Hepatitis B and C. After she had filled out the questionnaire and watched (again) the video on activities that can contaminate your blood—intravenous drug use, unprotected sex—and completed the brisk evaluation, Marleigh sat with a needle in her arm. It was almost relaxing, sitting and knowing she was making money doing it. The phlebotomist had gotten it on the third try. The veins she called "blue and plump and juicy" rolled away and hid after the woman's first stab. Marleigh could see the skin starting to bruise. Long sleeves again, then.

"So, they'll know when I come again these bruises are from donating, right?" Marleigh asked. The technician nodded. It took almost ninety minutes, and she left with a debit card loaded with fifty dollars and a promise of fifty more for each donation for her first month. A TV in the center announced that a movie star had "finally broken the glass ceiling" by earning more than her male costar in an upcoming blockbuster—twenty million for the six months that they filmed. Marleigh's body could never produce enough blood to make a million in her entire life, let alone twenty in six months.

The bus fare was just under three dollars round trip, so that wasn't bad. Gas in her Subaru was precious. Her time wasn't worth anything to anyone other than her and the boys, so any amount of money was worth her time. And since she was now in the OctoPharma systems, she didn't have to waste time on screenings. She just had to line up behind that day's donors and do the bare minimum. The new-donor bonus of two fifty was significant, so she had to take advantage. With each visit, she drank lots of water and tried to eat to add weight. You could give more blood the bigger you were. Marleigh had always been small. Just some more bullshit stacked against her.

CHAPTER FORTY-TWO

The boys hugged Lynetha and said thank you. They had such manners despite everything, her boys. They were packed up and ready to move on to the Econo Lodge Marleigh had found. Lynetha hugged Marleigh long and hard. "I wish there was more that I could do," she said.

"You gave us more than two months," Marleigh said. "I can't ever thank you enough."

"Let me know where you are when you get settled. Back on those tiny little feet."

"You know it," Marleigh said, wondering if that day would ever come.

Marleigh and her three boys piled into her car and drove across town.

Marleigh hated herself for being poor. It was humiliating to tell her kids no all the time. A *yes* would taste so good, rare and exotic. There were fewer and fewer people that she could find who were worse off financially than they were, fewer rungs to fall before they had absolutely nothing. The only homeless people Marleigh had noticed when she was growing up were the scary ones, the loud and crazies who danced without music on street corners or yelled at passing cars. It seemed entirely impossible that she could someday be like any of them, tending to her few remaining possessions like precious totems. But each day what she had shrank. Anything that could be sold was sold. She imagined herself disappearing a little bit with each item—shoes never to be replaced, cups and dishes, chipped, the waitressing smock that stayed folded in her drawer, increasingly more gray than black, if only she could wisp away. But that didn't happen. It never did. She had to live in her failure and her shame publicly. Her sons anchored her to the world, whether she liked it or not.

She tried getting drunk once. She'd watched her mother and then Jace forget their lives that way. Though it temporarily softened the edges of the world, she awoke with a blistering headache and parched, dehydrated breasts that couldn't feed Max. There was no escaping.

Her sweet boys tried to make the best of the small hotel room. "Two big beds!" Jason proclaimed. "Nicky and I get this one!" Max tried over and over to climb up the side of the bed, using his beat-up car seat for balance. The walls were thin, the windows breathed, and nighttime outside their hotel room door was loud and scary. Arguments rattled through the walls. Bottles shattered in the parking lot. Marleigh hugged her boys close. All of them ended up sleeping with her. In the mornings, she drove by the hotel kids waiting for their school bus pickup. Her boys were warm and safe in the Subaru.

Marleigh had enough cash for two weeks at the hotel. Every dollar she earned slipped through her fingers and into someone else's pocket before she had time to count it. She returned to OctoPharma, but for the first time failed the basic iron test. The simple finger prick made her woozy.

When she missed her payment date, generally handed in cash to the manager on duty, Marleigh returned with the boys from school to find her hotel room door locked, the key deactivated. What little they owned remained inside. She had her sons, their backpacks, her purse and car keys.

She parked in front of the office and left Jason with the car keys and told him only unlock the car doors for her. Marleigh flung open the door to the hotel office and demanded to be let into their room.

"This is a hotel. Nothing here is yours," the desk clerk said.

"We aren't going to stay. Let me back in to get our things and we will go."

"There's fifty-dollar lock service charge associated with squatters."

"You fucking fuck," Marleigh screamed. She was trembling.

"Calm down or we'll call the police."

"I said, let me back in to get my things."

"I can't do that without the service fee. If our business is done here, I'll have to ask you to leave the lobby. Otherwise, I'll have to call the police." Marleigh did the math in her head. Their clothes alone were worth more than fifty. She counted out the money and handed it to the clerk.

The boys followed Marleigh and packed. They were off again. Marleigh drove and drove.

"Where are we going?" Jason asked.

She found a well-lit street with no parking restrictions and maneuvered the car into a small space.

"Can we go home, Mommy?" Nicky asked. Marleigh had been running the air conditioner as high as she could, trying to keep the summer heat out. She couldn't idle the car all night. Gas was too expensive. Turning the car on and off at intervals would draw attention. What did Nicky consider home, anyway?

"No, sweetie," she said.

"What about our gramma?" Nicky asked. "Don't we have a gramma?" The boys had overheard Marleigh talking to Lynetha about her mother, her fear of having to go to her for help.

"No way," Jason answered for her. That kiddo didn't miss a thing.

"I have an adventure planned," Marleigh said. "We're going to stay here tonight."

Jason's eyes narrowed at her in the mirror, as they did more and more these days, wanting to question her but not having the words. She was suddenly so grateful for her son's deliberation, how hard he worked to pluck out just the right word. "What," Jason began, then hesitated, "are we doing?"

"Car camping. Your dad taught me about it when we went to Nebraska." *Ask me about Nebraska. Let's talk about that instead. Anything but why are we sleeping in a car, are you pregnant again, Mommy, what are we going to do tomorrow?*

Nicky tried out the word but ended up sounding like he had a stutter. "Camping," squealed Max, who squirmed in his too-small car seat. Car camping sounded better than sleeping in the car. Or temporary; let it be temporary, homelessness.

"Where's the tent?" Jason asked.

"No tent when you car camp," she said. "You stay in the car. You don't have to look for a soft place to put your tent. And you don't have to worry about animals stealing your food." Both older boys loved to eat, and Max's moods followed his brothers', so this detail was crucial. "And the ground can be hard and lumpy under a sleeping bag."

This was nothing like the Nebraska night she and Jace made love in the cab of his truck before rolling sleeping bags in the truck bed. The truck bed liner like ribs beneath them, they slept under the star-streaked sky.

· · ·

After two nights of parking inside the city, Marleigh realized her mistake when a man knocked on her window. "Do you guys need help? Are you okay in there?" Someone would call the police and report them. She relocated their sleeping quarters.

Leaning against the open door of the Subaru, Marleigh gargled with the last warm ounce of water in the 7-Eleven-brand bottle, the plastic creaking empty in her hand, and spat out the toothpaste. Using the toe of her shoe, she ground the foamy paste and spit into the dirt. That dark spot could be anything. This was a good place, a safe one. She didn't want to lose it, yet. Jason's breath stuttered in his sleep. He sounded just like Nicky and Max in the seat behind him. But Jason's rangy legs and pasta-stick arms hung long and limp against the edges of his big kid seat. She wanted carpet under his dream feet, his fingers to plump back out and clutch a string cheese that he'd nibble once from the top, then from the bottom, back and forth, her little bunny. But she'd picked any remaining mozzarella from the wrappers days ago. The fingers whose prints streaked the window beside him twitched as he dreamt. Max still slept in his car seat. Last night she squeezed the Motts for Tots juice boxes so hard that each boy got a taste of Very Berry and Awesome Apple (both with a hidden half serving of vegetables in every box). She should throw them away, but she won't let her boys see the car cubby empty.

"Where'd my little TV go?" Jason asked six months ago. The DVD player that had hung behind her seat for his entertainment as they ventured around town had been sold on Craig's list. Next was the plastic toy grill, the poofy white hat, her books, and the easel where she planned to teach the boys to paint and sketch, someday, when they were older. Jason never asked about the house the way Nicky did. Jason carefully avoided any use of the word *home*.

Each night, Jason helped her pick out clothes for the three of them from his very own suitcase, the one with Thomas the Tank Engine on it. She dressed him and his baby brothers before bed and stashed their bags in the trunk, out of sight. That way she could wake him just before preschool opened, give him a half a granola bar. That box was thinning. She had to reach deeper and deeper.

As all three boys chomped on breakfast, she pulled into the carpool line at United Presbyterian Preschool. They climbed out of the car, waving to her, and looked like every other preschooler, pre-kindergartner, and first grader, if a bit skinny. The carpool monitor smiled at her. And Marleigh knew her car didn't look any more lived in than the Highlander ahead of her, or the Suburban behind. She waved at the monitor like all the other mothers who would use the five hours of pre-K for skinny vanilla lattes or hot yoga, like once she imagined she might.

After bringing the boys to school, Marleigh went to Mark's house. They had dropped the pretense of a playdate, as all of their children were in preschool. He looked panicked when she arrived. She hadn't considered the possibility of his wife being home. He made her iced tea, and they sat in the fenced-in backyard where the children had played. Why had he gone to a park? There were two brand-new swings and a shingled playhouse. Ariel had everything.

No one would see them. She didn't know how she could have been so careless, so stupid, how it was possible that she could be pregnant. It seemed utterly unreal to her.

"It's impossible," Mark sputtered.

"I guess you're not only shooting blanks with that thing."

"It's not mine. There's no way. Are you sure it's mine?" How were men (and their mothers) always so certain they weren't the fathers?

"Of course it's yours," she said, dropping her face into her palms, massaging her temples. *Fuck fuck fuck fuck,* her insides screamed. "Don't freak out. I'm going to have an abortion."

"Thank God," he said, the man who had said countless times how desperately he and his wife wanted another child as he and Marleigh watched their children play at the park.

"Your life will be fine. I don't want this any more than you do."

"So, you really plan on ending it?" he asked, sounding more alive. Color returned to his cheeks.

"Definitely. I just need to add some shifts so I can afford it and whatever babysitter I'll need while I'm there." Marleigh realized she didn't entirely understand what having an abortion entailed. The mechanics couldn't stop her, though. It was the only choice that made sense for everyone—her, the boys, the father. This baby. What a shit show Marleigh would bring it into. There wasn't any room left in the car on the bad nights, anyway.

"I will pay for it," he said. "The cost of the procedure." The word *procedure* sounded more like everything Mark had detailed about what he and his wife had been doing to get pregnant, not terminating a pregnancy. He dug around in his pocket and found his wallet. He flipped it open and emptied it into Marleigh's hand, a compact stack of bills, several twenties on the outside.

"Mark," she said, knowing that this was the very least he could do but wanting to act like she wouldn't take the money. Did he always carry around that much cash?

"I'm sorry. I can't see you anymore. Not like that, not like anything." He pulled his hand away from hers. She closed her hand on the cash. "Please, take the money." He looked down at his feet.

"You need to be careful carrying around money like that," she said. "Don't want you to get rolled with your pockets full." Her joke made him more uncomfortable.

"I'm sorry. I wish I could do more. I hope that's enough."

"It'll have to be," she said.

CHAPTER FORTY-THREE

Marleigh now had four hundred dollars in her pocket to off a baby. She needed a plan. She wasn't going to dump all this cash into some seedy hotel. The boys were doing okay in the car, but she had to make a change and soon.

Homelessness was a type of profound aloneness that Marleigh had never imagined. It involved tremendous secrecy and occasional outright lying if she didn't want anyone to find out. And it wasn't a matter of want, but necessity. Tattoo artists tended to be a pretty open-minded bunch, but the word *homeless* conjured images of shelters, the smell of piss, creepy men reeking of wine trying to sneak into her cot and bedbugs, and filth and addiction and shame.

Over and over as a child, Marleigh was made to work on stains old and new, whether they were in outside layers of clothing or underclothes. "If you look like trash, you're trash," her mother said. No matter how clean she got her underwear and socks, there was nothing Marleigh could do to fill in the deep cracks around her mother's lips—unfiltereds carved them. No amount of regret-purchased cover-up would get rid of them. "Those people should have their kids taken away. Why'd they have them if they can't feed them?" Jackie said. Despite her self-righteous platitudes damning the poor, Marleigh's mom's *can'ts* rhymed with *aint's*, especially when she was angry, which was most of the time. Marleigh learned early that drunks said they drank because it made them happy, took the edge off, but it made her mother cruel and suspicious and full of blame for everyone responsible for her unhappiness.

There was no way Marleigh could call her.

. . .

From the phone at the shop, Marleigh called Belinda, the strange chorister and apparent black-market baby dealer. She'd held on to the card Belinda had given her. Marleigh agreed to meet the adoption lady because it meant a full meal and a chance to sit down. Belinda seemed a little crazy, but she figured she'd see what she could get. Belinda was probably full of shit anyway. Marleigh felt nothing about what was growing inside of her. She hadn't had much time or energy to experience her pregnancies after Jason.

They met at a bustling deli downtown. Marleigh didn't want to meet too close to school. Belinda was already there. She had ordered two ice waters, one for each of them, and a Sprite for Marleigh. She hadn't had a soda in so long. The smell of fresh bread and sauerkraut. Clanging cutlery. The sugary tang almost gave her a buzz. "Can I get a Reuben?" Marleigh asked Belinda when the waitress came to take their orders. Salt and bread and fatty meat.

"Whatever you like, dear," Belinda said.

Marleigh forced herself to slow down and chew. She wanted to save the second half to split for the boys. Belinda ordered a bowl of soup. She blew calmly on each spoonful before raising to her lips. "Go ahead and finish it," Belinda said. "I can tell you're still hungry."

Marleigh shook her head. When the waitress passed by, Belinda tugged lightly on her apron. "Sorry to bother. Can we get another one of those Reubens to go? No rush."

Marleigh nearly cried. Over a goddamn sandwich. She devoured the second half as well as the side of chips.

"There are so many women out there who all they want is to be able to get pregnant and have a baby of their own," Belinda began, once Marleigh had cleaned her plate. "You have three already. And while you can't give a family one of their own, you can do the next best thing. Think about the life you could give your children. Surrogate mothers make more because they're carrying the biological child of the parents, obviously. But I know several families willing to compensate you for your gift as well as take excellent care of you and your baby along the way. Compensation averages around thirty thousand, in addition to clothing allowances, medical care and vitamins." Her gift. She didn't see it as a gift, that's for sure.

"How much do you make in all of this?"

"A reasonable finder's fee"—Belinda used air quotes—"that's none of your concern."

Marleigh knew the hungry look childless women got around babies. The way they stared too long or unknowingly mirrored the cupping of her hand at the base of her son's neck or the gentle thump to encourage a burp to rise. The women who held nothing but swayed anyway. If she could hit rewind and return to when it was just she and Jason, she would do it in an instant. Not just Jason as an infant when she loved him so completely and felt herself so solidly the center of their universe that nothing else mattered or could ever matter, but now, to enjoy Jason as a self-sufficient little boy. To have the time and energy and money to catch her breath and know her boy as she did when he was her only. Those months when it was just the two of them, Jace deployed and Marleigh at home, had been the very best of her life.

But thirty thousand dollars to do what she couldn't stop her body from doing anyway. The thought of what that money could do made her head spin. Could she really do this? Would she? The money would change their lives. She needed to think. She needed to figure out where they would sleep that night. And Jason needed glasses.

That week, in first-grade eye exams, Jason learned he was neither stupid nor dyslexic. He just couldn't see. The school nurse performed the exam and warned Marleigh that a basic pair of prescription glasses ran around two hundred dollars. And that didn't include the optometrist's appointment.

Selling her blood, her personal shit that had once seemed important, and the boys' stuff—why not sell a baby, sell some couple some hope? Maybe next time she would volunteer to be someone's surrogate. That's where the real money was. "Okay," she said to the adoption lady over lunch. "Okay, I'll think about it."

"You don't have much time to make a decision," the woman said, canting her chin down and lifting her eyebrows at Marleigh. "Almost impossible to get an abortion after twenty weeks. Just because you're not showing doesn't mean the baby's not growing. I was in the church bathroom that morning." Until that moment, the woman had only referred to her pregnancy as a gift. Life, joy. She'd only used euphemisms instead of *options*. "It's already been a few weeks."

Marleigh needed this woman and any potential adoptive parents to believe that she loved this baby, that all she wanted in the world was to be able to keep her and raise her and love her, because of course this would be her girl after all those boys. She'd learned how her life worked out, what the odds were.

A buyer had to believe in the intrinsic value of something to pay top dollar. Art. Tattoos were useful and permanent and informed everyone around you, and yet customers still wanted to argue about price. But the art that hung in the cool, marble hallways of the Chrysler Museum (free admission and breezy air-conditioning, and oh God, the sketches and photographs in the modern section), no one argued that those works weren't valuable, whether or not they understood them. Marleigh exaggerated the drop of her mouth, the parting of her lips in shock.

"I haven't considered that." She curved her hand around her abdomen. Of course she had. And of course Mark thought she'd already had an abortion. "I love my children," she said. "No mother wants to consider giving one away." That wasn't a complete lie. She would go down swinging to keep them together. With the hand at her lap, she pinched the skin between her thighs tightly in her fingernails to try and force tears. This woman wouldn't beat her. Clearly, Belinda was primarily looking out for herself in this deal. After wooing Marleigh with food and soft surroundings, she'd made Marleigh open and exposed her weakness. "If you think I would ever consider killing this baby, I don't think I can ever work with you." She stood to leave.

"Sit down, Marleigh." She had dropped her voice low. It was calm and flat and terrifying. "I meant only that the clock is ticking, and you know it."

Yes. Marleigh was running out of time. Finally, the tears came. "No, I have to go," Marleigh said.

She walked out of the restaurant without looking back, and, of course, before the check arrived. The plastic bag with the second sandwich sagged in her hand. Marleigh hoped that she hadn't overplayed her hand. The private adoption, the money for this baby was her only hope now, but she had to get its money's worth. Marleigh needed to save the cash she had and plan her next several steps.

CHAPTER FORTY-FOUR

Jackie cried when she saw Jason, Nicky and the baby. "You're little men already. And you look just like your daddy," she said. "Especially you," Jackie said, grabbing Nicky's chin. He beamed. No one ever singled Nicky out.

At least she was the nice, sweet drunk when the boys met her. Probably just tipsy enough to offer them brownies and cookies. Did she have the ingredients for either? They needed full bellies and a place to sleep. Marleigh took care to keep things easy and polite. She and her mother knew their own score. Marleigh also knew she could never let her guard down or trust her mother, especially this kind, grandmotherly version of her. And she had to hide the pregnancy.

An addict loved Marleigh more at the perfect amount of drunk, loved her more than Marleigh had ever been loved or would ever be loved again. "You're going to do so much better than us. I just know it." In school, Marleigh's kindergarten teacher thought she needed to see the speech pathologist. Marleigh always said "mush" instead of much. Guess how mush I love you? At the wrong, too much, too drunk place, Marleigh's shit didn't stink. "You think you're better than your father and me? You put shit in, you get shit out. That's all you are."

On the rare, not-drinking-at-all days, Marleigh was nothing. Her mom couldn't or wouldn't have emotions. She was blank. All physical sensation, mostly discomfort and turn the heat down or up. As soon as she emoted, an addict got drunk again.

As they stood outside Marleigh's mother's front door, they each still had a large bag of their belongings, but that was it. Marleigh pawned everything that was worth something and plenty that wasn't. Her mother balked at the overstuffed car in her driveway. "What will the neighbors think?" Marleigh rolled her eyes. She knew what the neighbors had been thinking for the last thirty years. Marleigh took exceptionally good care of her car; she loved that Subaru and knew it should last her almost forever.

"Hi, Gramma," Jason said, standing still as she hugged him. "You smell nice."

"Listen to you, ladies' man." Jackie waved them all into the house. She had the windows open, but the house still smelled of decades of smoke. Since Marleigh's father left, *temporarily, you know how he is,* her mother did most of her drinking at home. She announced to her favorite bars that she was done being their sucker. So she bought her own liquor, the trash can perpetually full of black plastic bags that crinkled from the brown paper bottle bags she left inside. The house had suffered for it. She'd opened the windows, though. She was trying. She was trying. Marleigh needed to try, too.

"There's only one spare bedroom. It's not a palace," Jackie laughed and gestured around her. "But it'll do, won't it? Jason, how 'bout your mom and the little boys share that one. You can have the couch and guard the place at night." Her laugh turned into a smoker's bray and then a cough. Jason's eyes stretched wide.

"No one needs to guard anything, buddy," Marleigh said. "Grandma's just trying to give you some big-kid space."

Jason looked excited at the thought of space just for him. Marleigh wasn't the only one being constrained, forced to live with fewer and fewer items of her own. Jason likely felt the pinch deeper than his siblings. Nicky had never had much to call his own, Max had even less. When Jason was little, he'd organized his toys like shrines, by type. His few beloved soft toys—softies he called them, so often to Jace's chagrin—lived on his bed so that he could rub the puppy dog's ear as he fell asleep. Marleigh had reattached Pupper's left ear a dozen times; his rubbing was insistent and regular, though it only took him a few minutes each night to fall asleep. He rubbed the ear between his thumb and pointer finger and then gently twisted it between his fingers. And he had a Beanie Baby owl with big, glittering eyes that Marleigh gave him for his third birthday because his eyes had always been so big and bright.

Jason had a teddy bear that slept beside him, always. The bear wore camouflage, and his fur was less mottled, less worn than the others. Jace had taken him to a Build-a-Bear place, and they'd stuffed the bear and dressed it together. Then the sixty-dollar price tag seemed excessive. Now she could have stretched it to feed them all week. Maybe Jason so rarely touched it because he realized his dad could never give him anything else ever again. Or maybe it just wasn't as soft or cuddly as the other toys. But Jason always wanted the bear on his bed. If he knocked it onto the floor, he'd cry for her to come and pick it up. He used to, anyway.

Nicky brought a small bunny to school for nap time—Bun Bun—and except for regular washings, Bun Bun stayed in his school bag.

Jason had three Lego sets. One he'd completed with Jace and had asked Marleigh to glue it so it wouldn't come apart. He'd seen his friend's mom do it. His friend had tons of models, he told her.

"If you glue it, you can't take it apart and use it again," she warned.

"I know," he said. So, he built the other sets and rebuilt them over and over, melding all of the pieces into a gallon sized plastic bag so he could create new structures and machines. And he had a tool kit, mixed with some baking utensils like whisks and spatulas, on a small plastic work bench that he would share with his brother but never agreed to pass it down to him. The books scattered through the old apartment belonged to the library.

When they changed apartments, they whittled their belongings even more. And each time they moved or went to stay with someone, they shed more. Hopefully they could make this housing situation work and not have to pack up again.

Marleigh had felt numb for a very long time, but somewhere inside of her began to ache. She couldn't believe she ended up back here, in Ocean View. The house she had fought to escape her entire life. What had been the point of it all? The boys didn't know she was pregnant yet, so she had nothing to explain, not yet anyway. They were too young to recognize the signs. The signs had been so subtle, she might have missed them. And she wasn't as sick as she had been with any of them. Her body knew what to do by now. She wasn't sure what she'd say as her belly started to swell and bulge, but she had to come up with something—both for them and anyone else watching. Ideally, she could have this baby without anyone else noticing. Baggy clothes, keep the weight gain minimal. She wasn't a big girl. It could all be like it never happened. Half a year, really, that was all. She would get her family out of here for good.

. . .

Marleigh walked into the crowded diner and spotted Belinda sitting with a fidgety but perfectly dressed couple. Belinda squeezed her round body out of the booth to shepherd Marleigh to the couple.

"Marleigh, this is Warren and Holly Ennis." Holly had caramel and honey highlights in hair that cascaded over her shoulders. Her forehead was unlined, eyebrows dark and defined. Warren had the beginnings of crows' feet, but his hair was thick and dark. They looked like they should be on a magazine cover under the headline "How to be perfect."

Marleigh extended her wrist to meet Warren's outstretched hand. He stared at her tattoo. A delicate black outline of a woman's hand, fingers crossed in hope, nails slim and long and black. The words, *bruised but not beaten* thin as lace stretched up the pale underside of her forearm. "I-I got that way before this pregnancy." She pictured that hopeful, naïve, version of herself, confident that she'd beaten the worst life had to offer. Her words broke his stare. She shook Holly's hand. She wore a simple cotton dress that swished against her sandals. The soles were so thin she could feel the floor. Warren's eyes followed the flimsy loop of black bra strap that kept drooping down her shoulder. She pushed it back up.

"It's so wonderful to meet you," Holly said. "Your baby, our baby, will have the best of everything. Its own room and bathroom, first a nursery, obviously."

Marleigh pictured the three boys piled into a twin bed with her at the Econo Lodge. Jason dozing against Nicky's car seat in the Subaru. Max never recognizing the same place for more than a month at a time.

"Let's all have a seat," Belinda suggested, and summoned the waitress. "You can take the outside seat, Marleigh. Little more room." Belinda winked and patted her own ample midsection.

Marleigh's hand automatically dropped to the tight swell of her abdomen. Holly's eyes followed. She looked ravenous.

The waitress arrived, small notepad in hand. "What can I get ya, hon?"

Marleigh looked up from the menu and at Holly, then back down. "Can I have the two-egg omelet with spinach, bacon, and cheddar cheese?" Did Holly realize she was nodding as Marleigh ordered, apparently approving of her diet? She stopped. "And some water and orange juice, please."

"Coffee?" the waitress asked.

"No," Holly answered. Marleigh's eyes pulled wide. "Too much caffeine isn't healthy, right?" She blushed. The waitress left.

"So, you two are looking to become parents?" Marleigh asked.

"We have a daughter," Warren answered. "She's three."

Marleigh couldn't hide her surprise.

"My infertility appears to be secondary." Holly's voice broke on *infertility*. "We didn't have any problem having our first." Warren put a hand on her shoulder in comfort. Marleigh ached for that kind of touch. "We're desperate to give our Sadie a sibling."

Belinda said, "Marleigh here has other children. Healthy, beautiful children."

Marleigh ground her jaw. Belinda knew what her sons looked like. Of course she did.

"I don't want to talk about them," Marleigh said. "So, is it legal for people to buy babies?"

Holly gasped and turned to Warren.

Belinda slammed her meaty hand on the table, rattling silverware. "No one is buying anything." She smiled and reached across the table to pat Warren's palm. "We've discussed this. The Ennises will pay you expenses to keep you and the baby healthy, and you will agree to give the baby to them through adoption as soon as you deliver."

The difference between Belinda's explanation and buying a baby sounded like a very thin line.

"How far along are you?" Holly asked.

"About eight weeks," Belinda answered before Marleigh could speak. Holly's eyes glistened.

"With an ultrasound, the doctor can give you firmer gestational age," Belinda said. "Who's your doctor, Marleigh?"

"I'm between doctors right now." Not exactly a lie. "I delivered my boys at Portsmouth Naval, but my husband was alive then and I had Tricare. I don't have that now."

Belinda nodded and watched Marleigh. "They always say wait until ten weeks anyway until there's a definite heartbeat. You know what to do in the meantime, right, Marleigh?"

"Because of my previous losses," Holly stammered and looked down at her lap, "I-I can't attend any of the doctor's appointments until there's an ultrasound. It's too triggering."

"I don't have insurance," Marleigh said. She had stopped paying for that a long time ago. "Doctors and hospitals have to see me," Marleigh explained, air quoting *have*. "But they require upfront payments for everything." The truth, every word.

Holly raised her eyebrows.

"Some require a deposit before they'll hold an appointment." Marleigh also knew that the docs ordered far fewer tests and drew less blood without insurance to pay for the labs. Maybe being uninsured had its benefits. She had more than a month before she had to worry about labs or doctors.

"Is the baby's father, um, involved?"

Marleigh shook her head. "Not at all." She rested her hands on the table. Every so often they dropped to her lap, but just as quickly she placed them back on the table.

"But you know him?" Warren reddened as his wife spoke.

"I certainly did. Pretty well by the looks of me."

Belinda stepped in. "What Mrs. Ennis is asking is about the baby's biological father; is he healthy, what's he like, is he—"

"Yes, he's healthy. He's not a felon. I don't know what he got on his SATs."

"Does he look like you?" Holly asked. "Like us?"

"Are you asking if he's white?"

Warren sputtered his coffee. Holly tried to recover.

"Marleigh," Belinda chided.

"Sorry. Yes, he's a white guy. This kid could look just like you." She didn't tell them about Mark's red hair.

At the end of the meal, Warren pressed three twenties into Marleighs's palm. "Thank you so much for coming to meet us. We'll do everything possible to give this baby the best life. Take your boys to dinner tonight, on us."

. . .

It didn't take long for Marleigh's mother's hospitality to wear out. "The little ones get up too early," Jackie said. "You're eating everything in the house." When Marleigh and the boys had arrived, the refrigerator held only a box of wine, a few bottles of nail polish, greasy takeout containers, and a plastic bottle of eye drops. The plastic gallon of

Burnett's vodka disappeared from the freezer sometime that first day. Her mother must have stashed it in her room, drank it warm. All of them had been told and told again not to step foot inside there. Not that Marleigh had any interest in doing so. She knew exactly what she would find. She'd snuck into her mother's room plenty as a child, throwing away the empty bottles and pouring out any remainders she found. Covering up the bottles in the trash with newspaper.

"You've got to be saving a ton in rent. And you're not paying a babysitter. You're using a lot more water than I did. Electric, too. Those bills are a lot less when it's just me." Marleigh had planned to pay her mother something each month. Marleigh had expected a surplus, too, after giving up the apartment, and she needed to sock away just a little to get them out of here and back on their feet. When they talked initially, her mother was supportive. She knew Marleigh would pick up shifts bartending and tattooing again.

"How much do you want, Mom?" She wasn't sure how much more she could take. She had saved six hundred.

Jackie didn't answer. "I think it would just be better for you guys to move on." She avoided Marleigh's eyes, kept looking around and behind her. "Your father is coming home." What was happening? Her mother was shaky. She kept trying and failing to light a cigarette. Finally, she stood, grabbed her purse and made for the door.

Marleigh raced into her room and into the drawer where she kept her cash. Only seventy-five dollars remained. Jackie was pulling down the street before Marleigh raced back out the front door. Jackie had stolen everything Marleigh had saved, minus the seventy-five and the sixty dollars Warren Ennis had given her.

CHAPTER FORTY-FIVE

"Time to pack up, guys." How many times had she told her children this? Marleigh shoved her threadbare clothes into a plastic Walmart bag. Everything she had fit into two. She muttered as she worked, so angry and wildy desperate to get out of her mother's house.

"I'm all ready to go," Jason said. He looked up at her, his eyes magnified through his new lenses. She cupped his chin in her hand. "Good boy. Go help your brothers."

Marleigh wasn't a thief, though she was raised by thieves. Fuck her mother. She knew better than going back there. Marleigh would never steal, nothing major anyway. Not that she hadn't thought about it. If she could have stolen the right lenses for Jason's prescription in the cool, sporty frames, she would have considered it.

She inventoried Max's diapers and wipes as she loaded his tiny, stained clothing into the diaper bag. The supply dwindled. He had no pacifiers or toys. He soothed himself to sleep by sucking on his middle and pointer fingers. Where would they eat that night? What would they do? She buckled the boys in their seats and fixed her mother's house in the rear view.

The kids were starving, so she headed to that busy Wawa on Northampton Boulevard. She could slurp enough at water fountains throughout the day to keep her milk flowing. Thin, but still flowing. But Max was much too big to still be breastfeeding. It soothed him like the water fountain soothed her, keeping the pangs at bay temporarily, but not filling either of them. She had never decided to continue nursing him. It was just a basic sustenance. All Nicky wanted was Cheez-Its, and that could be dinner. All he ever heard from her was *no*. For just this once she could give him a *yes*. Wawas were risky. Brightly lit and with the sandwich counter separate from the checkout counter (not like a 7-Eleven where the cashier is responsible for hunting out cigarettes and plucking sweaty hotdogs off of the roller), there were eyes everywhere. And she had to walk out between two checkout lanes. She filled her arms like everyone else.

Marleigh hadn't realized that the Ennis family had that much money until Holly Ennis couldn't remember the number of bathrooms in her house. "Silly me, that's right—four. And a half! I'm always forgetting the new half-bathroom. It was out of commission so long during the renovation. Out of sight, out of mind, you know?"

Would it be like that with Marleigh's baby? Delivered, handed off. Out of sight, out of mind. She didn't judge them for having more bathrooms than they could count—just a little, anyway. She'd just never be able to tell her boys the kind of life the baby would get to lead when they were stuck living with her. As if they wouldn't trade places with a fetus in a heartbeat for a shot at a life like that? She thought Holly was kidding when she handed Marleigh a gift certificate for six months of prenatal yoga—an unlimited use punch card with a bright *no hot yoga-expecting!* sticker on it—just for agreeing to meet them. Those places thought of everything. Or when Holly offered her a grocery stipend because organic berries and spinach cost two times as much as regular, but "the pesticides on conventional produce have been shown to cross the placenta. They could show up in breast milk in trace amounts," Holly said.

"Don't worry." Marleigh tried to laugh it off. "I hate spinach." Those damp, sticky leaves and that off-green smell.

"But such important folic acid and iron! Better than any other source."

For a second, Marleigh considered asking her to buy her a pack of those overpriced cigarettes in the bright, primary colored boxes with an Indian on it. Wasn't that tobacco organic and non-GMO? It would be almost worth taking a nasty puff just to see her face. Priceless. Granted, tobacco use of any kind (as well as alcohol, marijuana, inhalants) would void their agreement. The one Marleigh had yet to sign. The contract they drafted for her consideration was oddly specific and very thorough. The hardest part was looking at Holly and Warren and seeing the future she'd worked for her and Jace.

She had to decide soon. Marleigh directed Jason to bring Nicky up to the Wawa cashier and ask where the bathroom was and if they could use it. The lines were unusually long. That must have been why the bottled water aisle was empty, and only a few loaves of bread remained on the shelves. Bread was too bulky anyway. She stuffed two small bags of Cheez-Its and animal crackers into the pouch of her sweatshirt and walked out. The boys knew to meet her at the car. "Mommy," Jason said as he climbed into the backseat. "Everyone in line was talking about a hurricane. Have you seen a hurricane, Mommy?"

"I have. Lots. Don't worry. They never hit directly here."

Marleigh drove to a familiar parking lot and handed the boys their treats. Jason tore into his bag and opened Max's animal crackers. Jason munched his ruffled chips happily; Nicky licked the orange dust off of his fingers. She slept.

When Marleigh dreamed of Jace, and suddenly she was always dreaming of Jace, he was kind, gentle. And sober. He was the Jace she knew before he packed all that goodness up in his seabag and left her, the beginning of such a long goodbye. Sometimes as she dreamed she knew she wasn't awake and that this Jace wasn't real. That reminder kept her safe. Other times, though, it was too seductive. She dreamt of the life they had promised each other. He played joyfully with his sons, was eager to get home to them each day. He walked Jason to a school bus stop, the pudgy, small fingers in his strong but careful grasp. He held her hand after waving his boy out of view. The rough callouses of his palm welcome and familiar against her skin. The weather was always breezy in her dreams. Leaves skittered across the sidewalk. She brushed a curl out of Max's eyes. He still had soft baby curls. She hadn't cut his hair yet. He couldn't demand a high and tight buzz, "just like Daddy's" yet. The dreams were sweet and hopeful.

Each time, she had to wake up. That kind, fatherly Jace had been gone so long now. He had no business showing up in her dreams. What good was he to them? Shit, she missed him.

• • •

The storm was coming; that much was clear. Normally the port town was protected by the barrier islands of North Carolina, and any major hurricane glanced off land and head back out to sea where it belonged. Regardless, Marleigh needed a haven for her kids. Even the outer bands of a hurricane could be frightening and dangerous.

Her old landlord told Marleigh she wouldn't see her without first and last month's rent and a full security deposit. "Don't bother if you don't have all three. That's the policy for non-payers. You're lucky I would consider renting to you." Even with what the Ennises gave her at each meeting, she didn't have close to enough.

They could go to a shelter, but those never seemed safe. And she had gone that route enough to know it was rough. She couldn't sleep. She had to constantly watch her cot and the boys' cots to make sure some creep didn't wander over to their space and start putting hands on one of them. And ahead of big storms, shelters relaxed their rules and looked more the other way. So, there were more fucked-up people in a confined space, which made everything worse. The neighborhood around her mother's house flooded terribly, so going there they could end up underwater or trapped for days without power, car flooded out, while her mother raged her own personal hurricane party.

She and the boys stayed at the all-night coffee shop until they lost power and decided to close. Marleigh wanted to fill the boys' bellies and take advantage of air-conditioning and the cushioned booth for as long as she could. She had looked up the highest places to park in Norfolk and found out that the city had opened parking garages downtown for free. But the streets were flooded already; the two main roads into downtown were impassable. She had waited too long to leave. She couldn't live without her car and couldn't risk driving into deep floodwaters. She stopped at an intersection. Ahead of her was an abandoned car, headlights barely above the water. She turned around, frantically scanning her surroundings for higher ground, but it was dark.

Rain lashed the windshield; wind shook the car.

"Are we okay?" Max asked.

"No one else is out here," Jason said.

She approached a cemetery and remembered hearing a story about cemeteries being built on high ground way back when so the bodies didn't wash away. True or not, that's where they were going to spend the night. She parked as far away from large trees as she could. Still, pine cones and pine straw pummeled the car.

The water rose, inching toward their tires. The wind howled. Trees creaked and bowed, dropped their limbs. The car shook. The sky was too dark to look for funnel clouds. She ran the car for fifteen minutes at a time to refresh the air. Opening the windows was out of the question.

Her indecision could get them killed. Marleigh had to stop behaving as if she had any choice.

CHAPTER FORTY-SIX

T he restaurant was noisy. Loudly scraped plates and coffee burnt
on the bottom of pots. Each of them—Warren, Holly, Marleigh,
and Belinda—had full plates of food. But only Marleigh was eating.
She was too hungry for restraint.

She was out of time. She knew that the couple would want her baby
more if they had to work for it. Wasn't that always the way? Anything
that came easily was cheap. But how far could she push it? Belinda had
to know it wasn't Jace's baby she was carrying, so she couldn't claim
last baby of a dead warrior. But she didn't want that woman making
her or her baby seem cheap, either. Meeting this couple was like the
strangest quick succession of dates she'd ever been on.

"I'm not sure I can do it," Marleigh said, pushing the last bite of
cheesy eggs and hash browns across her plate, not looking up. In
her mind, Jason's terrified eyes as the wind shook their car, Nicky's
wobbly chin as hail pelted his window, the way the storm didn't upset
Max, in his too-tight, too-short pants and soaked diaper.

Holly began silently sobbing. She had always looked so put
together, so smooth and expensive and rich. Thin and untouchable.
Marleigh lifted her eyes from her plate, just barely. Warren gathered

his wife into his shoulder. "I knew it," the woman said in a trembling, wet whisper. "I knew it would happen again."

Belinda stared at Marleigh, cold and flat. Warren cleared his throat. One arm around his wife, he twisted his coffee mug around and around on the table. *Again,* Marleigh thought, Holly's voice ringing in her ears.

"I know this must be incredibly difficult for you," Warren said. "I—we—can't imagine what you must be experiencing." Around and around went the mug. His voice was different. The façade of cocky pilot and his perfect wife cracked. "Please, though," he continued. "Marleigh, if you don't think you are truly prepared to move forward with the adoption, please just let us know now." He seemed to really love his wife. Mark had sounded like he'd loved his wife, though, too.

Again. Oh. It all made sense. They had already sat at a table like this and begun to dream of the baby that would be theirs. But they hadn't gotten it. Just like she had dreamed of the life she and Jace would build together as she was pregnant the first time. She knew the taste, the smell, the touch of that dream life—milky coffee, talcum, soft skin, insulated windows, a new, firm mattress. Books for the children. They had been crushed by hope just like she had, once.

A sharp jab to her ankle, hidden beneath the booth tabletop. Clearly a warning from Belinda, who must be worrying about her cut of the fees evaporating. Marleigh could read the couple, though. Growing up in the gym then bartending and tattooing, Marleigh could read more than faces and expressions. She knew every trick people played to hide pain. She knew when someone kept her face blank but carried pain in her muscles.

Some amount of pain was just part of it—getting a tattoo, motherhood, life. No one lived without getting hurt. Pain taught what was valuable. This couple had to understand that her emotions were on the line, too. She just had to imagine giving up Jason or Max or Nicky, and she could access enough pain to make it real, giving away the life inside of her. She took a deep breath and rubbed the bridge of her nose before opening her eyes, locking wet eyes with the wife.

"I don't have any other choice," Marleigh said. "I know that. I can't give a baby the life you can. But I don't have to like it," she said. And it was all true, each word. She didn't like what she was doing.

"This is good. Healthy," Belinda said. "None of this is easy, but we're all looking for the best possible outcome for everyone involved. Isn't that right?"

"I'm not backing out," Marleigh said. "I won't do that. It's just harder than I expected. I have always been a good mom. No matter what." She wasn't sure who she needed to understand this.

"I—I can tell," Holly said. "You obviously love your boys very much." Marleigh dropped her chin and nodded, her face tilted down to the hands clasped in her lap. Holly continued. "Thank you for trusting us. We'll love and take excellent care of this baby."

"Please don't talk about them." *This will help me take care of Nicky, Max, and Jason,* Marleigh reminded herself. Still, she felt dirty. And sad.

She would do it, she decided, with toast covered in the last bite of eggs, damp with butter. The night of the hurricane cemented it. She would have a baby and she would give it to these people. She was morning sick, a very good sign. She would eat well; her boys would eat well. She would never see these people again after she gave birth. They had more money than they knew what to do with, and if giving some of it to her made them feel less guilty for taking her baby, then so be it.

They negotiated the terms. Obviously paying money directly for a baby was unethical, and no one suggested that. But taking proper care of her body and eating well and taking vitamins was expensive. And minimizing stress was very important, too. Marleigh always worried about her boys, she explained. Nothing was certain for them—not the next good meal, school, housing. Nothing. In addition to monthly incremental payments to total thirty-five thousand, they agreed to a grocery stipend so that Marleigh could stock up on and prepare high quality foods.

"I have your first payment from the Ennises as well," Belinda told Marleigh quietly. "Ten percent," she whispered.

Ten percent was more than three thousand dollars. Marleigh's heart beat in her throat.

Holly owned a yoga studio. She was very focused on the mind-body wellness connection. She didn't seem like a yoga person. She was pulled too tight and on edge. Marleigh though yogis were supposed to be chill.

"Women need to prioritize their own health and well-being," she said once.

Marleigh's answer was, "Some of us are just hoping to survive," pleased as the woman's face reddened. It was good to keep them on edge, just a little.

Warren handed Marleigh a folded stack of bills, his palm to hers, a fifty on the outside. "For anything you need," he said, his eyes on her. Another man's cash in her palm. An uncomfortable wash of déjà vu.

Marleigh's neck itched. He gave her this like it was nothing. She couldn't let him see how anxious she was to count it and jam it in her pocket. He had no idea the money was already spent, had been spent a thousand times over—security deposit, first and last month's rent, pads to put beneath their sleeping bags on a bare apartment floor. "Thank you," she said, a light squeeze of his hand.

CHAPTER FORTY-SEVEN

Jason invited school friends to their apartment for the first time in his life. He was no longer ashamed. Marleigh's bed was the pull-out couch in front of the TV, and the boys shared a bedroom. Jason and Nicky had a set of secondhand metal bunkbeds that Warren Ennis assembled. Max had barely slept in a crib after leaving the NICU, so Marleigh found him a cheap toddler bed shaped like a racecar. The first payment changed their lives but left little to spare.

Marleigh lied to everyone she encountered—coworkers, the boys' teachers, the parents of the boys' school friends, and every other parent she ran into. For once, she wasn't lying about where they lived. Her secret was in her body. Growing inside of her was the answer to her every prayer. She lied to the boys, too. She never wanted them to know how close to the precipice they had been. How tenuous what little they had was. Had Jace taught Marleigh to lie? Lies were a survival strategy. Her lies kept her together with her boys as surely as lies ensured Jace could get his next drink just as her mother had gotten hers.

Lies had a way of becoming true. For different amounts of time each day, Marleigh forgot she was way past broke and nearly drowning. The lies were comforting. *My children go to a good school. Education will save them. Education is saving them. Seeing a different life than the one they lead will remind them to stay focused and work hard.* She was a good person. She was a good mother. Everything would be okay.

She had never made them any promise. It wasn't stealing if someone had so much they didn't notice what you had taken. They would get through this. She was building a stable life for them. Jason and Max looked like every other six and two-and-a-half-year-old. Nicky stretched out, a sudden growth spurt. They all deserved better than this. Sometime these narratives kept her in thrall for a couple of days, a week.

The colored cell phone bill arriving at the new apartment. Last notice, it said. That wasn't real. That was the lie. She balled up the brightly colored notice—the happy lime-green color was bullshit; bad news belonged in black and white not neon—and threw it away. Unopened pregnancy test boxes, shiny and wrapped, behind her towel under the bathroom sink.

"Change of plans, boys," she announced late one afternoon. Jason studied her, and Nicky studied his older brother. Max toddled in circles around her, rattling her keys. He loved carrying Marleigh's keys.

"Go bye bye?" Max asked. He always asked this when he played with her keys, always was up for an adventure.

"Yes, go bye bye," she said and scooped him into her arms. "We're going out to dinner." She could see on Jason's face that he was working through what this could mean. A dollar menu night was fun, though very rare. Grazing grocery store giveaways didn't make up for a lost meal. Marleigh had to prepare for weigh-ins and prenatal visits, and that meant she had to eat. Jason had already learned not to get his hopes up. He was already nobody's fool.

They drove to the sprawling pizza parlor. The strobing globe lights around the sign danced across her sons' eyes. The momentary rapture captured for Marleigh in the rearview mirror. They deserved this. They needed this. She would give it to them.

"We're eating here?" Jason asked. They'd only been here twice before. Once, Jason was invited to a birthday party for his friend Abby. Later, he'd told Marleigh about the refilled pitchers of root beer, baskets of breadsticks, and most of all, the game room. "Abby's parents gave every kid five dollars to play!" Marleigh'd tied a ribbon around several colored pencils she'd not yet sharpened and would likely never use and purchased a small sketch pad from the Dollar Tree for the girl's gift. Abby's birthday had been one of Jason's best days ever.

Marleigh unlocked the car doors. "Yep."

"Cool!" Jason said as he swung the door open. Before exiting, he leaned over to unbuckle his brother's booster and car seat. "Shut up about the game room," he whispered to Nicky and Max. "Don't make her mad." The younger boys nodded but didn't hide their disappointment. The last time they came here, she had snapped at Nicky when he asked for quarters for the games. "How about you appreciate the dinner we're having and stop trying to waste money on that crap!" It wasn't one of her finest moments.

She smiled when she thought of the Ennises' bills in her pocket. These boys made everything worth it. The hostess asked Marleigh, "Close to or far away from the game room?"

Jason's mouth dropped open at Marleigh's response. "The closest table you've got." They heard the machines from their booth—the ski balls rolling, air hockey table wheezing, the change machine plunking out quarters. The boys tried so hard not to look at the game room.

"Let's go ahead and order dinner, then I have a little surprise for you," Marleigh said. A good surprise, for a change.

The server appeared and asked for their order. All three boys stared at Marleigh. "Three lemonades and an icy cold milk, with a lid if you've got it." The boys knew only to expect water.

"Milky! Milky!" Max shrieked, clapping and bouncing in his seat. The waitress smiled.

"An order of breadsticks, please, a large Greek salad, and an extra-large pizza, half extra-cheese and half-pepperoni." No one was going hungry tonight, and she could stretch the leftovers across days.

"Isn't this expensive?" Jason asked.

"We've had a good week," she said. "We deserve to celebrate. Tonight, you're not allowed to worry, just enjoy." The boys wriggled in their seats in anticipation of a pizza feast.

Jason took a long drink of his lemonade before pausing to ask the waitress, "Um, are the refills free?"

She winked at him. "Sure are." Jason and Nicky slurped them in one strong draw. "*Aaaaah*," Nicky said, wiping his mouth with the back of his hand. Max happily splutter-gulped his milk.

Marleigh set three one-dollar bills down in front of both Jason and Max. They gasped and looked at each other, questioning. "Mom," Jason began, but stopped himself, taking the bills off the table before she could change her mind. She had worried he was going to try and give them back, man of the house and all. Nicky did the same. Marleigh lifted Max out of the booster seat and gave him a dollar of his own. He just wanted to be a part of whatever his brothers were up to. "Put the dollars in the change machine and watch out for each other. The money's gone when it's gone."

She knew they would watch one another. They took care of one another as instinctually as she cared for them. From her seat, Marleigh had a straight line of sight into the small game room, so she could keep an eye on the boys without having to get up. All four of them had a wish granted.

"Relax a minute, Mama," the server said as she placed a basket of yeasty breadsticks on the table in front of Marleigh.

Jason and Nicky raced each other on fake motorcycles. She refused to think about their father when the bikes leaned under their weight around a curve. Instead, she concentrated on their whoops of delight. Their childish trash talk. Marleigh nibbled on the dough and leaned back against the booth. She watched her sons act like children.

The next morning, her Subaru's gas light appeared as she pulled into the school parking lot. Marleigh walked the boys to their classrooms, then drove a mile to the cheap gas station. She could make a quarter of a tank last a week. She pressed her credit card into the pay slot on the pump. The machine spit it back out. Rejected. She must have pushed a wrong button. She rifled through her wallet, confused. She had plenty of money. A quarter tank of gas was less than ten dollars. She handed the cashier a ten-dollar bill. "For pump two."

Last night, the boys licked greasy fingers. Smiled as they turned their crusts into mustaches. That was real. She hadn't lied to the Ennises. Really, it was gung-ho Belinda who declared Marleigh pregnant. What proof did she have? Marleigh told her she didn't know what she was talking about that day at church. Marleigh hadn't gone looking for this opportunity. It had fallen into her lap.

CHAPTER FORTY-EIGHT

Marleigh's stomach had been upset all day at work. She needed to learn not to rely on Jason and Max's leftover crusts as the basis for her breakfasts. (Nick wolfed every bite of his food; no leftovers from him.) Who knew what kind of preschool germs they carried on their little bodies? At least she'd eaten something. This baby didn't care if the PB&J was originally made for one of its half siblings. Little kids were walking, talking petri dishes. She hadn't woken with nausea for the first time in weeks. Maybe, finally, the morning sickness was ending.

Each pregnancy had been so different that way. She was hardly ever sick with Jason. He was always the easy one. How was it with Nick? Why couldn't she remember? She was sick well into her second trimester with Max; maybe that was his early warning signal of the hell that was to come. Those pregnancies were so close together it was easy to juxtapose and compare. And confuse.

This was different. She needed a bathroom. She formed an *O* with her mouth and slowly exhaled. She could make it back to the apartment. She had to. She clenched everything below her belly button. Some urine leaked. Motherhood was such a beautiful thing, like everything else from ten thousand feet. She shortened her steps and picked up her pace. Only a block and a half to go. Was it the blueberries? She'd washed them. Produce was always the culprit, the worry in every restaurant she'd worked in. The health departments always focused on the temperatures of the meats, how hot were the soups, how cold the freezer, but it was the germs clinging to fruits and vegetables that were the scariest. Always the source of listeria or salmonella or E. coli. This line of thought wasn't helpful. She needed to get to the bathroom, get changed and get to work. Calories were calories and the food allowance was keeping them in an apartment and out of the car. Nothing could be wasted.

The Ennises offered her a stipend if she cut back her work hours so she could rest. Sleep was so important for fetal development; they wanted her aiming for nine hours of sleep each night. They'd never been thrilled that she put needles in peoples' skin for a living, so she agreed to end her night tattoo shifts by nine. She extended her daytime hours by two and a half. She paid off her back utility bills and set up a payment plan to begin to dig out of credit card debt.

Donna emailed her asking for her new phone number. She'd tried to send the boys birthday cards and they'd gotten returned. *Is everything okay? You're always welcome here.*

Maybe Marleigh would be able to start one of those educational savings accounts so that the boys could consider college or a trade school. She wouldn't have her sons selling themselves to the Navy with the promise of some future education. No way in hell. She practiced breathing like she was in labor so she didn't shit her pants in front of her neighbors. And Jason and Max hadn't had a big growth spurt in months, so one had to be coming, even if Nicky finally slowed. At a thrift store that meant at least thirty-five dollars apiece in new clothes. But she paid her rent on time and in full. She slept without the weight of anxiety for the first time since Jace died. She was making the right choice for all of them, and baby girl (she was certain) would live a life Marleigh couldn't imagine, the life of a princess. The life her older brothers deserved but would never have.

Key in the door and up the stairs, Marleigh barely closed the apartment door behind her before going into the bathroom. A twist in her stomach and it was over. Throw out the berries! She stood to wipe and then move on with her day. The toilet was streaked with ribbons of red that spiraled before breaking apart. A small purple clot sank to the bottom. She wiped again, another smear of red. Again. Less, but pink. A third time, nothing. She wiped herself raw and flushed. It's nothing. Nothing.

She had spotted early and often with Jason. With Max she'd bled hard once, certain she'd lost him. That was much worse than this. This was nothing. Overripe berries. She had an hour before she had to be at work, so she lay down on the couch and elevated her feet. She lifted her planner from the coffee table beside her and flipped to the page for the month. She'd circled an appointment in two weeks— *Doc at 12pm 13 weeks*. Marleigh lay down, tired. She only had a little while until the boys would be done with school for the day.

On their way home, they stopped by Harris Teeter and picked up ingredients for dinner, baked ziti with ground beef, something everyone liked. None of her boys was picky. Real hunger taught them to enjoy every bite. She still had plenty of Warren Ennis' off-books cash, which he handed her each time they met. She picked up a treat for herself, one of those individually wrapped chocolates, and boxed animal crackers for the boys. Everyone went to bed with full stomachs.

What was thirteen days until the OB-GYN appointment? It might as well be a lifetime away. What was a little blood? She wasn't squeamish.

Max listened that night, rapt, as Jason read *Where the Wild Things Are*. Max and Nicky studied their big brother as Jason paused and pushed his new glasses up the bridge of his nose. Everything was fine.

Certainly, everyone could wait just a few weeks. Marleigh wasn't certain of the truth. But just as she knew she would agree to give an unborn baby to the Ennises to keep her sons, Marleigh, knew, too, that she would lie as long as she could to provide Jason, Nicky, and Max a taste of the life they deserved.

CHAPTER FORTY-NINE

Warren Ennis stayed outside of the ultrasound room while the technicians booted up machines and Marleigh shivered under the thin gown. Her nerves and the cold room raising goosebumps down her legs, quaking her knees. It was just Marleigh, Holly, a nurse, and an ultrasound technician in the small, dark room.

"Deep breaths and relax." The tech squirted lubricant on the transvaginal ultrasound wand. The wand needed to be inserted. A thirteen-week pregnancy was too small to be detected by an external ultrasound.

Holly squeezed Marleigh's hand but looked away as the woman inserted the wand into Marleigh. Both of the women's fingers were cold.

"You can let him in," Marleigh said. Holly dropped her hand and opened the door for Warren.

"Just a second now," the tech said. Marleigh had forgotten how it hurt, the burning as the wand bumped against her cervix. There was no Jace. No one's hand for her to hold.

The wand probed deeper inside of her. "Ow." She grimaced. The Ennises turned to her. Their fingers were knotted together, white at the knuckles.

The technician pressed a button on the wall phone. "Please send Mrs. Holt's doctor." She turned the screen to face Marleigh and Holly and Warren. It was blank, had been powered off.

The doctor knocked once as she entered the room. She frowned, then told the technician to turn the power on to the screen. "I'm sorry, Marleigh, Holly. As you can see, there is fetal tissue here, but no heartbeat."

Holly collapsed into a chair. "Again." Warren covered her in himself.

The tech slid the wand out of Marleigh. She threw her plastic gloves away and spirited out the door.

Marleigh exhaled a grunting whoosh of air. Her ribs and lungs and belly emptied of the worry they held, the lies, the unknowing. She didn't have to hide anymore. She didn't have to choose which of her babies to save. In the space that relief made, a surge of sadness moved through her. She clutched her stomach and sobbed. She was saved and she was found out. She cried for this baby who may never have been. She cried for her sons' childhood, her own. She cried for Jace. Everything they had shared and lost. What she had survived. Marleigh cried in thanksgiving, gratitude.

Her fingers found Holly's and she held on. "I'm so sorry," Marleigh said. She meant it. She was sorry for the Ennises' sadness. Sorry for what she couldn't give them. Sorry for what was, again, taken from her boys.

Once she finally stopped crying, Marleigh put on her clothes and walked to the parking lot. Lighter, younger, somehow, than when she arrived. Warren intercepted her before she reached her car, his grip tight around her wrist. She panicked, imagining sirens and flashing lights, and tried to pull away. He didn't let go until Marleigh turned to face him.

"Please, he said," his face puffy and hair mussed. "If you ever need—"

Marleigh shook her head. She'd taken too much from them already. "No, I'll be fine."

He dropped her arm.

Walking away, she blew her nose and tightened her ponytail. She drove to the gas station and filled the Subaru, even topped off the tank. A full tank would carry Marleigh, Max, Nicky, and Jason more than four hundred miles, a quarter of the way to Nebraska.

ACKNOWLEDGMENTS

Marleigh Mulcahy and Jace Holt became real to me during a National Parks Arts Residency at Agate Fossil Beds National Monument in the spring of 2018. Without those windy, solitary weeks in Nebraska's Niobrara River Valley, I fear Marleigh and Jace would have remained indistinct sketches in my journal instead of the couple who haunt me still. The gift of time and space in that landscape is one I'll never forget.

Just as time and place are required to create, I don't know how to write without a community. Thanks to the Muse Writers Center, Women Who Submit, Hampton Roads Writers, Seven Cities Writers, and the community of writers I'm grateful to call friends, I don't have to. Michael Khandelwal and Shawn Girvan, you've turned a good thing into a great one. Janine Latus and Ellen Bryson, I hope you'll always let me learn from you. Allison Schoew, Gretchen Gillen, and Tammie Rue Elliott, you met Marleigh first and encouraged me to continue. Cindy Carlson and Mike Krentz, thank you for the opportunity to read and be read by you. Thank you to Koehler Books and my editor, Joe Coccaro, who taught me quite a lot. His sharp eye honed and tightened every chapter.

To Jessica Kliner, Kerri Furey, and Kathryn Fletcher. You're like sisters to me, except we never hate each other. Thank you for keeping me (mostly) normal, current on pop culture and loved like only girlfriends can.

To Mom and Dad, thank you for all of your encouragement and support whether we're far apart or near. I treasure our adventures and time together. Allison Wendt and Emily Weech, it feels like this novel and both of you are launching so beautifully into the world. I can't wait to see where you take your lives.

Camilla and Lucille, in alphabetical order since Milla gets sick of being last. This book publication isn't your first rodeo. It's just what we do. I wonder how many books you've both read since I started writing this one. Thank you for enduring my mismatched and unbrushed walks to the bus stop, as well as my inability to help you study for math or science. Witnessing both of you becoming yourselves is the greatest wonder of my life. You're truly the two best people I know.

This novel would not exist if not for the care, feeding, and coffee brewing from my husband, John. You are a writer-hype-husband and soccer stepdad and hiking companion beyond my wildest imaginings. Thank you for the steaming refills on the days I hunched over my computer, still in my pjs, and ignored you. Thank you for knowing when to suggest I *just go outside for a run*. I love you. Having you in my corner makes me feel invincible.

To anyone who has read this far. Thank you, thank you, thank you, from the deep, nougaty center of me.